SPY OP

A TASTE OF PARADISE

RONALD K MARSHALL

A JAKE HARPER AND TJ ALVAREZ NOVEL

THE WAR AFTER THE WAR SERIES
BOOK ONE

ISBN 978-1-7334517-0-3
Cover design by Matthew Worsman of Rock-A-Print

To contact visit my website ronaldkmarshall.com

ACKNOWLEDGEMENTS

Writers are readers. My writing is dedicated to my teachers. I was fortunate to have many fine, stimulating educators who instilled in me the love of reading and writing. And to the librarians and the public libraries with all the writers' books which inspired me. Other writers still do. One group of librarians, York County Library's staff were instrumental in helping bring this book to print. I spent countless hours in libraries doing research for this book.

I would like to acknowledge all the brave men and women of the armed services. Also, the many unsung heroes of the clandestine intelligence services. You are the protectors of our great democracy. I salute you.

My father, Cecil Thomas Marshall was one of the heroes. My hero. Recipient of seven bronze stars, one of two survivors of his Army company in the Pacific Campaign of WWII. Our family never knew of his awards until after he passed. He showed many signs of PTSD. Long before the disorder was acknowledged. Many victims of PTSD suffer in silence. Their families suffer with them.

I wish to thank family and friends who encouraged me to keep writing. Among these are:

Dr. Kenneth Martin Burtner and wife Amanda, Gary and Andi Sauerbrei, Ralph Chibaud, John and Janet Glenn, Russel Lowery, Gary and Rose Lamb, Secrette and Simon Mninski, Lindsay and Fernand Guidry, Janet Boyst, Robert Belangia, Mike Hunter, Mark Hunter, Kevin Marshall, Bert and Kathy Morris, Rick and Cecilia Burtner, Remy and Jonathan Bergeron, Eric Sprouse, Gail Hoffman Kot Hy, Eric and Elise Jones, Sean and Whitney Marshall, Patricia Roberts, Tracie McKay, Kenny Acosta, Pam Burgess, Janice Moore and Loretta Honnoll Ross. Thanks for your support.

Special thanks to Matthew Worsman of Rock-A-Print for the cover design.

I have taken liberties in the telling of the story. Names were changed, events fictionalized based upon people and events which inspired this story. Some are real, others are not. The technological aspects are based upon documented accounts of existing or proposed technologies. All errors are unintentional and mine.

This book is dedicated to:
All the women in my life
You made life worth living

Who's gonna care for the ones who care for the ones who went to war.
The War after The War
Mary Gauthier

Beware of pretty faces that you find
A pretty face can hide an evil mind
Johnny Rivers

When she was just a girl she expected the world
But it flew away from her reach
So she ran away in her sleep and dreamed of
Para-para-paradise, para-para-paradise….
Cold Play

…Kompromat is generally true, though photographs and videos are sometimes tinkered with to heighten the embarrassment. This makes it a particularly blunt and dangerous weapon……
Andrew Higgins and Andrew E. Kramer
Ivan Nechepurenko and Sophia Kishkovsky
"The Soviet Union Died, but Russia's Use of Sexual Blackmail Lives On"
New York Times January 12, 2017

The *Poseidon is an autonomous,* nuclear-powered, and nuclear-armed unmanned underwater vehicle…capable to deliver both conventional and nuclear payloads.
Status-6 Oceanic Multipurpose System
Wikipedia

PART I

1

Jake saw him walking through the crowds, moving in and out of the food court area inside Miami Dade Airport. Big tawny guy, like Jake just over six feet, but additional twenty pounds of natural muscle mass – good genes. He moved like a cat, eyes checking everything out, many women, some men checking him out.

Most people were in a hurry to get to their boarding station or, like Jake, grabbing an overpriced, quick bite before joining the hustle of the concourse gauntlet. Several people turned to look at this big man in a police combat uniform. TJ had more than once been taken for Dwayne Johnson, "The Rock" of Hollywood fame. Size and shade of skin, same big-boned face with the ever-present smile. Looks can be deceiving for The Rock in movies and TJ in real life. The smile was there as a welcome for the gals, a warning for all others. Jake stood, and TJ moved his way.

They clasped each other hand in hand, chest to chest.

"Hey bro, looking good. How ya feeling?" TJ asked, as they sat down facing each other in the corner booth.

"Okay man. Little stiffness, aches and pains, usual shit. How's the wife?"

"Deane's same as always. Better than I deserve. So, you're headed to the Bahamas? What's that all about?"

"Got hired by a man to go down see why his company is behind schedule and over budget. Some resort project. Maybe a month, who knows, may end up being longer. I needed to get away. Money's been tight."

"Sorry to hear that. Have anything to do with Joanna?"

"Pretty much. Her parents blame me for her death. Got my children convinced. They hardly talk to me. Monthly support is 'bout the extent of the relationship. Could lose the farm." Jake pushed a green tea across the table. "Almost forgot. You still drink it I hope."

TJ took the bottle, twisted the cap off and drank several swallows. He looked around. Several people were staring at him. He straightened up and nodded to a smiling lady strutting by. He looked back at Jake who had noticed also and was smiling that gotcha smile.

TJ grunted. "You may or may not know, I tried to talk to Joanna after you got sent to Walter Reed; sounded like she didn't want to talk. Never knew if she told you I called. Next thing I hear, you were at Fort Jackson and you two had gone separate ways—heard about the overdose, had to be rough on the children."

Jake shook his head, "Yeah. They've never talked to me about it. Hit me hard, felt guilty."

TJ's smile faded.

"Not your fault bro." He paused. "Sometimes I wish Deane and I had children. Other times I hear stories like yours, and I see what bad relationships do to people. Even worse, having known and seeing what the pain and devastation people experience when they lose a child…It was hard on Deane…she never talks about it…I try not to dwell on it, sometimes when I am out on an op, the what ifs creep in. Guess being a parent just wasn't meant to be."

Jake could see the momentary flicker of pain in TJ's expression, then the smiling mask reappeared. He knew TJ, he had his own way of dealing with loss. Discussion was not it.

"Took your twenty and came back here, became a cop, what's with that?"

"Yeah. Not many old military snipers, didn't want to continue as a trainer," TJ said. "Being a cop ain't so bad, only thing is too much bullshit paperwork, not enough action, so I joined the undercover unit. Deane's not too happy about it. You know we both grew up in the Hood. We recently moved into the home Deane grew up in, same area as I grew up. Lots of homies. The gangs are getting worse, more organized, more weapons, more crime of every kind. The cartels have recruited many of the locals. My brother, Leon, he and his homies are trying to keep their shit on the down and low, but the pressure and threats are becoming too much. Anything happens to him my mother would go to pieces. I decided I should use my knowledge to maybe get rid of some of these bangers. Make it safer for Deane, my family and the good guys.”

“Sounds like the shit we saw overseas.”

“Not much different, except this is my home. It may be the Hood, but it could be different. Bro, the Bahamas can be dangerous too. Quite a few of our joint task force operations dealing with the cartels involve the Bahamians running drugs and human cargo into the country, Haitians, Cubans, others. The DEA has a watch station set up on one of The Exuma Islands. They fly a hot-air balloon and surveillance drones, but still these guys manage to slip through. Better watch yourself.”

“Exumas? That’s where I’m headed. Speaking of which, I better head to my gate. Thanks for coming to see me off. Tell Deane hello. Remember, heroes are mostly dead. Think twice before volunteering, you were taught better.”

“Hey, maybe you should think about joining the feds, they like vets, especially smartass ones like you. And ‘women like men in uniform,’ isn’t that what you used to say?”

“Got a plane to catch.” Jake stood. They clasped again. “No feds. With my neck, doubt I could pass the physical.” He eased his duffel over his shoulder, released his suitcase handle and started for his gate.

“Keep in touch bro. Don’t wait so long.”

Jake saluted, hand behind head.

2

Nasau, Bahamas

The plane descended over Nassau--the Bahamas--turquoise water lapping up on white sandy beaches, ladies in skimpy swimwear sitting under umbrellas, sipping on fruity rum drinks in tall frosty glasses, palm tree-lined roads with resort hotels and tiki huts on each side, casinos-- Maybe he would get a chance to try his luck. Even if he had to work, should be plenty extra time to play, try to forget all the trouble he left behind. A much-needed R&R.

He had never been to the Caribbean. His parents had owned a small Cessna 182. They made numerous island-hopping excursions while he was living the soldier's life. He and Joanna were scheduled to fly to Aruba for their honeymoon, had to cancel due to her morning sickness. He was feeling slightly hungover, no comparison to morning sickness he figured.

The last leg with Bahamian Air was on a plane that reminded Jake of an Army jumper with seats added on each side. In less than an hour they were landing at a small airport, smaller than the York County Airport. About the size of Lowry's Airstrip not far from his farm.

There was a metal hangar with small planes and a couple private jets tied down on the tarmac. His plane was loaded with Bahamians and expats, like him. Not many touristy looking passengers. At the airport, they disembarked down a set of steps and filed single file into a low-slung concrete building, painted garish yellow, where other people, like the ones who were on the flight with him, waited to be told to load up for the flight to Nassau.

There was no air conditioning. Even though it was late afternoon, the temperature felt well into the nineties with a breeze which didn't feel any cooler. Jake wasn't sure where to go, so he took his duffel bag and a large rolling suitcase and followed the other arrivals out the doorway on the other side past a small, crowded seating area.

Underneath an extended overhang, sat numerous Bahamians and a couple expats, all of them smoking, a few had beer bottles in their hands. There were no cabs, no buses, some cars in various stages of disrepair. He looked around, didn't see anyone there to pick him up. Had there been public transportation, he would not have known where to go. Some of his fellow travelers climbed into cars and trucks and were driven off. Others headed across the steaming hot asphalt circular drive, went into a long commercial building on the other side. Sign said *Kermit's*. He saw someone emerge with a beer.

Not knowing what else to do, he decided to check it out. He found it to be café-like with a very limited menu. It was air conditioned and offered four brands of beer – Budweiser, Miller Lite, Heineken and Kalic. Jake bought a Heineken. Five dollars. He wouldn't be doing much drinking at that price. He walked over to a table with a glass wall facing the terminal.

Sometime later, an older model pickup truck pulled in front of the terminal. A tall, slender Bahamian emerged smoking a cigarette and joined the men sitting on the concrete bench against the wall of the terminal. The driver emerged. He was about five-nine, 180 with woolly hair dressed in jeans and a T-shirt. He walked over to stand at the metal rail facing the men, then he turned and started walking toward Kermit's. Must be his ride. He set his bottle on the eating counter, grabbed his bags and went back outside.

"You must be Jake Harper?"

The fellow had a sideways grin. "Welcome to paradise." He added a heh-eh-heh laugh, sounding like a cross between a donkey and a hyena—to Jake it was irritating.

"I'm Richard Costa, you can call me Rick. Come on. I have your limo over here." He let out another grating laugh.

Rick drove them down the road, staying in the left-hand lane. Jake kept his eyes locked onto the meandering road which Rick tended to straighten.

One side was bordered by rock, the other dropped into a vegetated void with occasional glimpses of ocean. They made a loop through nearby Georgetown.

"Lots of places called Georgetown in the Caribbean," Rick informed him, "Bahamas are a former British Commonwealth. The main road is called Queen's Highway, in honor of Georgie boy's wife, supposedly she was a black Muslim. Guess some of the royals have darkie blood. Many Bahamians are mixed breeds." He barked another laugh and looked over at Jake to see his reaction.

"No big deal for me. My best friend is Afro-Cuban," Jake replied. He saw Rick frown. At least he didn't laugh again.

After the ten-minute grand tour, Rick stopped off at a line of low slung, wooden shacks, reminding Jake of high school concession stands. Place called Fish Fry. Each stand served, what Rick called, island fast food. The air was heavy-- burning wood mixed with competing smoked meat smells. Jake's mouth watered—the tang of spiced meat: sausages, dark, swollen from the heat, chargrilled beef strips, shrimp skewers with peppers, onions and tomatoes, fish, the head still attached, the flesh ready to fall off the bone, potatoes and what looked like squid, which Jake learned was conch. On counters were jars of pickled vegetables and seasonings. Some Bahamians sat on stools, others were seated around Domino tables, cold, sweating bottles of beer turned upwards onto smacking lips, eyes filled with pleasure. Island music played through small speakers set into the open framework. This was more like what Jake expected.

Rick bought an order of conch fritters and a couple of beers. They seated themselves at one of the picnic tables next to a blue-painted shack. Rick began asking Jake questions. Jake gave him a brief rundown of who he was and about his career in the military. Jake found out Rick was from Saint Louis, was a union member, had lost his job when the company closed shop.

"Moved overseas, claimed it was due to the recession. That was bullshit. The company was anti-union, wanted cheap labor. The bastards. Lucky for me I got recommended for this job by a friend, the former manager who moved on to another project in the Caymans. The lucky fucker. Maybe I'll get lucky. Maybe Ned will send someone like you to take my place and he'll send me somewhere like the Caymans." He studied Jake for affirmation.

Jake didn't reply. He was thinking about Rick's seeming to not want to be here and what that meant. The old saying, "if it sounds too good to be true, maybe it is," came to mind. He looked around, seemed perfectly okay to him.

"Have you done other work for Ned? That how you ended up here?"

Jake swigged his beer, said, "no".

When Jake didn't elaborate, Rick said, "I heard you were coming, nothing else. You my replacement?" He looked at Jake expectantly.

"Ned hired me to come here to do whatever needs to be done. I needed a job and here I am."

Rick was puzzled to learn Jake had not worked for ESI and knew little about the type work they did. They finished their beers in silence, Jake checking things out. The one thing he noticed, no women—what's up with that he wanted to ask? Another strange land, surrounded by a people of another culture, his last experience playing in the back of his mind. Rick's probing, not being able to be open, was killing the buzz. For some reason, he felt this was not going to be a plum job in the promised land he envisioned. His neck was stiffening up. Stress did that, he was ready to go before Rick made him depressed.

They left there as the sun set over the horizon. A few miles along the winding Queen's Highway, with everyone driving like there is no tomorrow in vehicles made for right hand driving, coming at Jake's passenger side. No control of the steering put him on edge. Rick told Jake he would be sharing a house with him and his girlfriend Blakley, who had come for a visit. A visit, from the sound of it, Rick had no intention to end.

The house was a sky blue painted concrete ranch that sat on top of a hill with views through low shrubs which revealed the top of another home further down the hill. A spectacular view of the turquoise waters, shimmering with the fading light, like a giant jewel.

Rick's girlfriend Blakley was taller than Rick. A big-boned gal, whose roots on her scalp indicated dirty blonde, but her hair was sun bleached and tied back with a scarf. She had on a swimsuit top which barely covered grapefruit size breasts. Her skin-tight cutoffs revealed wide rounded hips and a crotch outline that made Jake blush. She noticed, made her smile. She gently squeezed his hand, her eyes lingering, boring into his.

Rick directed Jake to a back bedroom where he stowed his bags beside a regular size bed. There was a nightstand on the far side with a cheap vacation homestyle lamp, a small chest of drawers on the wall near the foot of the bed, and a closet with boxes and junk spilling out its open door. Back down the hall was a small bath. Jake glimpsed it, before they turned right to go to what was to be his room. At the other end was the front bedroom, obviously Rick's and Blakley's.

Returning to the open kitchen/living room which occupied the first half of the house, he saw Blakley had laid out a tray of veggies, cheeses and shrimp with crackers and cocktail sauce on the side. She added three beers, two on the table in front of the sofa and one in front of a hardback wooden chair on the other side. They snacked and Rick made a quick rundown of what Jake could expect the next day concerning the orientation. Jake asked about the Project, and Rick told Jake what he already knew, which wasn't much. Jake asked how and when they were paid. He had set up automatic deposit for his pay but forgot to ask for details when he was in Charlotte. The woman, who took down his info, had not provided any details.

"Ned gives expats salaries or wages plus a living expense allowance. I pay the locals by check bi-weekly, unless they agree to automatic deposit. Expense covers the basics. Meaning, you can't eat steak every day or go out drinking every night. Not that you'd want to; everything comes frozen, shipped in containers to the grocer. A few restaurants have stuff flown in. Otherwise only thing fresh is the seafood." He laughed his grating laugh again. "But while you're here, we can combine our money. That'll leave us enough to have some recreational vices. Do you do drugs?"

Jake had not expected this. "If you're referring to heavy recreational drugs, no, not since before I joined the Army. Had a hard time kicking an opioid habit after my broken neck, which resulted in my medical discharge. CBD oil helped. Smoked a little weed last night. First time in a long time. Alcohol is my drug of choice."

Blakley went to the refrigerator and returned with three more beers, set them down, and left. Shortly she returned holding a jewelry box. She sat back down, put the box on the table, pulled out a bag of weed and a piece of coral with holes in it, in which she placed a thumbnail piece of weed. Jake thought about declining but figured they would think him antisocial, so he took a few tokes as the pipe was passed around. Didn't take much to get him stoned.

"How do you get pot down here?" Jake gasped, trying not to cough after he took a toke.

"You can get almost anything here," Blakley said holding up a bag with a white powder in it. Rick shook his head. She ignored the admonition, turned a saucer over on the coffee table, put some of the powder on it, used a credit card to divide the substance into three lines, rolled up a ten-dollar bill, and snorted a line.

"Hope Jake's cool," he said to Blakley in a harsh tone. "You cool Jake?"

Blakley slid the saucer toward Jake. Rick reached out and stopped it, all the while looking at Jake.

"If you mean will I tell anyone? No. I'd rather not know, and if there is trouble, I'll swear I knew nothing about it. If that's cool, I'm cool." Jake locked eyes with Rick until he turned his stare to Blakely.

"Put that shit back. Sorry about that, Jake. Blakley likes to party, and she thinks everybody does too." Blakley frowned then snorted the other lines. She licked the plate, her eyes on Jake. She sat back, smiled at Jake then put the bag away.

Jake wondered just what kind of party girl Blakley was. He took his eyes off her and turned back to Rick, who seemed uncomfortable. "What else is there to do when you're not working?" Jake asked breaking the silence.

"Not a helluva lot. We get together with some of the other expats mostly. Got some interesting friends from down under. One guy you might like, Alec. What do you think Blakley, think Jake and Alec might get along?"

Blakley looked up and shrugged.

Rick continued, "Alec was Australian SAS, served in Afghanistan back in their early campaign. Doesn't like to talk about it. Guess it's that veteran thing. Big Elvis fan. Been all over the world on other projects. That's mainly what we do. Most of the young dudes play video games. The older ones get together for cards on Thursdays, Texas Hold 'em mainly. Not sure what the Bahamians do, other than fish, drink and get fucked up. You can get a hot card for satellite TV, no local stations. I brought a laptop, we do streaming. Friday nights, a place in Georgetown grills steaks and chicken with a side buffet for twenty dollars. Place has a bar and a Bahamian band plays island music, most of it American Fifties and Sixties R&B with an island beat." Rick continued drinking.

Jake, feeling the beer and weed, decided he needed to hit the sack. "What time do I need to be ready in the morning?"

"Not a partier. You'll learn." Rick said. "I head out about seven. I'll take you to orientation. That's the first thing. Usually takes half a day. After that I'll show you around, introduce you to some of the other subs and our Bahamian crew. Maybe Ned Junior, the boss's son will show up. Watch him. He thinks he runs things. I try to ignore him. His buddy Mitch the bitch is our tool manager. Pretty much all he does is get in the way. There's Amy, the boss's son's girlfriend. She comes around, hangs out, about all she's good for. She's supposed to be the person who does our orders and helps with the paperwork. I pretty much take care of that, making her unnecessary, but…anyway, you'll see."

Rick took a long pull on his beer.

"Tomorrow I have to tell the Fluor orientation people and the Bahamian authorities what your job is. Not sure what I'm supposed to tell them what it is you'll be doing."

"Tell them I'm in training and was sent here to give ESI another hand."

"The Bahamians don't like us being here. They tell you they can do anything. We're not supposed to bring anyone here who can do any work they can do. You see the problem. They've sent expats back because of this. Before you or I say anything to anyone, I need to check with Ned."

"What do I say until then?"

"Let me think about it. I'll let you know in the morning."

Jake stood up. "Wake me when you get up, if I'm not already up."

"Will do."

Jake went back to what Rick had said was his bedroom. It was damn hot. No air conditioner. There had been a window unit in the living area, another in Rick's bedroom. He had a ceiling fan. He walked back to the living area. "Is there not a central air system in this house?"

Rick laughed, which made Jake want to strangle him. "Most homes don't have them, including this one. We'll leave our bedroom door open and put a fan in the hall blowing our window AC air your way. There's bottled water in the fridge; we don't drink the tap water. I'm not sure if this home has a cistern or if it's municipal water. Has an odor."

Jake was used to his quiet Carolina farm. The noise of the fan kept him awake...that and the feeling he should have done some research before jumping at this opportunity. That's what happens when you're desperate and act on a tip made by a drunk in a bar. His neck felt like a knife had been inserted. If he had to do physical labor, could he hack it? And this fucking bedroom, like trying to sleep in a sauna. Memories of the Philippines, memories of the IED, memories he tried to keep buried.

At six, Jake gave up and slid out of the damp, uncomfortable bed. He felt certain he sweated away five or more pounds. In the kitchen, he found a coffee maker, filters and ground coffee. When he pulled the water reservoir on the coffee maker open, tiny insects scurried out. They were all over the kitchen counter. Coffee would have to wait. Pissing wouldn't. Someone was in the shower, so he stepped outside. Not quite dawn, the sky was filled with stars. Different constellations from those visible at the farm, different like every place overseas. The air had scents of the sea, there was a welcome chill. Jake was standing there enjoying the view, the door to the kitchen made a noise, he turned to see Rick.

"There you are. Thought you might have decided to get the hell out while you still can," he said with his laugh.

Not what Jake needed to start the day.

The day didn't get better. The drive was another harrowing adventure. Once they reached the project, the sun had risen. The first thing Jake saw were end to end mobile units, window air conditioners sticking out every ten feet. Men dressed in work clothes, hard hats in hand, came out each end.

"That's man camp. Most companies house their workers there," Rick said as they drove by. "That trailer behind there is where you'll start. That's the medical station, where they have you do a piss test. Anyone flunks the piss test is sent home. Ned pays your way here, you flunk, you pay your way back."

"I did a drug test before I was hired," Jake replied. "You mean I have to do another one here?"

"Everyone does. Construction policy. Administered by the Bahamian Government, another way to get rid of expats."

"Fuck man, why didn't you tell me before you offered me the weed last night?" Jake felt his anger rising. "You should have told me."

"Thought you knew. Ned's people should have warned you. They normally do. We've had to send crews back that flunked the test. Pisses Ned off. I doubt that little bit you smoked will show up. You've got an hour. Drink a lot of water. I'll see if I can get you some vinegar, they say that helps."

"Ned's people? You knew. You should have told me. Better still, you shouldn't have offered me the damn shit knowing I was to be tested. Seems to me you wanted me to flunk."

"Chill out dude. I'm sure you'll be all right with the piss test. I need to get in touch with Ned to find out your job title. The Bahamians don't want expats here taking the jobs, so they look for reasons to send you home, incomplete paperwork is one."

"You told me that already. What you should have also said and done, you didn't. I don't cotton to bullshit. And I'm not dude. You may call me Jake or Harper. I think it best that I don't flunk that piss test. Capiche?" Jake could feel the heat, his heart was pumping in his head, this motherfucker had pushed the wrong buttons.

They reached a guard shack. The guard waved them through. Out of nowhere, a grader came from behind a dune, Rick braked hard. The operator was a black man, dressed in colorful clothes, his hair twisted in a hive on top of his head.

"Motherfucking Rastafarians, have to watch those assholes, they won't stop. Only people on site who don't have to wear a hardhat, some religious bullshit. I hear they don't get drug tested either. Maybe you could say you're a Rasta."

Jake didn't reply.

They crested a dune and passed by more trailers that formed a loose complex with boardwalks joining them. A sign with an arrow said *Office*.

"That's Fluor's offices. Your orientation will be conducted there."

Further on were rows of shipping containers sitting off the ground on concrete supports. Signs on every other one designated the occupant's company name. Rick stopped at the end containers. He pulled a ring of keys attached to his belt, unlocked the heavy steel door padlock, went up the three wooden steps, cut on a light and went inside. Jake followed. At the end was a steel desk with a worn fabric-cushioned chair on casters. On the right was a smaller desk flanked by shelves holding a selection of boxes labelled hardware items. To Jake's left were other shelves lined with other boxes.

"Fucking Mitch. I told him to inventory this shit and put it in our other container. That's what I was telling you. He's a slacker. Thinks 'cause he's the boss's son's friend, he can do as he pleases. He should have been here by now. The damn Bahamians should be here shortly to check out tools and hardware, and that means they will have to wait. Fucking asshole."

"I've got to go see Jeff Taylor, our liaison with Fluor. Ned may have told Jeff your job title. if not, we'll call him. I'll be back in time to take you to begin orientation. When the Bahamians show up, tell them not to get on the computers. They like to visit the hardcore porn sites. Ned doesn't want them on the computers. Fucking Mitch. He better get his ass here. Oh yeah, here's the sign in sheet." He handed Jake a clipboard. "Have them sign in and check off the vehicles and any company shit they have out."

He left, leaving Jake standing there wondering what he was supposed to be doing. An overwhelming despair hovered on the edge of his consciousness, reminders of the withdrawal sirens' song that had played endlessly when he had attempted to go cold turkey from the pain meds. "If you can't control your addictions, they will control you," had been his mantra. The upcoming drug test threatened that control he had demanded of himself, another outsider had entered his life, putting him at the mercy of the fates. The stiffness and pain in his neck remained, a constant reminder of the dark void he once crawled out of.

3

Washington, DC

"Do we have anyone on the inside that we can trust?" Special Agent Robert Hardy was asked. He sat across the desk from the current Undersecretary of Homeland Security. The office was a shrine to America's who's who. Pictures and plaques lined the walls, individual and group photos, some outdoors, most indoors at ceremonies, taken with every president from Bush Senior to the present occupant of the oval office, and senior members of the intelligence services.

Special Agent Hardy was summoned to the Undersecretary's office first thing that morning. He was having his first cup of coffee, discussing his day's itinerary with another agent, when the office phone operator buzzed to say the Undersecretary requested his presence. The question was asked during the discussion concerning Operation Pink Flamingo, a joint task force operation involving the DEA, FBI and the CIA in conjunction with Homeland Security Investigations. SA Hardy was HSI's team leader. The task force had agents working from Washington, EL Paso, Miami, Mexico City, Guayaquil, Bogota, Exuma, and Guantanamo attempting to put together intel linking Castro's generals to the cartels and agents of foreign intelligence services, former and current, friend and foe.

The Undersecretary had received intel indicating the Castro family involvement. "Not much happens in Cuba without the families' implicit or explicit orders and profiting from any transaction. All intel indicates Cuba's leaders were in negotiation with a Russian group to purchase UAVs and submersible drones which would be used by the cartels to deliver drugs into the US from the islands and Europe through Africa. The President and his advisors are concerned. This could be another Cuban Missile Crisis, or it could be the President's people looking for more fire for their political rhetoric, playing to their spin machine." He stood and began pacing.

"The Russian oligarchs with Putin as their state head are intent on undermining the United States and our allies. When it comes to propaganda and cyber warfare, they have proven to be up to the challenge. They have begun broadcasting their damn political misinformation from a Kansas City radio station no less. This announcement of having developed a submersible drone with speeds capable of outrunning and outmaneuvering our underwater tactical capabilities and being able to carry heavy payloads and nuclear warheads, has caught the U.S. military off-guard. Our intelligence services, including our agency – hell, the entire defense industry – we've been napping. Nuclear capability is troubling, despite their rhetoric, the Russian oligarchs have shown no intent to have more nukes for Russia, or so some think. That doesn't mean they aren't above profiting from selling the capability to others. If these agents and cartels are collaborating with the Cubans, as the latest intel indicates, and they get their hands on these drones, it could be a game changer, right in our backyard. This intel is coming from other sources. We need humint confirmation. Do we have any feet on their ground?"

"Homeland has none at present. The other agencies, despite this being a joint task force, are playing the same old, "I'll show you mine, if you'll show me yours," game. I have put out feelers to all major cities' law enforcement drug units hoping to recruit a bilingual officer with cartel experience."

"Any possibilities?"

"One name was mentioned by our field supervisor in Miami, Thomas Jefferson Alvarez. He is of Afro-Cuban descent, grew up in Little Havana, has a brother who is a gang lieutenant, took his twenty from the Army, where he distinguished himself as a sniper. Four tours in the Middle East, then a trainer with The Philippine Scout Rangers, got out, joined Miami Dade SWAT Team, and for the past two years has worked in their drug enforcement unit, with over a year as an undercover agent. The field supervisor approached him. He seemed reluctant to leave his current position. Special Agent Swanson thinks with the right incentive, he possibly could be persuaded. I know of Mr. Alvarez. We have a mutual acquaintance who has spoken highly of him."

"Sounds like he should be our man. What incentive does Swanson think would bring him onboard?"

"Swanson thinks we should get Miami Dade Police Commissioner Arenzo Dominguez to give him a leave of absence so we can take him around the block for a test drive. Sounds like a possible win-win scenario to me."

"We need someone now. You're heading down to the DEA Exuma Station in a couple days. Stop over in Miami and meet Officer Alvarez. I'll talk to Miami's Police Commissioner and have him talk to the Alvarez man's SWAT Commander."

Hardy stood. "Thank you for your time sir. I need to make some calls to get things set up."

"Mr. Hardy, this operation is important. Everyone has their eyes on us, including the Director and the President's staff. We best not drop the ball."

"I understand sir."

"One other thing before you go. Have you given any more thought to this new tech implant program? We need some worthy volunteers. Sounds promising. Could be a career maker. Going to be part of this Space Police Force in the works. Give it some thought."

"I have and will sir. Thank you for your time." Hardy rushed down to his office. Undersecretary Cotton didn't have to say it, he knew this was a career maker or breaker. Maybe he should consider the implant program, be involved with the new Space Force. Might have to, if this op goes sideways.

One of the world's wealthiest cities was starting to awaken. Known for gingerbread houses, palm trees fluttering in the breeze from Biscayne Bay, and white edifices standing tall against cottony clouds in a soft blue sky. This was the city of Spanish and British colonial origins. The city where Ponce de Leon hoped to find the fountain of youth and a man named Flagler built a railroad. A place where native Americans were forced into slavery and desiccated by European disease. The city built by Bahamian and Haitian labor, only to become enslaved, then tortured and killed after the War Between the States. Now the second most Spanish-speaking city in North America, largely due to families like Thomas Jefferson Alvarez's, whose ancestors fled Cuba after the Castros took control. Most of them had been wealthy Cubans. TJ's family had not been.

TJ was on Calle Ocho headed downtown to a meeting with his SWAT commander. He had not said what the meeting was about. This was supposed to be TJ's day off. He had hoped to meet Deane for lunch at one of Little Havana's glitzy restaurants. The restaurants, cafes, bakeries, art galleries and tourist shops all dressed up with murals in muted pastels, lay silent behind palms and tropical shrubbery. Two more weeks until the art festival, when these streets would be teeming with artists, their art visited by tourists from all corners of the world and the usual criminals preying upon the unwary.

But not today. The heat had begun to subside, people were coming back out to enjoy themselves. He lowered his window once he left the surrounding streets. The smells of dank dampness, baked goods and spices, rich Cuban coffee and cigars lingered.

His trip began at the small pale green, brown wood-shuttered home with its small lawn in front. In back was the fruit tree-lined, fenced-in, spit size yard which was barely large enough for a patio where he grew potted tomatoes and peppers. This had been Deane's parents' home. She grew up here, two blocks away from the home he grew up in and where his mother still lived. In between was another world. Two blocks of weed-infested backyards behind homes that should have been declared unfit for human habitation. Older model cars lined both sides of the streets, often spilling over into concreted front yards.

Garbage, more often than not containing used injection needles and condoms, lay amidst the fly infested stench of discarded food containers, piled up on the curb waiting on pickup. Wild and unwanted dogs scavenged through the heaps, scattering the offal, which ran down the streets during heavy downpours, clogging already flooded drains.

After Calle Ocho, he turned onto Flagler Street. He had to zigzag his way around the barricades, broken pavement, mud and water pools, construction debris, and idled equipment. This was the renewal project. Supposed to fix the decaying infrastructure. Been dragging on for years, disrupting homeowners and merchants alike, driving many out of business and away. Looked as though bombs had been dropped and the construction crews were the occupying army. Little Havana mixed now with Little Guatemala, Little Nicaragua, Little Haiti, Little Columbia – all Little People-land, the tired and poor masses, politically and socially unwanted, powerless, always.

When he entered the commander's office, he saw the aging Special Agent Swanson of Homeland Security was present. He wondered what this was about. Swanson's earlier approach indicated more knowledge than TJ liked anyone knowing about him, his wife, his career.

"TJ, this is Special Agent Swanson of Homeland Security," his commander said.

"We've met," TJ replied. His commander raised an eyebrow.

Swanson spoke up, "I introduced myself to Officer Alvarez at one of our task force meetings."

"I received a call from the commissioner last night. He had spoken to someone high up in Homeland Security who requested I speak to HSI Special Agent Hardy. He requested I have a pow wow with Supervisor Swanson and yourself. Seems Homeland and other Washington agencies have a joint task force operation and they need someone with your capabilities to join them. Swanson will not divulge to me why you are their chosen one, neither would Hardy. Nevertheless, the Commissioner has directed me to consider an administrative leave of absence for you to assist Homeland and the task force in this operation. Agent Swanson wishes to speak with you in private." The commander rose from his desk and left the room.

Swanson turned his chair fronting TJ. TJ couldn't help noticing the big man's face was grim, forehead puckered by a frown.

"Officer Alvarez, when I introduced myself to you, you indicated you might consider coming onboard with Homeland."

"No sir. I told you I would consider working with Homeland Security on any operation as a part of a joint task force, which included my SWAT Team."

"This is a joint task force operation and we need your expertise."

"Since you seem to know all about me, you know I left the military several years ago. That was because I wanted to spend more time with my wife. If this task force needs me to go anywhere away from here, I would have to respectfully decline."

"You work undercover, which requires you to be away from your wife. This is what we need from you, to go undercover, just as you do now. This operation is considered a national security op. Uncle Sam will pay for your assistance in addition to your regular pay." He paused. TJ was staring at the wall behind his commander's desk. There was a map of Miami and Dade County hung there.

"Your wife works for the school district and does work for the VA. She has student loan debt, you are helping support your mother, and between the two of you, you are just getting by. Any emergency and you would in all likelihood go under. Think of the money as an insurance policy. I'm sure Homeland would throw in disability and whole life policies."

TJ felt like he was being asked to take a bribe. This whole thing felt wrong. This involved Deane; she would have to make the decision. He doubted she would agree. She had been against him going undercover with the gang unit. He could almost guarantee her answer would be no. She would ask where and for how long, that would be if she didn't say no immediately.

"I need to discuss this with my wife."

Swanson's face lit up. He nodded.

Before he could speak, TJ said, "She will want to know where and for how long."

Swanson's light dimmed. "This will be explained by Task Force Leader Hardy. He wishes to meet with us this afternoon."

"There will not be any need unless my wife says okay."

Swanson looked crestfallen. "He may be in the air on his way here, I'll try to reach him." He pulled out his cell and sat waiting for a connection.

When the connection was made, Swanson rehashed their conversation to Hardy. Swanson's eyelines tightened, as though he had been given bad news. After a couple minutes he stuck his phone out to TJ. "He wishes to speak with you."

TJ took it. "TJ Alvarez."

"Mr. Alvarez, I am Special Agent Hardy from the Charlotte office. I am on my way down to the Bahamas. Homeland's Undersecretary Cotton requested I make a stop in Miami to talk with you. I have been told you have expressed reservations about your participating in our joint task force operation. Your participation has been approved by your police commissioner and your SWAT commander. I understand you wish to tell your wife about this operation, I'm afraid that will not be possible. I will see you at 1400 hour at our Miami field office. Please hand the phone back to Special Agent Swanson. Oh, by the way, seems we have a mutual acquaintance, Jake Harper, good man, as I have been told you are also."

TJ handed the phone back. The heat rose up his neck into his face. He sat clenching his fists. He did his duty for Uncle Sam, had numerous medals to prove his distinguished career. This must be what men from his father's generation felt like back during the Vietnam War when there was a draft. His father joined and paid the ultimate price. Seems Uncle Sam felt his family still owed them. Deane would not be happy. He was not happy. Then there was that last comment…what did Jake have to do with this?

4

Miami, FL

The sun's morning warmth was fast becoming humid heat, the sulfurous smell of the green slime. The algae which threatened aquatic life and made professional fisherman lose money and the wealthy yacht and waterfront homeowners angry, was being pushed inland by a slight breeze. TJ put the window up on his F150 King-cab, whose black paint and once-shiny chrome were aged by the salty air and the polluted water that ran in the streets during the constant storms. Better than recent years when drought turned the everglades brown and Hurricane Irma flooded the area, causing everyone with any sense that could afford to, to flee northward. His mother's and their home were spared, no structural damage. But the area was like a landfill with trash and other people's outdoor unmoored belongings littering the streets and their yard.

He was there then, recently discharged from the Army and on duty with other emergency personnel as a member of the SWAT Team. Deane and his mother were happy because there were the usual scumbag looters taking advantage of the situation and he was available to protect their properties. He was happy in his new job and being home with Deane. Their lives had taken on the semblance of normalcy. He dreaded telling her that was about to be disrupted once more. She asked him the questions he anticipated, turned away frowning when he told her he didn't have answers.

"Why you?" she asked as she turned back to face him, the frown still there.

"I don't know that either," he replied drawing a deeper frown. "He mentioned he knew my friend Jake which puzzles me."

"He didn't elaborate?"

"He had me give the phone back to Swanson. I was stunned by the statement and did as requested. I tried to call Jake and got no answer, not even voice mail. I plan to keep trying. I'll send him an email later. Maybe this Agent Hardy will tell me something in a little while when I meet with him. The only good thing, I was promised extra money and insurance for both of us. I'm going to request they pick up the payments on my veteran's plan and pay your student loans also."

"You make this sound like a permanent assignment. Is that something you would consider?" She looked worried.

"Depends on what they offer. I like being home with you. That will be a major determining factor." He reached over and squeezed her hand. "No matter what they say, I will discuss what this means for us with you. I was told not to mention the offer to you. Don't say anything to anyone else. You know you are the most important thing to me."

"Yeah, how about your going undercover without talking to me about it? I'm still not happy about that decision."

"We talked about it."

"Don't try that with me. You had already put in for the unit before we talked. Is this another one of those scenarios?" She pushed his hand away and looked at her phone. "I've got to get back to the hospital, I have several veterans coming in this afternoon. This PTSD awareness campaign seems to be bringing them in. Making it tough to keep up. I don't care what they offer, you better not be putting your ass in the firestorm again. I want you as my husband, not as a patient."

"Okay commander." TJ watched, as she got up and walked away. Damn he was lucky to have her. Her fine shapely body still gave him a stir. Twenty-five years and their love life was still a marvel.

Hardy, unlike Carl Swanson, looked fit. He was TJ's height and a few pounds lighter, dark headed with brownish hazel eyes, tanned and probably had no trouble with the women. Had a ring, TJ figured he must be married.

He walked up to TJ when he entered the room. They shook hands as they sized each other up.

"I'm Robert T. Hardy. My friends call me Bob. Damn, if you don't favor The Rock. Our mutual acquaintance Jake Harper's description was on the mark. Must make for some awkward or fun moments when you're out in public. Jake told me a great deal about you. He thinks highly of you."

"What does Jake have to do with this?" TJ asked.

"Please have a seat Officer Alvarez. Jake has nothing to do with this, other than being your friend. He is not part of this operation. I'm certain he knows nothing about it and I need you to keep it that way."

They joined Swanson at a dark wood table with plain wooden, slat-back chairs. Once they were seated, Supervisor Hardy leaned forward, hands clasped, elbows resting on a folder which was embossed with **Homeland Security** amidst its logo in the center and at the top of the folder was **Operation Pink Flamingo** with **Top Secret** just below this.

"I am here to discuss Homeland Security's part of a joint task force with you. The op is made up of Homeland, ATF, DEA, the CIA, the FBI and NSA. Operation Pink Flamingo has been formed to determine whether Russia and Cuba are colluding with the Russian and Mexican cartels in the sale of Russian-manufactured submersible drones that are fast and can carry heavy payloads. These payloads could be people, drugs, torpedoes, even nuclear explosive devises. In other words, Operation Pink Flamingo needs to find out and do what needs to be done to prevent a potentially greater threat than the Cuban Missile Crisis which President Kennedy averted in the 1960s."

"What does this have to do with me?" TJ asked.

"You are Cuban American, you speak the language, and know the culture. You have family in Cuba. You grew up in Little Havana. You've been working undercover here in Miami going on two years. You know or know about the major players here and abroad. You have worked with drug task forces and know the ropes. You served in the Army for twenty years, where you learned Russian among other things. If I were a head-hunter, with this job description posted, you would be the person I was looking for."

"Have a job I happen to like. I was not and am not looking for anything else. Since you know my background, you know I was a sniper, mostly I worked alone. The same with doing undercover work, I work alone. You might say I don't get along well with others." TJ smiled his don't-fuck-with-me smile.

The room became silent, the only sounds their breathing and the hum of the air conditioner. Hardy and Swanson were zeroed in on TJ, their eyes locked on his.

"What Special Agent Hardy and I–" Swanson began saying, Hardy held up his hand and he stopped.

"Officer Alvarez, I understand your lone wolf attitude. I appreciate that mentality. If that were your only objection, I could work with that. There has to be more to it than that."

"What I hear from you concerns my Cuban heritage. I am an American of Cuban blood--never been to Cuba and have no desire to do so. Little Havana is not just Cubans. The closest any of them, including me and my wife, have been to Cuba is watching movies. I promised my wife when I left the Army that she and I would grow old together—the key word is *together*. I am all the family she has or knows. Not a lone wolf, I have her as well as my mother and a brother and his family. They all depend on me. As for my knowing the major players here and abroad, I have been working to get to know the kingpins in this area. Often our intel is faulty, a small fish is taken for a big fish and vice versa. I know about the major players abroad only from briefings—that is not my area of expertise. If you want my help here in Miami, I will do what I can for the task force… otherwise I will respectfully decline."

"Good. We can start from there. According to our intel, much of the financing is being done by laundering money in offshore accounts or through shell companies. A lot of that money ends up being used to purchase drugs for sale here in Miami. The money from the drug sales is reportedly used to purchase parts, hardware and software which is being shipped through shell companies to somewhere in the Americas to help pay for their growing operation. They are attempting to go high tech, adding drones to their inventory, possibly a submersible drone."

"We have no concrete intel who the players are—nationality, location, connections, the name of their operation. What we need from you is to use our resources and your sources to find out anything and everything known on the street about who the players are, if there are any new players, Mexican, Columbian, Cuban, Russian, whatever."

"Again, why me? Why not the DEA, ATF, CIA or other fed agents?"

"They have agents working this also. Problem is they look at this as competition. There has always been competition between the agencies. The DEA and HSI have no love for each other. The NSA and CIA are the worst. They take and often share with other clandestine organizations and create files they call top secret, meaning they can never be relied upon to testify in court— our intel becomes legally worthless in their hands. There are people within our own organizations and country that may be leaks. Loose lips and all that. Keep everything in house. Be wary of all outsiders. Most insiders know who the odd men are. You will be HSI's insider."

"Supervisor Swanson told you about the compensation we will be providing. Any questions with regards to this or the operation?"

"You talk as though I have agreed."

"You said you would work with us, that was if you could stay here. I am accommodating your request. It's a done deal. You will report to Supervisor Swanson. No one else is to know anything about this. Any questions?"

TJ knew he had been drafted. The only choice was to walk out, lose his job, which would mean losing any chance at landing another job in law enforcement, he was stuck.

"I have insurance, life and medical, as does Deane. Rather than having another policy, we would prefer you up the value of the policies, guarantee the payments. Pay her student debt. If this thing goes bust, I want a guarantee of relocation for me and my family members."

"I don't see any problem with those. And the operation?"

"Not at this time. I guess if I think of any, Supervisor Swanson can fill me in."

"That's right. He will get you started with the paperwork and introduce you to our team. Your commissioner and commander know you will be working undercover as part of the task force. That is the extent of anyone outside HSI to know. Anyone else says anything to you, get the hell away and follow the procedures Swanson will explain to you. Welcome to the team. Stay safe." Hardy stood, followed by Swanson and TJ. He shook TJ's hand and went out the door.

5

Great Exuma, Bahamas

Due to lack of sleep and boredom, Jake felt the weight of his situation. He sat at Rick's desk and attempted to get on the computer. Nothing doing. He needed the password. He leaned his head back against the wall and stared out the open doorway. The faint light of approaching dawn helped orient his position. He was facing east. Suddenly a figure appeared in the doorway. He was a light-skinned Bahamian, about Jake's height but much thinner, dressed in jeans, boots, and an untucked, faded blue, long sleeve cotton shirt. He was followed by a shorter, thin, darker skinned Bahamian dressed in similar fashion, only his shirt was brown. The shorter one had been laughing at something the other one had said. When he saw Jake, he stopped laughing. They both walked on up to the desk, grinning at Jake.

"You must be Rick's replacement," the taller one said in a sing song voice, "I'm Thaddeus, other Bahamians call me Yeller, 'cause my skin color. This is Terrence."

Jake stood and shook their hands. "I'm Harper. Not here to replace anybody. Where did you hear that?"

"Dat the word we got. Ever't'ing happen islands ever'one know. You see," Thaddeus said.

"You not take Rick's job, what you do?" Terrance asked.

"Not sure. Needed a job. Ned hired me to come to the Bahamas and help finish the project. What do you two do?"

"Whatever Rick say do. Where Rick and Mitch the Bitch?" Thaddeus asked. They both laughed like it was an inside joke. "We need get in other container."

"Rick had to go to the main office, and I don't know anything about Mitch. Rick handed me this sign in sheet and left. Said he would be back shortly." Jake heard a vehicle pull up, loud music playing, which ended when the vehicle was switched off, followed by the sound of voices. Other Bahamians of various sizes and dress entered, chattering away, seeming to ignore Jake and Terrence and Thaddeus. There was a screeching and metal on metal clanging sound coming from the container next door. One Bahamian dressed more stylish than the others, medium height, athletic, women would say good-looking, stepped through the rest, introduced himself as Rodney, took the clip board and walked back out, followed by the others.

Jake stood and went outside. The Bahamians came out of the open container, next to the one he was in. They carried boxes and tools, laid them in the back bed of the two trucks—the one he arrived in and an older, more beat up one. Music once more resumed, piercing the once quiet break of dawn. Jake watched the gathering mass of employees exiting the other container, ESI's Bahamian workforce. They piled in the front seats and back beds. The trucks drove off, disappearing over a sand dune. Jake looked around. Up and down the rows of containers, similar action was taking place. Soon vehicles and people on foot formed a steady procession following the same route the ESI workers took. It was as though some movie director had yelled "action" and everyone began the scene, following the predetermined script.

From the other container came the sound of voices, one was releasing a stream of expletives, another laughing. Jake walked over. Inside was Yeller and a tall, lanky, young, white guy, whose clothes looked like he had slept in them. He had a droopy, sleepy look on his face, looked hungover. They were stacking boxes on shelves.

He looked up, saw Jake. "Who the fuck…you the dude Rick said was coming to take over?"

"No mon, he say he be not Rick's replacement," Yeller said.

"You going to orientation; if so, you better git going," the white kid said.

"Rick said he would take me there when he got back from his meeting. I have no idea where I'm supposed to go," Jake responded.

The kid smirked. "Rick won't be out of that meeting for a couple hours. He's full of shit. The bastard. Come on I'll take you there. You got your paperwork?"

"What paperwork?" Jake's gut feelings had been right, Rick was trying to get him kicked off the project.

The kid walked past him, started walking toward the office complex. He didn't bother introducing himself.

"I'm Jake Harper. You can call me Jake or Harper. You must be Mitch?"

"You got it," he replied without stopping. "Mitch Beatty, that bastard Rick calls me "Fuckhead" or "Mitch the Bitch." He thinks because he fought golden gloves, he's some badass. One of these days, he's going to get what's coming to him."

Mitch walked fast. They went up the steps onto the deck that wrapped around and between the Fluor Daniel's office complex. At the far end, they entered a metal door. Inside was the plan room with wall to wall vertical open files holding the blueprints and other construction documents. There was a drafting-type, tilted table in the center. Mitch went through an opening into a hall, turned into the first office on the right. A well-dressed smallish man with glasses, kind of geeky looking, in his late twenties, sat behind a desk that took up most of the room. He looked up as they entered.

"Jeff this is Jake Harper. Rick was supposed to have him fill out his paperwork and take him to orientation. He should have been there already. He has no paperwork."

Jeff stood, extended his hand. "Jeff Taylor." They shook. "Thanks Mitch, I'll handle it," he said with a western twang.

Mitch squeezed by Jake and left.

Jeff opened a file cabinet drawer that was in the corner, pulled out a stapled set of papers. "You don't have a hard hat?"

"No, I'm afraid not."

Jeff took his sticker covered hardhat off the top of the filing cabinet and told Jake, "come on."

In the file room, Jeff opened a drawer and pulled out a hardhat, handed Jake the hat and the paperwork and told him to follow him. Jake looked at the first page after they exited the deck and headed toward the area Rick said was the man camp. It was filled out. "Who filled this out?" he asked.

"ESI's Charlotte office faxed that over. You need to initial and date each page and sign the last one. You'll need it for orientation. When you finish the drug test, come back and find me, I'll take you where you need to go."

"Rick said I needed to tell you people what my job designation was. He said you and him would call Ned and let me know. Did you see Rick?"

"Rick knew what that was. I don't know why he would have told you that. It's on the paperwork they faxed down. Don't you know what your job title is?" Jeff asked, walking beside Jake.

Jake wasn't sure what to answer.

A wind carried smells of the sea, salty, fishy, up from the bay. The tune that Mitch had been listening to played in his head--a song he remembered his mother used to listen to, only with an island beat, steel kettle drums and the island lilt making the sound different. Jake looked out toward the sea. There was a building with an antenna on a distant promontory. Closer in the remains of a wood boat, half-submerged in the sand and surf. The water turquoise. The rising sun played on the slight waves lapping onto the silky white sand. He could imagine the gentle splash of the sea, the cool rush that would take your breath away as you waded out into its salty pulse. This was what he had expected when he had been hired to come to the Bahamas.

They arrived at another mobile trailer. Jeff went up the weathered steps, Jake followed. Inside was a desk with a Bahamian female wearing a nurse's outfit. Jake looked around. A couple of Bahamians stood in the narrow hallway. Two large Bahamian police officers were outside two doors at the far end.

"Sir," Jake heard the nurse say. He turned, and her hand was extended. He handed her the paperwork. She flipped through the pages. "You must sign these," she said handing them back.

Jeff said, "I'll see you when you're through."

Jake initialed, dated and signed the pages. He saw he was listed as Assistant Project Manager on the line for job description.

The nurse drew blood. He had to piss in a vial; one of the police officers watched. Never had a man stared so hard at his penis.

He passed. The nurse handed him his paperwork and sent him on his way. They should give you Kool-Aid and cookies like the Red Cross does. Better still, would have been a shot of whiskey. Jake wanted to celebrate his success. Fuck Rick.

He headed back toward the office complex. The morning hum was a steady buzz of earth moving equipment, dump trucks, and pickups moving in and around the containers. He still had not seen any buildings under construction. They must be off in the distance, behind the dunes where most of the trucks seemed to be coming and going. The huge earth movers were probably building the golf course an expat he overheard on the flight in was talking about. The earthmoving equipment was operated by the Rastafarians Rick pointed out. No hardhats. Reminded him to put the one Jeff gave him back on his head.

The rest of the morning was spent listening to one company person talk about the company and the project. Then a long session given by the safety and security officer, who stressed their many hours without any major injuries and that, if you were to receive a life-threatening injury, the nearest hospital was ninety miles away in Nassau. Jake thought, not much different from when he had served overseas in the Army.

Exiting the office complex, he thought about his neck. The pain from the anxious stress had eased. Maybe the heat and salty air helped. Jake felt sweat trickling off his forehead and down his back. The breeze was still blowing, stirring the hot air, sun rays reflecting off the white sand, trapping heat between the primer-red, rusting metal containers.

Orientation ended at lunch time. Jake had no idea where to go, no way to get there. He headed back to the laydown container yard hoping Mitch or Rick would take him wherever they went.

As he neared the ESI office, he heard shouting. Looking in that direction he saw Mitch come running out of the supply container, Rick was running after him. Rick threw his hardhat hitting Mitch in the back with it. Mitch disappeared around the end of the container. Rick stopped and picked up his hardhat and turned just when Jake reached the office container.

"I'll kill that slack son of a bitch. Ned needs to get him, Amy and that piece of shit son of his out of here," he said to Jake.

"What was that all about?" Jake asked. Man o' man this fucker has a temper, he thought.

"He let those Bahamian fucks take both trucks. They're supposed to load the shit in one truck. If they all can't fit, they need to walk, like the other companies' men do. I've told him over and over not to let my truck be used to haul those niggers to the job sites. I need it so I can check on them, run to the airport, and go to lunch. He needs his ass kicked."

Jake had no idea how to respond. He was beginning to think Rick had a bully mentality. Lying, underhanded deceit and being a bully—to Jake these were signs of insecurity. People lie for many reasons. Experts claim the average person lies numerous times every day. A lie doesn't care from whose lips it falls. Most times the lie is meant to embellish a story, make the speaker look or feel better about themselves, or, told because the truth may cause the listener to be offended. These are what Jake and most people call "white" lies.

Then there are the pathological liars, the ones who either don't know the difference between truth and lies or do not care. It is said pathological liars have more white matter on their brain causing them to think more, but in a non-discerning manner. How do you know when they are lying? "When their lips move" was one reference often used. Jake noticed these people often punctuate any skepticism, often within their own thoughts, by saying, "I'm not lying." His ex-wife had been one of those.

Jake hated liars as much as he did bullies. From his point of view, bullies either acted this way as a self-defense mechanism to cover up their fear, or, saw themselves as physically or mentally superior, feeling an overwhelming desire to intimidate or harm those whom they preyed upon. Often one or both of their parents or another authority figure had intimidated or physically harmed them, reinforcing their own predilections.

Here was one of Ned's problems. Rick did not know how to manage people. He saw management as giving him the upper hand—another way to bully. Jake had been told by his father and in military training, good leaders led by example, encouraging, not demanding. The former manager, Rick's friend, had done Ned's company a disservice recommending Rick. Jake would have to tread lightly, not make hasty judgments. Rick saw him as a threat. But, if Rick tried to bully him, he would find Jake would neither run, nor back down. He decided to confront Rick. He would wait until he learned more.

Rick went in his office and called one of the Bahamians at the job site. When Jake entered, he heard him instructing whomever to bring him his truck.

The container pulsed with heat, no air moving, a reminder of daytime in the Middle East.

"This is the kind of shit I have to put up with every day," Rick said closing his flip phone. "Ned knows but refuses to do anything about it. He yells at me and tells me to handle it, then gets pissed when I tell him the problem is his son and his son's friends. I've sent them back to the states twice. They come back. Maybe he sent you here to replace them or maybe he has decided to get rid of me. I really don't give a fuck anymore."

"Any place near here where I can get something to eat, maybe within walking distance?"

"The man-camp serves bag lunches, mostly fried bologna and a bag of chips. I don't care to eat that shit. I was going to take you to one of the places around here, but fuckhead let them take our wheels. Rodney is bringing the truck. What kind of food do you like?"

"Whatever. Usually I pack something when I am on a job away from home." Jake sat in the only other chair, stretching his legs. "Hopefully I can get to the grocery store sometime soon. When do I get that food allowance you said we receive?"

"This Thursday. I can loan you money if you're short."

The truck pulled up in front of the office, radio loud enough to be heard over the noise of the motor and the AC cutting in and out. Rodney didn't switch off. The sound grew louder when he opened the door. Several other Bahamians came back with him. Rodney went to the wall air conditioner and plugged it in. The others entered and sat on the floor. Some had bag lunches and can sodas. Rick walked out. Jake followed. He closed the door to the office. Jake saw Rodney seat himself in Rick's chair before the door squawked shut.

They traveled several miles back toward Georgetown. Rick seemed to not be in a big hurry. There was not much in the way of oncoming vehicles, giving Jake a chance to enjoy the periodic views from above down to the flat expanse of the sea whose colors were three shades of blue. Off in the distance, like a mirage was another island, where Rick said people went by boat on weekends to cookout and frolic on the beach.

"The waters between here and there are infested with sharks. One of the top dogs with Fluor has a son that is one of their office flunkies. He got drunk and missed the final boat back. The crazy fucker swam back in the dark. No one knows how he managed, made him a topic of conversation. Every time anyone introduces him, they tell the story. Lots of people do foolish things out here. People stick their noses into local business, not smart. Just so you know."

"Was that a threat or a warning?" Jake asked.

"Fair warning. Most of these Bahamians have other enterprises. They will tell you they are experienced in almost anything. Some have worked on other projects in the islands. Most pick up work in the service trades, whenever and wherever they can. Many Bahamians have boats. They charter them out on weekends. Not all their charters are legal, if you get my drift."

Rick pulled into the parking area of a concrete block, tin-roofed building set back off the road. A white metal sign had Rosie's Diner in faded red letters painted on it. The lot was full.

Inside looked like any Fifties-era diner, not unlike the ones Jake had eaten in where he grew up. The same all along the Southern towns and byways he had traveled. The diners weren't much different either—white, blue-collar men filling their veins with fatty fried foods and ice-cold beverages—in the southern U.S., that was usually very sweet iced tea. The heavy-set waitress looked at Jake like she had never heard of iced tea when he ordered it. Rick reminded him of the water, so he changed his order to a Pepsi.

"Weird having a former British Commonwealth establishment that doesn't serve tea," Jake said when she left. He looked at the menu. Mostly rice, beans and fried plantains for vegetables. Guess I'll have to get used to it, he thought. He commented about this to Rick.

"Kind of hard for most these places to serve fresh vegetables. They don't grow any here, the ones shipped in come frozen. Wait until you go to the grocer. A small watermelon costs fourteen dollars." He saw Jake's brow rise. "Welcome to paradise." He let out a brief snort of his irritating laugh.

"Hope I can make do on that living allowance."

"You'll learn. Pooling our allowances will help. Be careful of former expats that live here. They're always trying to get materials, supplies and labor from the companies. They make stealing and selling to them sound like they're trying to help you out. It can get tempting. Happens quite a lot. A lot of the natives are descendants of pirates; many expats came here and have joined their ranks."

The food was seasoned well. Jake enjoyed it.

On the way back, Rick told Jake he needed him to take the truck when they got back to pick up a Bahamian named Rob who would be flying in from Nassau. "First we'll run by and pick up Blakely at the house. We'll take you around to some of the other places after work. Seems like every day here is hump day. Today happy hour is at a place near Georgetown."

6

Jake had never driven on the wrong side of the road legally, other than passing. Meeting other vehicles passing on the passenger side, felt awkward. He hugged the driver's side of the road. Twice he had to slam on brakes because of drivers passing on the curves, meeting him head-on. He had a difficult time remembering where to turn in order to reach the house. It took him three times as long to get there than it had taken Rick that morning.

At the door, Jake hesitated, thinking he should knock. Hell, this was his living quarters too. In fact, he had more rights to be here than Blakely. He opened the door entering the kitchen. There were dirty dishes in the sink covered in those minute insects. The air smelled of marijuana. He heard Blakely humming a tune. Jake headed toward the hallway, when he turned the corner, Blakely was stepping out of the tub/shower. She turned toward Jake, seemingly not surprised or embarrassed. She continued to dry herself, looking up at him smiling.

"Like what you see?" she asked laughing at Jake's red, shocked expression.

Jake said, "I'm sorry." He turned down the hall and went to his own bedroom.

She followed. Jake felt trapped. His arousal was a natural reaction, turning away to hide his embarrassment was something new. It had been awhile since he had been with a woman and Blakely was all woman. Jake didn't know what her game was. Supposedly she was Rick's girlfriend. He laid awake last night, thoughts of her on his mind, wondering if her actions were purposely seductive or naïve coquetry. There was not much doubt now. His mind was fogging—the little head was threatening to take control of the big head. When he was younger, after Ariel, his first love and lover and before his marriage to Joanna, there had been many casual sexual partners. That was a long time ago.

"You aren't gay, are you?" she asked causing him to turn from looking at her sideways to looking her dead in the eye.

"Not my thing. You're supposed to be Rick's woman. I try not to drop anchor in another man's port."

"How chivalrous. I'm not Rick's woman. He doesn't own me. I used to be a bartender at the bar he frequented in St. Louis. When the economy went south, the tips all but disappeared. Rick and I got drunk together one night and he told me he had been offered a job in the Bahamas. Asked me if I wanted to come. Ta da, here I am. I don't have a job, and he doesn't complain about my staying. That's the extent of me and Rick. Mitch didn't mind. He turned out to be too much of a kid. Ran his mouth. Bet you aren't like that." She reached out and rubbed Jake's groin. She started undoing Jake's zipper.

Reluctantly, he gently took her hand away. "I never thought I'd say this, especially to a good-looking naked lady, but I'm new to this. I've been told by friends that all I have to do is breathe on a woman and she ends up pregnant," he said with a grimacing smile. "Don't want any more children and, nothing personal, I don't want to catch something that keeps on giving."

Before he thought to block her, she yanked her hand from his and slapped him hard. "Go fuck yourself. I am not some slut that you can talk to like that. She turned and hurried back down the hall, went in the bedroom she shared with Rick and slammed the door.

He plopped down on the bed. The heat of the sun, the slap and the feelings he felt, reminded him how tired he was. It would be nice to lie back and take a nap. He wasn't sure why he had refused Blakely's advances or insulted her. He had a way of doing that. Joanna said the Army had made him callous. Perhaps? Joanna's infidelity did not make him want to be charitable. In his heart he knew it began before the Army.

Ariel Harper, a distant cousin, his kissing cousin, his first love, the one who had been his first in everything, the one who had disappeared without saying why or goodbye, sent away by her father when he found out about their lovemaking. Ariel, the one every woman would be compared to, and fall short. Ariel, a large reason he had stayed in the Army.

Sleep was reaching out for him, pulling him toward its embrace. He stood up. He needed to go to the airport. Blakely was supposed to go with him. He went back down the hall and knocked on the door. She didn't answer. He hesitated then cracked the door. She sat on the bed, still undressed, a laptop computer resting on her knees, her shaved sex shining. It was all Jake could do to keep from stepping in, undressing and taking his pent-up sexual frustration out on her.

"Did you change your mind?" she asked looking from his eyes back down to his bulging crotch.

"I'm sorry. I have a hard time saying what it is I should say. I meant no insult to you. I hurt people too often and regret how I handle situations, especially with women. It is my fallacy, not yours. I apologize."

She put the laptop aside, took her right hand and rubbed it between her lower lips. "I can see you're having a hard time." She had her eyes on his crotch, a lascivious smile played on her moistened lips. "If you think my pussy is diseased, you are wrong. I am picky when it comes to whom I give myself to. I am on the pill. If you like, you can use a condom or if you wish I can give you some relief in other ways." She licked her lips. "Looks to me like you would like some relief." She continued to rub herself, looking up and smiling at him.

Jake wasn't sure how to react. He felt himself blushing and chuckled nervously. "You're a trip. I guess you know that. Anyway, Rick needed me to pick you up. We need to get going. We are supposed to pick up someone from the airport." He closed the door. "If you're coming with me, get dressed and let's get going."

He moved away from the door and the temptation that lay on the other side. *Damn. Maybe I need to find some place other than here to stay.* Jake wasn't sure how much Rick knew. She had mentioned Mitch. Was that the reason Rick had it in for the kid. He heard her moaning. She wanted him to hear her moaning. Then she laughed.

A few minutes later she came out of the room and walked up to him sitting at the table. She extended her hand, trying for his nose.

"Smell that and tell me if it smells rotten to you." She laughed again. "Come on, lover boy. We shouldn't keep Rick waiting. He gets jealous. Wouldn't want that, would we?"

Something wasn't right with her and this whole situation. Jake had a bad feeling. Things were going to end quicker than Ned wanted. Damn, her sex did smell inviting.

They sat in the truck at the airport. The quiet lingered, became oppressive. Without explanation, Blakely got out and went to the café where he had waited the day before. Jake lay his head back and closed his eyes. On the way over, Blakely had said she applied for a job with Four Seasons as bar manager, so she could stay here. He asked if Rick knew. She said she was growing tired of Rick. She asked Jake if he had a girlfriend. He said no. He told her about his ex and kids, adding, his son was old enough to be her younger brother. She thought that was funny.

"Is that why you don't want me?"

"Maybe…I'm temporary. This project is almost complete. Ned sent me here to help finish up, then I'll be gone."

"Rick thinks Ned sent you here to take his place. He's worried he'll be sent back to St. Louis and return to being unemployed. Ned's a dickhead. How well do you know him?"

"Not much. I take it you don't like him?"

"I've met him a couple of times. He eye-fucked me both times. Him with his second wife and all his kids. When he's with you, he talks like he'd do anything for you. When he calls Rick, he talks dirt, yelling and cussing, acting like he owns him. Rick says he talks to Fluor's people the same way. He's a telephone bully, who thinks he's better than everyone else. You'll see."

Jake dozed off. His phone ring tone woke him. *No ID* showed. He decided he should answer.

"Jake, Bob Hardy. How are you liking the Bahamas?"

"Bob? Damn. How'd you know I was in the Bahamas?"

"Eric from Dilworth told me."

"I haven't seen Eric in months Bob. How did you know? What's going on?"

"Why don't we talk about this over drinks. I'm here for the night. Let's meet up at the Georgetown Inn, say nineteen hundred hours. I'll explain when I see you." The call was disconnected.

What the fuck was going on? Jake knew Bob as another member of a private billiard club in Charlotte. Eric the owner told Jake Bob worked for one of the federal agencies. Bob had not been forthcoming about his employment when Jake asked. They were friendly, not exactly friends. TJ said he should join one of the agencies. He doubted this was a coincidence.

7

Miami, Fl

The HSI field office war room had three people seated at computers. Agent Swanson, Carl, introduced them. Bridgette, Baker, and a Hispanic named Mariel, they were research and intelligence analysts. There were several others – Julia, Diego and Michel, who were interpreters.

"Occasionally we have other field special agents come in. For this op you're our main man." They had returned from the buzz of the operations room to Swanson's office.

"How you envision me in this op?" TJ asked. "Hardy said I was to use my sources. Those sources belong to my other operation. Don't see many of them any benefit to this op. Kinda pisses me off that I've been cultivating these assets, getting close, turning CIs, putting together my case. Now, I'm supposed to switch gears, throw that case in the can and go a different direction? Don't know why my commander and the commissioner would agree to this, think they were railroaded also."

"Hold on there, fella. You were selected because of these assets. You will continue working your other case. The pukes who killed those two cops, local law didn't think they were part of the Latin Kings' action with the Juarez Cartel, isn't that what you were trying to prove? That that traffic stop killing was too well prepared, the van disappeared despite an all-out shut down and search of the whole area. The Kings couldn't have done that without some big-time help. You've been on it for over a year, are you any closer to getting names, proving your theory?

"You probably weren't told, HSI offered to assist the DEA, they refused. We had information that the shooters' van had a plastic coating they removed. Rode right through the roadblocks and escaped via a boat owned by a Bahamian with connections to the Juarez boys. They shuttled them to Haiti, then across to Cancun, where we lost them. We offered this information to Miami Dade Investigators and they let it drop, saying not enough manpower. Shocking huh? Two cops killed. No one wants to act on the intel handed them. That's the kind of jurisdictional, noncooperation that has allowed too many of these dickheads to have a free ride. Nobody gives a shit about the deconfliction code, they only pretend to."

"How is it HSI knew and no one else did?"

"Because we have better intel. Despite lack of cooperation, HSI has better access to channels in matters dealing with national security."

"The local and national security faces a whole new level of threat, due to UAVs. When drones became more popular, we knew it was just a matter of time until they became a means for illegal transport, surveillance by criminals, and possible terrorists' use. As they grow more powerful, the potential for arming personal drones became a reality. They have become a major part of the cartels' current and potential arsenal to be used against each other, law enforcement, even industry, military and political leaders. This newest submarine UAV of Russia's ups the ante big time. We don't know without a doubt that it is beyond the prototype stage. We intend to find out. Miami is not HSI's only field office working on this."

"We have to be very careful, as Bob said. Not only are there agents from Russia, Cuba and the cartels in on this, sad to say, we have people within our own law enforcement and federal agencies who are on the take. Seems every time we get a hit on a possible, they already know we're listening or making a move. They use drop phones, constantly switching—whenever we get a known *ping*, they somehow know. We start all over again. Often, they use a technique called mirroring. You familiar with mirroring?"

TJ replied, "Yeah. It's where one phone retypes a text or message onto another phone. Makes it difficult to track the message and the recipient. Fucks up wiretapping."

"We try to get a sympathetic judge to give us a roving wiretap warrant allowing us to follow the target rather than the devise. That way we don't have to keep applying for wiretaps over and over—judges tend to become unsympathetic. Problem is we need a proven target to obtain a warrant. And we need to keep that target close to our shirts, like good cards in Texas Hold-Em, without having the other players reading the tell. You a card player?"

"Not really. Usually watch, don't lose any money that way. The few casinos I've visited, noticed the house usually wins."

"That's because they keep the card sharks out. They know who the 'players' are." Swanson used finger quotes to emphasize his point. "Unfortunately, we don't always know. We are now having to screen our people on a random basis. Ever taken a lie detector test?"

TJ leaned forward toward Swanson, resting his large arms on the table, hands clasped, "I'm sure you know I passed the test before I became an Army sniper, have top security clearance, revetted when I joined Miami Dade SWAT team, I have nothing to hide."

Swanson leaned back away from the table, distancing himself from TJ's glare. TJ noticed a grimace as he leaned back.

"I'm not doubting your veracity. But, everyone at HSI and other feds have security clearance, yet we still manage to find bad apples. No offense, Homeland's policy requires everyone to be tested. There are three different methods in use: the lie detector, a memogram device which reads brain waves, and HS has a specially trained person, referred to as the human detector. We test and randomly retest our personnel using different methods each time. One method gives us pause, then other methods are used."

"All detection methods are less than 90 percent reliable. I have been taught to beat the lie detector test. I was put to the test with a gun to my head. Do you personally know what that's like?" TJ kept his eyes locked onto Swanson's. "I also went through the extreme testing in case of capture, as a matter of course before becoming a Ranger, including water boarding. Does Homeland use those methods on the ones who give you pause?"

Swanson paled. "I served in Vietnam. I was held captive for over a year and subjected to levels of mental and physical abuse, you can only try to imagine. No. I would never use torture as a method of interrogation. Not only is it illegal, the veracity of information gained is unreliable. I hope you agree."

TJ eased back in his chair. He noticed the slight tremor in Swanson's hands. He had noticed it before and not thought much about it. "Don't know what to say to someone like you. Could say I'm sorry, but know you'd rather not be pitied. The best I can think to say is, I salute you." TJ did just that. "Would also like to shake your hand."

Swanson leaned forward, TJ half-rose and they clasped hands. "My father served two tours in 'Nam, didn't survive the second one, hated hearing people's empty pity. Also hate the 'thank you for your service' from those who recite that as if they care."

"You still must take one of the tests, Officer Alvarez, or rather I should call you Agent Alvarez."

"TJ what my friends call me. I'd be interested in taking that memograph test, just to see the results."

8

Great Exuma, Bahamas

The tall lanky Bahamian came out of the Georgetown Airport building. Jake recognized him as the person Rick had dropped off the day before. Once more, the dude that Jake now knew was named Rob, stopped to exchange words with a couple Bahamians that were seated on the concrete bench. He set a big black carry-on bag down and they did what Jake called the jive greeting—fist bumping, finger clinching, elbow smacking, with a couple other moves thrown in. They started talking. Jake could hear their sing-songy cadence and booming laughter. Rob turned his head, when the middle-aged one nodded his head in the truck's direction. Something was said, they all laughed again. Rob turned, headed his way, his broad face lit up with a smile. The passenger door opened startling Jake. It was Blakely. She too was smiling and waved. The guys on the bench waved back. She slid in next to Jake and patted his thigh high up, brushing his groin. Rob put the carry-on in the truck bed, got in the truck, slammed the door shut. Jake wondered what was in the bag. Rob had been empty-handed when he departed.

"What's up Blake," Rob asked. "You mustah be Mistuh Harper Rick's replacement. I be the main man Rob."

He stuck his fist out across in front of Blakely. Jake bumped his fist.

"Mr. Harper says he doesn't want to be Rick's replacement, Jake is a former soldier boy, got injured, medical discharge. He's finding it *hard* to adjust," Blakely said. "We going to show him around tonight, maybe after a few drinks and some other things, he'll loosen up." They both laughed.

Jake wondered how she knew about his time in the service and his medical discharge. Maybe Ned or someone in ESI's Charlotte office told Rick? Blakely and Rob chatted, as Jake drove. He heard names that meant nothing to him. The only other question and answer that really caught Jake's attention was when Blakely asked if Rob's trip had been a good one, and he replied, "Like always."

Nearing Emerald Bay, Jake watched the sun's reddish disk bob in and out of clouds, its shaky light shadowing the hilly land side along the island highway. Rob asked him to pull into a set of apartments called Sun Villa, a couple miles Jake guessed, from the job site. When he stopped, Blakely got out after Rob.

"Switch off," she said and followed Rob into the door of the lower unit he had been directed to park in front of.

The inside of the apartment reminded Jake of retro-fifties--vinyl furniture in bright orange and blue colors. The linoleum floor was worn smooth, the topcoat ragged in spots. The air smelled like a frat house after a night of partying—stale smoke, hints of marijuana, and the odor of alcohol, mainly beer, hung in the humid cold air blowing from a window AC unit. Seated on the blue sofa was Mitch and a darker-skinned, well-toned guy, looked to be in his early twenties like Mitch. They wore virtual headsets. They didn't even look up when Blakely asked if they had anything to drink. Jock type motioned his head toward the kitchen.

Rob followed Blakely into the kitchen. Jake sat down on the orange chaise thinking about the situation. He needed to find a way to get to the Georgetown Inn before seven. He glanced at his phone, almost four thirty, close to knock-off time for most job sites, Rick said he would need the truck. He got up and went in the kitchen. Blakely and Rob were leaning against the kitchen countertop drinking beers and talking. They stopped when he walked in.

"Rick is expecting us to bring the truck back to him. What time does he knock off?" he asked her.

"I've already called him. He's bringing the other truck. One of the expat crews stays in these apartments said he would wait to give the boys a ride.

Have a beer, relax. Tonight's hump night. Drinks and beer are half-priced during happy hour at this place in Georgetown. Most people from the project go there. Rick said this would be a good opportunity for you to get to know some of them, away from the job, when everyone is acting normal. Don't you ever let loose or are you always uptight?"

Depends on where and with whom, Jake wanted to say but kept his mouth shut. He opened the refrigerator. The only thing in it was beer. He took a Heineken, opened it with the opener laying on the shiny green vinyl tabletop wrapped in ripple-shaped aluminum edging, another circa fifties replica, maybe original. Rob and Blakely watched him. He walked back into the living area and sat down on the orange chaise. The room was paneled with yellowed wood, the ceilings Celotex panels, reminded him of his paternal great aunt and uncle's house when he visited as a kid, everything except the colors, here orange and green, theirs' grey and brown. His great uncle had been a funny man, always joking and laughing. His grandfather never liked him much. After he died, when Jake was fourteen, Jake asked his father why his grandfather disliked his brother-in-law. His father's answer shocked and amazed Jake.

Back in the early Sixties, after Jake's great grandfather died, several of his daughters and their husbands – Jake's other great aunts and uncles –had swooped in before the funeral, like vultures and took everything they had coveted, leaving Jake's great-grandmother with the bare necessities.

The next summer, for his great-grandmother's birthday, the whole family, for her birthday request, laid out a feast across long wooden tables set out on the lawn of her house under a huge red oak with Spanish moss dripping from its limbs. Jake's grandfather and four brothers along with Jake's father and other siblings and cousins were on one side, their sisters and husbands on the other side with their children. Sometime during the meal after the blessing and main course before desert was to be served, a comment about the raid on their parent's house was made, which led to an angry exchange. Next thing Jake's father knew, Jake's grandfather and brothers had pistols drawn, as did the in-laws on the other side, each threatening to kill the other. Jake's great-grandmother pounded on the table and demanded they put the guns away. Remarkably they complied. That was the last family gathering they ever had. The only man who had not pulled a gun, nor taken a side, was Jake's jolly great uncle. Jake's grandfather felt this sister and her husband should have been on their side.

Jake did not realize the story had taken place in his head while he was asleep. Next thing he knew, Mitch was taking his more than half-empty beer from his hand.

"Hey dude, you spilled your beer. You all right?" Mitch asked. "Blakely keep you up partying last night?" He threw a towel on the mess at Jake's feet.

"Something like that."

"You play?" the other guy asked.

"Not my thing. Who are you?"

"Nick Baxter. I'm here helping my dad. Our company is doing the project floor coverings. We're out of Little Rock. You from Charlotte?"

"South of there in South Carolina."

They shook hands.

Mitch stood and yelled, "I'm outta here, dude." He disappeared toward the back of the apartment. "You coming out tonight?" he asked Jake.

"Probably."

"I'll introduce you to my dad. He's a little older than you, but you guys probably will get along. He's cool."

Rick showed up shortly afterwards. Jake had expected a problem might arise between Rick and Mitch, but nothing was said. Rick grabbed a beer and asked Rob if he got what he needed. Rob said, "yeah mon, in back of dee truck."

Rick guzzled the beer and they left.

Jake had to ask, "What's in the bag?"

"Rob's big sausages," Blakely said. "These Bahamians like to play with their big sausages."

"Everything comes out of your mouth is always a joke, mostly about drugs and sex," Rick said.

"Your complaint is?" she asked. "Isn't that why you like me?"

"You think?"

"What about you, Jake? You ready to go out and have some fun?" She looked at him with a grin.

"Where we headed?"

Rick said, "back to the house so I can get cleaned up and change clothes. Somewhere you need to be?" He laughed his grating laugh. Blakely winced looking at Jake then laughed. "We'll head down to Georgetown afterwards. Guess you heard about hump day happy hour. Not really hump day anymore. This damn thing is seven days a week now. They're talking about working shifts. Ned called, and he's all for it. Said he'll be down here before Christmas to see how we're doing. Said you were my assistant. Guess I have two weeks before you take over."

"I don't think so. He never said anything like that when I interviewed with him. Why you keep thinking that?"

"Wishful thinking. Once you're here a while, you'll know what I mean. Ned's making all the money, let's everyone know it."

"Enough of this talk. It's hump day." Blakely said. "Only problem for you, Jake, is how few single, non-Bahamian women there are. Most of the pretty ones are already taken. Might make you reconsider your situation." She winked. Rick glanced over and she laughed.

Bob Hardy was sitting in the back corner, oak booth of Tandy Tavern in the Georgetown Inn. He was dressed in a blue knitted-cotton short-sleeve shirt, Khaki shorts and leather, buckled sandals. He looked like a tourist on vacation nursing, what Jake recalled, his typical tonic and gin. Jake was wearing a button-down, white shirt with Old Navy gym shorts and plain leather sandals. Jake ordered a Heineken from the bar and joined him. No one seemed to be paying them any attention. Bob raised his glass. "Cheers Jake. Good to see you."

"Why do I feel coming here wasn't to give me your regards, Bob?"

"Jake my ol' friend, you should not be so negative. Do you know why this place is called Tandy's Tavern? See that spit of land out there. Jessica Tandy and Hugh Cronin used to live out there. They entertained numerous actors, luminaries, including then King and Queen of England. Legend has it, she died in their grand home there and her ghost can be seen wandering the grounds. Much like the ghost I've heard you say could be your grandmother back on your farm."

"Thanks for that bit of trivia. Shall we get to the reason you called me to come meet you, Starting with how you knew I was here? Don't give me the bullshit line that Eric told you. We both know that can't possibly be true."

Hardy held up his glass to get the bar tender's attention. He walked up to the bar to retrieve his drink. There was no waitress inside the small tavern. Outside was a large deck area that stretched down to the harbor. Lights on strings lit up the main deck and lined the boardwalk down to some steps, several large boats were moored not far away. Off to one side of the main deck was a covered bar area. Tables and chairs were being arranged outside, extending from the wall out to the boardwalk.

Hardy returned. "Heard you were struggling financially. Eric told me about your troubles with that custom home whose contract fell through." He took a swallow of his drink. "You ever stop to think about how convenient it was a person sitting next to you in that oyster bar and grill, happened to know ESI was looking to hire someone like you for this job in the Bahamas?"

Jake looked hard at Hardy. "And I thought I got lucky. Guess TJ hinting to me that I should think about joining up with some fed agency was your doing also. I'm not interested. We're through here?" Jake stood to leave.

"Come on, Jake, I would never do that to you. I've known you since you got out of the Army. I listened and was sympathetic to how your wife and the VA fucked you over. I consider you a friend. I hope you feel the same toward me. Friends help friends. At least I try to help whenever and however I can. Sit down, finish your beer. Tell me how it's going."

Jake eased back into the seat.

"Let me get you another beer."

"No thank you, I'm fine. The people I came here with are probably wondering where I am. You know Wednesday, hump-day, happy hour get togethers. They're going to introduce me around. I would ask you to join us, but Blakely, one of the people I came here with, would probably think and say something crude."

"Blakely Carmichael, at least that's who she says she is. Has license, vehicle and voter registration cards and a passport that say the same. Funny thing, Blakely Carmichael, with the Social Security number used by this Blakely, died as an infant and is buried in a church graveyard outside Kansas

City, Kansas. She's just one of many questionable characters here in the Bahamas that we need to know more about."

"Who's we?"

"Homeland Security. Go to this hump-day thing. Meet me here, rather, will you meet me here later? I'm in room 207, registered as George Polk. Go on, you need to get to know these people. Be aware they may not all be who they say or appear to be."

"Like you?"

"Yeah. Like me. Only I wear the white hat."

"I can't promise anything. I Haven't had much sleep the last few nights. The house I'm sharing doesn't have air conditioning in my bedroom, never cools off. I'm so tired, even the alcohol has little effect on me."

"Tell you what, I'll get you a room here for the night. Maybe let Uncle Sam buy you a window unit tomorrow. All I ask, listen to what I have to say. Deal?"

"Against my better judgement, I'll take you up on the offer with the understanding, I made no promises."

Blakely, or whomever she was, stood by the bar talking to some older men. They were laughing. Jake would have bet his next newborn it had something to do with sex. She broke loose as soon as she saw him enter the circus-size tent, made a beeline in his direction.

"Where did you run off to? Rick and I have been looking all over for you."

"Walked around Georgetown. Ate at the Georgetown Inn and booked a room for tonight."

"Is that an invitation? I'm sure we could slip off in a little while for a quickie. That's probably all you'd be good for." Her alcohol-infused face flashed a grin.

"You're probably right. Guess I'll have to take a raincheck on tonight. Where's Rick?"

"Right behind you. The offer is there, if you change your mind. Come on, loosen up, have a drink."

"Rick look who I found."

Jake turned around. Rick walked up to them.

"Jake said he is staying in the Georgetown Inn tonight. I was telling him he shouldn't have done that. You need to buy him a beer, take him around. There are people you said he needs to meet. I'll wait at the outside bar."

For the next two hours, Rick led him around introducing him to people. Jake nursed three or four beers, throwing the bottles away before they were half empty. He wasn't buying, others kept insisting. When they met up with Blakely, she was standing with a tall, distinguished-looking Hispanic named Juan Carlos Diego. He was a Columbian, ramrodding the company responsible for the stucco work. While they were talking, the burly Australian former serviceman named Alec Wickham, the bloke that Rick had spoken about the previous night, came over accompanied by a rugby lock-size New Zealander named Marcus Barrette. It was obvious they were not interested in talking to Jake. Alec was fixated with Blakely. Marcus became engrossed in a conversation with Rick. The Columbian moved off

to talk to the man Walt Whitmire, Fluor's main man for the project.

Jake decided to make his exit. He told Rick he was heading out, he needed to crash. Rick didn't seem to think anything of it. He handed Jake the keys to the truck saying he and Blakely would catch a ride with Marcus and Alec.

9

J ake didn't bother to drive the half mile to the inn. He had to buzz the desk manager, a droopy-eyed Bahamian who gave him room key for 209. Adjoined Hardy's room Jake guessed. The room was small with a regular size bed, two end tables with lamps, a digital clock and a phone. A small closet was just inside the door with a chair and chest of drawers tucked into the recess next to the closet. The décor was Victorian era, accented by two rugs on the floor and frilly curtains behind which was a double window overlooking a recessed area of the courtyard deck. The sounds of a Bahamian tune, steel drums and all, could be plainly heard amidst the hum of voices and bouts of laughter. There was a small bath with a shower, pedestal sink and a toilet. Next to this was another door. To Hardy's room, he figured. As a precaution, he checked for exits in case there was a need to make a hasty retreat.

He tapped on the adjoining wall's door. As if he had been waiting, Hardy opened the door on his side. Jake entered noting the same musky, humid scent with a hint of potpourri. Same as in his room. Hardy sat on his bed. Jake took the chair.

"Hope the party dies down before it gets too late," Jake remarked.

Hardy chuckled. He was holding a gin and tonic. The bottles sat on the chest of drawers along with another crystal glass and a dripping decorative ice bucket resting on a towel.

"Care for a drink? Help yourself, gin and tonic, all I have. Alcohol is inexpensive, not so the room. Glad I'm not paying."

Jake made himself a drink, light on the gin.

"Meet any interesting people?"

Jake told Hardy about the people he had been introduced to. "Didn't notice anything I would suspect as being unusual. He laughed. "Everyone except Blakely, she seems to think with her pussy." Hardy laughed, Jake was exhausted, he managed a smile. "After what you told me, I think maybe this is her way of throwing people curve balls. She said something about Mitch, a kid who is the boss, Ned's son's best friend. Sounded like he had been the housemate before me. They apparently had something going on. Rick, her boyfriend and Ned's company manager down here, now have issues with each other."

"So…what is Ned's connection to you and why was I selected to come here?"

"Neither Ned nor his company have any connection to Homeland. I know Ned, does some government jobs. We were recently at a social event and he happened to mention the problems he was having with this project. That was the extent of our conversation regarding that. I heard from Eric about your financial woes. Your problem, his problem, my op. I had an aha moment, need and opportunity came together. I had a Homeland person keep an eye out, here you are. Interested in hearing me out? You said you would."

Jake took a drink. Been a long time since he had drunk a gin and tonic— not bad. "Wait a minute…you left something out. Just exactly how did this guy know I was in this bar? How long had he been tailing me?"

"That was the only day. I told him your telephone number and address. He waited for you at the McConnells' crossroad, followed you from there. You really should be more aware of what's going on around you. Learn not to be predictable."

Jake sat there twirling his drink. Fuck. This pissed him off. "Why should I? Before now, I never felt I had reason to. Not stateside. Why didn't you call me? Could have saved both of us a lot of time."

"You're right. Figured you'd be none too happy my nosing into your personal business. I apologize." He watched Jake, evaluating, calculating, Jake realized Bob always seemed to do this. "Anyway I hope this works out for both of us. What I have to say cannot be repeated to anyone. This operation is a matter of national security and I am trusting you to honor my trust. Do I have your word regarding this?"

"Bob, how did we meet?"

"A couple of years ago, right after your release from rehab. Don't you remember? We were in Dilworth Billiards, one of my rare tournament entries, you and I were matched up. It was your first time back in the tournament." Bob turned his head towards the sounds of merriment, a familiar song seemed to raise the crowd's enthusiasm.

Jake studied his movement trying to detect the sincerity. "I'm thinking your presence was calculated. You asked a lot of questions, but now that I think back, I believe you already knew the answers. You've been recruiting me from the git-go. Almost every time I came in you seemed to single me out."

"Jake, I talked to a lot of people. I liked talking to you. If you think my friendship was calculated, you would be wrong. I won't lie to you, because I knew your background and found out the reason you had stopped showing at Dilworth was for financial reasons, I did set out to recruit you for this operation. I figured we could both benefit and knowing I would be helping you was a major determination. Your military experience, operating in a hostile environment, learning how to ask the right questions, knowing that trusting the wrong person and intel can get you and your fellow men killed, those are lessons only experienced operators know. Hear me out, if you decide not to help, we'll shake hands and pretend this never happened. Before I proceed, I need your word this goes no further. Like I said, this is a matter of national security."

"I would never betray my country. You have my word on that. But, if you think telling me what you are about to say means I have agreed to do anything, save your breath."

"Fair enough..." He took a drink, looked out, twisted away from Jake, turned on the radio that was on his bedside table, the volume competing with the outside noise. When he turned back to speak, Jake had to lean forward, arms on his knees, his head up, increasing the tension and pain in his neck. "The Russians may be creating a situation potentially greater than what occurred during the Cuban Missile Crisis. Seems they have developed a submarine UAV that can outmaneuver and outrun any vessel we have in our arsenal. This UAV utilizes stealth technology, can carry a heavy payload, drugs and other illegal cargo. It can be armed with conventional torpedoes as well as nuclear armed missiles. All this they claim. Our intelligence services are scrambling to verify the threat. We have reason to believe our country's allies and even more importantly, enemies are very interested, as would be expected."

Jake interrupted, shifting his position to relieve the tension in his neck. "What does this have to do with me?" He slid the chair closer to the bed, the competing sounds made hearing difficult.

"Several of the interested parties are the cartels and some Cuban generals. Our listeners have detected increased audio traffic in this region. We know some Bahamians are involved with the cartels, running drugs and human cargo from numerous ports, namely Cuba, Haiti and the Dominican Republic into the Bahamas and the Gulf Coast States. The DEA has a station in the Exumas. I am here to pay them a visit. They are part of this operation along with numerous other federal agencies. Problem is there is little cooperation and sharing among our operational partners. We need someone to be our eyes and ears here. Someone to listen for anything that hints at this operation. We are certain they have operatives here."

"We know there are cartel members which are employed here. The DEA is having problems determining the key players. These people are sharp. They use disposable phones which they change regularly, makes surveilling them difficult. We need humint. I am hoping you'll be that man for us." He got up and fixed another drink. Jake handed him his glass telling him to make it a strong one.

Jake took a big swallow. "If I agree, who and how will I relay any information I gather?"

"Ever been on a dating website?"

"No."

"Quite a few people here are members of various services. Get them to help you get set up on Match and eHarmony. We'll have some of our people correspond with you through these services. They will use a predetermined code to verify their veracity. Be careful, the Russians and others troll these sites trying to hack in. You'll have code names. No code, no talkee. You interested?"

Jake noticed the music stopped. He twirled his glass back and forth on top of the dresser creating a ring of moisture. He picked up his glass and watched, as the circle opened on one part, the water retreating—like all circles in life, they are destined to be broken—where did that come from? He finished his drink. "I'm tired, my neck is making sitting here uncomfortable." He stood, twisted his neck back and forth, and looked back at Bob. "I need to sleep on it. In the morning, we'll talk more. I'll be up early. You can treat me to breakfast, and I'll let you know."

Jake's sleep was troubling. He lay awake thinking about Hardy's offer. He couldn't decide what bothered him more, the fact he was being recruited, or the financial reason for the recruitment. The turmoil played over and over in his head each time he became semiconscious during the night. He needed this job, but he had never trusted any of the federal agencies. The agents he had known, while serving in the Middle East, caused numerous problems, had no more scruples than the mercenary pukes that worked for the independent security services. Like the CIA, they treated him and his fellow soldiers as though they worked for them. Taking credit or placing blame, whichever suited their personal agenda. They rarely shared their intel, often when they did, it was faulty. Too many innocent civilians had lost their homes and lives so an agency could claim a major victory, all the while, convincing most Americans, many the so-called moral majority, the slaughter was righteous. Made Jake and other soldiers into an invading, merciless horde. Gave the Moslem extremists easily sold propaganda. Painted targets on every soldier's back.

Did he want to be one of their agents? If he did, it would be for the money—making him nothing more than another mercenary. Was he being self-righteous? Had he not done things for Uncle Sam, that could never be talked about with anyone other than those who had been there? He had never thought of the Russians as enemies until recent events had shown their leader, a former KGB man, had every intention of destroying western democratic values.

And the Cubans? He always wanted to visit the island, something many people who knew him never understood. Something he had no explanation for—a childhood fantasy, he did not know its origin. Its leaders had been at odds with the U.S. government since the nineteenth century. Jake tried and failed to find a logical explanation for its continuation. Hardy claimed their leaders were working with the Russians and cartels, threatening the security of the US. Was this agency propaganda? Another attempt to justify their bloated expenditures and budget? Did he want to be a part of this?

The alternative was to work for ESI for as long as it lasted and hope something else came along to keep him from losing the family farm and everything else. Was his disdain for the bureaucrats greater than his fear of an uncertain future? These thoughts continued until it was time to get out of bed. He needed sleep. Two nights with little rest. First Blakely. Then Hardy.

Daylight pierced his half-conscious dreams. He became aware of the hum of the waking world, unfamiliar sounds coming from the direction of the bay. His second full day in this tropical playground of the rich and those who catered to their desires. Most of the islanders simply trying to get by on the crumbs doled out.

Jake looked at himself in the small, gilded-frame mirror over the pedestal sink and tried the smiling therapy he discovered after he returned to the conscious world. Happened during physical therapy at Charlotte Memorial Hospital on the final leg of his "so called" recovery. He learned about mirrors and himself. Self-hypnosis. Fool yourself, change your thoughts. See what you want to see.

Mirrors, he discovered, are not all the same. Anyone who has been in a house of mirrors knew this. Apparel store and gymnasium designers knew to make a person's image more flattering. He began to wonder which him was the one other people saw, or did he appear different to each beholder. Which reflection was the real him? He tried to smile, to make his mood different, to do what the smile accomplished other times, make his worries and depression seem trivial. Many times, it worked, other times, like today, he saw his smile as the fake one so often used by salespeople and con artists to rid you of your protective shield. Was he being conned? Was he conning himself?

Hardy used the military-political catchphrase, "national security," as it was so often used, to sell the public on the never-enough weapons or to justify their imperialist's propensity. Was this an excuse to make Cuba another proxy battleground for the United States and Russia. Or were there Cuban generals, emboldened by the Castro reign ending, willing to enrich themselves and jeopardize their country's sovereignty and security?

TJ spoke to Jake on several occasions, when they were getting to know each other, about the Cuban American/ mainland Cuba dilemma. TJ's mother hated the Castros. Her romanticized longing to return to the place she left as an infant never ceased. TJ, his wife Deane and many younger Cuban Americans saw themselves as Americans of Cuban decent and felt no need to go back.

Perhaps Hardy was sincere in his desire to disarm Jake's self-defense mechanism. Calling out Jake's patriotism? Fuck that. Jake didn't need to hear that. Jake needed to know if Hardy, looking in his mirror, was convinced this time the threat to their country's national security, was real? If Jake decided to believe him, would he be able to look himself in the eye, feel justified when he started prying into these stranger's lives? Spying on the innocent along with the guilty, being the judge and jury, perhaps ruining their lives. Would the guilt be his? Could he set aside his cynicism for bureaucrats, generals and politicians, who exacted their agenda on a mission—morality never part of the equation? Continually, knowingly abandoning him and his fellow vets after they are no longer part of their arsenal?

Bureaucrats. Despicable societal leeches. He didn't owe them anything. Was he going to do this? He believed in his country, more than its leaders. Just like his father and grandfather, he was a patriot—when called, willing to serve. The gods must be laughing.

He tapped on Hardy's door. When he answered, Jake told him he would meet him outside.

Jake was amazed to see the outdoor deck area looking as if nothing had happened the night before. Several tables and chairs sat near the back exit. Ready for patrons who wished to enjoy the harbor view for breakfast, brunch or lunch. The kitchen was not open. No coffee, no sweet rolls, nothing. Hardy came out and they walked down toward the dock. The water was dark and still. No breeze, the few boats gently rocked at their berths.

"You look like shit. Guess you didn't sleep so well?"

"Takes a while for me to adjust. Stranger in a strange land and bed. That kind of thing."

"Did you come to a decision about helping me with this operation?

"If I decide to do this, I need someone I can communicate with in person. On occasion, not all the time. I'm not like others, I was never one to live online."

"The DEA's station is on a nearby island. I am heading there this morning. Maybe I can post someone there, without ruffling the DEA feathers. Anything else?"

"You said you would get me a window AC unit. Need that to happen today if possible. My plans are to have a place all to myself and my own vehicle."

"That might draw unwanted attention to you."

"Not if Ned decides to move Rick somewhere else and I take his place. Perhaps you can help with that."

They walked to the end of the dock. They started back toward the inn.

"Ned and I are not that close. All he knows is I work for the government."

"What good am I to this operation if he decides a few weeks is all he needs from me? Don't tell me you expected me to find out what's going on before the end of the year?"

Bob laughed. "That would make my boss happy. Let me see what I can do. Anything else?"

"I need some way to get in touch with you personally. And you haven't told me what kind of compensation y'all planned on my receiving."

"I'll be changing my phones constantly, as will you. Get on those dating sites. If you need to talk to me, send a message and I'll answer the best way possible, as soon as possible. I'm going into the lion's den, communication will be limited. Compensation? He laughed again. I figured Ned's pay would be sufficient?"

"Think again. I want at least what I was receiving as combat pay, plus a bonus if I get on base and a double bonus if I empty the bases."

"What if we match what Ned is paying and guarantee your VA disability and all back payments?"

"You guarantee a year's salary no matter how long this lasts. Including this year as a sign-on incentive. I'm signing on for one year only, which means I get two year's salary guaranteed. The way I see this, I have become a cheap mercenary whore. Those security company fucks in Iraq get that much for a month's work." Jake's phone was vibrating. He pulled it out of his pocket. It was Rick. "I'm headed that way," he said after Rick asked him where the hell he was.

"I've got to go. I expect to see the first year's money in my account. Plus, the VA offering. If that happens and the AC unit shows up ASAP, I'll know you people have decided you want me. See you Bob."

"You drive a hard bargain. Look forward to hearing from you Jake. Be careful here and online."

10

Miami, Fl

Lyndon, Leon was what he preferred, TJ's younger brother, lived two blocks on the other side of TJ's mother in the hood part of Lil Havana. His concrete block house had bars on the doors and windows with Kevlar shades hanging down inside. Anyone out at night was either looking for trouble or trouble was certain to find them. Drive by shootings were as common as newspaper delivery at the top tier hotels on the other side of the freeway.

TJ had his brother meet him at their mother's house.

"What's the haps ugly?" Leon asked when he entered the back door into the kitchen. "Why the meet?"

"Wanted to see if you gotten any uglier, makes me feel better." TJ stood from his seat at the kitchen table. His mother got up, hugged Leon. He was dark like their father. His face resembled their mother's back when she was their age, the exception a two-inch scar over Leon's right eye where a bullet had plowed a furrow in an attempt by a rival gang member trying to perform his initiation tap. The kid, a wannabe banger, was never heard from or seen again. Had happened while TJ was overseas. TJ found out about it when he applied for the SWAT Team job. His brother's gang membership, brought up in the interview, almost kept him from being hired.

They braced, went through the slap, bump, greeting ritual, ending in a bro-hug. Then they sat down. Their mother poured Leon a lemonade and left the room.

"How you liking the UC work, bro? That why you wanted to see me? Not a good idea meeting up. So, speak, tell me what it is couldn't be said on the phone?"

TJ locked eyes, not smiling anymore. "Feds goina bring heat to the Hood. Something big in the air. I normally try to stay out of your business, could get some bigtime heat for telling you this. Understand?"

Leon smiled but his eyes were flashing. "Then don't get into my business bro. Be better for both us."

"Can't promise anything little brother. Came here to give you a heads up. Need you to get the word out that anyone who hears any unusual rumors about big money coming in, possible connections with the Latin Kings, other bangers, the cartels, get in touch with you."

"We small time. The Latin Kings steer clear of us and we stay out of their way. There's no love between us and them. I do what you say, the truce be broken. They outnumber us and have bigger and more lethal weapons. You got t' understand, can't do this thing you ask?"

"Okay. I need someone in their organization. Think you can help me with that? I'm doing you a favor. Did this 'cause you my brother and would break mama's heart if anything happened to you. Plus, your wife and kids. All I need is for you to listen for anything unusual. Get me a name in their organization, someone high up. You don't need to talk to him, just tell me his name."

Leon sat back, his eyes shifted toward the living room. The sound of the television could be heard. Their mother laughed at something that had been said on the Spanish speaking talk show she watched. His eyes came back, he looked at TJ with a defeated stare.

"Bro, you know what I say could get not just me killed, but mama, my whole family. If it come out you one who say something, they goina think I tell you. There are police, who knows, even SWAT men who talk. How you do this, so they not know it's you?"

"Don't worry. have ways. No one ever know it me. I understand how this goina work. Its better you don't know. Help me out bro. I'll take care of you, you know that, get you some money to help out until this blows over."

"Don't need no money…This has to stay on the down low…I was approached by a member calls himself Daniel Diego, Double D tattooed on his hands, other tats on arms and neck. Tried to recruit me. Big guy, scary looking, rides a Harley Low Rider, hangs out at that biker club over near the old stadium. Came here from El Paso. Word is he has connections to the Juarez Cartel. Supposedly did some enforcement work for them. Be careful bro, these guys don't have rules, they do things to whomever, whenever they feel like it. They hear you asking of them, they'll come at you, our families, no warning."

"Thanks bro. You hear any blowback let me know. Text 999 to my cell you hear anything about the other, or need me, give me that signal and we'll meet. Give Sondra a hug and tell Tico and Jose Uncle T asked about them."

TJ stood, they hugged, he walked to the other room, kissed his mama's cheek and told her he was going back to work. He heard Leon slip out the back door. He waited, finishing his lemonade, then went out the back door and walked to his mother's friend's house a block back and a block over, where he left his truck.

"Talked to one of my CIs," TJ said to Carl, seated behind his desk, arms raised over his head, his face tight with tension or pain. "Gave me a name, a biker named Daniel Diego, supposedly a cartel enforcer, here from El Paso."

Carl lowered his arms, he sat forward gingerly, slowly he rose up, came around his desk. "Come on. Let's see what we can pull up on Senor Diego."

TJ followed him into the secure room. He waited until TJ entered then closed the door. The room was bathed in flashing lights from numerous screens, large ones on walls, others at individual desks, their operators' faces backlit. There were the *hums* and *thumps* of fingers on virtual keypads, muted voices speaking into mic sets. Carl walked over to the intel analyst introduced earlier as Mariel.

"Mariel, I need you to pull up what you can on a biker, possibly from El Paso, goes by name of Daniel Diego." He turned to TJ. "We'll wait in my office.

"Mariel is one of the best. Anytime you need info talk to the analysts, that's what they're here for." He slowly rocked back in his chair, locking his arms behind his head. "How you want to handle this Daniel Diego, once we get his bona fides?"

"Thought about that on the way over. My CI asked me not to confront Diego personally. Scared someone may have seen me with him, make his crew and family suffer the consequences. I know an undercover cop with vice. She's one of the best. I figure to have her put the moves on this fucker and get him where we can get our hands on him. My CI thinks he may be a good bet to know what the cartels have to do with the Latin Kings. Not much happening in Miami without the Kings knowing 'bout it."

"You know we're not supposed to involve the locals. That said, suppose we decide this is our best bet, let's say she gets him where we want, think she'll keep quiet, let us handle the interrogation? You do realize there is no other manpower, other than what you have seen here. You ever done an interrogation?"

"Sat in on a few. One in 'Stan, couple in the Philippines. From what I've heard and read, most of what I witnessed frowned upon, illegal, 'specially stateside. You ever take part in any?"

Carl grinned. "Yeah. I've been part of a few. Took training at Guantanamo, after my military career ended so ominously and before I went to work with the Secret Service. Most of what I know is old school, much of it frowned upon because of those sadistic pukes at Abu Graib decided to make movies which went public. The way I see it, anything goes. As long as you don't get caught, don't leave a corpse lying around. Just so we're clear, I didn't say that, you didn't hear it from me. There is a section in the new Military Code of Conduct. You can find it online."

Mariel tapped on the open door. Carl lowered his arms and motioned for her to come in. "Anything interesting? Maybe a good bedtime reading?"

She laid a printout on his desk. "This big ass dude has been in and out of the system his whole life. Nearly beat a kid to death when he was eight years old. His parents disappeared while he was in juvie. Taken and returned from several foster homes. Ran away from a low security juvie home at the age of thirteen. Arrested for one offense after another including resisting arrest, assault and battery, attempted murder, drug possession, distribution and illegal sales of weapons. Some were reported stolen from a National Guard Armory. Most recent warrant was for a triple homicide in Juarez. Never arrested, never tried, charges dismissed. He seems to be a lone wolf, but reports say he has been seen in the company of known gang members from Texas to California. If he's here, no one has reported to have eyes on him."

"Thank you, Mariel. Put him on our watch list. See if you can track him. I find it hard to believe no one has eyes on him. Look a little harder into this. TJ may be able to give you a number sometime soon."

She looked at TJ, smiled and left.

"Jesus. This fucker looks like he belongs in horror movies or one of those old spaghetti westerns as the bad hombre." Carl turned the printout around so TJ could see the picture.

The picture showed a man who looked to TJ like he could play guard on a football team or be a professional wrestler. The tattoos on his beefy arms were visible. His face was bruised, his lip swollen. "Looks like someone worked him over before they took the mug shot."

"Could be that resisting arrest charge. You really want to send a female cop to seduce this ape? I'm not sure I'd want to be in the same room with this fucker, even with a loaded revolver. You need an elephant gun for someone like him." He looked at TJ, shook his head.

Carl was right.

"Need a copy of this printout. Let her decide."

"If you decide to go forward with this let me know. That way you don't come back out I'll know to call in your old SWAT team and a hearse. Not that I've given your proposal the green light, you do understand this?"

11

Great Exuma, Bahamas

Rick was waiting for Jake out by the road. He had a knap sack, similar to, if not the one Rob returned from Nassau with.

"What's in the knapsack?"

"Caulk sausages Rob went to Nassau to get. What'd you think of your first taste of the island nightlife?"

"I was too tired to enjoy it. Doubt I'll remember many of the people there, their names, or what they do."

"You'll see some of them today. I want you to take the crew out to the site today. See what we do, get familiar with the work and workers."

Jake took the Bahamian crew out and helped them unload. Rodney and several others wanted to know when he was taking over. They didn't seem convinced by his denial.

The site was much larger than Jake had anticipated. He walked the three-story concrete structure where he dropped the crew off. He was told this and the other buildings around a large courtyard, where numerous swimming pools were being built, was to become guest lodging. There were crews getting set up to do the work at every spot inside and out. He rode to the other end of the project. A big guy with a handlebar mustache leaned against an older model Ford Bronco. He waved Jake over.

"Who might you be?" he asked. Jake noticed the veins spiderwebbed across his cheeks. His nose had the purple tone of life in a bottle.

"Jake Harper. I'm with ESI. And you?"

"Bartholomew Conyers. People call me Bubba."

They shook hands.

"What'd Ned send you down here for? Rumor has it ESI's about to be kicked out of here. Behind schedule and overbudget. You here to fix that, eh?"

"I'm supposed to try. Any ideas what the problem is?"

Come with me. They walked up a dune from the parking lot and into a two-story building under construction. There were crates everywhere.

"These crates have been sitting here for two weeks. They're the windows, glass partitions, shelving and the other shit that should have been installed over a month ago. I don't see any of your merry men, do you?"

Jake had no reply.

"Every building has the same thing. Your boss Ned is demanding more money. Says we're behind paying for work completed. Ricky boy makes excuses, repeats what Ned tells him. Ned's boy's down here with his girlfriend. Talking to him is like talking to a junior dickhead. Me and the rest of Fluor's people aren't going to sign off on work that hasn't been completed. Rick knows this. Now you do. Things better change fast or we'll bring another company in and back charge the hell out of ESI."

Jake went back to where he dropped the crews off. He walked through searching for the crews. When he finally found them, there were two men standing around talking for every man that was working. One of them was Rodney, supposedly the top man, talking and laughing with several other Bahamians that were not employed by ESI. When he saw Jake, he called him over and introduced him. Jake asked where everybody was.

"They doing what they told to."

"Show me," Jake said.

Rodney and the others looked at him as if saying who the hell you think you are. Rodney told them he'd catch up with them later. He didn't look none too happy.

Everywhere they went, Jake saw the same thing—one or two working the others standing around, like this was one big social club—reminded Jake of utility crews or county employees back home. Difference was, those crews were big in case they were needed for emergencies.

Jake was beginning to understand ESI's problems. But he didn't know names, their duties, and, he damn sure did not have any handle on who might be the players involved in Homeland's operation. If ESI was kicked out, he could lose out big time. There was one person that possibly could know something, he just needed to get her to talk about something besides sex.

Once back at the office, he stopped at the entrance to the storage container unit. Mitch was seated on a metal folding chair, a clipboard in his hand. A box fan was cut in an opening in the back blowing the heated air across his short dark blond hair. Sweat glistened on his forehead. There were stacks of boxes waiting to be checked off and put on their appropriate shelf. He didn't look up or acknowledge Jake's presence when he walked in.

"Morning Mitch. Appreciate your help yesterday."

Mitch was counting a row, his lips moving as he counted. When he finished, he checked it off on the clipboard, then he looked up.

"I wanted to talk to you. Seems you once stayed where I am now. Want to tell me about it? Is that what caused Rick to have it in for you?"

"What does it matter? That fucker is fucked up. So is that whore Blakely."

Jake chuckled. "Whore huh? Did you pay her for fucking you?"

"Hell no. I never fucked her. Did she tell you that?"

"Seems to me that's the way she is, tries to make it hard to resist, I figure you know what I mean." Mitch's blue eyes flashed but he didn't reply. "Yeah, she hinted you two had a go at it, and you ran your mouth."

Mitch's expression became pinched, angry looking. He looked down at the clipboard. "She's a whore. Rick is pussy-whipped, too stupid to see she's using him. Hope she fucks him over and dumps his ass. Wouldn't be surprised if she's fucking half of Fluor's people. She thought because I was Kendall's friend, I could get him to help her get on with Four Seasons. I told her Kendall couldn't do anything and wouldn't even if she fucked him." He paused reached down picked up a pack of Marlboro Lights and a butane lighter.

"I'd appreciate it if you wouldn't smoke that upwind from me."

He rose, started to light up, then laid the pack and lighter on a box. He held the unlit cigarette in his hand. "Kendall told me she had come on to him. He swears he didn't fuck her. In my book she's a whore. She had Rick kick me out of the house, she's part of the reason he's tried to get me fired. Sent me home once, even had Ned bring Kendall home twice. Mostly Rick's afraid Kendall will convince his dad Rick doesn't know what he's doing. He has it in for me because I'm Kendall's friend, same reason he does for Amy. Blakely may have told him I tried to fuck her, wouldn't surprise me. Even if I did, I would never admit it."

Jake came inside out of the sun. "You know anything about how Blakely is getting her drugs? Rick claims everything is easy to get."

"You kidding me? I don't know anything about that. I smoke some weed. That shit is everywhere. As for the other stuff, I wouldn't know who has it or where it comes from."

"I hear some of the Bahamians have boats, do side business on weekends. You know which ones I could talk to?"

Mitch flinched, his eyes darting past Jake and back. "Man, you shouldn't be talking that shit. Those fuckers don't like outsiders asking about their personal business. One expat about my age, almost was killed because he said something he shouldn't've. You a narc, some kind of law enforcement dude?"

Jake glanced behind him. A truck went by. When he looked back, Mitch had picked the clipboard up and was looking past Jake like he wanted their talk to be over.

"No. I'm trying to get a handle on why this project is so behind schedule and over budget. Talked to a guy named Bubba. He said Fluor was getting ready to kick ESI outta here. I need this job. I'm trying to figure out what is going on, that's all."

Mitch yawned and stretched. He started grinning. "Bubba is a joke. Nobody knows why they hired him. He used to be a backwoods guide up in Minnesota or Upper Peninsula Michigan, somewhere like that. I've been told he drinks a liter of Scotch every night. Look at his face, tells you all you need to know. Don't get me wrong, I like Bubba. Once you get to know him, he's fun to be around. Got a lot of great stories. He hates Ned, says ESI is making him look bad. His part of the work is behind schedule. Ned refuses to do the work until he gets paid. Bubba won't sign off on what's been done. It's fucked up. Look, I just wanna do my job, I don't need any trouble. Got nothing back in Charlotte. Besides, I like it here. You want my advise, talk to Jeff Taylor; he's the one knows whether Bubba is telling the truth or not."

"Where's Rick?"

"You think I would know? Could be checking on another shipping container or an expat crew coming in. All this shit came in this morning." He waved his arms around, cigarette in his left, the clipboard in his right. "There's supposed to be a couple more shipments coming. For all I know, customs may be holding them up. Rick hasn't been paying the fees, so Kendall says."

"That doesn't make sense, why would he not pay them?"

"Claims Ned doesn't see why he has to pay into the Bahamian Social Security System for everyone who comes here to work. Ned boasted he talked to the Prime Minister and got a waiver; local government people say that never happened. Creates all kinds of problems getting materials and subcontractors brought in. This woman named Julia Marshall, the Bahamian administrator, was in here couple days ago, Rick promised he'd talk to Ned about paying. Maybe that's where he is."

"Rick wants to know where I am, tell him I'm going to pick up an AC window unit at Role's True Value Hardware and get some groceries."

"You might want to leave him a note, 'cause I ain't goina say shit to that asshole."

Jake stopped at Fluor's office. Jeff Taylor had gone to lunch, or so a smiling, pleasant-looking oriental gal named Nancy said. She happened to be Jeff's wife and worked in the accounts receivable department. Made him wonder how many other girlfriends and spouses worked on the project or were on the island. From what he had seen at hump fest, there weren't that many women here. His celibacy seemed to be doomed to continue.

He got directions from her to the hardware store, where he picked up a 15,000 BTU AC unit. Hardy at least had taken care of one of his demands. Next stop, the grocer in Georgetown, which appeared to be several containers put together. There was not much to choose from in the fresh vegetable section, everything not very fresh looking, would have been taken off the display or reduced in price at home, and was more than twice the price of farm fresh. The dry good and canned aisles were sparse. Dollar General stores back home offered more. Selections were limited to single brands, most he was unfamiliar with, the prices unreasonable. The meat aisle was also sparse, everything frozen solid as if it had been sitting on dry ice and priced like it was on the menu at a fine dining restaurant, even the milk was frozen. Two grocer bags ended up costing more than quadruple what he was used to.

On the way out of Georgetown near his turnoff, he saw oncoming traffic veering around something in the road. As he drew nearer, he saw a young

Bahamian woman bent over picking up what appeared to be her groceries. She was trying to juggle them, while dodging the vehicles, only to lose them again. It was like a tragicomedy. Jake couldn't believe no one bothered to stop to help; most didn't even slow down. Jake pulled over, and the driver behind him blew his horn then wheeled around him.

Crossing the road, he noticed the frustrated woman was pregnant. She looked over at him, her tear-streaked face stung and angered Jake because of the callous nature of the other drivers. He reached out and took her arm.

"Come on. I'll get you across the road and you can sit in my truck while I pick up your stuff."

"Thank you suh. I be all right."

She tried to bend down and Jake held on gently but firmly. "No ma'am. You need to get out of this hot sun. Please come with me. I promise you I mean you no harm and I don't mind."

She looked at him trying to judge him. She wiped the tears from her eyes, taking her time to figure out why this stranger would offer to help. She seemed to realize the futility of her situation. She let him guide her across the road.

It took numerous trips for Jake, dodging sporadic other vehicles to retrieve her groceries and pile them next to his two bags in the seat.

Before he pulled out he introduced himself. "I'm Jake Harper. I'm here with ESI working on the Emerald Bay project."

"My name is Esmeralda Rolle. My husband, Edward he work on project too."

Jake learned she lived on the other end of the island in Rolle Town near Little Exuma Island. She kept telling him he didn't have to take her all the way there, that it was too far and she could hitch a ride. She had hitched rides on the way to Georgetown. Made no sense why she had been on the other side of Queen's Highway when Jake happened upon her. She explained, she had crossed over because the shoulder had gotten too narrow on the other side. Her bag had slipped, then tore when she tried to catch hold to it.

"Edward, he pay you, Mistuh Harper."

"That won't be necessary. This gives me a chance to see more of the island. You from here?"

"Yes suh. Edward family, they have heritage land. Family all over Bahamas. Rolle Town they property."

Jake figured as much. He kept looking over at her. She seemed to have relaxed. Her face was finely chiseled, dark skinned, much like TJ. He had noticed many of the Bahamians didn't inherit the more African characteristics, other than their dialect. He had not seen any schools, he wondered where those were.

Rolleville's outskirts, where she lived, consisted of small concrete homes, packed in close to one another with little or no yard. She had him pull into a short drive, wide enough for one vehicle, a two-foot strip of sand on each side separating the drive from a small porch of her house and the nearly identical house of the neighbor.

Before Jake could come around and open her door, she was out, her arms full of canned goods. He went up the few steps and opened the door for her. A Bahamian man about Jake's height, his right arm extended out to grasp the inside handle, his other arm wrapped around a squirming infant was shocked when he saw Jake. He stepped back and Jake stood aside letting Esmerelda go inside. She put her arm load down on the small wooden counter and took the infant who was reaching out for her.

Quickly she said, "Edward this Mistuh Harper. He work at project too. My bag broke and he give me ride. I say you pay him."

Jake reached out his hand. "Jake Harper. I don't want any money. I'm glad I could help."

"Thank you suh. You with ESI. T'ink I see you this mornin' talking to Rodney."

Jake tried to remember. "You were on the second floor talking to one of ESI's men, the big one. You both walked off when Rodney and I came up the stairs."

"I was talking to Alvin about getting' on with ESI. The com'ny I wid pour concrete floors. Say we be outta work by end of year. I need keep workin', new baby and all."

Esmerelda said, "Edward fetch otha groceries in Mistuh Harper truck."

Jake helped him get the other groceries in.

"I've got to get going. I don't know the job situation. Check with me later after I learn the ropes. Who knows there might be something for you."

Since he was in Rolleville, Jake decided to have a look. The damn meat was still frozen and the other perishables were being kept cool next to them in the bags.

Back on the main road, he took a right. Topping a hill, the view took his breath away. He pulled the truck over. Directly ahead on a cobblestoned street, on a corner two blocks distant, was a white-stoned church, with a high pointed steeple. On top of the steeple was a shiny gold colored cross. Behind the church on the righthand side, he saw the hill dropped downward, maybe a half mile to the emerald waters of a bay, where several boats, some with white sails, others motor yachts, rocking at anchor. It was as though an Impressionist artist had spread a gigantic canvas in front of Jake and painted a masterpiece.

He jumped out of the truck, his mind telling him to hurry, as though the scene might disappear. He took out his cell phone and snapped off numerous pictures. Were there other scenes like this one?

Sadly, none to equal that one. Jake forked left at the church and followed the street to where it ended at a dock. There were boats of all sorts tied up. What Jake noted were the cigarette and fast looking catamarans mixed in with fishing boats, the yachts and sailboats. He stopped and took it all in. On the dock were two white, well-dressed men talking animatedly to a large Bahamian. Jake stared hard, pulled his cell phone off the seat, zoomed in and took a photo. It was Alvin. What was he doing here at this time of day? He should have been at Emerald Bay working.

12

Miami, Fl

Margarette Elkins met up with TJ at a coffee shop near the airport. He almost didn't recognize her – she was dressed in everyday casual wear, her hair styled and with makeup not garish like the hooker coating he was used to seeing. She could pass as an everyday soccer mom.

"Wow. Never imagined you lookin' like this."

"What, you think I go around looking like a hooker all the time?" She sat down, took the coffee TJ had waiting and took a sip. "Honey and cinnamon, at least you got that right."

"Sorry. Just never seen you except on the job. How've you been?"

"Not doing without, how about you, you still married?" She smiled. "Of course you are. That's what I always liked about you TJ, you never tried to put the move on me, unlike most the douche bags I work with. Why we here? I know this isn't a social call."

TJ slid the pictures of Diego over to her and eased back, arms resting on the table, he took a swallow from his bottle of green tea, the glass nearly hidden in his massive hands.

Maggie's green eyes studied the two printouts. She read the short bio. "Nasty looking, not a mama's boy. What's this to do with me?"

"Got an op running. This twisted mother may be able to help me with locating the key players. Need to get him alone, have a talk, hoping you would help me." TJ watched as she took another drink of coffee. She spread the two pages on the table, her eyes went one to the other.

"Normally my johns are businessmen, white collar perps, top drawer pimps or pushers. Don't deal with the bottom feeders, have but moved up, safer all the way round." She tapped Diego's picture. "Definitely not my type, working him, I don't know how you planned on little ole me helping on this one. I don't see him hanging out in the areas I've been working."

TJ knew she was tough as nails, many perps found this out the hard way. She had a red belt in Ken Po, Korean contact karate's highest ranking, meaning she had used her skills to take her opponent's life. Almost cost her career, put her on extended leave, finally was cleared, that was when she moved into the undercover vice unit.

"You familiar with Clutch's?"

She brushed a strand of hair back behind her left ear. "Biker bar down near the old Orange Bowl. Not my usual hangout, I'm more Frederick's in South Beach. TJ, I'm not sure I want to help you with this one. But, I may know someone who can. He's another UC cop, Buster Brown you know him?"

TJ chuckled. "You got to be kidding me, Buster Brown?"

She stifled her amusement by covering her mouth. TJ noticed the big diamond ring.

"You married? When this happen?"

"I've been married, have two kids, a boy and a girl, two and four. My husband is with the DA's office, Tommy Lyles, you probably heard of him, most cops call him Tom Cat, because of how he dresses and prowls in the courtroom."

"Damn Maggie. How come no one knows this?"

"Better this way. About Buster Brown, if you like I can call him or give you his number. If anyone knows the bikers at Clutch's, it'll be him." She took out a cell phone from her small purse. TJ noticed she had a small pen shaped cylinder dangling from the strap connector, Deane had a similar pepper spray dispenser she kept with her. Maggie also had a snub nose .38 secreted in her purse, the outline hardly visible to the untrained eye.

"You talk to him, ask him about the bar and what he knows about Daniel Diego, *Double D* tattooed on his hands along with other tats on his arms and neck. Tell him you need to meet up, go over a case involving him. Don't mention my name."

She got up from the table, walked outside, TJ watched as she moved out into the parking lot and got into a Chevy Suburban. He went to the men's room to take a piss. She still was in her vehicle when he came back from the john. He went to the counter and bought a bottled water for himself and one for her. The sun was glaring off her windshield making it impossible to see her face, he could see her body moving, left hand patting the steering wheel, right hand out of sight. He saw a big grin on her face when she exited the vehicle. Her gait was jaunty like an actress doing an outdoor commercial. No wonder she was so successful working the high rollers.

"Your boy is an absolute freak," she said sitting back down across from TJ. "Buster says he's new to the scene at Clutch's. Comes in once or twice a week, shoots pool, drinks beer and tequila shots. Doesn't talk much except to the manager and bartender, a two-time loser, drugs, a registered pedophile. Now here's the kicker, I don't believe I can help you out, seems your boy is into some weird and kinky shit. Buster says his CI was told by the bartender that Double D likes the rough stuff, had a tranny back in Juarez, they like to play train and he was the caboose."

"What in the hell does that mean, *be the caboose*?"

"Be at the end, after others had been there, collect the whole load or take it where the sun doesn't shine." She laughed.

"Holy moly." TJ sat there stunned then he began to laugh. They both laughed. The few other people inside, the two employees and a couple of older patrons looked at them wishing they knew what was so funny.

TJ wiped his eyes with the backs of his hands and Maggie dried hers on a napkin. He took a pull off his bottled water, she poured hers into the cup of ice TJ had bought with the waters and took a drink.

"Got to figure anyone involved in pulling a train has to be kind of AC/DC, but never heard of this caboose shit before," TJ said. "You're right don't know how you would be much help with this one. What'd you tell Buster?"

"Just what you said. He'll meet us at the airport long term parking deck in thirty minutes. Who are you supposed to be? You know we UCs are suspicious of strangers."

"Can he be trusted to keep his mouth shut?"

"What do you think? Ever known a UC who didn't know how to keep his mouth shut? That's how we survive. But this is your call, tell him as little, or as much as you feel you should. We better get going."

Buster Brown was a beefy man with a bloated red face in a linen sports coat, his white dress shirt unbuttoned, wet with sweat, a gold cross nestled in among his thick chest hair. He leaned against an older model Cadillac. TJ drove past him, parked his truck, and waited on Maggie, who had parked on a lower level.

"Damn this heat and humidity. Should've moved to California, been a weed grower or some shit like that." He tossed down a cigarette, mashed it into the concrete with his stylish loafers, reached down with a grunt to pick up the butt, then eyed Maggie, as he straightened up. "Looking good, Mags. You outta vice?"

"Nah Buster, still trolling uptown. Buster this is TJ, he works with SWAT. TJ, Buster. You need me to hang around?"

"Man, anybody ever take you for The Rock? You his brother or something?"

TJ grinned. "All the time, kind of gets old. Probably no different from people asking you why your parents named you Buster Brown." He turned to Maggie. "If you could hang around, I'd appreciate it, might need your help after all." He turned back to Buster.

"What's on yo' mind? Why the meet? And oh, just so you know, my mother's name was Mary Jane. I don't say that cause I work narcotics, that really was her name, just like in the early comics, her character was Buster Brown's chick named Mary Jane, got it? Now can we get on with it. There's not enough air moving under here."

"Why don't we sit in my vehicle?" Maggie asked.

Once they were seated, TJ in the back, Buster in the passenger seat, the AC turned up full blast, blowing the burnt stench of cigarettes back into TJ's face. Buster turned to look at TJ. "Talk to me." His accent was Italian-Irish, could have been from New York, Jersey or N'Orleans.

TJ pulled out the two pages and handed them to Buster. "This the fuckhead Maggie asked you about?"

"I've seen this same shit. Yeah that's the one. Came to my attention a few weeks back. Mags told you my CI says he's a switch-hitter. Goes to show, you never can tell. Why you interested?"

"What else your CI tell you?"

"This is beginning to sound like a one-way talk, ever hear of tit for tat, buddy? Why's SWAT interested in this scumbag?"

TJ watched Buster fidgeting, nervous energy, he hoped that was all it was.

"I work undercover, just like you and Maggie--with a special gang task force. Word has it the cartels have something cooking with some of the major gangs along the Gulf, big money involved. This guy's name came up, I'm trying to figure out why he showed up. One of my CIs told me Diego might be a key player in this deal. Need to know why a hit man out of El Paso's a key player. I need to talk to him. Can you help me out?"

"You think this is narcotics?"

"Much more than that. I'm not at liberty to say too much. Let's just say, this may be bigger than anything since El Chapo. Could end up causing a war. That's all I can say. You help me, and you and Maggie can take as much credit as you like."

"You on the level? Maggie asked looking at TJ with renewed interest. "Why didn't you say this earlier? IF this is as big as you say it is, you can count me in."

"Why would you share?" Buster asked, a pained expression crossed his face, his eyes squinting, you could see he was having a hard time concentrating, the cogs not connecting.

TJ leaned forward, his hand on each of their seats. "I need to talk to this man. You in or not?"

Buster looked over at Maggie. She nodded yes. "How you want to play this?" Buster asked nervously patting his upper coat pocket. TJ watched wondering what this meant.

"Can either one of you get your hands on Rohypnol? Going to need enough to get this ape cooperative but not knocked out."

"How's this going to work? We know he's not much into women, not women like me. Most of those biker chicks could qualify for ultimate fighting competition. They're into each other, pulling trains, that kind of gorilla shit. I'm sure I can get Rohypnol, other than that, I don't see my being of any use."

She too was watching Buster's jitteriness. "Never heard of it being used on a man, guess it could work. What do you think, Buster?"

Maggie's question made Buster frown or was it something else, TJ was beginning to think Buster was jonsing. Wouldn't be the first time an undercover narc became a user.

After a pause, during which Buster retrieved a handkerchief and mopped his brow, even though the air was getting chilly. He said, "Diego swings both ways. I know a nurse works at the VA, hangs out with bikers, comes in Clutch's once in a while." TJ and Maggie stared at him like they found this hard to believe. TJ was wondering if Deane might know her or if this nurse could have seen him there.

"What? You think all these bikers are like this fucker? Bikers aren't all into outlaw shit, or, only blue-collar fuckers, working construction or slinging freight down on the docks. You'd be surprised how many professionals there are. The big timers usually are professionals, or they have dealings with that crowd. Who else has the money to buy and sell quantity? Heroin, coke, opioids, you name it, the biggest users are your white collar, uptown motherfuckers. Most of Clutch's members are uptown not small time. I'm surprised you didn't know this, Mags."

She nodded, her eyes not leaving Buster. TJ knew what he said was right. But what he figured Maggie was thinking, did this include Buster and this nurse?

"What makes you think this nurse would help us out?"

"Vickie can't afford to say no to me. She's my CI."

"OK. We get her get him out of there, bring him someplace we can question him. Then Maggie sits on her, makes sure she doesn't talk to anyone. Buster, you and I wear disguises. I'll question him, you be my backup in case this fucker becomes a problem. Also, in case your CI gets scared."

"Why don't I take Vickie away from there?" Maggie asked.

"Don't know much about Rohypnol's effects. She's a nurse. Plus, since she's the one he thinks he's going to be screwing, might help stop any suspicions if she's there when he comes to his senses. Either one of you got any better ideas?"

"Look my friend, I need another cigarette. Been trying to quit, these pills that are supposed to help, they give me the shakes, wire me up. Let me know when. See you Mags." He lit up immediately after exiting Maggie's vehicle. They watched as he walked off, shaking his head.

"What you thinking?" Maggie asked looking in the rear-view mirror. TJ had leaned back still watching Buster.

He turned his attention back to Maggie. "I think your friend has a problem. The question is, can we trust him?"

"I'll see what I can find out. When you want to do this?"

"I was hoping tomorrow. But Buster could throw a monkey wrench in my plans." He opened the back, driver's side door and got out. Maggie lowered her window.

"I'll do what I can to get some answers today. Let's touch base later." She put her vehicle in gear and drove off.

TJ felt he may have fucked up. Since he was near the VA, he figured he should drop by, see if Deane could help him find out, or possibly knew, who this nurse was. Vickie, could be an alias?

13

Great Exuma, Bahamas

Seeing the Bahamian named Alvin gave Jake a jolt. He wanted to get out and move closer, the idea of confronting Alvin for being here instead of at Emerald Bay entered his mind. He decided it was too risky. If Alvin was somehow connected to the operation, he could blow his own cover. He decided he needed to know more about Alvin. He put the truck in gear and eased off, hoping Alvin wouldn't see the truck and recognize it.

As he was leaving Rolleville, his cell tone rang out. Caller unknown was what his screen read. He hesitated. Not sure if he should answer. It stopped. Almost immediately started again before he could set it down.

"Yeah," he answered.

"This is Rick. Where are you?"

"Rolleville, headed back toward Emerald Bay."

"What the hell you doing up there? Never mind, you can tell me when I see you. Blakely and I are heading to Big D's, it's a restaurant halfway from where you are and the job site. It'll be on your left. We should be there in thirty minutes, no, make that an hour, I need to stop by and check to make sure the two dickwads, Mitch and Kendall, are still on site. They can close up." He disconnected.

Jake stared at the phone, closed it and checked his groceries once more. The meat was still frozen. He turned into a roadside store and bought a Styrofoam cooler and a bag of ice, fifteen dollars, he sure hoped Hardy deposited that money. He would check later on, if he could find Wi-Fi.

Big D's was another wooden hut similar to the ones at Fish Fry, with raised wooden panels that served as the roof which could be lowered to close the place down. It set back from a bay, the water across a dune, tropical trees and a couple palms added to the island feel. Jake sat on one of the wooden stools. The l-shaped countertop was polished to a mirror

shine with urethane over layers of vertical strand board. In one corner was a frozen daquiri dispenser, on the other end was a sink and cutting board next to which were lemons, limes, oranges, peppers, tomatoes, onions and globs of some white slimy sea creature. The back wall had various bottles of alcohol and a white marker board with felt marker writing announcing the food available.

A pretty, young Bahamian woman asked Jake his name. He had not expected to be asked this, usually the first question is what do wish to drink or eat. He told her. She introduced herself as Lilah.

"You on holiday or you work?"

"I'm here to work on the Emerald Bay project. Do you have any beers?"

A slightly larger than medium-size man came out from behind the back wall. "Lilah, the mon not here be questioned. Go check Maurice, see conc ready." She smiled at Jake, frowned at the man, ducked under the hinged section of bar top and walked behind Jake. He watched her twisting shapely rear disappear around the bayside corner. He turned his head back to the man. He had a toothy grin. He looked disapproving. "That be my daughter. She t'ink she all growed up. What I get you suh?"

Jake asked about the beer selection. Same four brands. He took what the man who introduced himself as Big D the owner, proprietor, cook and bartender, called a Hinie. Lilah came back with a five-gallon bucket from which Big D extracted another ugly ball of white glutinous looking flesh. She set the oblong chunk by the cutting board. Big D saw Jake's fixed stare.

"This heah conc, some folks call sea snail. Ever had conc fritters or conc salad? That our specialty." He pointed to the marker board. "Fresh from de sea." He immediately began cutting and dicing peppers, onions, tomatoes and conc. He put all in a bowl, squeezed lemon, lime and orange over the mixture saying, "juice cook conc." He set the bowl with a fork in front of Jake. "You try. You no like. You no pay."

Jake, a lover of all seafood, looked down at the salad, his reservation came, not from trying the conc, but wondering if something that had been pulled out of a five-gallon bucket, handled by hands he had not seen washed, said to be cooked, by juice from lemon, limes and oranges, was safe to eat. He hesitated, Big D and Lilah watching him, then he forked a small portion and tasted. It was amazing. Risk or not, he ate, savoring every bite. Big D and Lilah grinned and watched.

Another truck pulled in as he was finishing. Rick and Blakely had arrived. Rob was with them.

"Heh, heh, heh Big D what it is," Rick bellowed walking up and stopping next to Jake. Blakely followed taking the stool on the other side of Jake, an illegal smile playing across her face. Rob disappeared around the corner.

"See you tried the ceviche," Blakely said to Jake.

He had followed their entry, watched Rob disappear and seen Lilah's seeming glare at Blakely. He looked at her and said, "Yeah, first time, enjoyed it. You want something to drink?"

She looked across at Lilah. "I'll have a frozen daiquiri."

"Rum or tequila?"

"Coconut rum."

Rick and D had moved off to the side and were talking. Jake was watching trying to hear. Blakely was having none of it.

"Hear you played Sir Galahad today."

Jake fixed her glassy eyes with a stare.

"Coconut telegraph. No matter what happens on these islands, everyone knows. It's amazing." She sighed. "Also heard you were visiting with a friend in the Georgetown Inn last night, a nice-looking man." She lowered her voice. "Is that why you refused my offer?"

Jake chuckled. "If I say yes, does that mean you'll stop playing games Miss Carmichael? Or, maybe you should tell me your real name?"

She had picked up her daquiri then set it back down. "What the fuck are you talking about? Of course that's my real name. That guy must have sucked your brains out through your dick. My license and passport will prove it, fucking asshole licker."

All talking had stopped, everyone was looking at them. Rick started their way, his face twisted in anger. Jake stood, laid a twenty on the counter, said thanks to Big D and Lilah and turned to leave. Rick stepped in front of him, Jake saw his fists were balled.

"Your girlfriend isn't feeling so cheerful this afternoon. Y'all enjoy yourselves." Jake started to step around him and Rick reached out grabbed his arm. "Don't let her push you where you don't need to go. We both can't afford any trouble." Jake pulled Rick's hand loose and walked on.

Jake heard Blakely say, "You going to let him just walk away?"

He pulled out and drove on. Inside he was seething; part of him wanted to go back and take Rick apart and expose Blakely's false accusation. This was a first for him, walking away. He knew it wasn't over, maybe it wouldn't escalate. He doubted that would be the case.

His mind was churning. He had not seen any police since arriving on the island, other than at the clinic where he was drug tested. Was there a jail or did they only deport expats who broke the law? Like he said to Rick, he couldn't afford to find out. The coconut telegraph must really be buzzing. This could pose a problem for gathering information in this testosterone fueled environment, where even those so inclined hid behind machismo. He hadn't seen any available women to quash the accusation—at least create doubt.

He needed to find an Internet connection to send the pictures he had taken to wherever Hardy needed him to send them. He was supposed to set up accounts on the two internet dating sites. He needed help doing that. Perhaps Mitch knew how to do that? He would stop by the job to see if he and Nick were there. He needed to meet Kendall, get connected to the internet at the same time.

At ESI's container office, there was a small Ford sedan with rental plates parked out front. The equipment container's doors stood wide open, no one was inside. Inside the office, Jake found Mitch seated at the nearest table. Seated next to him entering something on the computer was a long-haired blonde, all woman, with breasts that strained her loose-fitting, frilly blouse; this had to be Amy.

She stopped typing, looked at him and smiled. "Hello," she said in a sweet sincere-sounding manner. "You must be Jake Harper. Kendall and I were like wondering when we'd meet you."

The young, all-American looking young man seated at Rick's desk rocked forward but didn't make any attempt to stand. "Yeah, my ole man said he was sending someone down here to check on things. When he told me, I told him not to bother. He never listens to me. I keep telling him Rick is the problem. Maybe if you tell him, he'll listen." He leaned back and put his feet up on the desk. "The Bahamians think you're here to replace Rick; Mitch and I started that rumor. Got Rick all nervous."

"Why did you do that?"

"I was here before him assisting Greg, another one of those guys from St. Louis. At least he had management skills and had done this kind of work. He was Rick's friend, should've never recommended him to take over. My ol' man thought I was too young and figured the Fluor people wouldn't respect me."

Jake figured there was more to it than that. "Been wondering when I'd get to meet you. Thought you might be avoiding me."

"I try to steer clear of Rick. I've been around, out on the job, up at Fluor's office. Amy started working from their offices to keep away from Rick. She tries to come here one day a week to make sure Rick hasn't changed the orders. Blakely is trying to take Amy's job."

"That two-faced whore," Mitch said. "Thought they were meeting you at Big D's?"

"I left them there to come here. Have the Bahamians all left?"

"Some have. Rodney, Alvin and a few others are working with an expat crew to finish the doors on Building One. Ned said Fluor would pay him soon as we get signed off on all the doors." Mitch said.

"That means they'll be making double time and won't be worth a shit tomorrow. All because Rick refused to pay the fees. I talked to my ole man; he deposited money to pay so customs would remove the lock on the shipping container where the last door units were. Rick said he was told not to pay part of the fees. That was a month ago before the money was deposited. I told him the money was deposited, he wouldn't listen. He doesn't know what he's doing. He's like a mindless bulldozer, fucks anybody gets in his way. Hope you tell my ole man he needs to get rid of Rick."

Amy finished doing whatever it was she had been doing and sat back.

Kendall stood and came around from behind the desk. He asked, "You done?" She said she was. They walked past Jake. Kendall turned back to face

Mitch, who had moved over to get on the computer. "We'll come back to get you in an hour. You going tonight, aren't you?"

"I guess so. You don't need to come back, Nick said he'd give me a ride."

Amy told Jake bye. Jake found it difficult not to stare. She noticed, so did Kendall, he went out without saying anything.

After they left, Jake took the chair Amy had sat in. "Mitch, can I trust you?"

"What do you mean?"

"You know how Blakely is. Do you think she is mixed up in something she shouldn't be?"

"You mean illegal? Possibly. I mean there's lots of opportunities. She does what's best for her. Like I told you, I think she'd fuck anybody if she thinks they can help her get what she wants. Why?"

"You said she might have fucked Kendall. Doesn't sound like he could or would be able to do much for her. Kendall has Amy. I don't believe Blakely would stand a chance in comparison."

"Amy and Kendall have known each other all their lives. They've talked about getting married. I told you Kendall said Blakely came onto him. I believe him when he says nothing happened. Like he told you, Blakely wanted Amy's job. Kendall would never get mixed up with Blakely in anything illegal, if that's what you're thinking."

"If Blakely is mixed up in anything illegal, you think Rick might be also?"

"Wouldn't surprise me. But he seems too much of a boy scout. The Bahamians don't much like him. He's a racist."

"If she is, who do you think she would be mixed up in it with?"

"Why you asking me this shit? I try to stay as far away from her and Rick as I can."

"I'm trying to figure out what's going on here. I don't know anyone and I'm trying to figure out what the game is and who the players are."

"You play cards?"

"I have been known to, why?"

"Tonight is card night. Lots of the people get together on Thursdays to play. They're playing at the metal contractor project manager's house tonight. Kind of a going away party thing. Their people are finishing up and lots of them will be leaving soon. All of us were planning on going. You interested?"

"Are you saying I may get some answers by going?"

"I told you, I don't know anything. This will give you a chance to get to know more people is all. You can go or not, doesn't matter to me. Rick and Blakely probably will be there. That's all I know, okay?" He turned back to the computer. Jake saw he was playing a video game.

"Sounds good. I need to get online and check my email. What's the password?"

"No password. I wouldn't go on any sites you don't want anyone to know about. They have spyware, Fluor does, and ESI does also."

"How did you find this out?"

"Jeff told me. Said I needed to keep the Bahamians off the porn sites. As if the Fluor people don't do such shit. Most of them have been to Cuba, even though it's illegal. All they talk about is the young pussy they got. Even the head of security, dickhead Don."

"Aren't there any non-Bahamian women on the island? What about wives and girlfriends?"

"Most of the people are single as far as I know. Blakely, Amy, and a few wives, that's about it. The biggest thing I miss is my girlfriend. You married?"

"Divorced, going on three years. Three kids. Was hoping there would be some island women I might get to know. So far, my opportunity seems to be limited. Not counting Blakely. Hope I can avoid getting that desperate." They both chuckled.

"Yeah, wish I had never met her."

"Someone recommended I try the Internet dating sites. You know anything about those?"

"Some of the dudes are on them. A couple guys claim they have gotten laid. Might want to ask Nick, he's on a couple of the sites. He's even brought some girls here he met online. IF you don't mind the spies knowing, who knows you might get lucky."

Jake got online and checked his email. Not much worth reading. Nick showed up while he was on the computer. He took the other vacant seat and he and Mitch discussed the video game Mitch had been playing. Jake interrupted to ask him about the Internet dating sites.

Nick said he met some freaky chicks on the ones he frequented. Need to read between the lines. "Most people lie, the chicks mostly lie about their age and post five or ten-year-old pictures or pictures of someone else. I ask every time and warn them if they're not like their pictures, I'll know when I meet them. A few I've met don't seem to get it. Makes for a bad scene. Fuck 'em, sometimes I do, most time, it's a waste. Probably the same for the ones your age, be careful, the ones you're after are probably looking for someone to take care of them, not like the ones my age."

"You might be surprised. Older women like to have fun also. In your opinion is it worth the effort?"

"For me it is. I get to talk to a lot of chicks, which, as you may have noticed, there's not many available out here. Who knows maybe you'll get lucky, that's the way I look at it." He stood and asked Mitch, "You ready to get out of here? We can head over to your place and get a game in before we head over to the card party."

"Jake wants to go with us, you cool with that?"

He looked over at Jake. "That'll be all right by me. You ready to go, dude?"

"Is your place where I went yesterday?"

"Yeah."

"I think I remember where it is."

"Turn everything off and put this lock on the doors when you're ready to leave." Mitch laid a long shaft keyed lock on Rick's desk. He shut his computer down and stood to join his friend Nick going out the door. "Be at my place by seven if you decide to go with us."

Jake worked almost an hour to get set up on the two Internet dating sites Hardy told him to join. He called Hardy's phone. No answer. He entered 111 and disconnected. Hardy called back in less than two minutes. He sounded cheerful and enthused when Jake told him about what he had witnessed. He asked how he could get the pictures securely to him. Hardy said send them to his number, that it was secure.

"After today, this number will no longer be operational. If you need to reach me, leave a message on the dating site. Your online partner will know what she's supposed to do. Also, I've decided to give you some backup. This person will meet you to set up a way to communicate, perhaps a drop site. They will mention having heard of Dilworth. You reply with the manager's name."

Jake told him about the incident with Blakely.

He laughed. "Not sure confronting her was the right move. Hope it doesn't come back to bite you. Maybe you should give her what she wants. You might consider using a body condom." He laughed again. Jake wasn't sure it was funny. "Your backup may know who these people in these photos are. I'll have them run through our system to see if we get any hits. Try to get Blakely's and this Alvin guy's phone numbers. Be interesting to see if they communicate with each other or anyone interesting. Could be they're using burner phones, which, in itself, may mean something. Continue to keep your eyes and ears open Jake, we and the DEA are getting increased audio traffic from these islands." He ended the call.

14

York County, SC

Major Bud Jenkins, formerly with Army Intelligence the CIA, then NSA, now worked as Chief Security Officer for his former commander Colonel Thurmond Pinckney Tindal, now CEO of Tindal Industries, a weapons manufacturing and sales company. Tindal had acquired a large portion of land, formerly a namesake, Pinckneyville, in upstate South Carolina, across the Broad River from where he now resided and where he had been a member of a hunt club for several years.

Upon the land across from Pinckneyville he built a palatial home, an architect's rendition modelled after the historic Charleston waterfront homes, Tindal's childhood homeplace, where his mother had been a live-in nanny for a wealthy merchant, his own father unknown. The grounds were immaculately landscaped with terraced stone stairs meandering down to an airplane hangar and a dock on the Broad River; fountains, a gated entrance and orchards cresting nearby hills on each side of a paved drive ended at one huge fountain, two cars distant from the columned entrance, which separated the house from a side entrance portico joining a large six bay garage which had guest quarters and a large research laboratory below ground. Bud Jenkins had his office down a long hallway from the lab connected underground to Tindal's office inside the side aboveground entrance, serviced by a private elevator.

Bud had taken the elevator up to Tindal's office. He remained standing, declining Tindal's request to take a seat. Tindal was seated at his large ornate, dark walnut-stained desk crafted from trees cut from the land where the structures now stood.

"The acquisition of Marberry Manufacturing has been completed. I intend to move the research group here. Is the lab upgrade construction complete and ready for the techs to be brought in?" Tindal asked.

"Yes sir. I supervised the construction to make sure every detail, particularly the security and monitoring systems, were according to the specifications on the plans. My office and your office have total access to the lab." What Jenkins didn't tell him was he had made sure his office could monitor Tindal's office and the guest quarters, but Tindal could be disconnected from having access without knowing. "Installed into your desk is a state-of-the-art virtual setup which you can access and control using voice commands. Would you like me to demonstrate?"

"No, that won't be necessary. As you know, we have Dr. Lisa Guthridge, the technical head of Marberry's research and development team, being flown in to meet with us. She should be arriving shortly. I expect her to be impressed. Tindal Industries needs her and her team. The major reason for the acquisition was to bring her and her team onboard. The drone project her team is developing will be unlike any our military has in their arsenal. I intend to see this project through and sell this to the Pentagon. We need her onboard. You will help me make sure this happens."

"I will do my best sir."

"I know you will… Bud, you and I have traveled many paths together. This could be the one that defines our success."

"Yes sir. I will roll out the red carpet. She is already aboard your private plane and has departed Charlotte Douglas. I have made sure the staff understands their roles. I was going to talk to the chef, but your wife sent word she would handle that. Is there anything else you wish?" He looked at his watch in hopes Tindal would get the message and tell him to get going. Which he did.

Dr. Guthridge was a tall, willowy woman that most people would pass on the street, only noting her height. She wore her dirty blonde hair in a bun, pulled tight giving her a school matron look. No makeup, her skin so light, she resembled a ghost. Jenkins' fantasy thoughts of her in a sexual way started when he looked at her profile picture taken with her hair down. Seeing her in person, as she descended from the plane in a stylish pant suit and long light sweater, made him have second thoughts.

"Bud Jenkins." He extended his hand and she gently laid her long fingers across his palm then stepped down from the plane by his guidance. She introduced herself and withdrew her hand. "Colonel Tindal regrettably had some urgent business to attend to." Bud lied, Tindal had yet to come down to greet anyone. "I hope you had a pleasant trip?"

"Yes. The view coming in over the mountains brought back memories. One could imagine what it must be like when the leaves are at their autumn peak." Her voice had a trace of Scandinavian with a husky feminine lilt.

One of the Hispanic staff took her bags out of the plane and placed them in the rear of the luxury golf cart. Bud helped her to be seated in the soft leather, sun-warm, rear passenger area, then he went around to seat himself. They started up the beautifully landscaped utility path which would take them to the upper terrace where Tindal should be waiting.

"You have an accent, Swedish perhaps?"

"Yes. My parents came here when I was young. Colonel Tindal is he a pleasant man?"

"I'm not sure what you mean by pleasant. I have known him most of my life, served under his command, now work for him. You will find him easy to talk to, if that is what you mean? He has been looking forward to this meeting, as have I."

She smiled. This was going to be easier than Dr. Perkins, her mentor led her to believe—frightfully exhilarating.

They were greeted by Mrs. Tindal and the house maid who left followed by the house staffer who took the bags.

"My husband will join us momentarily. Would you care for something to drink, water, tea, or something to warm you, I'm having hot spiced tea."

Lisa said she would have a water. Another staffer went to a side bar and came back with a crystal tumbler of slightly chilled water seated on a napkin, resting on a crystal coaster, upon which were laid lemon, orange slices and sprigs of mint. She set it down on an ornamental iron table next to where Lisa stood and resumed her station near the outdoor service bar.

Lisa held her linen-encased glass and stayed standing watching the magnificent orange and red tinged wisp of clouds above the glassy smooth surface of the Broad River. The sun light's refracting as it descended over the far nearly bare-leaved, wooded hillside.

"I never get tired of the view," Tindal said coming alongside her. He introduced himself. "Sorry to keep you waiting. Pressing business that needed immediate attention. Would you like to have a seat or perhaps lie down a bit? I find travelling can be as tiring as working at a desk."

"No thank you. A tour of your lovely estate and perhaps the lab would be my preference. I'm not physically tired, just weary of being confined to a cramped seat."

"Of course." His reply was cut short by several shots puncturing his words. Lisa flinched almost dropping her glass.

"Oh Thurmond," Mrs. Tindal said, "I thought you were putting a stop to hunting that land across the river."

"The purchase is in probate." He watched as Bud released Lisa's elbow. He turned from his wife toward Lisa. "I apologize. I am in the process of purchasing the land across the river which used to be a Revolutionary Era county seat called Pinckneyville. This will afford more privacy and, sometime in the near future perhaps, become a vital part of Tindal Industries. I am counting on you and your tech team to help make this happen. Together we will see your research and development project become the success I am certain it will be."

Mrs. Tindal interrupted. "Come dear. The air has a chill to it when the sun goes down. Let me show you our house. My husband gets carried away sometimes. I'm sorry about the noisy gunshot. Gives me a fright whenever it happens." She took Lisa by the elbow and led her away. Bud heard Lisa's incredulous amazement upon seeing the glass displays that comprised the walls of the luxury man-cave room that led off the terrace.

"That damn game warden," Tindal remarked after he determined the women were out of hearing. He had walked over and poured Bud and himself a jigger of Cognac in two of the tumblers. He handed one to Bud and took a swallow of his. "He went by the Harper place. No one was home. Found out the Harper man is in the Bahamas. Left last week. I told him to go there two weeks ago. Also told him to make sure no hunters hunted the land across the river. I don't know why I bother with him, he's a lazy, incompetent redneck.

Makes you wonder how he ever passed the exam. I need the Harper land along with the land across the river."

"Now that I've finished the lab, I should have more time to concentrate on other projects. I'll see what I can do about these two issues." Bud drained his glass and took a sprig of the mint off Lisa's drink coaster.

"I have to have this Guthridge woman. Let's concentrate on her today. After she leaves, you do whatever it takes to put these land problems to rest."

"Anything?"

"Anything that won't come back on us."

"I'll make some calls. The lights are on downstairs, I believe our guest will be impressed."

"Go ahead. When Mildred returns, I'll accompany them down. Dinner should be ready by the time we're finished. You will be joining us. We can talk afterwards."

Pietr Okneyev was surprised when Jenkins called him on his private line. "How did you get this number, my friend?"

"Like you, I have many resources. That thing we talked about. It is looking like you were right. I am assembling a team to make it happen. How is yours coming?"

"We too assemble a team. Your people, they follow our trail. They think pot of gold wait at end. We make think fool's gold." He laughed. "Why call? You have something for Pietr?"

"Soon. You have people in Bahamas don't you?"

"Pietr have people where he need. You have need?"

"To make things go better for my thing, I have a problem. He is in Bahamas on a construction project. Emerald Bay on Exuma. You must be careful, he is ex-Ranger, served overseas."

"I do this, what you do for Pietr?"

"He stands in the way of this thing we're putting together."

"What Ranger's name?"

"Jake Harper."

"I do this. You owe me. Understand?"

"Understood."

He disconnected and took the phone apart. Later he would call the Mexicans. They would have someone in the Bahamas who could take care of Pietr's man. Making sure nothing came back on him. He heard the elevator as he threw parts of the phone in his wastebasket, he pocketed the rest to discard elsewhere.

15

Miami, Fl

The VA receptionist paged Deane for TJ. Deane smiled when she saw him as she entered the reception waiting room.

"We had lunch, now you come see me at work. Is something wrong?"

"Somewhere we can talk? I need your help?"

Deane looked at her husband, twisted her head, keeping her golden-brown eyes on his, wondering what this was about. She went to the receptionist and told her she would be in the atrium if anyone came looking for her. They went into a glassed-in area where there were two concrete tables and benches surrounded by tropical plants and a small bubbling water feature which provided a soothing sound. TJ remained standing. Deane joined him. He was looking out at a landscaped alcove between the white stuccoed building and the asphalt parking lot. It was just the two of them.

"What's wrong TJ? You look troubled."

"Think I made a big mistake. Case I'm working on was supposed to be kept under wraps."

"You took the job, didn't you?"

He looked around then turned back to look at her. He rarely discussed his cases with her; it was mutual. They both understood. They agreed to leave their work at work. It was easier for them than most, due to TJ's long absences overseas and Deane's acceptance of being a veteran's spouse. Being a career counselor and working at the VA, she heard it all, was a terrific listener.

"Not here."

She reached out, squeezed his hand. His eyes were troubled. He was deciding what to say.

"I know not to do what I did. Person I talked to seemed off—should have listened to that little voice. I need to get ahead of myself to prevent damaging my case." He turned to Deane and leaned down to hug. "Don't know if this place has a listening devise. There are cameras and speakers in the corners. Just hold onto me like you're comforting me."

She turned her head and looked into his eyes whispering, "you're beginning to worry me."

"I'm sorry. Let's go outside?"

He started his truck, turned the AC on.

"Why all the secrecy?" she asked.

"Know any nurse name Vickie? Don't have a last name. All I know she supposedly works here."

Deane looked at TJ. "There are a lot of nurses that work here. The VA operates around the clock, like any hospital. There are three shifts. Some nurses are part-time, some fill in from other clinics. Do you know what kind of nurse she is, a department perhaps?"

"No. All I know is she hangs out with bikers. You know any Vickies like that?"

"None I can recall hearing about or talking to. TJ, I'm in the therapy, psych department, most nurses avoid socializing with us. They come in do whatever is required and leave. Rarely are they present when I'm with a patient."

"Know anyone in personnel you can ask?"

"TJ, what am I supposed to tell them why I'm checking on nurses named Vickie?"

"Say you saw her name on her name tag and need to ask her something about a patient. This is important, wouldn't be asking if it wasn't." He reached across the console and brushed her hair back from her eyes. She was looking down, her hands clasped in her lap.

She leaned her head into his hand. "I know. I'll try to think of something." She reached to open her door.

TJ thought of something. "Ever talked to or heard the name Buster Brown?"

She hesitated her hand on the handle. "You mean like the shoes?" She looked back over her shoulder, a quizzical smile on her face.

"Yeah, like the shoes."

"Why you want to know? I can't betray any confidentiality."

This gave him hope. "You don't have to. Check his folder, see if nurse Vickie's mentioned."

Deane got out of the truck. "I'll try. If I find a name, I'll text you. You going to be home for dinner, or should I get something on my way?"

"I'll let you know. Call me or text me when you're ready to head that way Thanks Deane. I love you."

"I love you too. Please be careful."

He hoped he was wrong about Buster Brown. Why had Maggie not known about his condition? For that matter, how much did he really know about Maggie? Carl had told him not to involve the locals. This was beginning to look like he was about to get screwed from both ends. He headed back to Homeland's office.

He told Carl, he had planted some seeds and hoped they grew into something.

"You better throw a bunch of fertilizer onto them. Hardy sent us a picture from the Bahamas." He slid a copy across the desk, three guys—one big man of color in plain looking clothes, a tanned white man and a Hispanic looking man, both dressed like wealthy tourists or yachtsmen. The white guy had his finger pointed into the chest of the colored man. "The Bahamian black guy is named Alvin Moss, he works on the Emerald Bay Resort project, for now. He has his seaman's credentials and a boat, Bahama'Mama, anchored in this port. Bahamian officials say he is clean We have our doubts. His family has a history there, even has a place called Moss Town. The white guy is Boris Brezinski, a known associate of Russian mobsters, wanted by our boys in connection with extortion, drug smuggling, trafficking and prostitution. The other man is unknown."

"My friend is down there working on that project. Hardy knows him. Maybe I can talk to him, see if he knows this Bahamian."

"Hardy told you not to be talking to your friend or anyone else about your involvement." Carl leaned back, stretched his arms over his head, and moved them side to side. "I think this op is going to have to be my last. Get my back operated on, take my wife on a cruise while I recuperate. Ever think about what you'd do when you retire?"

"Try not to think about it," TJ replied.

Mariel knocked. "Carl, Diego got a hit on that phone for Brezinski. We tracked him onto a yacht anchored in Rolle Town Harbor. We just intercepted a radio transmission originating in Belarus. It was encoded. We sent it to Washington. They're working on it."

Carl rocked forward. "Good work. Tell the others to keep at it."

"Russians in the Bahamas. Radio transmissions from Belarus. Sounds like something is getting ready to happen. We don't want anything happening here without our knowing. You need any fertilizer money?"

"Not at this time. Hope to know something soon," TJ replied. "Think I'll go sit outside Clutch's, see if anyone interesting shows."

The sun was falling behind the downtown glass towers, one of the many places in Miami where the money changers made and broke people with the touch of keys on a upscale version of a typewriter. TJ had heard that the total amount of paper money available would only satisfy the demands of less than 10 percent of the general population if there was another panic and run on banks like had occurred during the crash of '29. Several of the richest people could clean the treasury out if they were to liquidate their assets.

He was thinking about this when he drove by in front of what had once been the Miami Orange Bowl, now the Miami Marlins Ball Park. Across the avenue, under the overpass, was Clutch's, a fixture before the Orange Bowl was demolished. It was now surrounded by upscale sport bars and boutiques. He pulled down the alley that ran behind the buildings. There were dumpsters, electric transformers and a couple fenced in outdoor patios. Clutch's had the largest area because it was at the end of the alley. Nearest the building were motorcycles, mostly chopped down Harleys, all chromed up with customized lights, buddy seats and storage compartments, several had been completely designed and built from the wheels up, costing more than a luxury automobile. Buster had called it, this was not some seedy biker bar.

TJ watched from the back of the lot. The patrons came and went. There were a few females dressed in designer jeans and leather jackets, looking like they came off a vamp modelling runway, their high-heeled black leather boots clicking on the pavement, numerous body parts pierced with rings and dangles. Most of the men had polished chrome domes sparkling under the string lights strung across the bike parking area. All had tats, some more prominently displayed than others. There was a burly doorman wearing dirty looking jeans and a leather vest sitting on a stool, checking the patrons in. TJ noticed a bulge under his left arm. Every time the door opened the sound of heavy metal echoed off the walls of nearby buildings. He used his cell to take photos. It vibrated. Deane.

"Hey darling, headed home?" TJ asked.

"Where are you?"

"On a stakeout. Were you able to find out anything?"

"Possibly. There was a Victoria Lombauski whose name was listed in Mr. Brown's folder. She has been suspended without pay, pending a review. That's all I could find out. You coming home for dinner?"

"Not looking like it. Could be late. Gotta go. Love you."

Maggie was standing on the passenger's side of his truck. He unlocked the door.

"Thought I might find you here," she said as she dropped a bag in his lap and laid her designer purse on the console between their seats. She was dressed in an all leather outfit that left little to the imagination. She had nose rings and skull bone earrings that looked heavy and painful. Her eye makeup, black with cat whisker sweeps at the corners, her raven hair pulled back in a ponytail. Barbie biker look.

He looked in the bag. There were several small ampules inside.

"Rohypnol. Should be enough to stop a horse. We were right about Buster, he's on leave, failed the piss test, crystal and opioids, being treated as an outpatient at the VA. I called his number, no answer, no voicemail."

"You thinking you and I can do this alone? Too risky."

"For whom? TJ, I know you better than that?" She looked in the backseat and saw a baclava, his riot shotgun and a stun gun. "You were out here looking to take him by yourself."

"Could be dangerous. Can't go in there with you, don't want you going in there without backup."

"He's not going to do anything in there. Queer his deal, no pun intended. Besides I'm not going in there alone. Look out your window."

TJ had been staring at Maggie. As much as he felt he was betraying his love for Deane, he couldn't help himself. When he jerked back around, it startled the shit out of him. Carl was standing there dressed like Marlon Brando in the fifties motorcycle gang movie, leather cap and all.

He moved the guns over and climbed in the backseat. "Fine stakeout man you are. I've been standing out there why you gawked and gabbed."

"What the…? How…? I must be dreaming." He looked over at Maggie then back at Carl, they were both laughing.

"Don't be so surprised son. Been a long time since I was on the street."

"You two know each other?"

"It's my job to know the people in my area. The commissioner called. The vice commander called him saying one of his undercover vice officers had made an inquiry about a joint task force sting. I told you not to involve the locals. I had to do damage control. The commissioner called Maggie in and we had a sit down. She's now part of our operation. Thanks to you. After talking things over and trying to figure out how to salvage your play, I decided I needed some excitement. Haven't worn these clothes in twenty years. Surprised to find I still fit in them."

"You can't handle that guy. What about your back?"

"Steroid shot. I don't plan on wrestling him. The tough guy at the door, he's probably an undercover cop. Maggie will badge him. He will have to help if the perp decides to play rough. With the shit Maggie requisitioned, it shouldn't come to that. I've arranged for us to use a room across the street in the stadium."

"No way to know he's in there, could be wasting resources," TJ said.

Maggie opened her door. "Might as well let the cop at the door know I'm here." She strutted up to the doorman. He stood up. They chatted. She flashed her badge concealed in her palm. He didn't look happy. A couple came in while they talked. They chatted some more, she walked over to her suburban and called Carl.

"He's here. I saw him seated at the end of the bar. Cop Tobey's upset, said he's been working this gig, thinks we're going to queer his play."

"I'm going to have to go solo guys. There's no way I'll be able to get near him if I bring someone in with me. Besides this is a members-only club. Tobey will let me in, but not you. Bring the roofie bag and my purse over, so he doesn't see, drop it through the passenger's side window the next time someone goes in."

Carl insisted on making the drop, thought he looked less conspicuous. TJ wanted to laugh. When he came back and sat in the passenger's seat, TJ said," you stand out like a sore thumb. Good thing no one was paying attention."

"I wore this at a policeman's benefit. We were doing a Men at Work song."

"You're a man of many surprises."

They watched Maggie enter the club.

"How long should we give her?" TJ asked.

"No idea. This date rape drug is a new one for me."

"Might be surprised. Heard talk of MDMA back in your day."

"I spent two years on an ROTC scholarship, met my wife and shipped out. Not much partying for me."

TJ jerked forward. "Oh shit, see that guy and gal getting ready to go in the club. That's Buster Brown, undercover cop. He knows Maggie. The gal is Victoria Lombausky, his CI. They're both on suspension, his for his drug issues, hers from the VA. This could be a disaster for Maggie. Fuck. We got to do something."

"Nothing we can do without creating a bigger fuck up. We just have to sit tight, let it play out."

"If she's not out of there pretty soon, I'm going in."

"And do what? Have a shootout? You could get a lot of people killed, including Maggie, our perp and possibly yourself. If not, the whole operation will be blown. The press would have a field day. Can't let that happen. Stand down and let this play out."

After what seemed forever, Maggie came out. She was on one side of Diego who was having a hard time putting one foot in front of the other. On the other side taking most of Diego's massive weight was Buster. Behind them was Victoria and another man. They were all laughing and whooping it up. Tobey tried to stop them. He looked upset. He said something to the other man, who waved him off. They staggered over to Maggie's Suburban, put Diego in the back. Buster climbed in beside him, then Victoria. The other man lurched around to the passenger side and Maggie gave a thumbs-up, climbed in behind the steering wheel.

16

Great Exuma, Bahamas

Filling out the information on the two Internet dating sites made Jake wonder if there were any women worth knowing. He wasn't sure what he should say about himself, especially knowing Homeland's people would be reading it. He read what he entered over and over. If he was going to be on there, he needed to sound sincere. Everybody lied Nick said. Okay, so what lies could he tell and sound convincing? What kind of woman would he want to get to know, if he got responses? He scrolled through the pictures of the women. Some looked damn good, others, he wondered why they would post a picture not trying to look their best? Which picture was real? What picture should he post for his profile? He scrolled through his photo library and posted one of him on his porch holding Rustler, a mixed-breed rescue pup from the local shelter who was killed by a hunter's truck as he sped down the road, hurrying to get to his tree stand. The picture went with his profile of being the lover of nature type, a self-proclaimed environmental nut, who enjoyed travel and adventures in the great outdoors.

He took his groceries to the house. Not much doubt Rick and Blakely wanted him there about as much as he wanted to be there. He placed the window AC unit in the opening, just as he figured, it was smaller than the opening. He measured the hole and wrote what he needed down, relocked the window and left to go to Mitch's apartment.

The sun had set before he reached the apartments. It took them a while to open the door. The air reeked of marijuana and cigarette smoke, several butts were in an empty beer bottle, smoke coming from its mouth.

"I'll follow y'all," Jake said when they finally ended their game, grabbed a cooler of beer and jumped in Nick's rental vehicle.

"The place is down toward Rolle Town. In case we lose you, we'll pull over before the turnoff. It'll be on the left past Big D's."

Jake had no problem staying behind them at first. They turned off the pavement onto an unpaved winding road, barely wide enough for two vehicles, with steep drop offs on alternating sides in the curves. He drifted back so he didn't have to eat the dusty sand kicked up by Nick's vehicle's tires which made visibility difficult. Memories of the dismal deserts of the Middle East.

Nick's lights disappeared, then his brake lights suddenly reappeared. Jake had to brake hard. They turned right, he had to reverse course to catch them. Shortly they took a left onto a road with numerous homes on alternating sides of the road, their lights lighting the moonless night sky. Vehicles lined the road.

Jake found a place to park down the road a ways, walked back to where the noise was. The yard was full of people. He saw a few familiar faces. He went inside. There didn't seem to be any Bahamians present. Ceiling fans churned the hot, smoke-filled air. At a long table ten card players sat, beverages of choice and stacks of chips, red, white and blue in front. Behind the players, were other people, predominantly male, in single or small groups, talking to one another or watching the card game.

The room to the right was the kitchen, packed with people, coolers and picked over trays of snack foods, crumbs and droppings on the counters or mashed into the vinyl floor. Mitch was in the back talking to Jeff's oriental wife, behind them, separated by a couple of familiar faces, was Jeff and Rick. Jake was turning to go to another room when someone grabbed his arm.

"Hey," Blakely said falling into him pushed by some guy trying to get past her. She obviously was plastered, her face flush, her eyes unfocused. "Don't be mad wit' me," she slurred.

Jake tried to pry her hand off his arm. She was not going to turn loose. "Blakely, your fingernails are digging into my arm. I need to find the bathroom, let go of my arm?"

She loosened her grip, swaying away and back, but she didn't let go. "I'll show you." Her words coming redolent with puff-laden alcohol. "We can go together." She grinned, turned and pulled him in spurts toward the area where the card game was happening. They veered right, went down a hallway, bumping into other people. She was bouncing off the walls, like the steel marble of a pin ball machine. They entered another room, Nick was on the sofa with a bunch of other people, they were engrossed in a video game. A cooler was open, sitting behind the sofa. Jake reached down to get a water. He grabbed an extra one for Blakely. She was swaying, her eyes squinting, her head turned toward a door with light coming from beneath it.

"Damn bathroom door is closed. Come on."

She pushed through a small screened-in porch into the back yard. The smell of reefer wafted through the air. Several people were standing around passing the glowing ends of a couple doobies. Blakely stopped took a proffered hit; Jake declined, left her. He walked over a dune. He was about to unzip, when he heard a stumbling shuffle then Blakely bumped into him, once more grabbing his arm. She sighed, let go of Jake's arm to pull down her jeans, tried to squat, but fell over. Jake reached down, held her in a squat, heard her steady stream.

"Oh shit. I pissed my pants," she said attempting to pull up her pants. Jake held on to keep her from toppling forward. She giggled then started hiccupping and crying. Jake sat her down, walked a few feet away and relieved his bladder. After zipping up and turning around, he felt Blakely pulling on the waist of his pants. She had taken her pants off and had crawled over to where he stood. "Help me up," she cried.

Jake reached down and pulled her up. She wrapped her arms around him and tried to kiss him. He pushed her back, holding her at arm's length.

"I'm in trouble," she mumbled. "I need help. I'll do anything." She bent her arm reaching for his crotch.

He blocked her attempt. "Blakely, we've been through this. I told you I don't mess around with another man's woman, especially one that I work and live with."

"Let me go." She struggled to get his hands off. He let go and she sank to her knees. "I'll tell Rick and the police you raped me." She rubbed her pants back and forth in the sand, a crooked sneer on her face. "Everybody will know."

Jake opened one of the water bottles and handed it to her. "Drink it. You need to sober up. You're pitiful Blakely. Stay away from me."

"You're, like, right about that," Amy said. She was standing on top of the dune. "You're nothing Blakely but a scheming whore. Don't worry Jake, it's not like I didn't witness the whole thing."

"Like, go to hell, Miss high and mighty, goody two shoes. Your boyfriend says you aren't worth a fuck in bed." Blakely tried to stand and fell back. She lay there.

Jake walked up the dune to where Amy stood. "Somebody needs to tell Rick where she is."

"Not me," Amy replied. "She like needs her ass kicked." They looked back down at her. She hadn't moved. "I'll tell Jeff, he can tell Rick. You wouldn't like by chance be willing to give me and Kendall a ride back to our place. Like, you know, Kendall can't handle his alcohol. He's like out of it. Mitch put him in the back of the truck."

"I drove here by myself. Tell you what, I'll take the other truck and y'all can follow me?"

"I've had more than my share, can't get used to driving on the wrong side of the road."

"Why doesn't Mitch drive y'all?"

"Mitch said he would but not now. I'm like scared Kendall will come to and try to drive. If you don't want to, I'll like see if I can get someone else."

She turned and headed back down the dune. Jake glanced back at the inert Blakely then hurried up beside Amy. "I guess I owe you for saving me from Blakely's bullshit. Think Mitch will drive the other truck back?"

"If I tell him to, he will."

He fished the keys out of his pocket and handed them to her. "I'll see if I can find Jeff to tell him. Where's the other truck?"

"Wait for me out front I'll like take you to it."

Jake went around the outside of the house to the kitchen where he last saw Jeff. He was with Nancy, no Rick. Jeff asked if he had seen Blakely. "Amy said she will like show you where Blakely is."

Jeff and his wife frowned then laughed. "Like where is Amy?" Jeff asked.

"She went to find Mitch. She asked me to drive Kendall and her back. I said I would. My guess is they're in the back room playing video games."

He went back out the kitchen door and walked around front. Juan Carlos was there talking to another man. The other man walked away when Jake approached.

"Hello Senor Harper. Good to see you?"

"Hope I didn't interrupt anything?"

"No interrupt. That man was looking for someone, he not say who. He said he go in back to look. Hard to get in front door, no."

"Yeah. That's why I came around the outside."

"You like party?"

Jake looked over at the corner. He thought the man was standing there. He looked at Juan Carlos. "Not much on crowds. I don't know many people. Most of the people I met the other night aren't here and it's too smoky and noisy for my liking." He looked at the corner again, no one seemed to be there. Perhaps it had been an optical illusion created by the bright stars.

Amy came out. "Hello Carlos. You ready, Jake?" Carlos looked at Jake with a tilt of his head. "Kendall is like out of it Jake is driving us back to our place Carlos."

"He nodded his head. His manner dignified. "Sr. Harper, perhaps tomorrow you come eat and drink in Georgetown."

"I don't know anything about tomorrow…"

"Come on. He'll be there." She pulled on Jake's arm. Jake looked over at Carlos as he turned to go with Amy. Jake shrugged; he shrugged.

"You know Carlos is Columbian?"

"Yeah. He told me. Why you make your question sound like you're accusing him of something?"

"Kendall and Mitch think he may be into something. Like you have to ask them. He seems nice to me. Just looks at me like funny sometimes."

"Not trying to be critical, but you know you say the word 'like' over and over when you talk."

"I'm sorry. Most of the people I hung out with in school, you know like that's the way we all talked. I'm sorry. Now I'm going to be self-conscious about it."

"Cool or Kool was the word when I was in school. Drove the sergeants crazy when I was in boot camp. It's hard to break habits."

They arrived at the truck. Kendall was laid out in the back.

Jake forgot Kendall was in the back until he heard him bang against the side when they went into one of the steep curves. He slowed down.

Amy was resting her head against the passenger side window, until the curves kept swinging her head back and forth against the glass. She slid over and rested her head on Jake's shoulder. "Do you mind my resting my head here?"

He did because it kept him from being able to flex his neck, but he told her it was okay. Her hair smelled good, mixed with the sweet and sour alcohol smell of her breath.

"What is it with you and Kendall?"

"Kendall and I were at UNC Charlotte. He was like their quarterback. I went there because of him. We've known each other like forever. We started dating. He like lost his scholarship because some sorority bitch accused him of rape. I stood by him, now I'm not sure."

"What makes you say that?"

Jake knew this was a typical story. Amy seemed more mature than Kendall. Family money, power and having athletic ability, Jake once was that boy. He knew Kendall's mistakes had nothing to do with what he had to lose. He did it because he thought he could get away with it. A hard lesson the Army taught Jake the fallacy of. Ariel's leaving had been what hardened his heart—love was a cruel teacher.

"Like, Blakely may not have been lying when she said Kendall had sex with her. He denies it, so does Mitch. Like I know they're both lying. Mitch said she told him she managed a strip bar outside St. Louis, where she met Rick." She rubbed her head into his chest, and an old too familiar feeling of the good times with ex-wife Joanna flashed into his head. "I heard you, like, tell her no?"

"I have not nor will I ever have sex with that woman." He looked to see if she caught on to his statement. She was staring ahead, seemingly oblivious to the reference. "I'm not sure we should be having this conversation."

"My mother says all men think about is sex. She's like all down on men because our daddy cheated on her. You think she's, like, right?" She had her eyes turned up looking at him.

"Probably." They came to the end of the sandy road. Jake turned right onto the Queen's Highway. Amy had leaned away so he could turn, she returned her head snuggling into the tender area under his upper arm onto his chest once again.

"Like, Rick asked me to go to bed with him and Kendall's dad looks at me like he's undressing me. Everyone here does the same thing." Jake had to flex, he rolled his neck and cleared his throat. "Am I making you uncomfortable?"

"Why are you telling me all this?"

"I'm sorry. Kendall says I talk too much." She was quiet for a couple miles. "We like stay in a house right past where Mitch is staying. I don't feel so good. Would it be okay if I lay my head in your lap?" She didn't wait for an answer. He hoped she didn't notice his arousal.

He thought about what Blakely had said about being in trouble and needing money. She had managed a strip club. Most clubs Jake knew about were owned and run by organized crime figures, controlled by men like his ex-father-in-law. Blakely?

He remembered the pleading look in her eyes. She was scared. Rick was paying her living expenses and he had never seen her carrying a purse or paying for anything. Was Rick paying for her drugs? Jake couldn't help but think her desperation was bigger than wanting more drugs. Did it have something to do with her former life, was that why she came here? Was Rick involved, and who told her about Hardy? Damn he wished he could avoid talking to her.

He pulled into the apartment complex, gently shook Amy until she looked up, confusion showing on her face. She slowly sat up. Jake had to help.

"I'm sorry. Where are we?" She looked around. "Oh. Go back on the highway, it's not far, something like the second, maybe third road on the left." She yawned and slid over, once more resting her head on the side window.

Jake helped her out of the truck. They managed to get Kendall into the small yellow- painted stucco cottage and let him drop down onto a sofa. He curled up and lay still. Amy asked Jake if he wanted to crash there? It was tempting, so was she. He figured it best to leave.

On his way back to his, Rick's and Blakely's place, he thought about the lack of companionship, being tempted by these young women. Perhaps those internet dating sites would help. Maybe they would be more than a Homeland message board.

His bedroom was hot, despite the noisy fan blowing the AC unit-chilled-air from Rick's and Blakely's bedroom down the hall toward his room. He installed the AC unit and stuffed a towel around the leftover space to keep any flying insects or centipedes from coming in. He turned it full blast and changed into a pair of shorts, a T-shirt and sandals. It was then he noticed his duffel bag had been moved, someone had pulled things out of the closet and failed to put them back. He went through his things. Everything seemed to be there. Who could have been here? How did they get in? He was almost certain he had been here since Rick and Blakely. Most likely they left Big D's, went straight to the party. He had locked the door; it was locked just now.

He went to the front door again. No sign of any tampering. He checked all the windows. They were locked with no signs of entry. There was another door off the kitchen which he had thought to be a pantry when he was putting his groceries away. Behind it was a narrow staircase. He went down the creaking wooden stairs. At the bottom, to the right, was a small garage with a small boat that had seen its better days. The battered garage door was bolted and locked with a corroded hasp lock. On the left-hand side was a washer and dryer, a work bench with nothing but cobwebs and dust on it, and, an access door to the outside with a simple lockset, no deadbolt. Easy enough to slide a stiff card in between the lock and jamb for quick entry. He pulled the door open. It grittily brushed the floor without much effort.

Out back was a large yard with clotheslines stretched in rows not far from the house. There were numerous footprints in the sand piled up outside on the concrete pad at the door.

Who had been here and why? Seemed to Jake, the mess in his housemate's bedroom was the same as he recalled before leaving earlier. Whoever came here had looked through his stuff. Nothing missing, not that his clothes, toiletries and shit would be of any value except to a desperate vagabond. That kind of person would have taken as much as they could handle and left the door standing open. He immediately thought of the man talking to Juan Carlos. Why he couldn't say, just a feeling.

He went to the refrigerator and grabbed a beer. It was nice outside, a light breeze blowing. He took a lawn chair off its hook on the wall, opened it and sat down facing the distant bay. A boat, lights twinkling, floating like a UFO on the night darkened bay, moved into sight briefly and was gone. It was quiet, lots of stars lighting the sky, different formations than he was used to seeing at the farm and the places he'd been stationed. Down toward the bay, on the next street down, he could see the tiled rooftop of another home, filtered light from a streetlight flickering in and out of view behind the wild foliage of the bushes on the other side of the road. No streetlights polluting the sky back at his farm.

His neck ached. He questioned his motive for being here. He wished he could go back to the farm. His financial woes forbade doing so.

That asshole from the hunt club, Thurmond Tindal, had offered, constantly badgered him, to sell. An attorney had bought the land surrounding his farm from the Hill family heirs, it had been their ancestral land grant holding. He had started the hunt club and when he tired of it, had offered Jake first shot at buying his land, but Jake's military pay was not enough, and he had no borrowing power.

Tindal had bought the land, cut the beautiful mixed hardwoods and replaced them with pines. Jake's farm looked like an oasis in the middle of a bombed-out war zone. During hunting season, it often sounded like one also. But at night, it was one of the most peaceful places Jake had ever known.

Now here he was staring up at a strange sky, dealing with a deranged sex fiend, working for an absentee company boss he knew nothing about – no make that two counting Hardy with Homeland. He was still unsure about what it was he was supposed to be doing, and who was friend or foe. Not much different from your military days Jake. Thank God for TJ, he had always known whose side he was on. He needed to call him. He got up to get his phone and another beer.

17

Miami, Fl

TJ answered on the second ring. "Hey bro. Try to call back in an hour or so. Gotta go."

He hated cutting off Jake. He wanted to talk to him. Hardy said not to, he couldn't understand why. Fuck it, fuck them. Jake was his best friend, one of his few friends. He would talk to him whenever he wanted to.

He was ready to tell Maggie to step out of her SUV, come back to his truck. Carl had his door open, revolver resting on his arm out the window. The blue emergency light was pulsing on top of his roof, his bright lights were shining into the vehicle, lighting up, blinding the occupants. He and Carl hoped Diego was out of it, the other unsub unarmed. They debated calling for backup, Carl made the call not to. TJ told him he had his police equipment. He quickly briefed him about his plan.

TJ spoke into the mic of his under-hood-mounted loudspeaker unit, "Driver, show your hands and step out of your vehicle. You on the passenger's side show your hands. Do not get out of the vehicle. Everyone else, keep your heads and eyes facing forward. Do not move. Driver, out now!"

Nothing happened. TJ looked over at Carl. "What the fuck is going on?"

"Your guess is as good as mine, podna. I hope we're not going to have any gun play. Tell them backup is on its way."

TJ set down his riot gun and picked up the microphone again. "Backup's on its way. Driver out. Show hands now. Comply or you will be treated as potentially armed and dangerous suspects."

They saw Buster raise up from his place in the back seat and do something to the unsub in the passenger's seat. The SUV began rocking. Shortly afterwards, Maggie exited the vehicle, walked back their way.

"What the fuck is going on up there?" Carl asked coming around from the back to TJ's side of the truck. Maggie looked haggard. Her eye whiskers were smeared.

"The passenger calls himself Renaldo, he says he is an owner and manager of Clutch's. He had a nine, apparently down in his pants hidden by his coat. The Cubano bastard, no offense TJ, he wanted to make a run for it. Buster pinned his arms and I grabbed the revolver. I gave it to Buster. Now what are we supposed to do?"

"Diego must be out of it, is that the case?"

"I guess I gave him too much. Vickie says he should be fine."

TJ reached in, cut his emergency bar off. "What in the hell was Buster and Vickie doing?"

"I don't know. Shocked the shit out of me when they came in. Vickie pushed herself onto Renaldo and Buster kept buying the drinks and distracting Diego. I just played along. Diego wanted an orgy, Renaldo was all for it, we all acted like it would be fun. I didn't know how to let you guys know what was going on. I figured I'd go to some sleazebag motel and play it by ear. I knew you were back there. Your move might have worked if it wasn't for that cabrone having a weapon. So now what do we do?" She wiped some hair that had come loose out of her right eye, smearing the whisker into a smudge.

TJ and Carl looked at each other.

"We can't let this Renaldo go." Carl leaned back against TJ's truck. Vehicles passed overhead on the freeway, making a rumbling sound on the bridge connections. "You think Diego could be questioned or is he too out of it"

"You might want to talk to nurse Vickie. Ever since we got into my vehicle he hasn't moved."

TJ yelled, "Oh shit," and started running toward Maggie's SUV, Glock by his side. Popping sounds, almost drowned out by the big rigs bellowing exhaust and hissing brakes passing overhead, reached Carl and Maggie simultaneously with TJ's exclamation.

Turning toward the vehicle they saw the passenger side rear door fly open, Buster fell out firing back into the vehicle, dragging Vickie as another *pop* and a flash of light came from inside the vehicle. The other rear door flew open, Diego rolled out, shouting something in a bear like bellow, a semi in his right hand, having fired the last shot they witnessed.

Diego struggled to get to his feet, pulling on the rear door. TJ yelled, "drop it. Stay down." Diego slowly swung his bald head, the semi aimed at TJ. TJ slid down face first, his right arm extended with his Glock, his left arm and hand sliding on the pavement, skin being torn and peeled by the grit, the arm helping to steady his aim as he fired off two rounds. They both caught Diego on his right side in the shoulder stopping him from being able to fire off any rounds in their direction.

Carl and Maggie ran up, helped him to his feet. The front passenger door came open, a head appeared, then disappeared. "Renaldo is getting away," he said trying to catch his breath, partially leaning on Carl, "I think he took his weapon off Buster." He pulled his right arm off Carl's shoulder and started running in the direction he saw Renaldo headed. "Carl you need to help Maggie check on the others. I'll go after him." He started running not waiting for Carl's response.

Carl yelled, "I'll call for backup," to TJ's disappearing back. Maggie ran up and took the semi from Diego. Carl went around to check on Buster and Vickie. Vickie had a switch blade stuck in her side, she was bleeding profusely, her eyes closed, breath coming in gasps. Buster lay in a pool of her blood, half the top of his head blown open above the left eye. Carl reached down, felt no pulse. He started to pull the knife out of Vickie's side.

She had opened her eyes when he touched it, put one weak hand on his and said, "Don't, leave it." Blood bubbled over her lips and dripped off the side of her face.

He eased her off Buster and leaned her against the rear wheel. He pulled his phone out, his hand covered in blood. He wiped it on his blood streaked shirt and dialed 911.

"Officer down, send ambulances need backup." He gave their approximate address. A few vehicles had stopped. He went around to the other side. Maggie was standing over Diego who had a lopsided grin. He was looking down at his lap, blood was pooling around his right side. "Think he'll make it."

"A big part of me hopes not. How about Buster and Vickie?"

"Buster's gone. Vickie may not be far behind. You okay?" She was shaking. "I called 911. Help is on its way. I'm going to move TJ's truck and go after the other perp. Think you can handle this?"

"What am I supposed to say? How do I explain this cluster fuck?"

"Say as little as possible. I'll talk to the commissioner. Keep these people away." Some of the other drivers had gotten out of their vehicles and were walking their way. The sound of sirens, came from several directions, bouncing off the walls, echoing in the cavern-like tunnel under the freeway. "Don't mention anything about TJ, me and Renaldo. We'll take care of him."

He hurried back to TJ's truck, adjusted the seat forward, and eased through the gawking bystanders whom Maggie was warning off, waving her pistol and badge in the air. He looked at her wan face as he pulled around her vehicle and two others, then floored the truck, its big hemi rumbling, pushing him back into the leather seat. The first responding vehicle's lights were reflecting off the rear-view mirror as he sped away. He took the first right, going underneath the freeway, cut down an alley, then slowed down, scanning the buildings and other side streets, hoping to catch sight of TJ and/or Renaldo.

18

Great Exuma, Bahamas

Jake was on his third beer when he heard the truck coming up the hill. Rick pulled up next to the low wall that divided the small front yard from the street, went around and retrieved Blakely. Her waist was wrapped in a towel, her limp arms and jean encased legs draped over Rick's arms as he climbed the two steps and walked up to where Jake sat watching. Jake slowly got up, opened the door. Rick glared at him, went in the house.

Shortly Rick came thundering out, the screened door slammed behind Jake, who remained seated.

"Get up."

Jake remained seated.

"Get up muthafocker. You goina get your ass kicked."

"You better go back inside and cool it, Rick. Don't let Blakely get you into something you really don't want to get into. I didn't touch her, if that's what you think. Best cool your jets."

"Focking liar. Left her lying there, her pants off. People saw you. Get up muthafocker."

Jake got up. He had ten years, several inches and twenty pounds on Rick. "This isn't Mitch you're calling a liar. You really don't want to do this."

Rick lunged at Jake. Jake sidestepped him, stuck out his leg and used his right arm on Rick's back to speed his momentum. He landed on the lounge chair, taking the chair and Jake's beer with him. He slowly got up and turned toward Jake, his fists clenched. "Focking fight like a man, asswipe faggot."

"You think knowing a little boxing makes you a man. Where I come from there is no such thing as a fair fight. There are no rules, and losers don't have a ref to stop the damage."

Rick picked up the chair and swung it. Jake took the blow on his arms and shoulder, his head, and more importantly, his neck, tucked in under their protection. He felt the jolt, but he was already in motion. He came around with his left and caught Rick behind his ear sending him flying off the porch. Jake threw the bent and ruined chair aside, the blood rushing in his head, murderous rage threatening to overwhelm him. Thankfully, he was able to prevent the click, when every thought and instinct would push him beyond control. He shook his head, twisted his neck, stepped down off the porch and kicked Rick in the ass, as he tried rising. Every time he moved Jake kicked him again. Rick tried rolling and received a kick to the groin for his efforts. He curled up into a protective ball.

"Rick, it's only going to get worse and more painful if you try anything more," he hissed, breaths coming between clenched teeth. "Listen and listen good. I have not touched Blakely, not tonight, nor will I ever. Talk to Amy, she'll tell you. She witnessed every bit of Blakely's little charade. The reason her pants were off is because she took them off after she pissed on them. Now we can talk about this tomorrow or we can finish this little game tonight. I suggest you go inside and sleep on it." Jake reached down to help Rick up. Rick slapped his hand away.

"Ok. Have it your way. I'm going in there and go to bed. I think you should do the same."

Jake reluctantly started up the steps, then stopped. 'Nah fuck this bullshit. This can't wait until morning.' He turned around and went back down the steps. "There's shit going on around here; I believe you and Blakely are right in the middle of it. Blakely told me she's in trouble and needs money. Tonight, I came back here, found somebody had been in the house, went through my shit. I believe this has something to do with Blakely, and I think you know what it is."

Rick rolled onto his back and sat up with a groan. He sat there, one hand massaging his groin saying nothing. Jake waited. He started to repeat himself when Rick looked up with a pained and angry squint.

"You don't know didley shit. You got it all wrong. Ned's the one with money problems. His fockwad son's legal troubles is where the money went focker. He sent his son down here 'cause he don't want him there with him."

This gave Jake pause. Rick was probably right about Ned and his son Kendall. But, there was more to this than that.

"Blakely said *she* was in trouble, needed help."

"You full of shit. Blaming Blakely for what you did."

"Keep on thinking that Rick. I happen to know Blakely was a bartender and manager of a strip club, that's where you met her. Strip clubs are owned and run by organized crime. Is that why Blakely came here? My bet is she owes them money. There was a man at that party. I just caught a glimpse of him. He was big, not dressed like the others at the party. I think he may have been the one to come here, went through the house looking for something. I believe Blakely knows what, possibly you too. I need to know what's going on."

Rick struggled to his feet. "Who told you that shit about Blakely? Was it Mitch or the bitch Amy? Maybe you should ask them who *their* focking source is? Why don't you tell me who that man was you stayed at the Georgetown Inn with last night? Is that why you tried to fock Blakely to prove you not a faggot?" Rick had a crooked smile.

Jake wanted to put his lights out. He needed answers. "That man was a friend from back home. I had a separate room, one with air conditioning, unlike what I had here. Not that I give a shit about what Blakely or you think. What I'd like to know is who told Blakely?"

"You told her you had a room, asshole. You tried to get her to come stay with you."

Jake stared at Rick, smiled and shook his head. "Are you that thickheaded? Why would I ask Blakely to come stay with me if I was there with my friend? Are you and Blakely swingers? Is that why you put the move on Amy?"

Rick began opening and closing his fists, his face twisted in anger.

"Who told her about my friend? Who does Blakely owe money to? What was the person who came into this house looking for? Is it drugs?" Rick's eyes darted aside just for a second.

"That's it, isn't it? You said you could get anything here. Were you talking about the Bahamians, or is it bigger than that?'"

"You don't know what you're talking about. You need to go back to wherever you came from." He pushed by Jake and stumbled into the house.

Jake thought about stopping him, decided to let him go. He had shaken the tree. Now, he'd see what fell out. He tried calling TJ again.

19

Miami, Fl

The alleys between the buildings for the most part in this section of Miami were unlit. The roar from the overhead traffic made hearing almost impossible. TJ had stopped running and was moving more cautiously. Renaldo couldn't be too far ahead. TJ felt certain he would try to work his way back to Clutch's. He would feel like a caged animal and the club was his lair. TJ worked his way around the place where he had left Carl, Maggie and the others several blocks over, the emergency responders' lights reflected off the walls on a couple of nearby alleys. As he veered away, he heard the sirens of what sounded like two different ambulances echoing down the tunnels created by the buildings.

He felt his phone vibrating in his cargo pants. He paused and looked trying to shield the lit face in case Renaldo was nearby… it was Jake again. He saw he'd also missed two calls from Carl. He tapped Carl's name and he heard the trill of the phone reaching out to connect.

"You have him?" Carl asked. TJ could hear the familiar rumble of his truck exhaust.

"No. Go to Clutch's block the alley," TJ said softly into his hand, "Copy?"

Carl responded "copy."

TJ heard what he thought was his truck's rumble two blocks over, behind and away from his position, headed in the direction of the club. He hoped Renaldo didn't start shooting for everyone's sake. How had Carl gotten his truck and himself away from the scene of their fiasco? The incident was the textbook hazard of working undercover. If you're the good guy, you can't search anyone without raising suspicions, whereas the bad guys could search you. Catch 22, double jeopardy, they may be carrying, you shouldn't.

TJ could see the lights from the Mariner's complex, he was less than six blocks from where Carl should be. Had he been wrong? Had Renaldo gone to ground somewhere between there and Clutch's? Had he doubled back? Was he shadowing him, maybe waiting for the opportunity to put one into him? Was he setting up on Carl? Had he already made it back to Clutch's?

TJ had not taken part in urban warfare, street by street, house by house searches in real-time situations. He had received the training in the Army and with the SWAT team, but his military experience had been solo, the lone stalker, setting up, using other personnel's intel to do his thing, sometimes waiting for days, other times aborting when the mission was blown or called off. As a sniper member of SWAT, he was called in after all other efforts failed. When he joined the undercover unit, he was once more solo, the penetrator, the calculated risk-taker. This situation called on his training, not his experience. Had he miscalculated?

His truck sat idle at the entry to the alley. He saw the top of Carl's head over the driver's seat, in a state of perpetual motion, then he became still, his eyes visible, watching him approach. TJ came up beside the driver's door, the windows were all down.

"Nothing?" TJ asked.

"Nada. Think he could be inside?"

"Your guess is as good as mine. How'd you manage to get away from back there?"

"Left Maggie to take the heat. Called the commissioner. He wasn't too happy to be wakened, even less happy to hear what happened and that his department is left with cleaning up the mess. We have to find this Renaldo dude. You can bet Diego's going to lawyer up."

"He's alive?"

"Yeah. At University Med, guards posted outside the door. Buster bought the ranch. Vickie's critical. Maggie's being held for observation and questioning. I told her say nothing, then skedaddled."

"I think I need to go see if Tobey has seen him. I think fire law requires a second entrance and exit."

"It would have to be out front. You take your truck. I'll walk around. I'll take your riot gun with me. You got another weapon besides your rifle and Glock? My 45 is in my vehicle a couple blocks from here."

TJ pulled the rear seat up and unlocked the safe he had mounted under the floorboard. He removed his sniper rifle and M4 each in their own bags, pulled out a locked box and removed his father's 45 inside its holster wrapped in a cloth with an extra clip. "

"That was my father's. Don't let anything happen to it. I've got a stun gun. You want it also?"

Carl said, "No. I'm not sure I could handle two weapons at the same time. Might get confused, fire them both."

TJ tucked his Glock into the back of his pants, slid the stun gun into his right lower cargo pants pocket and returned everything else into the safe, locked it and said, "Time to lock and load, boogie down."

"Give me ten minutes to get in place." He looked at his phone. "That will be twenty-three hundred twenty. Don't shoot unless you have to. Wound, don't kill. No more collateral damage. We can't afford another cluster fuck, especially these rich ass civilians." Carl started walking fast around to the front.

TJ waited. There was one cycle left, probably Diego's. Tobey was nowhere to be seen. TJ got out of his truck and waited outside the door, two more minutes. The music wasn't playing, there was no chatter or laughter sound that he could hear. He wondered where Tobey was situated in the bar. And Renaldo? He would step inside and be ready to hit the deck if anything didn't immediately look right. He wished he knew the layout and where to look first. No collateral damage-- didn't need to be told that. He pulled out the stun gun, checked it, held it low and reached for the knob. Locked. Fuck. He looked up. A security camera was up high in the darkened eave. Dumbass you should have looked. So much for a surprise entry. What now?

He stepped back into the shadows, texted Carl apprising him of the situation. Carl texted back saying there was a camera at the front also.

Carl called him. "Looks like we have a potential hostage situation. That is, if he's in there. Normally I would say call in the feebs or the U.S. Marshal fuckers. We do, and we lose any hope of questioning him. The press will swarm in here like flies. The whole operation looks to be shot to hell. Any ideas?"

"The only option I see is for us to both blow the locks off with our guns and go in from front and back. Tobey is either inside or gone. If this were a hostage situation, you would expect to hear noise, people frightened and pleading. Only noise is some kinda music. What about it?"

"Can't risk being wrong. Maybe he's not in there."

"Won't know unless we go in. Better than sitting out here all night wondering." TJ wanted this. They were running out of time. The shooting would bring the police. "What if the police show, then what?"

"It's all over. We go home with our dicks in our hands."

"Hold your position. I thought of something." He disconnected the call. He had his rappelling rope in his box. He ran over to his truck, took the rope out, got into his truck, backed it up as close as he could to the door, tied one end to his trailer hitch and the other to the door handle. He tightened the rope up then goosed his motor. The handle exploded out with the part of the door it had been bolted to hitting the motorcycle, sending it tumbling onto its side. TJ jumped out and ran back toward the building, the remains of the door rocking on the hinges as he dove inside, his already wounded left arm cradling his right which held his Glock pointed ahead. Tobey was seated at the end of the bar which was on the right-hand side. He turned his head, staring at TJ, a shocked, concerned look on his face. Renaldo was behind the bar with his semi nine wavering from the back of Tobey's head and in TJ's direction.

"Put down your weapon Renaldo," TJ shouted. A gangsta rap disc was playing, louder than TJ expected. "You have no way out. You shoot that policeman, and if I don't kill you, you'll take the big slide. But before you do, you'll pay in ways you can only imagine. Put it down, the worst that can happen is you get deported."

"Why you do this to me? I not know you."

"You ran when your friend killed those people. That makes you an accessory. I may be able to get you immunity, that is if you put down your weapon and give me a good reason why you ran. You shoot, and the deals off the table."

TJ could see Renaldo was not sure whether to trust him.

"Tell you what. I'll put my weapon down on the floor and you lay yours on the bar. You let Tobey walk out of here and you and I will talk about getting you out of here without going to jail. I swear on my Cubano mother's grave, you won't go to jail."

He was fidgeting. Not good. Tobey was saying something to him. TJ could not hear because of the music.

TJ was good at texting without looking at his phone, using either hand. He reached back with his left hand and pulled his cell out and texted Carl, *start banging on the front door yell FBI.*

"Renaldo the Feds are on their way. Your best bet is with me. You should know they will use the Patriot Act, and you'll end up in max. No lawyer. No rights. Forever in solitary in a ten by ten cage." Tobey said something to Renaldo, and fear contorted the Cuban's face.

Carl started banging, yelling, "FBI, open up."

Renaldo and Tobey looked that way. Renaldo and Tobey pivoted their heads back, Renaldo's eyes bulging, looking quickly toward the front and back to TJ.

"They kill me. No matter where I go, they'll kill me." He pulled the gun from Tobey's head and was putting it under his own chin. TJ dropped his cell phone, brought his left arm back to brace his right when he saw the uncertainty in Renaldo's eyes and the semi starting to move due to Carl's actions. He took his shot. The revolver flew out of Renaldo's hand. Tobey fell forward, and TJ jumped to his feet and ran around the bar and tackled the stunned Renaldo, whose trigger finger was now half gone.

"He was as cool as an icebox cucumber dildo in a hot pillow joint down on the strip," Carl said to Bob Hardy over a secure line. "A money shot if you ever saw one, right through the trigger guard. This guy is an ace. Wouldn't want anyone else covering me in a free fire zone. Has good instincts. Figured Renaldo would go to roost. Pulled that door off, went in like a one-man assault team."

"I'm glad you like the guy," Bob replied.

"Like him? Hell, I love him, if I leaned that way, I'd ask him to marry me."

They both laughed.

"Where is everyone now?"

"Diego is in the hospital under police protective custody, as are the two women, Maggie the Vice UC and Miss Lombauski the CI. I talked to the commissioner; he's agreed to keep this under wraps as much as possible. I told him the women and TJ deserve medals. I have Renaldo secured in our clinic, sent TJ home. Wanted to stay, be part of the interrogation. I told him he could have a go at it tomorrow."

"Anything good so far?"

"The guy is scared shitless. He says we can't protect him. Nobody can. They have people everywhere, he claims. I asked about his countrymen here and in Cuba. if they were in with the Bahamians. He laughed. He said the Bahamians were too fucking dumb to be in with anyone. He called them mules with boats. He clammed up when I asked about the cartels. Refused to acknowledge if they were who he was afraid of. His eyes said otherwise."

"What about Diego? What's their connection?"

"Said Diego dropped in whenever he came to Miami. That was news to us. He refuses to talk. I lied, told him Diego was dead. He demanded immunity. Said the other Cuban policeman promised him immunity. TJ said he told Renaldo the worst would happen to him was he would be deported if he put down his weapon. The lamebrain waved his cauterized and bandaged stub of a finger saying it was proof he had put the gun down." I had to laugh. He acted insulted. Carl laughed along with Bob.

"I'm going to let him think about it for the rest of the night. The lights are set to go on and off, along with screams and high-pitched wailing like someone is getting the shit beat out of them. Our team will have a go at him again in the morning. We need to get Diego out of University Medical and into our clinic. We can play the two against each other. I think Renaldo will break if we threaten to throw him in with Diego. That's about it, how about your end? You think Renaldo is right about the Bahamians?"

"No. Not with what we have so far. The Harper man is having a hard time with a woman named Blakely Carmichael, her ID doesn't check, see what our people can come up with."

"What about those Russian transmissions coming from that yacht to someone in Belarus, and those pictures that show a Bahamian talking to the Russian and an unsub that I sent?"

"I have talked to the Harper man, who took the cell phone photos and warned him. I also have added another couple of people for backup. I plan to stick around in the Bahamas another week until after Christmas, see what shakes out. Let's plan on daily updates. We need to keep this in-house as much as possible, I'll see what I can do to help with having Diego moved."

20

Great Exuma, Bahamas

Sleep refused to happen. He was still wound up from his confrontation with Rick. Jake had closed the unlockable bedroom door and wedged a chair under the knob so anyone trying to enter would have a difficult time getting in. He doubted Blakely or Rick would try. He wasn't sure the earlier intruder might not return. If only he had his Remington 12 pump shotgun that he kept loaded by his bed at the farm.

His neighbor had texted him on his regular cell leaving a message to call him. It was too late to call him. One of the things bothering him was why TJ had not called back. He hoped nothing bad had happened. With TJ he felt certain anything bad would be for whomever had been the other party.

Jake shifted his neck on the pillow, th incidents and stress were causing his neck to stiffen and ache. He rolled side to side, tossing and turning, nothing helped, too many issues. His restless mind drifted back to his own problems: Rick, Blakely, Ned and ESI's possible money problems, the other man at the party's identity, possibly connected to Blakely and Juan Carlos. Could the unknown man be his backup? Not if, as Jake suspected, he had been the one that broke into the house and went through his stuff. Had he broken in looking for something Blakely and Rick had, or, had it been something he thought they might have?

He needed to get to know more about the Bahamians, especially Alvin and potentially Rob and Rodney, maybe the Bahamian woman's husband

Edward could be someone to talk to about the others. And Blakely? Jesus, he wished he could steer clear of her, but she was in the thick of everything.

And ESI? Was Ned in financial trouble? Bubba had said Fluor was considering cancelling ESI's contract, kicking them out. Amy said Ned had told Rick not to pay the Bahamian fees, Kendall said the money was there, Rick was the problem. Had Rick used the money to help Blakely?

He wished he had brought books. He always did some reading when he went to bed to help take his mind off the daily grind. A chapter or two often allowed him to relax, turn off the bedside lamp, do his meditation, drift into sleep. No books, he had not seen any reading material anywhere he'd been on the island. What did the children do? Another problem to solve. As if he didn't have enough already.

Jake finally drifted into the dream world. His problems followed him there. He couldn't remember the dreams in detail. Naked women and images of his parents, Ariel had made an appearance, Joanna and his children. Some strangers were chasing them for what reason the dream never revealed. It was threatening, Jake who was the observer, felt and could not find a way to help them from whom, what or why? When he awoke, the fitted sheet had pulled loose from the mattress and he was tangled up in it and the top sheet. The room was still dark and frigid. He should have changed the AC thermostat when he came to bed. After untangling himself, he picked up his cell phone to check the time, 0500, his usual wakeup time back at the farm. He lay there trying to sort the dream(s) out. No such luck. He was certain his presleep thoughts had much to do with what happened in that ablative mind-clearing, mental computer-sorter world, called dream land.

He got out of bed, cut the AC unit off and headed down the hall to the bathroom for his normal post-military routine which wouldn't be normal without his coffee or breakfast of fruit and nut enriched, old fashioned oatmeal, not that instant crap many people preferred due to its ease of preparation. How were his bowels supposed to move and his kidneys clear, not to mention the caffeine jolt of dark roast coffee feeding the addiction and the food filling his stomach? Another problem to be solved. He would stop at the local quick mart he had seen near the job site to see what was available there.

Exuma Quick Stop didn't have fresh brewed coffee, so Jake got a green tea with ginseng and honey, TJ's favorite. The snack aisle had an assortment of biscuits, which Jake looked at in dismay, by site they resembled cookies. He asked and was told by another patron that they were the same as cookies. He grabbed several varieties and went out to the truck. The gas gauge showed the truck was near empty. He walked over to the pump, $6.50 per gallon, more than twice the price of premium grade back in the Carolinas. They wouldn't accept his credit card; he decided not to use his money.

The sun had tinted the northeastern sky, a glowing splash across the horizon as he pulled up to the security station. The Bahamian security man emerged slowly from his seat. He checked the window sticker and made a mark on his clipboard, slowly walked back, then waved Jake on. Jake pulled up to ESI's laydown/office containers. No one was visible, but the office door stood open. Inside he found two expats seated at the desks. One drinking a Coke, seated behind Rick's desk, was about Jake's size and looked a few years younger. The other was a skinny short kid in his early twenties with short sandy blond hair, picking his nose and licking his fingers. Grossed Jake out. They looked fresh and perk.

"You must be the new manager the Bahamians told us about," booger eater said in a Carolina country tone.

"I'm Jake Harper. Who are you two and how did you get in?"

The older one, entered something into his laptop, stopped, looked up and said, "Rodney has a key and let us in. I'm Wynn and that's Berry. My company is Carolina Frame and Door. We're out of Midland, North Carolina, here to modify the frames in building two." He went back to tapping something into his laptop. Booger eater Berry was playing a video game on ESI's computer.

"I'm from south of Charlotte, near a town called Sharon. I've been through Midland a few times on the way to the beach," Jake said twisting his neck, frustrated by not knowing the situation.

Berry laughed. "Blink and you miss it." He continued his game and Wynn continued on his laptop. It was as though this was their office and Jake the intruder.

"Thought you guys were going to do this work last night?"

Wynn looked up, closed his laptop. "My partner Tom and his helper Luke worked the night shift. Rodney has gone to check on their work then bring them back here when they reach a stopping point. There are a lot of fucked up door frames on this job, more than three times the number we were sent down here to fix. Ned's not going to be happy when he gets our bill."

"How'd that happen?"

"Fucking Bahamians don't give a shit. Nobody is checking behind them like they're supposed to."

"Who is *they*? ESI?"

Booger eater glanced at Wynn then at Jake. "Don't you know?" he said with a smirk.

Wynn spoke up before Jake could respond, "ESI's man is supposed to go through with Fluor's person, check everything. No one takes the blame, but each sub is responsible for their work. In this case, the doors won't work in the openings. if they're out of square, opening the wrong way or not plumb, we come in cut the frames, straighten them up and reweld them. That's all we're supposed to be here for. But Kendall has us installing the doors and closers in some cases. Doesn't matter to us, as long as we get paid."

"Kendall?" Jake asked, "I thought Rick had to okay the work?"

Booger eater laughed his snippy laugh again. "Rick rarely goes out to the job site. He leaves everything up to Kendall, who leaves it up to Rodney for the most part. Rodney always works the night shifts when we're here, gets paid double time, half the time he just watches or simply goes off somewhere. Brags he makes more money than you managers."

"Does Ned know this?"

"Ned knows what Fluor's people and Kendall and Rick tell him. He goes ballistic whenever we turn in our bill. Long as he pays, I don't give a shit," Wynn stood when the sound of a truck out front echoed in the early morning quiet. He came around the desk with his laptop and grabbed his hardhat.

Jake walked out first. Rodney pulled up in one of the beat-up older model trucks. Two expats got out of the cab and two Bahamians climbed out the back of the truck. Alvin wasn't one of them. Wynn and Berry walked over, started talking to the other expats. Jake went over to the driver's side.

"Mornin' Mistuh Harper," Rodney said sounding chipper.

"Morning Rodney. Were you out here all night?"

"Yeah man," he said, as Wynn and Berry took the seat in the front, Berry in the middle.

"I need to talk to you. You coming back here after you drop them off?"

"Gotsta come get the other niggas when they get here," he replied showing a toothy grin.

"Let's get going," Berry said as though he was in charge.

Rodney returned, picked up the others, left without talking to Jake. No Alvin had come back in the truck and no Alvin left in the truck. Tom and Luke said they had not seen him where they were working.

Mitch showed up earlier than the day before to open the tool container, disheveled as always. Rick didn't arrive until 0800. He didn't look at or speak to Jake, no comments, no job missions, nothing. The other two expats, Tom and Luke, left with him shortly afterwards.

Mitch came out of the tool container lighting up a cigarette. He stepped away from Jake, making sure his smoke didn't come his way. Mitch said, "the motherfucker was awfully quiet this morning. Did he say anything to you?"

"No. The truck I'm in is nearly empty. How do y'all pay for gas?"

"Rick and Kendall have the credit cards. Kendall should be coming this morning to the manager's meeting. You going?"

"Didn't know anything about it?"

"Maybe Rick didn't want you there."

"What time does it happen?"

"Nine o'clock at Fluor's office."

Jake walked up the middle of company container boulevard. It was nearly deserted. The workers had removed themselves to the job site and the managers were headed into the office complex. Jake's military mindset was appalled by the seeming lack of discipline and order. The older people here, like elsewhere in society, seemed to have lost their will to enact any discipline into the conscience of the younger generation.

His father blamed it upon the liberal sixties with too many families split apart and children lacking a strong male figure, raised by uncaring or overburdened mothers who turned their children loose, expecting society to help raise them. His generation blamed it upon too much media and lack of social interaction.

Jake believed every citizen upon reaching the age of eighteen should have to serve two years in the military, social services or in other community service organizations. Part of the service at home and part abroad in a controlled environment, where respect was earned and given. He doubted that would ever happen.

As he walked up the steps to Fluor's office complex, his phone chirped, indicating he had a text message. It was messages plural: one from his neighbor saying he needed to call as soon as possible; another was from TJ reading 'call me'; the third was from ESI's office informing him Ned would be flying in on Monday. Jake tried his neighbor. The call went to voicemail, not unusual for the rural connectivity in his home area. He left a message saying he would call back later. He was concerned. Twice his neighbor had tried to reach him. Had something happened?

Kendall was off by himself at the far end of the long row of tables and metal folding chairs down the middle of the meeting/ trailer room. He didn't acknowledge Jake's or anyone else's presence. Most of the others present were strangers to Jake, many looked at him, some nodded their head, only one person bid him "good morning," a guy sporting a sunburned complexion making him look like a fisherman in from days at sea. He introduced himself as Thomas Devereaux, manager of a company called Basics Metal Works located in Huntsville, Alabama. He started to say something to Jake. Jake's attention was caught by Rick's coming in with Jeff Taylor. They sat at the other end of the table near the dais, next to the two Fluor men from down under, Alec and Marcus. Rick quickly looked past Jake as he scanned the room, nodding to several people. A large well-dressed man in khaki pants and a dress shirt entered with an average size man similarly dressed but with longer hair combed back behind his ears.

The larger well-dressed man called the meeting to order and announced he would be leaving Emerald Bay and that the other man Charlie Davenport would be taking over as senior project manager. There were murmurs among the others seated at the table, not all looked or sounded pleased.

Charlie told everyone he was surprised to have been given the responsibility, but he guaranteed everyone that he would continue to make their lives as miserable as Dave had. A few chuckled. Jake noticed Alec

Wickham and Marcus Barrette, Rick's buddies, seated next to Rick, looked downcast and red-faced angry.

Jake turned to the Devereaux guy, who had seated himself next to Jake and remarked, "those two next to Rick don't look too pleased."

"Alec thought he would be given the nod. He has more experience than Charlie. Charlie's been with Fluor longer." He chuckled. "Charlie used to be a psychiatrist, married to some wealthy woman with a big house on Pawley's Island. This is his second career, like a hobby, can be stubborn, but gives everyone a fair shake, but doesn't abide bullshit." He stopped talking and nodded toward the podium. Jake turned back, watched and listened.

"Alec will take over my duties and be my assistant," Charlie stated, sounding more like a professor than any construction manager Jake had dealt with. "Any complaints see Alec. Any praise, I'll be happy to listen." More chuckles ensued.

After this Charlie walked over to a large white marker board with each building listed along with its status. He asked Fluor's managers to enumerate the status, then asked the subcontract managers for the timeline when their work would be completed. ESI's work had the most deficiencies and negative responses. Rick made numerous excuses, trying to deflect the blame, but Charlie was having none of it.

"This project's completion date is 385 days hence. It has been pushed back for the last time. There can be no more delays. Fluor's people and most of the other companies' people will be leaving for Christmas next Friday." He looked briefly in Jake's direction then his deep-set eyes bore into Rick. "I understand Ned is coming Monday, he tells me he has sent another manager here to help get his company on track. The only person here I do not recognize is you sir. Would you please stand. Introduce yourself." Everyone's eyes were on Jake.

Jake stood, introduced himself and sat back down. He felt like he was a specimen under a microscope.

"Mr. Harper, I'll tell you what's been said to Ned and Rick, ESI has until the new year to give us reason to believe ESI can comply with our schedule or Fluor has ordered me to bring another company in to complete the contract. I…"

Kendall interrupted, shouting, "That's bullshit. The delays are caused by Fluor's not paying what we've billed you people. You cancel and we'll sue." He stood and stormed out.

"Like father, like son," Jake heard one of Fluor's managers on the other side of Devereaux say. Most of the people chuckled.

"Rick, Mr. Harper, I hope you understand."

After the meeting, several managers from Fluor and the other companies came to Jake, introduced themselves, offered to help anyway they could, and wished him good luck, which sounded more like condolences. All appeared to be like all other construction managers he had known. He couldn't see any of them as being the type to get involved in major crimes. But then again, Jake knew white collar crime was more prevalent than most people were aware of and was the least likely to be prosecuted.

Noticeably absent in coming forward to say anything to him was Rick and mates, Alec and Marcus.

Jake needed a credit card for fuel. Kendall and Rick were nowhere in sight when he exited the building. Thomas Devereaux had followed him out, stopped next to him and stood there as Jake looked toward ESI's office while others filed out past them, going on to wherever they usually went.

"Are you from Charlotte?" Thomas asked, as Jake looked back at him wondering why he had stopped and seemed to want to talk.

"A place southwest of there. ESI is from there, I guess that is why you ask. I'm sorry, I'm trying to figure out what to do for transportation. My company's truck is almost empty. I need to find Kendall or Rick. They have the company cards."

"Come on. You can hitch a ride with me. I'm headed to Rosie's for a late breakfast."

He had a rental car parked on the entry side of the office complex. Once they were on Queen's Highway headed south, he shocked Jake by saying he had been to Charlotte and went to a place called Dilworth Billiards. He paused, Jake looked at him wondering.

"I guess you met the owner Eric?"

"Never been there actually. Bob Hardy told me I should mention this to you, said you'd know what to say. Have you been there?"

"Quite often." Jake looked at him harder. He was one of those people who, even when they're smiling, look like something is eating them up inside.

"You seem surprised. Guess you thought I would be someone else."

"Have you always worked with Basic's Metal Works? I mean…you're with Homeland Security right, or am I mistaken?"

He frowned. "Need to watch who you say that to. We'll talk about that another time."

They rode the next several miles in silence.

"Here we are. Looks like the others beat us here." They turned into the crowded crushed-shell parking lot, a weathered sign said, "Rosie's."

Jake's phone vibrated. It was his neighbor.

"Hey man, I've been trying to reach you," Patrick said.

"Sorry, been kind of busy. What's up? Has something happened?"

"Katie told Ben somebody broke into your barn. Wasn't anything missing he didn't think. He checked your house, the doors were all locked, but he said your digital clocks on your stove and in your bedroom were blinking. Could have been a power surge, but with the barn thing we kind of wondered. When I couldn't reach you, I called the sheriff's office. They wanted to know why I was calling instead of you. I told them you were on a job and I couldn't reach you. They said they'd send a patrol car by on each shift. That may or may not happen, you know how that goes."

"I'll try to give them a call. So, nothing seems to be missing, could be some of those damn fuckers that work for Tindal or some of his hunt club fuckers snooping around. Seems like something always happens whenever hunting season gets going. Thanks Patrick."

Thomas Devereaux had exited the car and was leaning against the sun-soaked front end. Jake opened his door.

It was as if Patrick hadn't heard him. "Speaking of Thurmond Tindal. He tried to buy back my property. I told him I wasn't interested. His man, Bud Jenkins, wanted to know if I was in touch with you. I told him you were out of town on a job. Hope that was ok. He seemed anxious to talk to you. I'm sure it's the same ol', same ol'. Mr. Tindal's buying up all the land round here. Hear he has a contract on all the timber land between you and me and is buying the land across the Broad River where the old historic town of Pinckneyville used to be. Rumor has it he's got a government contract. Has he contacted you?"

"No," Jake hurriedly replied. "He's tried to talk to me before. Like you, I told him I'm not interested. I'm sorry Patrick I need to go. I appreciate your calling. Let me know if anything else comes up." Thomas was standing outside, his sunburned skin getting more exposed, anxiously waiting. It was getting hot in the car even with his door open and the windows down. But once Patrick started talking it was difficult to get a word in or stop him from saying what he had to say.

"He's putting in a guard shack out at his entrance and tall ass metal poles with cameras on them all along the road. There has been a lot of air traffic overhead recently, Ben saw it when he was helping dig a pond over there behind his big ass garage. Saw several private jets land and take off from there. Molly and I have seen a shit load of government SUVs and a couple limos on the road this week."

He paused a moment to catch his breath, trying to remember what else he was going to say. "Rumor has it Mr. Tindal may be setting up a training camp on his land. Could be he's going into creating a dude ranch is what I figure. I talked to Red the game warden; he says he doesn't know what Mr. Tindal is up to. We both know that's bullshit. Ben was id'd by a couple of SLED and Federal Wildlife Agents with Red standing there when it happened. Some of this has been going on for a while, guess you knew most of it. Kind of makes you wonder what's what." As usual, Patrick didn't care for a reply so hung up. Thank goodness. Jake was running sweat, as was Thomas who had been needlessly waiting.

Jake hurriedly stepped out of the car.

"You should have gone in. That was my long-winded neighbor. He's watching after my place and taking care of my animals while I'm away." They started walking across the hot sandy parking lot. It was nearly full just like the last time Jake had been here.

"Everything all right?"

"Seems someone's been snooping around. Probably one of my neighbor Thurmond Tindal's men or a member of his hunt club. It's deer season. Fuckers are always coming over onto my land. I've lost six dogs in the last three years. Fucking hunters claim they run their deer, which is bullshit. The deer are used to my dogs. Wish there was open season on those motherfuckers." Jake chuckled. Thomas was looking at him strange.

They sat down at the table where another three men vacated the only possible table not occupied. Once they ordered Thomas leaned toward Jake and spoke so low Jake watched his lips to understand his question.

"Did you say your neighbor's name was Thurmond Tindal?"

"Yeah. Why, do you know him?" The possibility worried Jake. He wasn't sure why.

"There was a Colonel Thurmond Tindal, retired Army, CIA, NSA, now I hear he's a weapons' dealer or something like that. How well do you know him?" Thomas took a drink of his Coke then leaned back across the table.

"He was a member of the hunt club that leased the land around my property. Then he bought the land. I would have, but I couldn't afford it. He introduced himself to me as Colonel Thurmond Tindal, said he had been in the Army like me and had a home in Charleston. Been trying to buy me out. His people have been a thorn in my side, including the game warden, whom he has in his pocket. Never said anything to anyone I know about the CIA, NSA or how he got his money."

"Has to be him. That man has a lot of political friends. I never met him, but he was said to be a shrewd but ruthless asshole. Does Hardy know he's your neighbor?"

"Not as far as I know. Thought we weren't going to get into name calling in here? Rick's buddies are looking over here. Bet they're wondering what we're talking about."

Thomas leaned back. "Fuck Alec. That Aussie asshole tries to bully everyone. Getting him to sign off is like getting your teeth pulled through your asshole."

Jake laughed. Alec said something to Marcus and Rick, and they all laughed.

"Marcus is Alec's assistant fuck mate, maybe literally, wouldn't be surprised. Claims he was on the New Zealand All Black Rugby Team. From what I know about that team, I can't see how that could be possible."

"I played rugby while I was stationed at Fort Polk and taking classes at LSU. There were a few players I figured leaned that way. From what I've seen in the military and out, sexual orientation doesn't necessarily indicate you aren't aggressive, ain't mean as hell. Some of those people had to learn to be tough to survive, others hide their inclination behind a shield of bravado."

"Don't ask, don't tell. I'd rather know, especially in combat where I might be exposed to bodily fluids, blood and such. Did you ever think about that?"

"Tried not to. Here comes our food." Jake watched Rick and company leave. The rest of the meal was spent talking about the Emerald Bay project.

Once they were seated in the car, Jake asked Devereaux what he knew about the operation. He had received the same briefing as Jake from Hardy.

"I've been living on a boat on the northern end of the island, same place you took those photos. Hardy visited me after he met with you. You know pretty much everything I know about the operation. Homeland installed equipment onboard, allows me to monitor transmissions. My boat is as fast as many of those cigarette boats docked there. I had Coast Guard training and worked a couple busts while I was with the bureau, guess that's one of the reasons Homeland picked me for this op. Maybe you can come by and we can take her out. You a boat person?"

"My family had a lake house. Grew up with ski boats, fishing boats and pontoons. Nothing like what you're talking about. I'd love to go out do some fishing, touring around, see what your boat can do."

"Could be useful for this operation. Homeland is paying me for letting them equip it. might as well use it. You say you have a list of suspects. Maybe I know some of them."

"First off. How much time do you have? Do you have to get back?"

"I'm the boss here. What few men I have left are good at what they do. Mostly expats and a couple Bahamians. ESI is one of the few companies here with majority of the employees being natives. Like our company, most brought in trained employees. Made my job easier. It's Friday, most the managers come here after the meeting, as you may have noticed, then they fuck off until the end of the day. They have assistants who handle things and do the payroll. What you got in mind?"

"Do you know Blakely, Rick's girlfriend?"

"Who doesn't? She is either a big prick tease or everybody's been banging her except me. Why?"

"I can't put it together." Jake told Devereaux what had been happening with Blakely and Rick. He pulled over at Fish Fry. Not many people were there. He listened to Jake while watching the shack owners getting ready for the Friday business.

When he finished recanting his misadventures, Jake said, "I'm not sure what Blakely has gotten involved in, but I would bet someone's got their hooks in her and she's in over her head. I'm not sure how much Ned, Rick, Kendall and Mitch know either. Blakely, Alvin and Rodney are the first on my list to find out what they know. Blakely should be at the house. If you've got time, I'd like to swing by there and have a one on one with her."

"Tell me how to get there. I got nothing better to do. According to my instructions, I'm supposed to watch your back. I'll wait in the car and keep an eye out."

"That might be better. If it's just me, she might feel less intimidated, maybe open up."

"Open up? Hardy may be right you might need a body condom." He laughed.

"Wasn't what I meant." Jake wasn't sure this was just a Freudian slip.

21

The glassed-in interrogation room was in the same building as Homeland's Miami field office. It was between the operation center where Swanson and his team worked and the clinic. Diego had been transferred and Renaldo was seated in a bolted down metal chair on the other side of a metal table across from TJ. Swanson was seated next to his interpreter, also named Diego. They watched through the one-way glass.

TJ sat staring at Renaldo, who was trying to avoid looking back, his boyish Latino face puffy, eyes lined with fatigue from the night where he had been bombarded with bright lights and screams. He looked down at his bandaged joint. He started squirming, his hands fidgeting, going from his lap onto the table. He grimaced then tried to smile, like he had thought of something amusing about his pain. TJ didn't move, his face placid, letting it play out.

Several minutes went by. "Why you hassle me, man? I not do anything. Look my hand, fucked up, no reason. I want lawyer, going to sue, this make me rich man."

TJ didn't move, didn't say anything.

"What with you, man? Why you look at me like that? I no talk without lawyer, so fuck you." Renaldo wrung his hands, then jerked, his face twisted with pain, having forgotten the finger until his other hand made contact. His eyes started tearing. He wiped his running nose and eyes on the back of his unbandaged hand.

TJ waited then spoke calmly, "Accessory to murder of a policeman, twenty years to life; fleeing the scene of a crime, add another year; possession of an illegal firearm used in the commission of a crime, eight to ten; threatening an officer of the law, eight to ten; taking a hostage, six plus; resisting arrest, one to two; harboring a fugitive and terrorist, life in a max. You'll never see the light of day except maybe an hour inside a ten by ten cage. On the bright side, you may be taken to Guantanamo. You'll be back home in Cuba. We don't have to provide you with a lawyer. No one knows where you are and won't unless they read your name on the suspected terrorist list provided to the legal team at Gitmo. I'd say I'm not fucked. You are." TJ sat back with a smile.

Renaldo's eyes were wide open. He started shaking. "This no right. I no kill anyone. The man killed he no say he policeman. He tell Diego woman who get out of car a policeman. He offer help Diego escape. We know him. He do drugs, he want drugs, money. Diego say no. Buster he point gun. Diego, threaten shoot him. I scared tell Buster Diego no have drugs. Woman name Vickie she tell Diego do as Buster say. Diego he sit up stab Vickie. Doors open, Buster shoot, Diego shoot. I know not what to do. I run. Go my club. Tobey see blood on me, say we no call police. I scared, think police come kill us. He no want to listen. You break in, shoot me. This no right. Need medicine for pain, need see lawyer." He sat back trembling.

TJ chuckled. "You spend the night thinking this story up? I don't buy it. If you were to get lawyer and decide to plea, maybe you get twenty, no probation. But see that's not going to happen. You an illegal, no guarantees for you. Like I said, no one knows you here. To us you a terrorist. We know you work for a cartel. Just like your friend Diego."

"This not true. I have green card. I businessman, own club. Diego no friend. He friend with other owner."

"Let's see." TJ reached into a chair next to his, brought up a folder, opened it and leafed through the pages, held one up. "Says here, Clutch's is owned by Mango Investment Partners Limited." He pulled up the next page. "This is the Florida State Corporate Charter. It says Mango Investment Partners Limited is a holding company owned by a Swedish Company, Holtzhauser Limited of Zurich. Our State Department is investigating Holtzhauser for suspicion of laundering money for the cartels. Your name is not listed, nor is there any other individual listed as owners of Clutch's. Care to explain this?" TJ kept fluttering the pages given to Carl that morning, which Carl then briefed him on before he came into this room.

Renaldo seemed to be puzzled, did not give a reply.

TJ continued. "Where you get money to open Clutch's? You came here with your mother in '98 at the age of ten. She never became a citizen. She work for a cleaning service, lives in the barrio. There no record of your employment, yet you say you able to be owner of a club located near Mariner's Ball Park. Where you get the money?"

Renaldo sat there looking down at his hands like he was about to cry. He did not look up, remained silent.

"We pulled your record. You were sent before Social Services and a magistrate for truancy and stealing food from a vendor, held at a juvenile detention center; your mother got you out. You never finished school, no charges, suspected of having gang association, possibly a small-time drug mule. Yet you able to be a part owner in Clutch's. No one could possibly believe you magically came into legal money. You said you a dead man, tried to take your own life. Who is they?" Renaldo looked up, did not speak. "Diego's looking at the max. Unless he cuts a deal. What you want to bet, he will be willing to testify against you. He knows this *they* would want him to give you up, rather than him saying anything about them. In prison *they* might take care of him. He knows if he goes to the max, *they* will get to him. But you, you right, you dead meat, no matter what. Unless...you tell us what we want to know. We your best hope, your only hope."

"You can no help me. They find me. I'm dead. No one can help." He sat there, tears running, his body shaking.

TJ got up, put the papers in the folder, tapped them on the desk. "Bet they couldn't get to you in Cuba. Think about it." He left the room.

Carl and HSI's Diego were smiling when he entered the observation room. "Good job, podna. Think you nailed his ass to the wall."

"Yeah. He's right you know. No matter what, he's dead meat, and it won't be quick and painless. Gitmo's his best option. What about Diego, he conscious?"

"That fucking ape, acts like the shitstorm we dumped on him was a lullaby. Appeared to sleep right through it. Guess those roofies stayed in his system longer than expected. I talked to him. Asked a few questions. He claims he doesn't remember anything. Bastard knows he was drugged and knows what to say, or not to say."

"Does he know who we are or where we have him? Did you mention Gitmo?"

"No. No. No. You can try the Gitmo threat, but I have a feeling what you said to his buddy in there…guess he knows what will happen, since he probably is the one who dishes out the punishment."

Diego's bed was in an upright position, his arms and legs strapped to the bed frame. TJ stood on Diego's right hand side, the one that was in a sling with a strap wrapped around his massive body and secured to the bed.

"Comfortable?" TJ asked having decided to use a different approach.

Diego didn't respond.

"OK." TJ reached out, squeezed Diego's upper shoulder, his long muscular fingers digging in, searching for the ammo entry, his thumb searching for an exit. Diego's face contorted. "Fuck you, motherfucker. You're a dead maricon, you and your whole family." TJ kept the pressure on, Diego jerked, the bed shook and squeaked. "I've been threatened by far more terrifying assholes than you, yet here I am. Do you know who I am or where you are?" He squeezed again, he felt wetness on his fingers, he knew he should be wearing gloves, this switch hitter, who knew what diseases his body contained. "Diego, you shouldn't have threatened my family, that wasn't nice.

"See I know who you are. I believe you're what's called *the fixer*," TJ said slowly, deliberately. "When people you work for have problem, someone didn't do what your employer thought they should have done, you come in and fix it. Well you see, this means you and I have something in common, I have the same occupation. You have become a problem, my employer isn't happy with your employer, there was an understanding. No more. Your fucking Mexican Patrone thinks he come here, fuck us.

"Out of curiosity I would like to know why you here, who you working with?"

Diego flopped his head while he attempted to shrug. It was to no avail, the restraints, TJ's grip held him in place. Tears came into Diego's eyes, his sun-darkened pallor became noticeably paler, his face looked like a half-deflated balloon.

"Why don't you tell me what you and your people did to piss my people off, maybe I can fix it without causing you a whole lot more pain."

Diego's wide-eyed-contorted stare was fixed on TJ's grip.

TJ pushed past the bandages, dug deeper. "Damn, I bet I could touch my finger to my thumb."

Diego moaned.

"Bet you enjoyed torturing your prey before you finished them off. I understand completely. You ever skin any of them while they were alive? That and using acid are the most gruesome ways I've witnessed for causing a slow painful death. Waterboarding doesn't usually get the answers you want. Me, I prefer a little less messy approach, cutting dick and balls off, taking out one or both eyes, removing the tongue. Got any stories you'd like to share? Always like to add to my repertoire."

Diego began convulsing, then vomited. The vomit went all over the front of TJ's pants and his canvas sneakers. TJ let go of Diego, went over to the sink, took a towel and cleaned the filmy yellow gunk off his pants and shoes using the antibiotic soap from the dispenser. He looked like he pissed on himself when he finished. The smell was nauseating.

"You're going to pay for this, cabrone." TJ went out the door.

Carl was standing there, restraining a nurse. She looked up at Jake, fury plastered across her face. "I will be reporting this," she hissed.

"No. You will not," Carl said quietly with authority. "Your report goes to me, and I will not accept it. That man in there is a murdering terrorist, who stabbed a woman then shot and killed a police officer last night. You will go in there, clean him and the room without saying a damn thing to him, or I will bring you up on charges. Am I clear?"

She glared at Carl, tried to remove his hand, and said, "I will do as you asked, but I will inform Dr. Benitez about what I witnessed. It will be between you and her."

"If anything is said to anyone else, I will bring you up on charges." He released her. She went in the room. TJ and Carl watched her.

TJ looked at Carl. "I hope she doesn't say anything to him." Diego's lips were moving. Her back was to them, but from Diego's irritating look, it appeared she wasn't talking to him. "Does she work for Homeland?"

"Yes and no. This clinic is ours. She works for Dr. Benitez. She is bound by a confidentiality agreement and has a low-level security clearance. Fortunately, I caught her before she could barge in there. She reports this, I could end up in hot doo-doo. Hopefully, Dr. Benitez will convince her to keep quiet. They don't know who you are and probably never will. Deniability. I'll make sure the tape disappears. But…what in the hell? You trying to make him think you are here as his executioner?"

"I was just checking his wounds."

"That never happened… I'm talking about what you were telling him. Sounded to me like you want him to believe he was arrested, the cops turned him over to us, a rival gang, you really believe he'll fall for this?"

"Happens more often than most people know. Many of my informants should be behind bars."

"I know that. That's not what I'm asking ol' son. Do you believe that motherfucker will believe it?"

"You got a better idea?"

Carl didn't reply. They kept watching her as she cleaned up Diego and the floor, then worked on stopping the bleeding and rebandaging his wounds. Diego kept talking. They never saw her say anything. She came back out.

With a flat tone, her eyes flaring as she looked from Carl to TJ. "He says, he's not Mexican, not a fixer, and it was self-defense. That you say you are going to kill him."

"I need you to report to Dr. Benitez immediately. I will join you shortly."

She stormed off down the hall. After she had turned the corner, Carl turned back to TJ, flexed his back. "This could become a problem. Anyway, you know Diego seemed to want to talk to her. Maybe we should let one of our female agents play the good guy role." Carl saw the puzzled look on TJ's face. "Something bothering you, son?"

TJ walked back to look in the door at Diego, who looked back at him, a quizzical expression playing across his bulbous head. He stood back, turned around to face Carl, then started hurrying back down the hallway. "Tobey. What do we know about Tobey?"

Carl hurried to catch up. "Tobey. The cop outside Clutch's? What about him?"

"How do we know he's a cop? TJ replied. "Why did he try to stop Maggie when they were leaving? Why was he the only one inside with Renaldo when I broke in? Who was running Clutch's when we left and why was it closed early? It may be coincidences, but something tells me it's not. How quick can your people run a check?"

"We have easy access to most federal data bases. I can call the commissioner about the locals. That may take a little longer."

"You might want to tell him to put trusted guards on Maggie's and Vickie's hospital rooms—no access, police, detectives, or anyone. No telling who's in on this. I'm going to need access. Tell him that."

"In on what?"

TJ stopped. "Whatever it is. Diego was willing to stab a woman and shoot a policeman. I think Buster Brown and Vickie, his CI, knew more about Tobey, Diego and Renaldo. Possibly, their connection to whoever brought Diego here. Before I talk any further to Renaldo or Diego, I need to know if my assumption is correct."

"I'll see what I can find out," Carl said.

"I'm on my way to the hospital. Call me soon as you know something."

Tobias Totelokov, aka, Toby Tyler, aka Tobey Tobiski, was amazed that he had been given a free pass by the man who called himself TJ and the fed, introduced as Carl Swanson. One call TJ, he helluva shot, bad for Renaldo Espinosa, his supposed partner.

The woman cop thought he was local. He almost laughed. If she only knew. It was shocking when she came out with Diego and the dude named Buster and his woman friend and Renaldo. He tried to find out from Renaldo what went wrong with Diego. Renaldo brushed him off.

Next thing Renaldo shows up, blood on face and clothes. Scared customers. Babbling away. Had to clear the bar. Not know who hear what. Who they talk to? By the time Renaldo answered most of his questions, the one he heard called TJ and the fed, called Carl, showed. Good thing Renaldo was so scared. Lost nerve to shoot himself or him. He felt certain the half-breed wouldn't shoot. This TJ was a damn good shooter.

His contact say he should get out of town, lay low. First, he needed to find out what the feds and cops know. He thought his controller would want to know. Would be pissed the feds the ones have Diego and Renaldo.

Get out of town. He was. He needed to get to harbor. Leave the states. He was told who to go to. Controller say this man help him get away. Did not make sense. This man on the watch list. He didn't see any other choice.

22

Great Exuma, Bahamas

The house was in a mess like a party had taken place, air smelled musky, the everywhere-he-went traces of marijuana and beer. His room had been tossed, all his clothes lay in piles on the floor and bed. He turned and went back down the hall to Rick's and Blakely's bedroom door. It opened with difficulty impeded by clothes and personal crap piled in heaps. The chilled air created by the buzzing window AC unit hit him, making his sweat tingle across his forehead, on his neck and down his back.

Blakely, her bathing suit barely covering her, lay on the bed in a fetal position, her back to him, not moving. He walked the few steps over to the bed, pushing clothes out of the way with his steel-toed sneakers. She didn't move, he thought she was asleep, either that or passed out. Her being dead entered his thoughts and he hesitated.

"Blakely," he said loud enough to wake her, if all she was, was asleep. "Blakely you okay?" He saw her stir. She remained curled up, not moving. Jake reached down and rolled her over. She had a black eye, and dried blood lay in streaks snaking down from her lip, giving her a ghoulish look.

"Go away." She tried to roll back over. Jake kept her from doing so. She half-heartedly tried to brush his hand off her shoulder.

"Who did this to you?" he asked.

"Why should you care? I asked you to help me. Just go away."

"I'm going to call the police."

She looked at him, tried to smile, then grimaced making her look ever more macabre. "Don't. The police won't do anything."

"What's this all about, Blakely?"

She slowly tried to sit up, her face masked in pain. Jake saw bruises on her other arm and on the tops of her breasts. She flopped back down. "What does it matter to you?" She slowly reached up, pushed her blondish, tangled hair back off her face.

"I think you're in over your head. Does Rick know? Is he part of whatever you're messed up in?"

She looked away. She seemed to melt into herself. "Rick doesn't know shit. All he worries about is who I might be fucking." She tried to laugh. "He thinks I'm fucking everybody." Tears ran out of her eyes. She tried to rub them and winced when she touched her right swollen, blackened eye.

"What were they looking for Blakely, is it drugs?"

"It wasn't about drugs, Rick or me, it was about you. He wanted to know about you."

Jake had not expected this. The break-in the night before was about him, not Blakely?

"Blakely, you need to tell me what you know. Whoever did this to you didn't do it because of me."

"Really? Just so you know he thinks you are working undercover for the DEA. He wanted to know what I told you. He said you were a narc, is that why you came here?" She touched her lip, pulled her fingers away and stared at the pinkish streak.

"No, I am not DEA. Why would he be asking you this Blakely unless he's worried you are spilling the beans on whoever you're dealing with? You've got me mixed up in your shit and you better tell me what it is or I 'will' go to the DEA."

She started crying and reached out to Jake. He pulled back. she wrapped her arms around herself. "I didn't plan for any of this to happen," she said, her voice trembling.

"It started back in St. Louis. A customer tried to supply the girls with drugs—uppers, downers, a little reefer. I smoked some, but pretty much stayed away from the other stuff...He offered to give me a cut. In return, I had to keep my mouth shut. The people I worked for they wouldn't just fire me if I allowed it."

"I have a little girl. My mama has her. This man told me if I didn't deal, keep my mouth shut, something bad would happen to my family."

"Why didn't you go to the authorities or tell your boss?" Jake asked. He pushed her back to see her face when she answered.

She smiled. "He was a cop." Her tone had grown harsh.

"What does Rick have to do with you coming here?"

"It's just like you were told. Rick was a customer. Told everyone about his job offer. Boris, my boss heard and saw an opportunity. His people are everywhere, so it seems. Things were getting slow at the club. Girls were leaving. Boris said they might have to close the place. He told me to play up to Rick, see if I could find a way to come to the Bahamas with him. They had bigger plans for me. I had no choice. Boris paid for my mama to take my daughter away, I came here."

"You playing me? Was this his idea?"

"Yes and no." She looked at Jake, her eyes trying to say something. Jake wanted to give her some ice for the bruise.

"What do you mean?" Jake knew it didn't matter, but he couldn't help but wonder if her come-ons weren't all pretense. A part of him wanted it to be otherwise.

"Boris' man here, Victor told me to do whatever I had to to find out what you were doing here. Rick thought you were here to take his place. Victor wanted to know if that was all there was. When you met with that other man, things changed. He said I had betrayed him. He described what was going to happen to me and my family." Her breath caught, she gulped, the tears flowed.

"Yesterday, last night, I didn't mean what I said. I'm sorry. I was going to pieces. He came here and waited until you and Rick left. I had thought about drowning myself—I had put on my swimsuit. He came in from the basement, tore the place up, then started in on me…I thought he was going to kill me. He has given me until tomorrow."

"Tomorrow. For what?"

"Find out what you know. He said he would make sure you no problem after that. Oh Jake, they won't let me leave. I may never see my family again. I think he intends to get rid of you. Then me, if I don't buy my freedom or get a job so I can stay here and continue helping them." She reached out and grabbed hold of his arm.

Jake tried to pull loose. He needed to stand up, move around, think about what she said. She tried to pull him to her, like he was her lifeboat. He pried her hand loose. Something was in the works. Sounded like it was drugs since they thought he was DEA. They knew he had met with Hardy. Had they followed Hardy back to the DEA's station? Was that why they figured he and Hardy had to be DEA? He needed to tell Hardy see what he had to say.

"You said you had to continue helping them. How are you helping them?"

She pulled back and didn't say anything, just stared at Jake, trying to decide what to tell him. "You swear you're not DEA?"

"I swear."

"But your friend, he is a fed, isn't he?"

"No. He is not DEA." Jake could see she did not believe him. He had to think of something believable to say about Hardy. If this Victor knew about Hardy's presence at the DEA station, then any story line had to explain why he was there. "My friend works for the company responsible for surveillance equipment. They have government maintenance contracts." Sounded good, he hoped.

"Oh." She kept studying Jake, trying to decide what to say.

"This place is going to have a casino, several marinas, lots of heavy hitters will be coming here. They want to get in on the action. Victor said they had time and money invested in me. They need me to keep them updated on what is in the works. I am supposed to cozy up to everyone who might know something. That was what Boris told me before I got here. Now they treat me like they own me. If I want out, Victor said they would consider a quarter million dollars to buy my freedom. When I said I couldn't get that kind of money, he said I would have to earn it."

"Did he say what you had to do to earn it?"

"What do you think? He said long as I had a good body, I should use it to make money. He said there were other ways to make money faster. But now he's worried about you. He thinks you are DEA and I might be a snitch. He will need proof I'm not saying anything to you, he said."

"What kind of proof?"

She looked away and started trembling.

Jake reached over, touched her chin to turn her face back toward him, she resisted. "They want me out of the way, and you're supposed to help them. How? Tell me Blakely, what do they want you to do?"

"That's why he hit me. I told them I wouldn't do it. He said I would or my whole family would suffer. Then he hit me again and said that they would make me watch what they did to my family, then they would do the same to me." She was shaking and sniffing. She slowly turned her head to look at Jake. "I can't do it. What am I going to do? You have to help me. They're going to kill us both."

Jake wondered how much of what Blakely said happened. He had witnessed her histrionics—seductive vixen, vindictive provocateur, and now scared victim. How could he be sure she had not implied his role in her game to take the heat off her or someone else. What he did believe was she was in over her head and intended to drag him down with her. Thomas was waiting in the car. He needed to get going.

Blakely sat with her back against pillows looking up at him, her eyes imploring, pleading, the same way they had been last night. Before she threatened him.

"I don't want my family to die. What should we do?" she asked.

"Who knows about this, besides me?"

"Boris and Victor, now you."

"Who have you been dealing drug with? Are the Bahamians Rob, Rodney or Alvin involved?" Her eyes flickered. "What about Alec and Marcus?" She seemed to sink into the pillows.

"I told you, everyone knows where to get almost anything." She said. She pulled her knees up and wrapped her arms around them, pushing her breasts up, the ugly bruises made more prominent. Jake could see her nipples and chastised himself for looking. "None of those people have anything to do with Victor. As far as I Know they don't even know him."

"How are you supposed to contact him? I need his number if you've got it."

Her eyes widened, she rocked forward, wincing. "He'll know I told you. You can't call him."

Jake leaned in over her, could smell her. "I'm in this because of you, Blakely. He will kill me you said. You want my help, tell me how to get in touch with him or I'm going to leave you to take the heat on your own. You see, unlike you, I can go back to my home. I have people there who will help if anyone comes snooping around." Jake stood back up straight, flexed his neck, his eyes boring into her. He wanted to shake the information out of her. She turned away, grabbed her phone, scrolled through and handed it to Jake. He entered the number into his phone.

"Rick will be here soon. It's Friday. Everyone goes to Georgetown on Friday." She sniffed and frowned. "He'll think I have engaged in rough sex. That's the way his mind works."

"Get up. Clean yourself up. Put on makeup."

"What about you, will you be there?"

"I guess so. You should come up to me and apologize for yesterday and last night, so Rick can hear. Although he may not want to. If Victor is there, let me know without being obvious."

"Jake, I want us to be friends. I need you for this. I don't want you to hate me."

"I hope so, Blakely. Don't lie to me or use me and maybe we'll find a way out of this. I've got to go."

Thomas was parked up the street out of sight. He had the radio on, volume low, AC turned down, blowing into his face, fluttering his hair, his eyes closed. He jumped when Jake eased in and closed the door.

"Some lookout you make."

"Sorry. How'd it go?" He looked over at the clock on the console. "Maybe I should ask, how was it?" He chuckled.

"Didn't need a body condom." He put the car in gear. They started down the hill, back towards Queens Highway.

"Anyone come by before you closed your eyes?"

"Too early. The Bahamians will be at Georgetown outside the BSC Bank, lined up, partying down, waiting their turn to get in and cash their check. Some expats will be hitting the bars or going back to their place, waiting until later to head out."

"Yeah. Blakely told me."

"Did she say anything interesting while you were rolling around in there?"

"Someone named Victor thinks I'm DEA. He knows Hardy met with me and is at the DEA station. I told Blakely Hardy was a friend and the reason he was there was because he works for a company that works on surveillance equipment."

"Nice. That's a good out. Did she buy it?"

"Who knows. The most intriguing thing is a man named Victor wants me out of the way and Blakely is supposed to help him." Jake told Thomas what had been said.

They reached the Queens Highway. Jake got Kendall's cell number from Thomas and called to ask him to fuel the truck up and leave it at Mitch's. He said he would get Mitch to do it. He and Amy had other plans. Jake hoped it happened.

"Could be this was the guy at the party last night, do you think?" Thomas asked after he disconnected.

"Possibly. Possibly Juan Carlos was talking to him. I didn't get a good look. He was large is all I know."

"You say he talked to Juan Carlos. He should remember what he looks like. Ask him tonight.

"Do you have a way to communicate with HSI?" Jake asked. "I need to give them Victor's telephone number."

"Not directly. I was told to go through you. The only other option for me would be to go online to reach the main office by email or the information phone number."

"How long have you been with HSI?" Jake asked.

"So far this is it. Like I told you, I'm hoping to make it fulltime. As for the rest of the story…well… truthfully, I worked undercover for the FBI until I was axed when the current administration came into office. My superior pissed someone off, and I was guilty by association. My last assignment was investigating a construction company. Basics Metal Works was one of their subs. A college friend owns Basics. He hired me as an assistant manager, my bona fides showed I had worked for another company that had gone bankrupt." Thomas chuckled. "I had worked part time for a company when I was at Pitt, along with my friend. I knew a few HSI guys from my UC work for the Bureau. One of them introduced me to one of their field supervisors who told Hardy about me. How about you, how long have you worked for them?"

"I'm a cherry. Friend of Bob Hardy's and he railroaded me into this assignment, along with introducing me to Ned of ESI in a roundabout way. My first with HSI and ESI. Served overseas in the Army—eighteen years, just reupped for four more, then got DDed on a medical. An IED satchel bomb blew the personnel carrier I was riding in into a heap of scrap metal and I suffered a broken neck. Wife took my kids, left me—'she got the gold mine, I got the shaft'—here I am. Now someone wants to finish the job. I need some kind of weapon to protect myself. Got any ideas how I might get my hands on one?"

"I wish I did. You get caught in the Bahamas with a weapon and you go to jail. They throw away the key. Sticks and shells are about the only thing available. Only good thing is, the law applies to everyone."

"What about tasers or pocketknives?"

"Law says no unlicensed person can carry any weapon with intent to use illegally. The list of weapons includes almost anything and everything, including pocketknives, even sandbags, believe it or not."

"Damn. Hope the bad guys play fair. Otherwise I'm fucked." Fucked or not, Jake would damn sure carry his pseudo-pocketknife.

23

Miami, Fl

The traffic around the U, as it was called, was horrendous. Friday's traffic was always the worst, especially during football season. TJ parked on the upper level of the parking garage. He got out, retrieved a change of clothes—the smell from Diego's vomit had necessitated having his windows down with his AC on high to neutralize the hot, humid autumn heat. He put on his khaki cargo pants and canvas high top sneakers, then caught the elevator down to the third floor which had a connector to the hospital for personnel only. He slipped in when a couple of nurses were exiting. He caught their attention, but they didn't say anything—too caught up in their own conversation. He hurried down the corridor to the nurses' station and asked where the critical care wing was. The woman behind the desk hesitated to answer. She scanned something on her computer. TJ repeated his request, she turned her face up with a how-dare-you look, then answered as if it pained her, "Next floor up. Elevators are down the hall on the right." She nodded in the opposite direction TJ had come from.

The elevator seemed to crawl upward. The doors opened into a waiting area. TJ looked right and left. No sign of any police presence. He went down the corridor to the right where he saw a nurses' station. Several nurses and what looked like a surgeon with face masks dangling around their necks, were moving around the raised desk, behind which sat two other nurses. You could sense the tense buzz, but they moved like nothing out of the ordinary was happening.

One of the nurses looked up at him with a sympathetic expression when he asked where Victoria Lombauski's and Margarette Elkins' rooms were. She asked if he was family. To which he flashed his police ID and told her it was an emergency. She looked their names up on her computer and gave him directions. TJ trotted off in the direction she had indicated. Maggie's room was the closest. There were no policemen outside her door, he tapped on the open doorway and walked in. Maggie was propped up watching tv.

"They send you here to question me too? Or did Carl send you here to warn me to keep my mouth shut?"

"Sorry to disappoint you. There were supposed to be policemen watching you, where are they?"

"My trustees took off about five minutes ago. You didn't answer me. Why are you here?"

TJ walked over to the closet. The clothes she had worn the night before were hanging there, her high heel shoes on the bottom shelf. "You need to get up and get dressed. Carl and I believe Tobey or his friends may be coming after you. And Vickie."

"What are you talking about? Tobey is a cop, you're not making sense. Is this…"

TJ interrupted, "I don't have time to explain. You've got to hurry." He threw her slip and dress onto her bed. "Where's your purse? You have your weapon?"

Maggie hesitated. "Wait outside and close the door."

Within minutes, she came out carrying her shoes and purse. "They confiscated my badge and 38. What's going on? What is this shit about Tobey?"

"Come on. We've got to get to Vickie's room."

They hurried down the corridor past other patients' rooms, some with nurses inside who looked out as they rushed by. TJ could hear Maggie's bare feet slapping the cold hard linoleum tiles right behind him. They reached a corner, the hall branched right and left. He stopped and looked. Four men he took to be policemen were congregated outside a room several doors down. They were laughing, talking as if nothing was going on.

"Stay back," he said to Maggie when she came alongside him. "You need to stay out of sight. There's four cops, two plains-clothed and two uniforms.

I'm going down to find out what's going on with Vickie. You need to not be seen, especially by Tobey. He's not a cop. I'll explain later."

"I'm coming with you." She tried to go by him.

He stuck out his arm and grabbed her, pulled her back and turned to face her. "They'll take you in or possibly worse. We need to get you out of here. Vickie also, if I can figure a way to do so." TJ turned and Maggie grabbed his arm.

"Wait. I've got an idea. Come on."

"I need to make sure she's okay."

"And I need to get into a nurse's outfit and get an orderly and a gurney. Come on."

TJ hesitated then went with Maggie back to the nurse's station. Twenty minutes later, after an animated discussion with the head nurse and one of the doctors which included a warning from TJ that Vickie's life was in danger, the hospital would be sued if they didn't help them, they relented. TJ gave them Carl's number and told them Carl would back his story, but they couldn't wait.

TJ, Maggie, in a loose-fitting nurse's uniform and wearing a surgical mask, accompanied by an orderly and doctor, who insisted on coming, hurried to Vickie's room. TJ lagged back at the corner, figuring the police might be suspicious of him showing up at the same time as the others. The doctor wanted to question TJ's motive, how Vickie could be in trouble with the other police present. TJ reminded him once more of their earlier discussion about the possibility of there being a crooked cop, that Vickie was going with Maggie and him as a protected witness. The other police could not be made aware of this. The doctor said he would help them move her to a safer place. Then he would need more proof TJ and Maggie were telling the truth.

They were able to get Vickie loaded onto a gurney, took her down to the emergency room floor to a private room. Maggie came to get TJ after the others had gotten into the elevator. The doctor stayed with them, checking Vickie's vitals, warily watching TJ and Maggie. Before signing the two women out, he called Carl. They loaded her into an ambulance and Maggie rode with her to HSI's clinic where Doctor Bertrand had her transferred to a room not far from Diego's.

Carl called TJ on his cell. "This Tobey Tyler apparently took his name from an eighties' Disney movie, only the main character's name had no e in the spelling. We ran his name and description through NCIC and his prints through AFIS, nothing under that name. Interpol's files had a Tobias Tobelokov, aka Tobias Tobiski, wanted in connection with a former Soviet group operating in Germany Diebe im Gesetz, Thieves in law in our way of speaking. I've sent you his photo that was sent to us. Have a look."

TJ pulled his truck into a parking lot. The photo was grainy, but from what he could see, it bore a strong resemblance to their Tobey. "You're right. Any idea where he might be found?"

"We checked phone records of our buddies, Diego and Renaldo, got matching phone numbers, but the service providers are refusing to verify the phone numbers' information without a warrant. The secretary's office will take care of that."

"We called, went to voice mail, no recorded message. We started pinging both. One just stopped pinging, last ping was in the Little Havana area. I am passing by there now. I notified the Coast Guard. Dispatch says they have a boat in the area and will be there within thirty minutes."

"I'll head that way. Should take me about ten to fifteen minutes. Let me know where to meet you."

"I'm playing a hunch. There's a former Soviet Federal policeman who immigrated here not long ago who is now a multimillionaire, made himself rich by investing in real estate. The feds have had him under investigation for quite some time. They have an undercover operative inside his organization, seems the fed agent reported this Tobias as an employee of this real estate businessman. Get this, this businessman, Andrei Bolstoy is listed as part of Holtzhauser Limited of Zurich. One of his real estate holdings is a marina at Coconut Grove. He has a yacht there. The other phone pinged near there. My hunch is that this Tobias dude is headed there. I'm about five or ten minutes away."

"My ETA is less than ten minutes. I'll see you there."

Coconut Grove was not far from University Hospital, even closer to Little Havana, but a world apart. Rows upon rows of docks, all filled with boats of various sizes and shapes, some fishing vessels, numerous sailing boats, and many mega-yachts.

TJ had never been out on a boat. As far as he knew, the only boat his family had been on was the one that had brought his grandparents from Cuba, and he doubted they were anywhere close to being like the least of these.

He pulled up to the maintenance office building and waited. Coming in with the windows open, the air smelled clean and salty, with a hint of marine life. When he parked a breeze stirred the clean ocean air smells and mixed in the noxious odors of TJ's vomit incensed clothes in the rear cargo area, along with gas and diesel fumes from the open bay doors of the storage and maintenance building. Unpleasant, but nowhere near the odors from the sulfurous algae rot emanating from the Gulf.

Shortly Carl came wheeling in, driving his black Yukon. He parked next to TJ's truck. Got out donning a western reed-woven hat, with the brim turned down, matching his pearl studded western cut tan shirt, tail hanging over his blue jeans ending at his alligator skin boots. He looked like he was headed out to mount a horse, not a yacht.

"Where's your horse?" TJ asked with a grin.

"Didn't have a chance to change. Good thing you did. Damn, smells like you hauled a sick drunk in this rig."

"Know what the name of his yacht is?" TJ asked as they headed for the office.

"*BolsToy*, if you can believe it. Guess he figured that was catchy."

They walked in through the bay doors. There was clanging, air ratchet sounds, and several forklifts could be heard, one inside, one or two more could be heard through the bay doors on the other end of the massive metal building, where they saw a long dock, waves lapping against its pilings. The office was to their right. Behind a huge glass pane was a middle-aged man, dressed in a clean maintenance overall suit, unzipped revealing a flowery dress shirt open at the neck. He was seated at a desk, tapping the keyboard of a computer, several monitors sitting just in front. On the other side of his desk was a long counter, behind which was a younger man and row after row of metal shelving filled with various parts. A bell jingled when they opened the door, Carl followed TJ inside, stepped over to the desk. The man kept tapping, glanced up with a smile.

"One minute please."

TJ walked over to the young man behind the counter.

"Can I help you?"

"We're here to see Andrei Bolstoy. Do you know where we might find him?" TJ asked.

The older man stopped tapping and looked over at TJ, then at Carl. Before the younger man, his name tag said Gary, could answer, the middle-aged man said, "What's this about?" Not the reply Carl or TJ expected. The question and their facial expressions indicated a familiar wariness.

Carl pulled out his ID leather holder and flipped it open. "We're not here to have a discussion. A simple answer will do, or better still, you could take us to wherever we might find him."

"He's on his yacht. Is this official business?" His nametag said Mick.

"Mick, unless you want to be brought up on charges, you need to get up off your ass and take us to him."

Mick sat back, an insolent smirk on his face. "Do you have a warrant?"

"I don't need a warrant." Carl leaned down with his hands resting on the desk, staring into Mick's eyes. "That ID is all the warrant necessary. Either you get your ass up or we will cuff you and have US Marshal's crawling all over this place in a matter of minutes. Your computers and all your records will be confiscated and you and your man over there, what's his name TJ?"

"Nametag says Gary." Gary paled looking over at Mick with a pleading expression.

"Mick. You and Gary will be held for seventy-two hours, while we decide what all to charge you with. You'll need to hire a damn good and expensive attorney and wait while the wheels of justice turn. Now, you've made me waste more time than was necessary. Are you and Gary going to do as I directed or are you going to make me waste more time?"

Gary said, "I can't afford to go to jail, neither can you." He looked at TJ, who was resting his massive arms on the counter, then at Mick and finally Carl. "Mister I'll show you, but the yacht is out at its berth in the harbor."

Mick said, "Gary, son, you need to stay there and keep your mouth shut. These men have no right to threaten us."

Carl stepped around the desk, pulled out a set of cuffs, yanked Mick's arms back and cuffed his hands through the arm of his chair. "TJ cuff Gary."

TJ pulled back off the counter and before he could begin heading around the open end, Gary said, "We didn't sign on for this dad. I'm sorry." He came from around behind the counter and stopped next to the older man he called dad. The resemblance was noticeable. "Please don't arrest him. He is just trying to protect our family. Other people have been here, they showed badges, said they were FBI, they told us not to talk to anyone. We can't afford any trouble."

Carl looked at the two of them. "If I tell the feebs to jump, they better say how high. Mick, I'm going to release you. You and your son are going to take my colleague and me to see this Mr. Bolstoy. Are you willing to do that?"

"Dad," Gary said. His dad nodded.

TJ and Carl accompanied Mick and Gary out through the metal building, several employees stopped what they were doing and watched as they walked through. They went to the end row of docks and onto the dock then continued out the vibrating dock past all the boats until they reached the end.

Mick pointed out toward a large yacht tied to its lone dock which led to a spit of land at the entrance to the harbor. "How does he get from here to there?" Carl asked.

"He has a smaller craft up on deck and his crew shuttles him and his guests back and forth." Mick replied. "He has security. No one is allowed near his vessel. Only way there is from here. You have to have permission, invitation only."

"I need to speak to him. How do you contact him?"

"Two-way radio in my office."

"Why didn't you tell me when we were back there?"

"You didn't ask?" Mick said smugly. He and Gary grinned. TJ tried not to be amused. Carl was not.

"Wasting my time. I warned you. Here's what we're going to do. You and your son are going to take TJ and me out there in a boat. One of those you use to tow boats or do whatever you do with your boat. How about that?"

"I told you that is not allowed. They might shoot us," Mick said.

"TJ, while I radio Mr. Bolstoy and Gary here gets the boat ready, would you please retrieve your weapons, including your sniper rifle? You see gentlemen, TJ here is a highly qualified expert weapons man, can shoot a target further than you can see with the naked eye. Any weapon pointed in our direction better not be visible to him, just so you understand."

Carl had Mick contact the Coast Guard. Carl identified himself and was connected to the intercept vessel's Captain Peter Conroy, who told him they were within five minutes of reaching the harbor. Carl told them he would meet them at the *BolsToy* anchored inside the entrance to the harbor.

Mick radioed the *BolsToy*, Carl took the mic from him, when Captain Hector Jakovski answered. He said, "Captain, this is Carl Swanson, Homeland Security is Mr. Bolstoy on board?" The captain replied in the affirmative. "We shall be coming on board, would you please inform Mr. Bolstoy and tell his security people not to try to stop us. Over." TJ came back in carrying his scoped rifle, his Glock in his holster. Carl told him to wait in the warehouse with Mick while he retrieved his weapon. The *BolsToy*'s captain kept trying to get Carl or anyone to answer him on the radio.

As they climbed aboard the service boat, they heard then saw a motorboat speed away from the *BolsToy*, headed out of the harbor. TJ put his scope on it. "There are two people onboard. The pilot, another man, could be our boy Tobey."

"Fuck," Carl said as the boat disappeared. "At least we know there is a connection."

They slowly motored out. Carl told Gary to take his time. They would wait for the Coast Guard patrol boat, then go on board. He told TJ to keep his scope on the *BolsToy* and if any other boat or person tried to leave, "do whatever is necessary to stop them."

The CG patrol boat came in the harbor and turned toward the *BolsToy*. Carl directed Gary to signal their boat with his horn. Carl stood and waved as they approached and came alongside. Two guardsmen had weapons trained on TJ, who put his rifle down and stepped away, hands up. Carl pulled his ID holder out and held it up, shouting his rank and name to the men, one of which was Captain Conroy. They came alongside, Carl climbed up the ladder and spoke to the captain. One of the guardsmen came down to the service boat and told TJ he would stay with Mick and Gary, that he should go aboard the patrol boat.

Once on board, the patrol boat captain hailed the *BolsToy* to prepare for boarding. Captain Conroy and two of his armed men accompanied Carl and TJ as they stepped off onto a loading platform. The two Coast Guardsmen disarmed the two security men and they entered a dock station with two huge jet-skis up on lifts, then climbed up to the next level housing the sleeping quarters. The guardsmen searched them and came back accompanied by a middle-aged man of medium build and a gorgeous young blonde-headed woman, both in expensive looking housecoats. The man in a foreign accent, sounded German, was demanding answers for what was happening. The guardsman with them was grinning.

"Think I interrupted them doing the dirty deed sir," he said.

They proceeded up to the next level. A nice staircase ended at one end of a luxuriously appointed living area with a bar and several seating areas each with a center entertainment zone. One end had glass doors that looked out onto a large outside open area with another bar and dining tables with seating. Beyond was the harbor. The other end was closed off. The guardsmen went through the door, one after the other, weapons ready. Shortly they came back accompanied by a man dressed as a chef followed by three other people attired in food-stained, wait staff clothing, one man and two women. They too spoke in harsh, heavily accented tones, slaughtering the English language.

Carl wanted to know where their captain was and Mister Bolstoy. They all either shrugged or continued to jabber among themselves until Carl shouted, "Shut up!" Captain Conroy asked one of *BolsToy*'s security men where the captain was. He pointed up. When asked where his boss was, he shrugged. Can't argue with well-trained mutes.

Captain Conroy, Carl and TJ went through a side door, climbed up a narrow set of steps, coming out into a control room which had all the latest instruments and two small steering wheels. The medium-sized, swarthy man, possibly Mediterranean, dressed in formal captain attire, rose quickly. He had been seated next to a burly man with Slavic features—a long thin nose and small chin, a heavy brow over close set beady blue-green eyes and light brown short hair. He was dressed in khaki colored dress pants and a silk light blue shirt underneath an unbuttoned thin silk navy blue blazer. He was sockless, wearing shiny, expensive looking loafers, one of which was swinging back and forth on top of his crossed knees. He didn't bother to get up.

"Gentlemen, what meaning of this?" the captain asked.

Carl approached the other man, stopping a few feet away. "You must be Andrei Bolstoy. I am Agent Carl Swanson, Homeland Security. This is my associate Agent Alvarez and the other gentleman is Captain Conroy, US Coast Guard."

He arched his bushy brows, looking bored. "Agent Swanson of Homeland Security, my boat is a sovereign vessel registered out of the Cayman Islands. Would you please explain the reason for your presence?"

"You were harboring a known terrorist that we saw fleeing this vessel less than twenty minutes ago. That gives me all the reason I need to board this vessel, question you or anyone else on board. I can search your boat, without a warrant, detain you or anyone on board and have Captain Conroy seize your ship and tow it wherever I please. That said, I would like you to tell me where Tobias Tobolokov, the fugitive who left this vessel in your motorboat is headed."

"Oh yes. Your infamous Patriot Act. To answer you, I truthfully do not know any man by this name. I know of no one having left my vessel. I have been in my quarters up until Captain Jakovski asked me to come up here. Is that not so captain?"

"Yes sir." He looked at Carl. "I try tell you, but you disconnect. I want tell you Colonel Bolstoy was in quarters and ask not be disturbed until cocktail hour. I page Colonel Bolstoy. The boat it leave to pick up guests from other marina. The man onboard he deckhand. No Tobias. Is true."

"Colonel Bolstoy? How is it you have the title Colonel? Were you in the military? No. You were KGB then FSB, as I recall. Another crooked Russian oligarch pawn who killed his master and took over his enterprises. Perhaps you're still a Russian secret policeman."

"I am a businessman. That is all. As I said, I know not this Tobias you seek."

Carl looked at TJ who shook his head. "Then you won't mind while we wait for your other guests to return."

"Would it matter?" Andrei asked.

Carl said, "No."

"Would you please allow my people to return to their duties?"

Captain Conroy told Carl he would need to return to his vessel while they waited. TJ said he would wait with Captain Jakovski. Carl told Andrei Bolstoy he would stay with him.

After they left, TJ walked around admiring the rich tones of the teak, the shiny chrome and the polished brass that made up the captain's cabin. He stared out through the three hundred-sixty-degree thick clear glass taking in the view from high up off the water. Some seagulls flew by, diving down then pulling up and circling back around.

"Nice up here. How'd you get the job?"

The captain sat back down in one of the captain's chairs watching TJ. "I in navy, stationed Black Sea. Andrei and I do business together. He make investments, gas, oil and other. Make wealthy. Come America, buy real estate, decide he want boat. He think of me. I say I do this for him."

"You from Russia?"

"Leningrad and Sevastopol before come here. You familiar with Russia?"

"No. I'm American from Miami."

"You Cuban, no?"

"Yes. My grandparents came here after the Soviets helped Castro take their country."

"I been Havana. Castro no more rule country. You visit Cuba?"

"No. Have family there, never see them or talk to them. Does your boss do business in Cuba?"

"No. We go Hemingway Marina. Travel. See country. I stay with boat. Many senoritas, many not like Russians leave. I enjoy visit. Maybe go back. See other cities, more senoritas."

"Do you like America?"

"Yes. Like very much. Our presidents like each other. Many Americans blame Russia for spying. America spy on Russia, Russia spy on America, keep each other busy. Andrei, he say make money no matter what government do. He businessman, our president's businessmen, everyone make money. That way of world. You agree?"

"I wouldn't know. You go ashore here much?"

"Not much. Andrei have me stay with boat."

"Ever go to a nice bar called Clutch's? I believe your boss the owner."

The captain looked away then looked back. "I know no place called Clutch's. I shop at big mall, go restaurant, not go bars." He stopped talking and pointed. "See boat come back. Our deckhand and the guests."

TJ looked. Five people were on the boat, two couples and the man piloting the craft. "Where's the other deckhand? There were two people on board when the boat left here."

"You mistaken, only Benitez on boat."

"Captain, you a liar. Guess you goina be going ashore, be our guest until we hear the truth. Come on we'll be joining the others. No party tonight. Boat's now confiscated. No more Cuba for you."

"You no do this."

TJ grabbed his arm, pulled him out of his chair and shoved him toward the door that led down to the others. He picked up his rifle and pushed the captain who had stopped and was trying to turn back.

"You think we not know you, your family. You make big mistake."

"No asshole, you just made bigger mistake. I'll make sure to handle your questioning personally." TJ used the butt of his rifle to shove the captain who grabbed the handrail to keep from falling down the steps.

Andrei Bolstoy was seated on one of the plush sofas sipping a sparkling drink. Carl sat across from him in a matching chair. The Coast Guardsmen sat stone-faced at the bar and the two crewmen were a few feet away, standing awkwardly, glaring at them. TJ pushed the captain over to where Andrei sat.

"The boat is returning." Carl looked up at TJ and stood. Andrei started to rise. TJ fixed him with a look and motioned with his rifle to sit back down. "Tobey is not onboard, just one crewman and two couples."

Andrei rose. "I must send my men to help with their arrival."

"I will go with the guardsmen and the crewmen. I want to question his guests, see what they have to say happened to Tobey."

"This is preposterous." He looked from TJ to Carl. "You must not allow this. I told you I do not know anything about this man Tobey. I–"

Carl turned to him. "Sit down and shut up."

Andrei hesitated, his beady eyes squinting, then he sat back, a smug grin on his face. He had spoken much harsher words to the peasants and those wealthy criminals back in Russia. Those he would accuse of crimes in order to receive their bribes so that they might not go to prison and lose everything. Some ended up in prison anyway, others paid and paid until he decided it was time to come to America. Bribes worked here almost as well. Money to political action groups, grease for business wheels. This pompous bureaucrat would soon wish he had not treated Andrei this way. This man would know he fucked with wrong man. He looked over to his captain, who feigned an attempt to stand, started to protest, the one called TJ stepped closer to him. Andrei reached over and placed his hand on his arm. The captain looked at Andrei, who shook his head, they both eased back. He knew Hector, named for the mythological literary figure, loyal, noble Hector. He listened as the man Carl continued.

"You are under arrest. You and everyone here, including your guests. You will be taken to port and held for questioning." He turned to the guardsmen and told them to take the two crewmen and go with TJ. "Please inform Captain Conroy we are seizing this ship, and all people on board are to be detained for questioning."

24

Great Exuma, Bahamas

The truck had been fueled. Thomas told Jake they had more than enough time before they went to Georgetown to go to Little Exuma so Jake could see the boat he was living on. Thomas said Jake could use the secure computer to place a message on his dating site for Homeland.

Mitch wasn't there. He texted saying the key was under the seat. Jake retrieved the key, locked the truck and rode with Thomas, figuring he would be less conspicuous this way.

Jake asked Thomas to stop off at Big D's. He wanted a conch salad and hoped D or his daughter might be willing to shed some light on Blakely and who the players were on the island. After what had transpired the last time he had been here, he was wary about how he would be received. He told Thomas and he laughed. "You know we have to be careful, for all I know D could be involved, and, there's always that coconut telegraph."

Thomas said, "I didn't know much about D, other than, like everyone else on the island, he wants to bargain for any excess materials." Thomas said he was never one of his "customers."

The hot sun shimmered off the white sand when they stepped out of the truck. Maurice and Lilah were seated on the stools talking when they crested the dune that separated the parking from the small outdoor restaurant. Lilah quickly stood up, raised the hinged section of the bar and waited for them to be seated. Maurice disappeared around the bay side of the building. Lilah tilted her head, her dark eyes studying Jake and Thomas, a merry quizzical expression had taken a home on her young lovely dark face.

"Hello Mistuh Harper. 'Membuh me? What might you and yo' friend like?"

"Heineken," Jake replied.

Thomas said, "Make that two. Where's your restroom?"

"Round corner." She pointed the way Maurice had gone. After Thomas left, she placed the two beers on the counter. "You want anyt'ing else?" she asked making herself sound coquettish, a gleam in her eye.

She was at that age when the world seemed to hold no promises and didn't have to. It was the age when hormones rage, when Ariel had given her heart and body to Jake, or, so he thought. She too had flirted with Jake, and he had fallen, only to be hurt when she disappeared, taking his heart with her. Joanna said he didn't know what love was. Maybe he lost knowing how. He loved his children, a different, yet somewhat deeper, scary kind of love. Lilah was somewhere close to the age of his son. His lower limit of fantasy was someone he would consider having children with, if he had to. He really didn't want any more children, but would continue to live by the philosophy, 'if you're going to play, you best be willing to pay'. That had ended with Joanna. He hoped.

Not that he didn't enjoy the flattery. He wanted to feel love, to be loved. Not that he didn't want sex—sex without love was nice for release. Once over, he mostly felt empty or guilty. Unfortunately, his little head hated his abstinence.

"Your dad around?"

"No. He be heah shortly. Is there anyt'ing I can do for you?" She said again trying to sound older.

"Lilah, can you make a conch salad?"

Her face dropped. The smile faded. "Maurice go get conch. He be heah soon, make you conch salad." She seemed hurt. Youth's rollercoaster of moods and emotions.

"Lilah, I enjoy listening to you. You're one of the prettiest and nicest people I've met since I landed here. If I was twenty years younger, your dad would have to keep his eyes on me. I also wanted to tell you and him I'm sorry about what happened yesterday with Blakely."

Her smile once more lit up her face. "You not dat kind of friend with that Blakely, are you?" She frowned.

"No. Rick is her boyfriend. She's not my type?"

"Oh no Mistuh Harper, you not what she say you is?"

"No way. You see Lilah I have three children, my son is your age, my daughters not far behind. Someday you'll meet some man and he'll make your heart feel like it will burst. When it happens you'll know. Don't give yourself to anyone else until it happens."

"Amen to that," Thomas said as he sat back down. "Been around there watching Maurice catch and wash a conc. That's it in that nice "clean" bucket up on the counter, delivered by yours truly. Maurice busy taking a smoke break."

Lilah came out from behind the counter. She told them she was going to check on Maurice.

When she disappeared, Thomas asked if Jake had seen D.

"Lilah said he'd be here shortly." They both drank from their beers. The beers were only slightly cool.

"You learn anything else worthwhile or was it just a lecture about birds and bees."

"She doesn't like Blakely. Could be jealousy. Other than that, not much more than trying to keep her hopes in check."

"You sure do have a way with women."

"Yeah, my ex-wife thought the same thing."

They hadn't heard a vehicle, but suddenly Big D stepped through the beads that separated the back room from the bar. "Afternoon suh and you Mistuh Devereaux. You wouldn't happen to be Mistuh Harper's friend Miss Carmichael talk about?' He laughed. His broad face bright with mischief.

"Not funny," Jake said. "She say anything more amusing after I left?"

"I too busy to pay her much mind. Mistuh Rick and I talk about you. He say your boss come Monday. Make you top man instead of him. Maybe you and I talk 'bout doing little tradin'."

"Uh oh," Thomas said, "here it comes. Big D's wheeling and dealing."

Big D's broad faced smile grew broader. "You leavin' soon I hear Mistuh Devereau, hope not too late you and I do sum bus'ness?"

"You-- do business with Rick?" Jake asked.

"We talk. Talk t'everyone 'bout trade. You interested?"

"What do you have to trade with D, free bar tab?"

"Sumtin' likum dat. Ever't'ing 'cept wife and daughter." He laughed again. "You have sumtin', you come see me 'fore you talk sumbody else."

Thomas asked, "what do you plan to do with the materials you trade for?"

"Me build big restaurant. Big t'ings happenin' Exuma. Soon many people come from ever'where. Gots to be ready."

"D, you be willing to trade information, if I said I would help you out? You know, I scratch your back, you scratch mine." Jake looked up into his smiling eyes.

"Info'mation sumtimes worth lots to sum people. Don't hurt to listen."

"Bet you hear everything. You been here all your life, am I right?"

"Most of it. Went culinary school New Orleans, two years. Other than dat live here." He studied Jake, trying to decide where this was going. Maybe trading with him was going to be too expensive. Rick and Blakely said he said he was cool, but, that he act uptight, askin' 'bout drugs. When asked about man at Georgetown Inn, Blakely say the Harper man say his friend worked on equipment for DEA. D had already heard 'bout man and him being DEA. D knew he could be problem. He needed to find out, maybe give a little, get a lot, the way D like to do business. "What info'mation you lookin' for?"

Jake could see the wariness, hear it in D's sudden change in tone. He drank the rest of his beer. "How about another beer and a conch salad. That's what I came here for." He turned to Thomas, who was studying D also. "What you say Thomas, another beer and a conch salad sound good to you?"

"Another beer and some conch fritters for me," Thomas said, giving Jake a knowing nod.

After Jake finished enjoying his second conch salad in as many days and nursed his second beer near to the bottom as D pointed out before disappearing into the back once more, Jake turned to Thomas, "think he'll deal?"

"Can't hurt to ask, hopefully. Better get on with it, we need to get going."

Jake wondered out loud where Maurice and Lilah disappeared to.

"Maurice was sitting on a five-gallon bucket smoking a joint when I came out of the pitiful excuse for a bathroom. Damn thing make a backroad Arkansas service station bathroom look uptown, if you know what I mean. He offered me a toke. I declined. My bet Lilah and her ole man are enjoying the bay view, probably talking about us also."

No sooner had Thomas finished, D came back through the jingling bead curtain.

"You ready talk bus'ness?'" D had what Jake saw was a different smile on his face and his eyes were more squinty.

"Seems everybody knows everybody's business on the islands. No doubt, if anyone does, it would include you. What can you tell me about Alvin and Rodney?"

"Rodney, he know people, celebrities and such. They takes him out on boat, plays golf with him. Bet you wouldn't think Rodney play golf. Pretty good so's I hear. Alvin, like Rodney, they heritage land people, family always be here. Alvin, he a captain, have fishing boat, been doing long time. Anybody could tell you this, why you want to know?" D rested his hands on the bar. "You want 'nother beer?"

"Not yet? What do you know about the foreigners with boats up at Little Exuma?" Jake asked.

"This info'mation, it not come free. What you do for Big D?"

"You need materials you say, like I said I can get you those. How much depends on what you can give me?"

"And you Mistuh Devereaux, how you figure into this bus'ness?"

"This is between you and Jake. ESI has offered to take my company's surplus metal, seems they have some metal work to be done and my company is leaving. They won't need all of what will be left. The rest will be up to ESI and Jake, that is, if he takes over running ESI's work. I'm going to leave this up to you two. Jake, I'll be waiting in the car. I need to get going, so don't be too much longer." Thomas pulled out a twenty and laid it on the counter. "See you D."

Big D leaned back on the icebox behind him. "Mistuh Harper–"

"Friends call me Jake."

"Mistuh Jake, you have to be careful asking too many questions about other peoples and their bus'ness. I think listenin' better than askin'. Lots of people talkin' about you. I hear good t'ings and I hear other people askin', they worry 'bout who you are and why you here. You worry wrong people, bad t'ings can happen mon, you hear what I be sayin'?"

"I was hired by the man who owns ESI to come here to find out how I could get ESI back on track. I'm sure you heard Fluor is threatening to terminate ESI's contract. If they do, I'll be like all their employees, out of a job. I need this job. I am in debt up to my ears. In order to try to save ESI and my job, I need to figure what the problem is, that means knowing who the people are and anything else to do with what's going on. No one knows me and no one seems to want to trust talking to me. From what I've seen so far, Rodney and Alvin are the head Bahamians and before I approach them, I'd like to know something about them and anyone else that could help answer my questions. Ned is coming Monday; like Rick told you, he's going to want some answers. I'd appreciate it if you could help me out. I'm willing to barter with you, but you have to agree to keep quiet, just like I will about you."

"Not sure how I he'p you."

"Anything you hear about me or ESI. Who's asking or saying anything? Do what you always do, listen. Look I need to go. Think about it. If you help me, I'll find a way to help you." Jake laid another twenty on the bar. He shook D's hand before leaving. D told Jake to come back later. Jake told him it would probably be lunchtime Saturday before he could get back.

The bright equatorial sun had a faint orangey halo. Clouds were moving in and the breeze had picked up in intensity as they drove toward Rolleville. Jake felt even more unanchored on this island world. At home he would have heard the news and weather on the television and radio, pretty much knowing what was happening nationally and locally. Even overseas, morning briefings and others with radios and the internet knew more about back in the states and locally than he did here. Ned was coming Monday and he didn't know shit.

"You mighty quiet Mistuh Harper," Thomas said trying to sound Bahamian.

"I feel I'm spinning my wheels, digging myself deeper in the sand, getting nowhere. Ned's coming Monday. I don't have much concrete information to give him. He may shit-can me. Hell, Fluor may shit-can ESI's contract, then I'll be out of here."

"Welcome to the club. My boss wants me gone here middle of next week. Might be able to convince him to give me until the end of the year. I liked being here, working for Basics, helping HSI out with this investigative work.

I keep hoping HSI will bring me on permanently. When you talk to Hardy put a good word in for me."

The sight coming over the hill above the bay into Rolleville was just as breathtaking the second time as it was the first. Thomas slowed down and they went down the hill to the harbor area, past where Jake had seen Alvin and the two men. Thomas parked and they went out onto a dock, one row over from where he had seen them. Jake followed beside Thomas watching for any sign of anyone looking their way. They boarded a sleek boat nearly forty feet long tied up near the end of the dock, everything was stark white inside and out, then again Jake noted most boats were mainly white.

"It's a Silverton 39 Motor Yacht has two 385 hp Caterpillar diesel engines."

Jake stopped, his attention drifting, taking in the details. He shook his head.

"Not a very large kitchen, serves my needs, all I care about. Two bedrooms down below, small split head, wc on one side, small shower on the other—cozy tiny water home. Look around. The computer is in the salon, password *fryFly2myst8*. Here, better write that down," he said when he saw Jake shake his head. He took a pen and pad off the kitchen counter and wrote it down.

"Damn, I'm having to share a bug-ridden house with Blakely and Rick, and you get to live on a fucking yacht."

"My part of the divorce settlement. She got the house. I got the boat. Homeland equipped the thing with useful items, which I'll show you when I get back. I'm going to take a quick walkabout, see if any of our friends noticed. Small community here, people like to snoop and gossip, helps with security, but pretty much kills privacy."

Jake took a quick tour, kind of cramped, livable, he could get used to it. He found the computer, entered the password, was soon logged onto his dating site, sent the coded message which would alert Hardy to call him.

While he waited for the call, he checked out the messages and photos from women who responded to his photo and profile. Some sent questions, some posted provocative photos, several wanted to jump ahead of the getting-to-know-you-question and answer stage, requested email address and phone numbers. Jake was intrigued by the whole situation, not expecting much, but pleased to find the number of women ranging in age from late teens to early forties, who responded. Clearly some were not whom they appeared to be. He wondered how many were members of escort services trolling for men they could take advantage of. Another issue came to mind, was Homeland monitoring his site, could some of these supposed matches be checking to see what he would say?

As he was pondering the possible, responding to a few interesting looking and intelligent sounding profiles, his cell vibrated. Hardy.

"Jake you were supposed to get a disposable phone. You need to get several, who knows if this number is compromised."

"Been kind of busy, in case you haven't noticed. There aren't a lot of places to purchase phones." Jake needed his neighbor and others to know they could reach him, thought disposable phones were unnecessary. After all, no one was supposed to know the connection. Why bother with him, he was supposed to be undercover. And how was that working out?

"Nonsense. Do it, okay?"

Jake told him where he was. Hardy was concerned he was possibly exposed to the two men who had been with Alvin. (No shit.) He told him about his talk with Big D, then he told him the story Blakely had provided, about Boris in St. Louis and Victor here in the Bahamas. They both wondered if Victor might have been the other man on the dock and the man at the party the night before. Hardy said he would put the names into the system, see if they could come up with a match or possibilities. Hardy was concerned about Blakely's claim regarding his own presence and the threat on Jake's life.

"These people don't play by any rule book, and they certainly aren't worried about the police or Bahamian laws. They'll take advantage of any opportunity. They could be gone before anyone knows they were ever here."

"How am I supposed to defend myself? I don't like being threatened and defenseless, like being that one-legged man in an ass kicking contest, your opponent having a stiletto mounted in the tip of his shoe."

"You're there for as long as it takes to gather information. We arm you and you get into a jam we wouldn't be able to come to your defense without causing an international incident and exposing the whole operation."

"In other words, you're saying good luck Jake you're on your own. Anything happens, fuck you. Homeland is worse than the Army, at least the military acknowledges you, even when they're fucking you."

"Sorry Jake, that's the nature of the beast. Lots of unsung heroes on the walls of our building. You want out, then say so and I'll get you out of there."

Jake thought about it for a second or three. He had never been afraid of dying. He always felt his service was noble. He had been proud to wear the uniform, he didn't always agree with the leaders in the field and especially in Washington, but he believed in himself and had never questioned his own motives or actions. There were bad guys out there and he thought of himself as a good guy carrying out his mission to the best of his ability. His mission, the reason he was here was to stop a threat to his country—yet to be verified threat. On a personal level, save his farm—his prime reason. If that meant being a mercenary, well, he really didn't see he had a choice.

"You still there?" Hardy asked.

"I'll hang in here a little longer, but, if it comes down to me or them, then you better be prepared to deal with the consequences. I don't intend to be a sacrificial lamb."

"That's why I sent backup. You're with Thomas, on his boat, I'll see about another agency friend getting in contact with you shortly. HS is monitoring your location by pinging your phone. Assume they are doing the same. Change phones often and let me know when you do. Believe me, I am doing everything I can to keep you safe my friend." He dropped offsite.

Thomas made some noise to signal his return startling Jake. He turned around to face him. Thomas pulled out a bottle of Irish whiskey and poured a jigger or two in two glasses, handed one to Jake. "Drink up. Afraid I have some bad news." He drained his glass, as did Jake.

"Seems to be par for the course."

Thomas plugged a fresh earbud into his phone and handed it to Jake. He touched play on the screen, and the sound of swishing water and screeching and groaning of boats at berth could be heard followed shortly by voices speaking in a foreign language, Jake took to be Russian. He listened to the muddled conversation for a minute, looked up at Thomas with a shrug and frown. "I don't understand a damn thing they are saying. I take it you do?"

"I learned several languages while with the Bureau; Russian is one of them." Thomas rattled off a few words. "Our friends are discussing their travel plans once their mission is complete. Seems they intend to be leaving tonight. Meaning the mission is imminent. Said mission, take care of you and yours truly. One of them warned the other about the handling of the agent—"do not drop this and be sure to wear the second skin." Sounds like some kind of neurotoxin in play here. That muffled sound is probably due to them wearing respirators. This is serious. Guess you remember The Skipel Incident in Salisbury, England and the other couple who stumbled across the discarded atomizer in some trash a while back.

"Shit. We need to contact the Bahamian authorities. Get a hazmat team to check this boat out."

"You're talking delay. We don't have that kind of time. Oh hell, they're on the move." He punched in camera on his phone, zoomed out and snapped a few pictures. Most were in profile, one man turned to the other and Thomas got a full facial of him. "We need to follow them."

They rushed off the boat and stayed as low as possible behind the other boat and followed at a distance. The two Russians went up the dock to the parking area and got into a white Ford rental car. Thomas and Jake jumped into Thomas' rental. Thomas floored it out of the parking area to take pursuit.

The Russians didn't appear to be in any hurry. Jake and Thomas were able to come within sight of them before they rounded the corner of the church.

"Don't seem to be in a hurry, do they? Jake said as they topped the hill heading away from the harbor area.

"No, they don't. Kind of makes you wonder where they intended to put this dirty deed into action."

Jake was watching the car in front. It was not picking up speed as expected leaving Rolleville. He was having a hard time seeing due to the amber glare of the setting sun on their windshield. "Something isn't right. Do you think they know we're back here? Maybe the pursued doing the pursued isn't the case. Perhaps they lured us out here, to take advantage of a remote, no witness scenario. The Taliban used this over in 'Stan, teaching or taught to them by the Soviets."

"Then I guess we shall have to see who is better at this cat and mouse game. Who says we don't have a weapon?" Thomas patted the steering wheel. "Never had a chance to test the Bureau's defensive driver training I received. Better tighten your seat belt." Thomas pressed down on the gas pedal and they closed the distance on the other vehicle. "Good thing we're equally matched, size for size, makes a more equal fight."

Jake tensed up. His butt hole clinched. He didn't like not having control of the vehicle or the situation, his life was in Thomas' hands. He was pushing his right foot into the floorboard. No brakes for him. Thomas closed the gap on the Russians. The passenger in the other car swiveled his head staring back at them, the driver's eyes were visible in the rear-view mirror. Their car picked up speed.

Jake had no idea what Thomas intended. They raced down the curving Queen's Highway, tires squealing on the sharper curves. The ocean water rising and falling from cliff to beach as they went up and down on the undulating road, the evening light flickering and fading with the landscape.

"Do we take their vehicle out, perhaps over the edge or do we take them so we can maybe question them? If they survive, we need to consider the neurotoxin. I say take them out of commission permanently." Thomas said sounding on edge.

Jake had never liked killing. On the battlefield, he remembered every time, from the gut wrenching first to the last time he had fired the deadly shot. That was kill or risk his own and his fellow soldiers' lives. Kill or be killed was that not what this was all about?

Only they weren't wearing a uniform and Thomas was asking him to make the call. Would these men's spirits follow him into his dream world, another black mark on his soul? Jake never believed there was such a thing as a righteous kill, though he had told himself otherwise when he read or heard about brutal murders or people who committed major terrorist atrocities. He joined the Army after 9/11 wanting to exact revenge. Satisfaction never really came after he fired fatal shots. Tribal. Invasion for invasion. Revenge for revenge. He learned to live with that choice, could he live with this one?

"It would be good to know why they wanted to get rid of me and who else is involved. No matter. We have to stop them. Do whatever you can, if they survive, then we'll deal with them, if not, we'll have to live with the consequences."

Thomas floored the accelerator going into a curve, cutting into the oncoming lane. When they came out of the curve, there was a truck coming at them head-on. Thomas swerved back into the other lane, missing the truck by less than a foot, then swerved back into the oncoming lane, not letting off the accelerator. They caught the Russians by surprise. Thomas jerked right then quickly back left tagging the passenger side rear bumper sending the other car spinning.

Thomas hit the brakes and Jake watched as the Russians vehicle began a roll as though in slow motion, time seeming to have slowed down as well. He stared as the vehicle's roof sent sparks flying, the front end skidded into an escarpment, bounced off it, veered back across the highway in front of their car and slid down an embankment out of sight. Thomas had locked their brakes, the tires squealing and smoke rising, floating in the rush of air created by the two vehicles.

They both jumped out as soon as their car came to a halt. The smell of burning rubber from their tires filled the air with the acrid odor. They ran to the edge and peered down where the other car had gone. It had plowed a path through the shrubby vegetation and lay on the passenger's side on a small touch of beach thirty feet below, steam rising from the hot metal and from the motor being cooled by the damp sand and the bay's water washing up underneath. There was no sign of the two occupants. Jake looked around. He could see no way to get down there.

"We need to get away from here, before someone sees us," Thomas said. "We'll notify Homeland, let them get in touch with the local authorities. Tell them about the neurotoxin. If they survive, they'll have a lot of explaining. Maybe you'll get your answers. Come on. Let's get out of here."

Jake was amazed at how nonchalant Thomas seemed to be taking the consequences of his actions, their actions. Not seeming to be concerned if the two men were alive. Not what you would expect from an FBI man.

"You go. Get the car away from here. I need to go down there."

"You got to be kidding me. Someone sees you down there…" He saw the determined look on Jake's face. "Ok. I'll move the car out of sight and go down there with you."

Jake used his sneakered feet in a futile attempt to remove the glass off the highway. Didn't have to be an attorney to know he was contaminating a crime scene, one that he was complicit in the commitment of. He looked down. No sight of either man. He began a search for a way down, all the while thinking Thomas was right, if someone came along and saw him, he could possibly be creating a legal problem for himself. He also thought that he could be putting Thomas' and his life in danger from the neurotoxin if the containment was ruptured. He needed to know if either of them was alive, making them a continued threat legally and personal health-wise, and, to a great degree, ethically—this was a new type warfare, one that Jake was not entirely comfortable with.

Jake heard Thomas approaching.

"You know we're being crazy," he said as he drew near. "I moved the car down a ways. Got it off the road. I have no way of knowing if I'm blocking a drive or just some seldom used trail."

Jake didn't reply. He set off at an angle away from the other car on a crusty footing that crunched and broke loose every few feet. Thomas could be heard further back. Jake was following his own shadow in the setting sun. He could hear Thomas trying to catch up and cursing under his breath each time his booted feet slid. Fifteen minutes or so he reached the shallow spit of land. Jake stopped, listened for Thomas to join him and for any sound coming from the other vehicle some fifty feet away.

Jake whispered to Thomas, "I don't see any movement." There was pinging heated-metal sounds and the wind-charged surf, created an eerie feeling.

They crept through the ankle-deep sea until they were less than two steps away. They listened. Nothing except the swish of the rising surf. The two men lay in fetal balls, one wedged under the steering wheel airbag, the other pinned against his door, partially submerged. They weren't moving. Jake moved forward, cautiously reached in and touched the driver's neck. No pulse. Thomas watched.

"This one's dead. Not much doubt the other one is also."

"I hope we haven't been exposed to that neurotoxin. We'll know soon enough," Thomas said. "Good thing the Bahamians don't have a sophisticated police force. We're leaving all kinds of physical evidence. Could be there'll be a hazmat team to contaminate the scene. We need to get out of here. Contact Hardy. Hhave him get a team here to search these guys boat and check the car.”

"He's not going to like this. Neither do I personally. I need to know who else is involved. I want to go onto their boat." Jake looked over the car. Devereaux was shaking his head.

"No way, man. You can't risk any other possible exposure. Leave that to the experts. We can talk after we get out of here.”

25

TJ went with the guardsmen to meet the returning power boat. Benitez expertly guided the boat into the loading port in the aft section of the yacht TJ assisted Captain Conroy and one of the guardsmen, giving a guiding and steadying hand to the two couples, directing them over to the Coast Guard vessel. They demanded an explanation, protested, threatened legal and political reprisals—one claimed to be a resident member of the President's Key Biscayne Golf Club. President's a personal friend. Captain Conroy remarked how nice that was.

Benitez, looked shaken, was immediately separated from the guests. TJ led him aside.

"Where did you pick up these people?" TJ asked.

Benitez stared at TJ and shook his head.

TJ repeated the question in Spanish. Same results.

"You will go to jail, be deported after we learn what you know. You tell me what you know, maybe you get to stay."

He shrugged.

Carl and the other guardsman brought Andrei Bolstoy, Captain Jokovski, the chef and the crewmen down to join the others. Bolstoy began apologizing to the others. Carl told him to shut up. He then told Captain Conroy to take Bolstoy and Jokovski onto his boat while he talked to the guests. There were immediate protests from all. Thomas Palmroy stepped forward introduced himself to Carl and demanded answers, informing Carl about his residency and presidential connections.

"Key Biscayne Golf Club, is that where you were picked up?"

"Yes. At my private dock. I demand you return us there immediately."

Carl continued, "The other man that was on the boat with the helmsman, did he get off there?"

"What other man? That man, the helmsman, was the only man on the boat. What is the meaning of this?"

"You're sure there was no other man on board?"

"I have no reason to lie. I resent your implication." He reached into his dinner jacket and pulled out his cell phone. "I am going to contact my attorney, you–"

"Son," Carl said to the guardsman, "take that cell phone and all the other guests' phones as well. Search them for weapons and escort them onto your boat."

Carl turned away from the awestruck guests, their threats and dismay bouncing off his back as he walked over to join TJ and Benitez.

TJ told Carl Benitez refused to answer. "May be wrong but I think he doesn't understand English or Spanish," said TJ.

Carl rattled off a question in Italian and Benitez's face lit up. Carl and Benitez continued for a couple minutes, the questions and answers growing more and more animated—hands and mouth punctuating the conversation. Afterwards Carl told TJ, "He says he does as ordered, if not he and his family would suffer the consequences. He's more afraid of them than he is of us, says, even if he goes to prison and never sees his family again. I had Captain Conroy order air and maritime search of all vessels in the area; hopefully we'll get lucky. Maybe Tobey still has his cell, and we'll get a ping. For now, we'll take these people to the Coast Guard Station for questioning."

Captain Conroy met them as they brought Benitez over to the Coast Guard patrol boat.

"Agent Swanson, we don't have room on board the *Marlin* to keep all these people separated."

"I need to take them in for questioning and have the *BolsToy* impounded," Carl said.

"May I suggest you use the *BolsToy* as a temporary detention facility? I will request permission to keep the Marlin tied up and my crew assist in quarantining your guests for questioning until another vessel can be dispatched."

"Excellent idea," Carl said quickly, "I'm glad I thought of that." Carl saw the not so amused expression on Captain Conroy's face. "That was meant as a joke, Captain. Have your men do a thorough search of the BolsToy for any weapons, and communication devises. Then escort our guests back onboard beginning with the three couples, place them in the salon area. Take the chef and his staff back to the galley; I believe that's what the kitchen is called." Captain Conroy nodded.

"Make sure one of your crewmen keeps an eye on them while they prepare us a nice meal. Wouldn't want them doing something to the food to make us sick or worse, not to mention the kitchen knives. The father and son you have on board the *Marlin*, Mick and Gary, should remain on your vessel to be joined by this Italian deckhand Benitez. Agent Alvarez and I will keep Major BolsToy and Captain Jokovski company on the quarterdeck. Maybe our guests will be more forthcoming after the fine dining and refreshments. Oh, by the way, you wouldn't be kin to the author Pat Conroy, would you?"

"He is my wanta-be uncle, sir."

"Perhaps you could regale us with some stories to lighten things."

Captain Conroy grinned. "I'll do my best. They don't have to be true, do they?"

"Story telling is an art; leave facts to the historians' and lawyers' fabrications."

"Aye, aye sir."

"Captain while you're taking care of my requests, I need you to stay with Agent Alvarez and his guests while I make some calls."

"You may use the *Marlin*'s comms if you wish sir. They are secure."

"Thank you, Captain. I believe I shall. Speaking of which, post a man watching the BolsToy's comms."

Carl asked for privacy from the crewman manning the comm center. Crewwoman and womaning would probably be politically correct, he thought, since it was a she. Not that he ever felt being politically correct applied to the military. You're getting old, Carl. Maybe it was time to retire.

He called into Homeland's field office. When Baker answered, he asked if they had received any pings from Tobey's phone. They had not. Carl told them to keep listening. He called in to the Coast Guard Command Center and spoke to Vice Admiral Donovan, apprised him of the situation and requested the Marlin's crew remain until further notice. He had decided to quarantine the *BolsToy* for use as an auxiliary field office, thinking perhaps *BolsToy* might receive communication useful to the investigation.

"I need to keep the guardsmen and I want you to remove your vessel from the *BolsToy*. I am in the middle of a covert operation and I need to discreetly secure this vessel."

Vice Admiral Donovan wanted more details. Carl told him he could not discuss the operation with him, that if he had any questions, he should consult HSI headquarters. Vice Admiral Donovan said he would do that. Unfortunately, he would not be able to do so until tomorrow.

"You will honor my request forthwith. Your directive from HSI will be sent very shortly, are we clear?"

"I have a dinner party tonight. I will wait here thirty more minutes for the directive."

Carl disconnected and called Agent Hardy.

"Agent Swanson. I was just before calling you. There have been some ominous developments on my end. I hope you're having better results."

Carl told him about what occurred and of his request to Commander Donovan.

"I will notify Washington. He'll get his directive immediately." Hardy told Swanson to hold while he made a call. Several minutes later, Hardy came back on the line. "On its way. You should receive a copy of the directive very shortly."

"Good. What kind of ominous developments have happened on your end? I hope it doesn't mean anything regarding TJ's friend Jake Harper. He would be upset and that might affect his usefulness on this end."

"Agent Alvarez would have no need to worry, nothing has happened to Agent Harper. An unsuccessful attempt was made by two Russian agents to assassinate someone using a chemical agent, unknown at this point. Agent Harper and Agent Devereaux heroically sent their vehicle off the road, killing both provocateurs. I have requested a hazmat team be dispatched. Could be some political blowback from the Bahamian authorities I'll have to contend with. Our shaking the tree seems to be working. As for Harper, I gave him the option to bail out. He has decided to remain. There are others here that are involved. We need to find them. He is our best bet. I hate using him as bait, I would be even more regretful if anything happened to him. He's a soldier, he knows the risks, as we all do, that's all I can use to assuage my conscience."

"Same here. I really like Agent Alvarez. The man has nerves of steel. Like I said before, I'm glad he's on my team. Hopefully we can get some useful intel out of our guests on this end. Several of them have political connections, all the way to the president. I'm debating on cutting them loose if they have no valuable information. Part of me says if they're friends of Bolstoy, they could know something useful or pose a media risk once they are set free. What do you think?"

"I agree. Fuck their supposed political connections. This operation is about securing our country from a possible, looking more likely, terrorist threat. Do what you have to, let them deal with the Justice Department later."

"That's what I hoped you'd say. Good luck Bob. I'll let you know something soon, I hope. We lost Tobey. He hopped a boat out of here. We've got a search underway. He may be headed your way. Thought you might like a heads-up."

"I'll keep him in mind. Good luck to you also Carl. And, keep Agent Harper's involvement contained. Agent Alvarez does not need to know he is working with us."

Carl did not understand the last request. He wondered why the secrecy involving those two.

26

Jake went on-line, left a message, spoke to Hardy who said he would get a hazmat team on the way. He told them to wait there, keep an eye on the boat until someone arrived to relieve them. He also gave Jake some interesting info about Blakely—no information about any daughter, nor could they find a record of her supposed mother. Her connections to Boris and Victor were probably real. Jake wondered if these were the two dead Russians and what all this meant about Blakely. Hardy told him what he already knew—be wary of Blakely. Hardy said he was sending Jake a photo of a person of major interest calling himself Tobey, aka Tobias Tobelokov or Tobiski, or Toby Tyler. He fled Miami in a boat, possibly headed to the Bahamas. This reminded Jake he had not talked to TJ. He knew not to mention this to Hardy. They disconnected after Hardy admonished him once more for not changing phones.

Jake went back to the Internet date site. A woman's picture caught his attention. Her name was Elena. She sounded interesting. She was a nurse, lived in New Orleans. He sent her a message, then disconnected. He decided it was time to move on with his life, find someone to assuage his feeling of hopeless despair, maybe these match sites were the answer. If nothing else, he could maybe recreate a sex life. It had been too long, Blakely reminded him of his pent-up desires.

Being back in the enemy's sights, with the possibility of dying from someone else's hands besides his own, was invigorating, though he wished it was more overt instead of covert. Being a passenger in a murdering machine didn't seem right, it was like the IED that had nearly cost him his mobility and life, a chickenshit way to fight. Jake often thought he belonged in the time before gunpowder when you met the enemy eye to eye, hand to hand.

Thomas was standing guard on the dock. He brought Jake back to reality when he came back on board, startled him.

"Bit jumpy, are we? HSI has sent a man to relieve us. We need to get going to the Friday meet, greet, eat and drink ritual, perhaps another attempt awaits."

"You really get off on this, Don't you?" Jake asked standing to follow Thomas up onto the dock. "Did you ever serve in the military?"

"Regrettably no. Went straight from college to the FBI. Mostly did investigations, lots of paperwork, never fired my weapon except on the firing range. Always wanted to be on the front line, fighting the enemy with more than a law book. So yeah, I do find this exciting. Come on now, you're not regretting the deaths of those Russians who intended to kill us, are you?"

Jake wanted to tell him that only insane people kill without remorse, but figured he'd be wasting his breath. "Am I glad it was them and not me? Absolutely. But their death means we're no closer to accomplishing the mission. This is not a take-no-prisoner scenario, do you understand?" Jake could see anger, then a humorous mischievous expressions cross Thomas' face.

"Ok, you're the boss. I'll follow your lead. Just so you know, I'll do whatever to protect me and you. That is what my orders are. I want to be perfectly clear about that."

The Friday event took place under the same tent as the previous social event. Even at this early twilight time there was a queue. They had to wait to purchase a ticket which could be used to purchase quarter chicken or a steak, with a salad and baked potato. Jake decided to go with a steak. Once he was seated at one of the side tables away from the others, he began to eat and enjoy his beer. He had almost finished his meal when Blakely zeroed in on him, seating herself on the side opposite Thomas.

"This your new boyfriend?" she asked laughing. She had on heavy makeup covering her earlier wounds. "I am kidding, ok? I just wanted to thank you for talking to me." She leaned in closer; Jake could smell alcohol and reefer. "Did you talk to Victor? He hasn't shown up. I'm still scared. I'm glad you are here."

Jake pulled out his phone and showed her the pictures of the two dead Russians. There was a sharp intake of breath, she looked closer, her eyes enlarged. "That's Victor. Where did you get this picture?"

"You're sure?"

She continued to stare at the picture. "Of course, I'm sure. Is he dead?"

Jake ignored the question. "Do you recognize the other man?"

"No." She looked up at Jake. "Who are you? How did you get these pictures? Why are they on your phone?"

Jake stared at her. Their eyes locked. "Someone sent them to me. Seems our problem with Victor is over. What I want to know is why they would send me these pictures and not you?"

She sat back, leaned away from Jake, her eyes still locked on his. "How should I know?"

"Got another question for you Blakely." Jake scrolled back through his photos on his phone, Hardy would not approve of him having his original phone, he pulled up an older photo of him with his children from the last time he had been with them, a year before his life-threatening injury. "These are my children Blakely. You see they depend upon me. Anything happens to me and they would probably not be very happy. You claim to have a daughter who has been threatened. How about showing me pictures of her."

Blakely stood up. "You accusing me of lying? My daughter is with my mother, like I said. You have no right talking to me this way." She started to turn, Jake reached out, grabbed her arm. Several people standing in the food line were watching.

"You claimed you were threatened, and so was I. I showed you what that threat meant to me. I need to know this threat to your daughter is real. Or, have you made this whole story up and the threat to you is for something else you're involved in and have drug me into?"

She jerked her hand free and ran off. People continued to look at Jake, some with grins, others shaking their heads in disapproval.

Thomas sat quietly listening to the conversation. Jake told him what Hardy said on the drive over.

"Ever think about being an attorney? Might have missed your calling. Although in a courtroom that would probably have drawn a reprimand from a judge for badgering the witness. And, you may have lost a lot of the jurors," he said nodding to the people watching from the other side of the tent. "You have given the rumor mills a lot to work with. Should prove interesting." He chuckled. "Here comes Rick. Let me handle this." He placed his arm on Jake's shoulder to keep him from rising, stood and moved to intercept Rick and his two friends from down under. Charlie Davenport moved in and met them all. They were some twenty-five feet away. The band started playing, most of the people had moved outside to listen or dance. Those remaining inside watched in fascination the animated discussion taking place with the two top Fluor operational managers and the others.

Jake thought about Blakely. She was like a mirage, seeming to be there only because you want to believe there is something more. A shadow person—when the earth moves further around the sun, they disappear. That's what Jake hoped, he knew too many people like her. He had experienced the result for himself, caught up in something more than bargained for, looking for someone to take the weight so they can live with themselves. Who was pulling her strings? Why had she chosen Jake? Or was there someone out there who held a grudge against him. And that same person or persons had their hooks into her?

Another alternative was Blakely was one of those people born outside the system. Had never existed as far as the records show. Perhaps a daughter that exists that way as well. Either way, Jake was linked up with her. The threat no less real. Wishing Blakely would just go away wasn't going to help. He needed to find out what she was caught up in before he could know if it had anything to do with him and his mission. That meant getting her alone, away from Rick, hopefully before Ned came Monday. She posed a problem for ESI. Ned needed to be made aware of this.

Jake was thinking these thoughts as he watched Thomas, Charlie, Alec, Marcus and Rick huddle together, each glancing his way. Rick and friends with squinting, angry eyes. At the same time, Blakely hovered at the deckside of the tent staring past them at him like a confused child wondering why the adult was so angry with her. Her quirky moods were a thing of wonder. Was she mentally unbalanced or in over her head? Jake would bet the latter, maybe more than a bit of the former. Fear can do that to you. If only she would be honest, he would try to help.

He rose from the table and walked back the way he had come, then circled around the tent up onto the deck. The band was on the other side playing a fifties tune with a Caribbean beat, steel drums providing the rhythm. There were lots of people seated at tables drinking, talking, watching the dancers in front of the band. Jake decided to confront Blakely. Before he could reach her, Juan Carlos intercepted him.

"Mister Harper, I am glad you come. Let me buy you drink."

Jake looked past him. Blakely had disappeared. "A Heineken would be fine thanks."

Juan Carlos and Jake walked to the outside bar. Juan Carlos purchased a Kalik and a Heineken. They moved over to a table. Thomas came out with the others and he and Charlie came over to join Juan Carlos and him. Jake stood. Charlie motioned for him to sit.

"Rick seems to have a problem with you and Blakely. He has accused you of trying to get into her pants, despite her refusal. Personally, I have seen how Blakely is, and, would understand if you have misread her signals. Being on this island without available women can be a problem. I am against men bringing girlfriends here for that very reason. My wife has only been here one time in two years. Thomas says he has room for you. I think you should move away from any temptation and either take Thomas up on his offer or seek other accommodations. I hope you agree. ESI has enough problems and from what I understand, you were sent here to help solve them. I hope this will be the case."

Jake was angry. He smiled. Hoped to make himself look and sound sincere. "I think you're right. I believe I will seek other living quarters. However, for the record, I have not made any passes on Blakely. Perhaps you should ask her how she got the black eye and bruises. I assure you it wasn't from me. I appreciate Mr. Devereaux acting as an intermediary. if need be, I would be willing to prove Blakely's disingenuousness with witness' accounts. I hope that won't be necessary. Hopefully, my word will suffice. I will try my best to prevent any further embarrassment for her, and wounds to Rick's pride."

Charlie stood back up. "Mr. Harper, I would like to put this behind us. Far as I'm concerned, there's need not be any record of what occurred. Thank you. Gentlemen. Enjoy the rest of the evening. I plan to." He went to the side bar, ordered a drink, and walked off to join a group near the band.

Juan Carlos and Thomas were enjoying their beers, pretending to listen to the band. When Charlie was gone, Jake said, "thanks Thomas. For nothing it seems."

"You're welcome. I listened, did what I could to defuse the situation. Charlie was ready to send you guys packing, ESI's on Fluor's shit list as you're aware. Tell him Juan Carlos."

Juan Carlos brushed his dark hair back out of his handsome face. Jake saw a recent wound near his ear.

"How'd you get that scar? Jake asked.

"Truck run off road coming from Columbus Day celebration. Mexicans and some Bahamians think I dead, leave me. Others come along, get me out of truck. Rise from dead. You may not be so lucky. What I try tell you at party. Blakely talk to man you see talking to me. I see him threaten her before you arrive. He threaten me not say anything to anyone. He say he looking for Victor. Told him I know no Victor. He angry. Left when he see you. "

Another Blakely lie. She said she didn't know the other man in the picture. Unless there was another friend of Victor's.

"Thanks Juan Carlos, for telling me this." Juan Carlos tipped his beer, Jake and Thomas tipped theirs to him.

Thomas said, "Juan Carlos rumor has it you were forced off the road, is that true?"

Juan Carlos looked around to see if anyone was close by, "I wasn't that drunk. I think person who run me off road a Bahamian policeman." He looked around again. Two Bahamian policemen were on the other side of the deck on the opposite side of the band from Charlie and his group. They were talking to some other Bahamians.

"Why would a policeman run you off the road?" Jake asked.

"Our company not hire Bahamians. Our president friend with Bahamian Prime Minister. They have arrangement. Other Bahamians not like this. Ned, he think he friend with Bahamian Minister, hire Bahamians, officials not care unless he pay all fees. We pay fees. Everyone must pay fees. Rick not listen.

Do what Ned say. Cause ESI big problems. Thomas and I talk about this, we think you need talk to government administrator Miss Marshall. Have Ned pay fees to her. Problems go away for ESI."

"I think ESI has bigger problems. There seem to be too many Bahamians not doing anything. Ned needs to get rid of the excess personnel."

"Before Ned do this, must pay fees. You talk to Miss Marshall. She maybe help once pay fees. Bahamians they not like this. Must not know you think this."

"What do you know about drugs being carried by the Bahamians?"

Juan Carlos shook his head, smiled. "Why people think because I Columbian, I know about drugs. We stop cartels. Drugs everywhere. Legal and illegal drugs become new currency over world. I not do drugs. Bahamians have boats, fish, carry illegal drugs and people, hear Mexicans, others pay them. Not my business. Be careful who you talk to. I say no. I not involved, run truck off road. Do not talk to me drugs. Better not talk about drugs." He turned to Thomas. "Tell him Thomas."

"He doesn't want to have anything to do with drugs. He thinks some of the problems with ESI's Bahamians are due to their drug involvement, maybe Blakely is involved. If you hear anything let him know. Isn't that right Jake?"

Jake was watching Blakely. She was talking to Alec and Marcus. They kept looking his way. No telling what shit she was stirring.

"Earth to Jake." Jake looked at Thomas, then Juan Carlos. "Juan Carlos what do you know about Alec and Marcus?"

"Talk to Alec about work. Same with Marcus. He over ground crews, build swimming pools. Pool work almost complete. He leave soon. Alec seems not like Hispanics, never friendly, only talk work schedule."

"Juan Carlos if you ever see that other man that threatened Blakely and you, steer clear and let me know."

"Why? He threaten you?"

"Someone broke into the house, went through my things and roughed up Blakely, so she said. I'd like to find him and learn if it's true and what he was looking for." Jake stood. "I believe it's my turn to buy the beers. Juan Carlos? Thomas?"

Juan Carlos stood, said he needed to leave. "We start early tomorrow. Plan finish main work Friday. Everyone leave for Christmas. Hear your friend Alec go Graceland, big Elvis fan."

"That's funny." They all chuckled. "Thanks for the beer and info. I owe you one."

"You owe nothing my friend. Good night."

Thomas walked with Jake to the bar. They purchased two more beers.

"Interesting what Juan Carlos said. Blakely knows way more than she has let on. I need to get her where I can talk to her without anyone else around. If not, Hardy needs to find a way to talk to her. Maybe Ned can make Rick send her packing and someone from Homeland can have a talk with her."

"I wonder if there is another person here or if the other person with Victor was the one Blakely talked to at the party?"

"I was wondering the same thing. Hardy said another HSI man would be contacting me." He showed him the picture of Toby and told him what Hardy said. "Keep an eye open for this guy." Thomas hardly looked at the picture.

"Maybe the guy back at the marina is the other man sent to watch your back."

"You 'bout ready to head back. I want to see if the hazmat team found anything and talk to Hardy about this latest shit on Blakely."

"We can stop by, pick up your things on the way. You can bunk on the boat until you find something else. I'll be leaving Wednesday and may not be returning except to move my boat."

"Does Hardy know this?"

"No. My company boss and friend informed me earlier Guess he's not for letting me stay 'til the end of the year. Need to know what Homeland decides."

They drained their beers and left the way Jake came earlier, around the outside of the tent. As they neared the front of the tent Alec came around to intercept them. Jake stiffened expecting a physical altercation. He decided his best bet for the much bigger Aussie was to kick him in the balls or take a knee out, lower his defenses.

Thomas noted Jake's shift in gait. "Easy now Jake," he muttered, "maybe he just wants to talk."

Alec stopped several feet away. He saw the anger in Jake's face, the wariness in Thomas' stance. "Blakely sent me out here to talk to you mate.

Was up to me there wouldn't be much talk You want to listen or you prefer to be sent packing back to that y'all land where the men sound like a bunch of pansy faggots."

"What do they call people like him down under Thomas? Boonies, no bogans. Does your boyfriend Marcus know how you really are, or does he like his mates boganish."

Alec and Jake closed the gap between them. Thomas found himself sandwiched. His shoulders were pushed into their chests. He looked up into Jake's set-jawed face then glanced at Alec's snarling one. "Much as I'd like to see you two go at it, I'd hate to have to bail you out of that place the Bahamians call a jail Jake. At the least, you'd both be deported. Alec why don't you say what you came here to say and you two forget this macho bullshit. Another time, another place, how about it?"

"Alec. What are you doing?" Alec looked back over his shoulder. Jake looked past Devereaux and him, Blakely stood near the front of the tent. Thomas could not see her without moving but he heard the crisp warning alarm in her voice. "Back off please. Go make sure Rick stays with Marcus. Jake, we need to talk."

Alec stepped back much to Thomas' relief. "This isn't over, mate. You do anything to upset or harm her again, I'll take you apart."

"Wouldn't get my hopes up, mate."

"Please you two. I appreciate your sentiment, Alec. I'll be fine. Jake and I need to set the record straight."

Jake noticed this was a different sounding and more mature acting Blakely than previously witnessed. She hugged Alec then he walked back out of sight.

"Thomas," Jake said, "how about keeping an eye on the threesome while Blakely and I have our little chat."

Thomas looked at Jake then Blakely, turned and walked around front to make sure no one was waiting out of sight, though he wasn't sure what he could do if they were. He would like to stay to hear what was said, figured Jake would fill him in later. He checked Blakely for any weapons, none were visible, her tight-fitting shorts and top didn't leave much room to hide anything. She had something in her rear pocket. Looked to be a cell phone.

Jake walked up to Blakely.

"Why don't we go to the dock down toward Georgetown that should give us some privacy."

She looked up at Jake and smiled. "You not afraid to be alone with me?" Jake frowned. "I'm sorry. I promise to behave. Lead the way. I enjoy the sunsets. Kinda romantic, don't you think?"

"No offense intended. I'd rather not have you behind me."

She squeezed his hand. "No offense taken." They threaded their way through the parked vehicles in front and in the narrow strip next to the tent.

"You think I'm a bad person?"

"Not for me to judge anybody."

"Who are you, Jake? I know you're not just some manager sent here by Ned to take Rick's place. I had my suspicions and did some checking. When Robert Hardy of Homeland paid you a visit, suspicions kicked into high gear. No one could find anything linking you to any agencies. Did find out someone had been checking up on me. I knew they hadn't found anything. Or I would have been notified or taken in for questioning, maybe worse."

"I should have backed off, but Victor shows. Victor and his friend decided to play hardball. I told him I had not been able to find out who you were, he went ballistic. I knew there was something more to your story than you were willing to let on. I tried to talk to you earlier, but you seemed not to be forthcoming. Who are you, Jake? Who are you working for besides ESI. Is it the DEA?"

They stopped at the edge of the boardwalk of the marina dock. The lights, music and buzz from the tent party a hundred yards distant surrounded them, covering the sound of the surf, the rhythm of the waves vibrating under foot.

"You know more about me than I do about you. I know your real name is not Blakely and have every reason to believe you don't have a daughter. Who are you, what is it with you and the Russians?"

She turned to face Jake. "I need to know who you're working for in order to know if I should trust my instincts, open up to you. If I'm correct, I believe we could possibly help each other. Tell me are you working for Uncle Sam?"

"You probably know already. Are you?"

"Yes and no." She looked away.

Jake reached out and took her chin in his hand and turned her face back to his. She winced. "I'm sorry I forgot about the bruises. What does no mean?

How can it be yes and no?" She started walking down the boardwalk toward Georgetown. Faint music could be heard coming from the Georgetown Inn, losing the competition to the band at the tent now at their back. "You're a double agent. That's what no means. So where does your loyalty lie? Tell me I haven't fucked up by admitting anything to you."

She stopped. Jake walked around to face her. Tears were running down her cheeks dripping onto the tops of her breasts, exposed within her low-cut blouse.

Her voice and cadence changed. It was like she became a different person. "I was born in Ukraine on the Russian border. My father's parents were killed when Soviet Union was broken up. He convinced my mother to leave, we moved to Germany, then United States, to St. Louis. We were undocumented. They both died in an automobile accident when I was twelve. My father's sister was married to a William Corminsoy. They took me in."

"I spoke numerous languages, made it easy to major in language at college, where I was recruited. My uncle was an agent for the Soviet Union. Americans know I'm agent for Soviets. My uncle and Russian GRU do not know I am an agent for America. So I thought, Boris found out, maybe. Victor threatened to kill me if I don't help kill you. He wouldn't have beaten me or threatened me unless he knew something."

Jake didn't know what to say. He stood there watching her cry. A part of him wanted to believe her. The same part that wanted him to fuck her. He could do neither.

"I think it was you and Thomas killed Victor and other agent, I saw scratch and dent on Thomas' car. I was happy, also scared, thinking who else is here? They must know, and they will not stop until you and I are dead. You must see we have to help each other. I want to trust you, I have no one else."

"Why all this sex stuff?"

"Part of training. But that was not all. I find you attractive, and I thought if I get you in bed, I could know who you are. Then, after threat, whether I could trust you."

"And Kendall and Mitch?"

She wiped her nose on her hand, her eyes with her fingers, winced and tried to smile. "Orders. Same with Rick. I'm not proud of this, but I don't feel guilty, if that makes a difference to you. I think it would be different with you Jake, but I understand no means no."

"Are drugs part of your business with them?"

"They're Russian mob. They deal in everything that can make them money."

"I asked about you, are you involved in their dealing?"

"I was, still am. I'm tired of it all. But you can't just quit. There's only one way out and I think that choice has been made for me. I asked my contact to help me, to pull me out. He thinks there's a chance I'm wrong. He says I need to hang in here, thinks I am too deeply embedded for the Russians to suspect me, says there has been no intel pointing that direction. I haven't reported anything about your involvement in the deaths. They don't know I'm talking to you about an alliance. They would not approve. Agencies don't like to share."

"Why should I trust you?"

"I don't know Jake. That is something you must decide and fast. Both our lives are in danger."

"Why don't we start by you telling me your real name."

She smiled. "My real name is Blakely Anastasia Lyubov, my parents were Rom, gypsies. Most of my names deal with love, free love. William Blake, the poet, *"Can this be love which drinks another as a sponge drinks water,"* from the time of Enlightenment. So you see I was meant to live my life a prisoner of free love. What do you think?"

Jake stared in wonderment. "Hard to imagine you could make this all up. You never cease to amaze me. This alliance you mentioned, which side are you seeking to recruit me for?"

Her eyes that had taken on new life while explaining her name, suddenly grew angry, sparkle turned to fire. She was reaching into her hip pocket when Jake's attention was split by a sudden noise coming from behind him.

"Watch out Jake," he heard Thomas say with a grunt, "she has a weapon."

Blakely pushed Jake aside, rushed toward the sound of a scuffle. There was a crackle and a flash of light. Jake caught sight of Thomas and another man jerking in a strange mimicry of a dance being performed, like two prone lovers on the boardwalk. The second jolt rendered both nearly senseless. Jake rushed over and locked his arms around Blakely, his right hand seizing hers, using a pressure point to make it possible for him to use his left hand to take the taser devise from her. He retracted the leads and pocketed it.

"You trying to kill them?" he asked. She seemed to deflate. Trembling she turned to Jake burying her face in his chest.

"I saw one then another coming towards us. I just reacted."

There was the sound of other voices coming from the direction of the tent. He gently pushed Blakely back.

"Come on. We've got to get them and get out of here before others get here."

Jake pulled Blakely loose. She hastened after him to Thomas and the other man, his right hand poking up in the air as if he was trying to point to something or someone. It was Tobey. He reached down and pulled Thomas up onto his knees.

"Can you stand? We need to take this guy and get the hell out of here fast."

Thomas grunted. "Jesus. Felt like my whole body was on fire," he said pushing himself up with Jake's help. "Damn that hurts."

Tobey was trying to rise, his attempt seemingly futile, his face contorted in anger. Jake turned loose of Thomas kicked him in the head, rendering him unconscious.

Blakely let out a blow of breath as if she had been the one kicked.

Jake looked over to Blakely. "Blakely go meet whoever is coming, tell them whatever. Buy us some time. Go."

Blakely's face twisted from the unconscious Tobey to Thomas, then Jake, her eyes seemed to take it all in as she made a hasty decision. She grabbed Jake's arm, stared into his eyes as she kissed him hard on the lips, clutching him tight and whispered, "this is getting nasty, be careful," pulled back, turned and trotted off.

Jake lifted Tobey and with Thomas' meager help placed Tobey's unconscious body across his shoulders in the fireman's carry position, his sore neck protested every jolt as they moved off as fast as possible toward the lit end of the boardwalk in the direction of Georgetown. He doubted they would go unnoticed for very long. He hoped it would be enough time for them to figure something out.

27

Miami, Fl

The Coast Guard patrol boat had been untied, left the harbor with the second in command taking control with two of the crew. The other guardsmen remained with Captain Conroy and the others on board the *BolsToy*. They sat around the large dining table, Carl at the head of the table, the chastised and clearly irritated Andrei Bolstoy on one side and Captain Conroy on the other. TJ was seated at the other end with Captain Jokovski next to him along with the sour-faced Thomas Palmroy on the other. Palmroy's wife, a buxomly, foreign-accented redhead fifteen years younger was seated, along with the other guests in the middle. The serving staff performed their duties. The chef made a couple entries with guardsmen posted in the kitchen and the corners of the galley, content because they had been fed first at Carl's insistence, much to Colonel Bolstoy's chagrin.

They had finished their meal, along with several bottles of expensive wine. Carl, Captain Conroy and TJ limited their wine consumption to a glass each. Captain Conroy entertained the ladies with tales of misadventure and Coastguard victories, bringing smiles and laughter from all but Jokovski, Bolstoy and Palmroy. Carl was convinced Palmroy's recalcitrance was due to his involvement and fear of discovery.

Carl pulled TJ and Captain Conroy aside. "Gentlemen I am going to question the men separately starting with Mr. Palmroy. Agent Alvarez, you need to do the same with the women. Your good looks have caught the eyes of these ladies it seems." TJ blushed. "Start with Mrs. Palmroy. Be casual, gentlemanly, gain their trust, make them want to confide in you. I think Palmroy is in this up to his eyeballs. His wife may not know the details, but, like most wives, she knows plenty. Same with the other women.

"Captain Conroy, I want you to keep the stories going, along with the alcohol. Careful, don't want them too inebriated. Just enough to loosen their tongues is the objective." Conroy nodded, a smile, almost a grin surfaced on his tanned countenance. He liked telling stories. On duty, he was a hunter and gatherer, considered one of the best. Off duty, he was the life of his wife's social circle. Interrogation was not his forte, much to his wife's exasperation and his two teenage daughters' delight.

"Let's break these people's world, crack it like an egg. There's an omelet in the making and Uncle Sam wants to know all the ingredients."

When they re-entered the galley, the women were chatting merrily, the men were huddled together. Two of the men, the one caught enjoying an afternoon delight and Palmroy's friend from the boat, broke off and returned to their seats. Carl walked over to join the other three, ignored complaints and demands and told Palmroy to join him in the Captain's quarters. He saw TJ approaching Mrs. Palmroy, all the other ladies following his advance, plastered smiles giving Carl pause. He went over to Captain Conroy, told him to hold off on allowing any more alcohol for the time being. Palmroy stopped, watched TJ help his wife stand with the aid of an upturned palm.

"Where is he taking my wife?"

"Perhaps the ladies' room or another suite. What's wrong don't you trust your wife?"

"If he lays a hand on her—"

"Looks to me like the opposite is more likely. Don't worry, Agent Alvarez is a perfect gentleman, in and out of bed, so I've been told," Carl said, smiling. "The quicker you answer my questions, the quicker you'll rejoin your wife. If you don't answer to my satisfaction, you may never enjoy your wife's company again. I'm sure she'll manage quite well without you."

Carl wasn't sure where the Captain's quarters were. Palmroy continued his objections and threats as they walked down the corridor. He glanced in each room, there were signs they had been searched, drawers stood open, clothing on the beds, sheets pulled back, closet doors open. The guardsmen had done their job. They almost walked past the Captain's suite. A picture of Colonel Bolstoy in full regalia sat on a dresser catching Carl's eye.

Carl told Palmroy he found the place. Palmroy walked past and turned to Carl just as one of the guardsmen hurried to meet them.

"Sir. Captain Conroy sent me to deliver this." He handed a note to Carl. Carl read it, then told the guardsman to wait with Palmroy in Bolstoy's suite until he returned.

Mrs. Palmroy came up beside TJ, showing no signs of having consumed the copious amount of wine, he assumed she drank. She had a stern look on her blemish-free face. TJ sensed she was trying to contain anger and humiliation. Her form-fitting, silk slacks accentuated her well-toned legs, TJ could help but notice, as she moved ahead down the corridor. He walked more quickly to come alongside her. The only sounds were their feet on the carpeted floor, both treading lightly, like two cats in an alley.

TJ said, "Let me check this one?" She stopped and he opened the suite door. It showed signs of having been searched—male and female clothes lay on a queen-size bed. Scents of some expensive perfume with undertones of sexual fluids could be detected coming from the tossed linens. He asked Mrs. Palmroy to make herself comfortable. There were two plush white cushioned chairs on each side of a dark cherry wood end table. TJ cleared a path, took a towel off one and signaled to her to be seated. He sat in the other chair.

"You sure you wouldn't prefer I get undressed and lie on the bed," she said tilting her head to one side, a steely edge in her words, fire emanating from her eyes. "Or are you the kind who prefers to rip the clothes off their prey?"

TJ felt humiliated and angry. "Not inclined to do either. Perhaps you hoping I would."

She jumped to her feet and came at TJ palm raised. TJ abruptly stood, grabbed her wrist as she swung toward his face, intending a slap. She attempted to raise her other hand only to find it locked to her side. They were inches apart, eyes locked, her wine-scented breath coming in bursts from her parted lips, her body tense. "My husband will have your head on a platter," she snarled. "Do you have any idea who we are?"

"No and I could care less. Right now, you and your husband are on board a vessel, under the command of Homeland Security and will be held indefinitely unless you answer our questions and allay our suspicions you and your husband not involved in a criminal enterprise."

"My husband has political connections, including the president. My father has similar friends, including the Kennedys and former President Nixon. We will not be treated like common criminals as you will soon learn."

"Criminal perhaps, *common* not the description I would choose." He released her hands. "Please do not try to assault me again or I will be forced to place you in restraints. Let you feel what being committed feels like. Sit down. Please," TJ said a tight smile forced on his face."

She hesitated, took a few steps away, came back and settled into the other chair. "You know you remind me of one of our yardmen. You're Cuban. You don't have a heavy accent. Your family probably came over when Castro kicked the criminals out. I bet you live in that squalid area called Little Havana. You have been given a little authority and wish to take it out on those you resent for having what you wish you had."

"Good. Seems you have all the answers. Why don't we start with your presence aboard the *BolsToy*. What's the relationship with Colonel Bolstoy?"

"My husband and I own Trinational Hedge Fund Corporation, Andrei is one of our clients. My I use the loo?"

TJ walked over to the bathroom door and looked in. The place was a mess. He opened the glass shower door, there was a large dildo on the white round, two-person bench made into the marble surround. He almost laughed. "Help yourself." He stood back to let her enter and enjoyed her gasp as he was closing the door.

Carl texted TJ, '*cut it short. Will need to cut them loose soonest*'.

Shortly she came out, walked over to TJ and said, "That your idea of a joke?"

TJ waved her back toward the chair. "You know Mrs. Palmroy, I think I owe you an apology. A lovely lady with a much older not-so-handsome husband, I took you as a trophy wife. My mistake. I believe you probably the brains of your company. Am I right?"

She stood there staring at TJ. He could see the emotions playing across her face, her eyes searching his for his intent.

"Will was my father's best agent. He has a brilliant mind, very charming, great sales ability, a great romantic, with a sense of humor. You underestimate him at your own peril. I have two brothers, they thought they should have inherited the company, and would have, had not William and I made a pact. We have a good marriage, two lovely children and many friends in and out of business. Our business is run ethically, people trust us with their investment portfolios, many far in excess of millions. Andrei is one of them. We are aware of the accusations made about him. We did our own investigation. Since he came to America, he has been completely above scrutiny. Despite the investigations concerning the allegations, like our president, despite the witch hunt and impeachment, neither committed any crimes. You are wasting our time. Our attorneys will bury you. I suggest you limit your liability, perhaps an arrangement is possible. Our security department would welcome someone with your abilities."

"Thought you had me pegged as a yardman." Silence. She smiled. "Mrs. Palmroy, I believe you and your husband have become involved, knowingly or not, in activities that could ruin your business, reputation and freedom. I think maybe you are innocent of the planning. I'm not so sure you or your husband will be able to prove your ignorance of Bolstoy's involvement in illegal business, which, by all appearances, appear treasonous. Your political friends will soon not be returning your calls. If you know or suspect anything, now is the time and place to speak up. Perhaps an arrangement is possible."

She simply smiled at TJ like he was an errant underling.

"Someone is always misinterpreting data, Agent Alvarez. The truth is in the details as interpreted by the listener. Nothing is absolute. Perhaps you are listening to the wrong message or messenger." She paused. "This is so tiring. We must get this over with."

TJ was not sure what she meant. To him she seemed to be justifying lying—duplicity without admission of anything—the new political double-speak. Fuck that.

"What do you know about Bolstoy's club called Clutch's, Double D or Tobias Tobelokov, Toby, the other man on the boat that Bolstoy sent to pick you up?"

Mrs. Palmroy shook her head. "If we are done here, and I do believe we are, I would like to rejoin the others Agent Alvarez."

TJ nodded. "I'm sorry, but I must insist you wait here while I consult with Agent Swanson."

Carl was waiting with the others in the dining area. When TJ entered, they moved up into the Captain's control room.

"Anything useful, Romeo?"

"Not much. According to her, their relationship with Bolstoy's business. Her father's investment firm, which she and her husband took control of, invests his money. She claims they investigated him and he's clean. She also threatened to sue us. If she knows anything, I doubt we'll be able to get past her lawyers in time to be of any help. What did her husband say?"

"Pretty much the same crap. Hardy called before I could start my inquiries. Seems our boy Toby showed up in the Bahamas. A couple agents captured him with the help of Blakely Carmichael, who, by the way, claims she is a double agent. For whom is not exactly clear. Our agents believe after she aided in his capture, she also aided him in his escape. Both have disappeared."

"Hardy also informed me we must release the Palmroys and guests. He received a call from the secretary. Somehow, the big nuts in Washington knew about our venture, probably from the Coast Guard Rear Admiral or some other agency. The president gave the order." TJ started to speak. "I know this is a hot pile of shit. We are told this is a top priority investigation, a matter of national security with the brass balls pulling out all stops. Then this. Fucking pisses Hardy off. Goes double for me."

"What about the *BolsToy*, Bolstoy and Captain Jokovich and crew?"

"Hardy says nothing was said about them. We'll take them into custody, but, with regards to the ship, Captain Conroy and crew have been ordered by our director to stand down and resume their normal duties, which creates a quandary with regards to this vessel. Hardy left it up to me. I have no fucking clue about what to do with it?"

"Can it be disabled? Make it where it can't move. Leave the crew on board."

Carl scratched his unshaven chin, TJ heard the rasping sound, reminding him that he had not been home, seen Deane, showered or shaved in over twenty-four hours himself.

"I need to ask Captain Conroy about this. Maybe he can give us something useful. Meanwhile, you may as well bring Mrs. Palmroy back to join the others. I'll have Captain Conroy have a guardsman or two escort them ashore."

TJ and Carl need not have bothered. Mrs. Palmroy was with the others when they came down.

28

Great Exuma, Bahamas

The weight of Tobey bouncing on his neck became unbearable. Jake heard him moan then start to fidget. He stopped, tilted him, he slid off onto his feet, then crumpled. Thomas helped hold him upright in a sitting position., while Jake pulled Tobey's belt out of his pants, slid the ends through two belt loops and wrapped them around both wrists and buckled them together. He used his own belt and a strip torn from the bottom of Tobey's shirt to gag the mumbling, rugby full back sized captive. Jake was winded, bent over, straightened. "Go get the car and meet me at the Marina loading ramp."

"Jake, he may not be alone. I think we should stay together."

"We have to chance it. If the police come, the shit will hit the fan."

They heard the sounds behind them growing. Thomas didn't like this. The Bahamian authorities may know about the earlier incident and, as incompetent as they seem, they would like nothing better than locking up expats. He took off running, cutting his way through the vegetation, hurtling the low fence behind the long, low concrete building which housed numerous shops, tourist traps and a store that sold alcoholic beverages. He stopped to catch his breath, to check Jake's progress.

The dim lights and the uneven concrete surface made walking difficult. Pushing an unwilling, semi-conscious resisting force was almost impossible.

"Listen Tobey, if the police catch up to us, I may be in trouble, but you'll be in far deeper shit. We need to pick up the pace."

Didn't seem to faze him.

Jake was listening, watching for anything out of the ordinary in their immediate surroundings. He smelled Tobey's acrid sweat-infused muskiness, mixed in with the smell of the not-so appetizing smells of dead creatures of the sea, gasoline and diesel, hints of beer and sweet alcohol concoctions, whiffs of the bile-inducing stench of vomit. He heard approaching sounds of others behind them, the creaks and groans of the boats offshore tugging at their moorings. There was a slight breeze, lessening from the dying day. Not far off came shrieks of laughter and shouts of merriment. The sounds grew louder as he approached the docks out from the Georgetown Inn.

Two coupled revelers, their backs to them were walking toward the sound of the band at the inn. Jake felt conspicuous, scared someone would look around and see his unsightly muffled prisoner. He couldn't help but feel eyes bearing down upon them. Lights had come on along the dock, soon they would be where everyone at the inn would be able to see them.

Tobey decided to make a break for freedom. The revelers heard the slap of his shoes coming toward them. They turned to look, just as Jake caught Tobey's bound hands, wrenching him back. The surprised revelers' faces flashed shock. The women's faces contorted with horror when they saw Tobey's gagged mouth. The men grabbed their partners and they all started running toward the inn.

Jake shoved Tobey harder, wanting to get by the inn, two more blocks to where he hoped Thomas would be waiting. By the time he sensed then heard the noise from behind him it was too late. The jolt reawakened an old memory from his Army Ranger days when he had been tasered as part of a training exercise. It hurt then and hurt like hell this second then third time. He fell to his knees with the initial shock, then fell face forward with the second, his muscles spazzing. The third time jumbled him totally.

He tried to see who had done this. His mind was trying to formulate an answer as the pain slowly subsided. Who? Blakely? Who else? His head hurt. He registered the warm wetness of blood. The images wavered, someone leaned into view—Thomas. Was that earlier? Time seemed to stand still. Thomas drug him up, half-carried him. They stumbled away. Voices echoing around them.

"I knew I should have stayed with you," Thomas said once they were safely in the car. "How did she get a second taser?"

Jake was feeling his head, saw the blood on his hand. He checked his pocket. The Judas hug and kiss. "Seems Blakely is a woman of many faces and talents," Jake croaked, feeling like he was on a storm-tossed ship.

"Where could they have disappeared to? I would have seen them had they left by auto. I was in the only moving vehicle. Had to be by boat. That means they are out there on one of the boats. Too bad we can't muster a search," Thomas said. He looked over at Jake messaging his neck. "Many of the Georgetown Inn revelers were coming toward you. Someone alerted them. Must have seen you with Toby, then witnessed the flash of the taser arc when you were tasered by Blakely. You all right? Do you need medical care?"

"Go by the house," Jake said, wishing he felt better. "I need to search her shit. Doubtful, but maybe she left something we can use. Hardy's going to be pissed." He was dazed and puzzled. Seemed Thomas left something out. If only he could remember. He needed to find Toby and Blakely. How had Toby gotten here so fast from Miami? Blakely's look, like she knew him. Damn his head hurt.

"Yeah. He won't be the only one. Rick, Alec and who knows who all will be pointing their fingers at you. Me too. This could get ugly."

Hardy didn't say much when Jake relayed the news. Jake thought he had lost the connection.

"Thomas thinks there is going to be an investigation."

"Already is. The car off the road with no one inside and a hazmat team probe of the car and the quarantine boat has created a diplomatic problem. The prime minister has demanded answers from our state department. Blakely's disappearance will bring more questions with no satisfying answers to give. Hopefully, she will turn up. Seems doubtful. You're right, how did Toby get there so fast? Had to be by air. It is odd she would taser Toby, then help him escape. You say she looked like she may have recognized him?"

"Everything is fuzzy right now, but yeah, seems she did."

"We need to find them."

"Thomas and I are headed to the house. Perhaps Blakely left something useful behind."

"This thing about her claiming to be a double agent. We underestimated her. You need to get your things out of that house. Thomas..." The call was on speakerphone. "...you two need to get to Thomas' boat and stay there."

"Maybe Jake and I need to take a fishing trip."

Jake spoke up. "That may look suspicious. Ned will be coming Monday. I need to have a report for him. I want to find Tobey and Blakely."

"Thomas, you know anything about St. Louis?"

"Some. Once did an investigation there when I was with the bureau. Why?"

"I think maybe you would be the best choice for investigating Blakely's background and ties to the Russians. Less chance of alerting whichever agency she may have been an agent for. You interested?"

"Yes sir. My job is pretty much complete. My boss didn't sound enthused about letting me stay here until the end of the year. I was supposed to leave Wednesday. Probably be best if I went there sooner. Jake could stay on my boat."

"Good. I'll see how soon we can book you a flight out of there. From this point on report to Agent Swanson in the Miami Field Office. Jake the heat is going to fall on you. If I pull you out now your use to us in this op will be finished. You sure you want to stay?'

"Rick will be the number one suspect. He will blame me. The blame for Blakely's disappearance will be there whether I stay or leave. Leaving will make me look guilty to the authorities. I need the job. I'm staying unless Ned fires me, which is a real possibility, especially with what has happened between Rick and me. I feel responsible for letting Tobey and Blakely get away. If they left by water, there is a good chance the Bahamians are involved. I want to see what I can find out."

"We all dropped the ball with regards to Tobey and Blakely. Ok. Stay. Talk to Ned. Act normal. Go to work. If it starts to go sideways, Swanson will give you a heads-up."

"Normal? Wish I could feel normal."

"Leave Blakely to us. Get back with Swanson after you get settled in. That goes for you too Thomas. Check your messages for flight information. Let Swanson know if anything else happens."

Hardy was reeling from the earlier call from Homeland's Secretary. She asked him about the operation. He told her everything that happened to date. He wondered why she herself was talking to him directly instead of going through the undersecretary. Why his reports had not been given to her? Perhaps they had, he dared not ask. Political pressure, he had to have Carl release the Palmroys and guests.

Carl was as upset with the news as Hardy was.

"The news' rumor is the president is going to replace her and others. The head of Justice is under fire. More heads are on the block. Congress is issuing more subpoenas, and the Democrats are pushing and threatening, hoping to finally have the votes. The president out for blood. More talk of a government shutdown—too much partisan politics ruining everything. Good thing this is my last rodeo."

"May be my last as well. I don't intend to leave under a white flag. I'm sending Thomas to do more background on the Carmichael woman. I've instructed Jake to distance himself from the investigation and get on with the ESI work. He needs to steer clear of his old housemate. ESi's boss is coming Monday. Jake thinks he might get canned. Who knows we might all get canned? I hope he doesn't end up in a Bahamian jail. State might not get him rot, especially if there is a government shutdown."

"While you're checking on Toby's flight and Blakely connection, I need you to book Thomas the soonest flight possible to Little Rock. Send him the itinerary. Tell him to take ground transport from there under someone else's name. You are now in charge of our end of the operation. Follow up with the people you have in custody before someone pulls the plug."

"What about the *BolsToy*?"

"I'll have to think on that. I'm tempted to sink it, make a reef out of the damn thing. Take Bolstoy, Jokovski and crew in for questioning. I was going to sneak home for Christmas then head to Cuba. My wife will be pissed. I may have to rethink our strategy. I have gone dark as far as anyone who asks should be told. No normal channels of communication – code-com, if possible, from now on. Anything actionable, take action. I'm turning everything over to you, keep a close eye on Harper and Devereaux. Don't let them become the fall guys. And don't you become the fall guy. Watch your step; I think someone, or somebodies, are trying an end run, just as we suspected would happen."

"Don't worry about me. Be careful in Cuba. You may be the one state lets rot if you are caught, especially, like you said, if there is a shutdown."

29

York County, SC

Bud Jenkins was watching Lisa Guthridge on his monitor. Her tall, lithesome appearance in clothes had been deceiving as he had suspected and hoped. She showered and lay down on the bed without bothering to cover herself. Even lying on her back, her pert breasts stood out like two snowcones. Her waist was that of an athlete, firm and toned. She was a true blonde, her pubic hair trimmed into a heart shape. Must have a lover; no woman would shave herself like that unless she did. No, mention of a significant other in her vitae. No matter, he doubted that person would be following her here.

His voyeurism was interrupted by an incoming message: *Russians failed in attempt on Harper man. Russians pose no future threat. Do you wish further action?*

Damn. No word from Pietr about the failure. Maybe they weren't the only team. *Observe only for now. May be another team.*

The Guthridge woman would be leaving tomorrow. Jenkins looked forward to her return. She had verbally accepted their offer. The project was a go. Tindal would be putting pressure on him to take care of the Harper man. Perhaps he needed to put a backup plan in motion. Time to work on that later. For now, he was going to enjoy the view and dream about this lithesome creature's return.

Lisa lay there staring up at the ceiling. She was tempted to look at the tiny camera her sweep had indicated was in the recessed vault. Instead she decided to put herself on display. The Jenkins man had been visually undressing her since her arrival. She would play him, make it easier to learn his secrets. Mark would not like it. Maybe she was fooling herself into believing their relationship was more.

She wondered who this Harper man was. She had overheard Jenkins mention his name, only to be cut off by Tindal at dinner. She would ask Mark about him once out of here tomorrow.

30

Great Exuma, Bahamas

The house was dark. Jake went around to the basement door. Thomas entered the front door. He turned on the basement stair light, waited for Jake in the kitchen. Everything in the kitchen and living areas were the same mess as they had been when Jake was here before. He looked, her clothes and toiletries were still here. Tonight's events showed no signs of having been planned. He washed his hands and the blood off his head as best he could since the bathroom didn't have a mirror. It was merely a scratch. No more fresh blood showed when he dabbed it with toilet tissue.

"All her stuff is still here. She must have been as surprised as we were by Toby's appearance. You think she may be planning on coming back here?" Jake said to Thomas. Thomas was seated on the sofa, Rick's laptop on his lap.

"Doubt it."

He hurried to his room and started packing his things. When he picked up his other pair of tennis shoes a note fell out. *Jake call this number,* was all it said.

"Hey Thomas," he said coming back into the living room, "have a look at this." He tossed the note onto the laptop whose screen saver picture was of Blakely on a beach in a bikini.

Thomas picked up the notepad page and read it.

"Nine eight five is a Louisiana area code. My children live there," Jake said.

"You can have Homeland check the number. We need to hit the road."

Once they were back on Queen's Highway, Jake used one of Thomas' burner phones to call the number placing it on speakerphone. It was a robocall recording.

"Mr. Harper, this is your last warning. You and your amateur friends are creating problems which must stop immediately, otherwise it will get extremely personal. We know about your farm with the cute neighbor's daughter taking care of the animals. We also know where your children live. We have sent you a little show of our intent. Do not doubt our ability. We are watching you. I repeat, this is your last warning."

"What the fuck do they mean they have sent me a little show of their intent?"

"I don't know, Jake. We need to let Swanson hear this. I think you need to do this before you get in touch with your ex-in-laws and kids and the neighbor watching your farm."

"Shit. Fuck. Joanna's folks and I haven't talked since the funeral, which didn't go so well, my children stopped taking my calls shortly afterward."

"I don't know, Jake. Maybe Swanson will have some advice."

"Pull over as soon as you can. If only I could get my hands on those bastards."

Jake had Thomas place the call to the switchboard. After several relays, he reached Swanson then handed the phone to Jake. Jake asked for Thomas Alvarez, instead Swanson came on.

Swanson sounded surprised by Jake's call. Jake heard voices in the background, one was TJ's. He asked to speak to him, only to hear Swanson tell everyone to give him privacy.

"Agent Harper, you have been instructed not to speak to any other agent unless given permission. Permission to speak with any agent here is denied."

"Agent Alvarez is a personal friend and–"

"Especially Agent Alvarez. Agent Hardy's explicit order. Now what can I do for you, son?"

Jake wanted to tell him to kiss his ass. He had to fight to keep his emotions in check.

"Agent Harper, did you have something to talk to me about? Agent Hardy filled me in concerning your situation. I take it you are not calling regarding Agent Devereaux' flight?"

"Agent Devereaux and I just left the house I had been sharing. While there I discovered a note in one of my shoes." He read the note to Swanson, trying hard to not sound angry or unsettled. I need to call my family and my neighbor to warn them, possibly go home to do so personally.

Swanson hesitated briefly. "Perhaps this warning event has already happened. Could be what happened today,"

"And if it hasn't? This is my family and friends."

"If I were to give approval for you to do this, you would lose your job with ESI, podna. There is no way we can allow you to compromise your participation in this operation. As far as Homeland is concerned, you don't exist. Let me see what I can do. Meanwhile, stop all actions and simply concentrate on your ESI position. Let them see you have taken this threat seriously. How does that sound?"

"I don't like it. I will wait to hear what you say can be done. But, with all due respect, I won't wait long. As I said, this is my family and friends. Anything happens to them then there will be hell to pay for all responsible."

"That sounds like a threat son."

"No sir. I don't make idle threats."

"Put Thomas on."

Jake handed Thomas his phone and exited the car. He walked over and looked out over the bay. The moon light winked in and out of some wispy clouds. Jake was torn. This was not some foreign enemy threatening his country and way of life, this was too personal. If anything happened to them, because he failed to act, he wouldn't want to live with the guilt. It would be, kill or be killed.

Thomas came and stood by Jake.

"Agent Swanson has delayed my flight until Monday. That gives me time to close things down and inform my boss/friend of my taking time off."

"And keep an eye on me."

"That too." Thomas didn't tell Jake Swanson said if the heat came down for the Russian's deaths and Blakely's disappearance, they would be on their own. He would do what he had to do.

Jake looked over at him. "You know if I decide to leave, there is nothing I won't do to make that happen. I like you Thomas. If it was your family and friends, I wouldn't stand in your way."

"I know. You need to ask yourself, why you? Only you. This seems personal. If I were you, I'd be wondering if someone has singled you out. All along. Blakely, the Russians, possibly Tobey. Have you thought about that?"

"Yeah. And I can't think of why they singled me out. I was a nobody. A former soldier whose only threat since leaving the military was my ex-wife and my financial situation, which led me here. My ex-father-in-law once threatened me, but he wouldn't threaten me with doing harm to mine and his own family. I can't think of any reason for it being personal. But it is."

Thomas figured he might could slip away without being noticed. It would have to be just him. "You know we may be left on our own if there is a government shutdown. My first inclination is to get off this island. How, is the problem? I don't think the two of us better go to my boat. I could possibly get one of my neighbor boaters to give us a berth, but I would hate to be seen coming or going from there."

"What about getting someone to move your boat to another location. They could pick us up at another dock, take your car and get back to their boat."

"And what about tomorrow? All boats, coming and going must log in or out with the authorities. Best to wait until daylight to see if the police get involved. We need to stay out of sight for tonight. Maybe this will blow over or Blakely will show up."

"And what if something happens to link us to the Russians' deaths?"

"There is no reason for them to be looking at us. Our immediate problem is finding somewhere to stay out of sight tonight."

"Maybe Mitch would let us stay at his apartment for tonight. Doubt the police would look there. Besides, if this does blow over, I maybe can stay there until Ned comes and I find out whether I still have a job."

"You willing to bet your freedom on that?"

"Unless you can think of an alternative. He hates Rick and wasn't too fond of Blakely. That's where I'm going. You think of something else, let me hear it."

31

Miami, Fl

"How we going to handle this?" TJ asked Carl.

Carl's face was mottled, his forehead knotted, he kept alternating hands to swipe at the sweat which had continued to drip off each time he made a swipe. The coast guard vessel had left with Palmroy and his guests. Colonel Bolstoy and Captain Jokovski had vehemently protested the restraints and their impending removal from the vessel. They stood at the other end of the runabout's launch pad like two scolded children, incredulous that Carl threatened to scuttle the ship and send them to Guantanamo unless they shut the fuck up.

"You go with Mick and son in their vessel and take Captain Jokovski with you. I'll take Bolstoy and his crewman on their vessel. From the marina, you'll take the captain in your truck, and I'll take my two in my vehicle back to the field office." He twisted from side to side. "What's with you? You stand there not so much as a single drop of sweat and I feel like I've been in a sauna."

"My Cuban or Afro blood I guess. Maybe age helps."

Carl nodded like he agreed. "Think maybe I'll head back to Montana or somewhere out west when this is over."

"We going to let Mick and son go free?"

"Doubt they know anything. I'll put the fear of God in their head. That should keep them quiet. Not that it really matters since Palmroy and friends are loose. Did the crewman help you disable the ship?"

"Yeah. But anyone, particularly Mick and son Gary, could fix the problem I would bet."

"You're right. We could hold them for a few days without charges. Then the shit will really hit the fan, if it doesn't before then. Their family and employees will create a stink. Guess I'm going to have to use news' contacts to create a major crime bust story." Carl felt something was wrong with him and the op. Another one of his premonitions. Often his gut instinct was right. "I need some air. What say we load up and go where some air is moving. November and still too hot."

TJ looked out the back bay. The sun had disappeared, gold and rust-streaked clouds stretched over the horizon. Soon it would be dark. The air was not as hot, the wind dying. He looked more closely at Carl. "You sure you okay man? It's really not that hot."

"Never been much for the water. I'll be all right once we get on dry land and back to the office." He wiped his brow with his open palm, his round face scowling like he had eaten something bad. "We need to stay on high alert. Who knows how many others have heard about our little maritime adventure? We can't afford to let any more of these fuckers get away. The director is about ready to pull the plug."

TJ helped Carl load the reluctant Colonel Bolstoy on his runabout, then he shepherded the crewmate to the helm and watched as they slid back out of the rear launch area, Carl seated in the rear directly behind the colonel. It took some prodding to get Captain Jokovski to join Mick and his son Gary on board their boat. The son eased off from the *BolsToy* and was pulling around to the Marina side when TJ and his crewmates heard a sharp crack echoing across the bay. Before he could react, another crack sounded off, the captain slumped forward, his head having exploded like an overripe melon. A piece of his skull slid across the boat's deck ending up inches away from TJ's face after he dove off his bench seat. Gary and Mick had dropped down, their faces masked by horror, eyes darting from TJ to the captain whose body slid to the deck, unseated by the rocking boat.

"Stay down!" An unnecessary order, Gary and Mick were paralyzed. No way would they have moved even if he had ordered them to abandon ship. TJ unsheathed his scoped rifle, then moved forward, crawled over the captain, reached over Gary, switched the boat off. He took the cap Gary had been wearing and slid it up above the transom, nothing. The sounds of other boats could faintly be heard, competing with the drumming of his heartbeat and the slap of water against the side of the boat. He eased back from the captain's seat, pulled his scope into focus using the backrest for support. He focused in on the direction the shots sounded from. He thought he saw movement from the top of the marina, a brief glimpse, then gone. He turned his attention to the other boat. The runabout was rocking in the waves halfway to the marina. No sign of life. TJ had heard only two shot retorts. He wondered if anyone on the other boat had been hit and who that might be.

The assassins most likely had skedaddled. He stepped in a crouch over Gary and slid into the captain's seat, restarted the engine and eased the throttle forward. Keeping his head as low as possible, he maneuvered their boat forward keeping the runabout between their boat and the marina. He cut the throttle letting the momentum carry their boat forward, turning the wheel, so they bumped alongside the other boat. TJ reached out and grabbed hold onto the edge of the other boat locking them together.

"Carl, it's TJ, you okay?"

"I'm not hit, if that's what you mean. The colonel has a gaping wound just above his heart. He may bleed out if he doesn't get medical help immediately. We have a radio on board, need someone to radio for help. I've got my hands full trying to stop the bleeding."

Remarkably Mick stood on shaky legs, climbed in the other boat and Gary slowly responded to TJ's order to hold onto the other boat. TJ took his rifle and jumped up and over into the other boat to help Carl.

Carl said in a hoarse shout, "Notify the Coast Guard—do a closed-channel 911 emergency request, air-vac needed immediately. Tell them to get Captain Conroy back here asap." He turned to TJ, who had laid his rifle down, taking over compressing Carl's blood-soaked shirt against the wound, "Captain Jokovski?" TJ looked at Carl's red pock-marked with ancient wounds, flour-white stomach and torso then up to his face. Carl had glanced into the other vessel.

"Damn. My gut said something bad was about to happen. This whole op is fucked."

TJ watched Carl, half-listening to Mick's terse demand for medical response for a gun-shooting emergency.

"This goina bring the local police and news crews." TJ said.

"Like I said, this op is fucked." Carl turned to Mick talking to Captain Conroy and said, "tell him to hurry."

Carl turned back to watching TJ holding tight his bloody shirt on what was Bolstoy's sucking wound with one hand and applying pressure to the back-exit point with another shirt part with the other. The blood pool was starting to thicken on the once-white boat deck. "Could you have made these shots?" he asked TJ who tilted his head up to look at him, his handsome face contorted with thought.

TJ shook his head. "No. It was two shooters with spotters."

What makes you think that?"

"The shots too close together, over water with a breeze, each shooter was an expert, but not possible with amount of time for a lone assassin."

"Military reports testing a new scoped rifle with auto-adjusting capabilities."

"Sound signatures were different. It was two and two, from top of marina."

Carl turned and stared at the marina. Only then did he notice the numerous boats near them and gathered on the docks. Most had their running lights on, twinkling as the boats bobbed up and down making his unease more acute. "Did Captain Conroy give an ETA?" he asked Mick who had been listening to TJ's analysis.

Mick shook his head. "You want me to radio back?"

Carl hesitated. He needed to ask Captain Conroy if Palmroy or guests had used their cellphones. He would have to wait. "No. Seems others have already heard. Mick and Gary followed Carl's nod to the onlookers. "Who has access to the roof of the marina?"

"There's an access door for maintenance. Sometimes the employees go up there for a smoke break."

"Not likely a stranger would know about that, would they? You and your employees have some explaining to do. You two will be held for questioning by the locals. You are to say nothing to the police or the news nerds. If you do, I will have the feds throw the book at you. You will tell your employees nothing. Got it?" He looked from one to the other. They nodded.

Mick asked, "what should we say?"

"Tell the police nothing. This is federal. Tell your employees the same. Do it now. Radio whoever is in charge at the marina."

Mick did, adding a threat of firing if they did.

"Now, what I want to know is how much do you know about Colonel Bolstoy's business?" Agent Alvarez Mirandize them. TJ did each one. Carl did the crewmate. He sat on the deck, head in hands. He nodded his head when asked if he understood.

"The books from the marina will be confiscated and gone over with a fine-toothed comb, as will all your personal emails, bank accounts and your places of residence. If there is anything you know," Carl paused to let that sink in, "I may be able to help you out. Lawyering up and not cooperating won't make me or my employer happy. You won't like what will happen to you, that I guarantee. Speak now of your own free will or suffer the consequences. Who wants to go first?"

Mick and Gary stared at each other. Gary shook his head, his father hesitated, then said, "Mr. Bolstoy has had numerous foreign guests coming and going over the last year, most not very friendly. Two weeks ago, two military looking men met Captain Jokovski and one of the earlier guests at the marina. They went to the top of the marina and were up there for more than an hour. When they came down, Captain Jokovski told us Colonel Bolstoy had asked for quotes on upgrading the equipment mounted up there. As far as we know there is nothing wrong with the equipment and these people didn't look like the type to do that work. Like I said, they looked like jarheads, clean-cut, straight-backed, very fit looking. They conversed in a foreign tongue, sounded Hebrew to me. We felt it strange he would bring in outsiders for the work. That is part of our responsibility and Mr. Bolstoy had not said anything to us. That is all we know. We just handle the marina, other people's business is none of ours, Mr. Bolstoy makes that clear to every employee.

Carl stared at Mick the whole time he was talking. He seemed to be telling the truth. Military type? Foreign maybe? Hebrew? Seems, Captain Jokovski and Colonel Bolstoy had become a liability.

"Did any of the guests aboard the Bolstoy look familiar? Have they been to the marina?"

Gary spoke up. "We have lots of people coming and going. This is a busy marina. We could lose our jobs for talking to you."

"Son you may not have a job anymore unless it's making license [plates or such in a federal pen for obstructing a federal investigation."

"Who is going to protect us and our families from these people? Dad and I have families to think of."

"You might want to ask yourself who is going to care for your families if you are in prison," Carl retorted. "You and Bolstoy's other employees have become my guests and will remain so until I am satisfied you have provided me with the right answers to all my questions."

The onlookers were staring up, TJ looked and saw the chopper descending toward them from the mouth of the bay. Coming from shore was the sound of sirens. The cavalry had arrived. Within minutes a cage-like metal sled descended from the chopper and Carl had Mick and Gary help the guardsman load Colonel Bolstoy into its cradle. Carl got on the radio and had the message relayed to the helo to lower the basket once more. They loaded Captain Jokovski's body. He told the person on the other end to take the two men to the coast guard station.

"We need to save Bolstoy if at all possible," Carl said. "Keep his presence in house." The chopper disappeared. They motored the two boats to the dock. Captain Conroy returned, cleared the way. A Miami Dade patrol boat came alongside. Numerous police and emergency personnel were anxiously waiting on the cordoned off marina dock. Carl reminded their three in-custody men of his directive not to speak to anyone. He went on board the patrol boat.

"Do you know if the Palmroy's or any of the others used their cell phones after you left?"

Captain Conroy turned to his second in command and told him to ask the crewmen guarding their guests about any cell phone usage and what may have been said. He was back within minutes saying Mrs. Palmroy talked on her phone and seemed very agitated. One crewman said he didn't hear what was said. Another said he heard Agent Swanson and Alvarez names as well as Bolstoy and Jokovski,. He said when she noticed him, she switched to a foreign language he couldn't understand. Captain Conroy and Carl looked at each other.

"Have that crewman get with a language expert. May be the break I need to allow me to bring her in for questioning," Carl said. The second hurried off to get the crewman.

"What about the director's orders?" Captain Conroy asked.

"This incident changes everything. Contact your commander and ask what he wants you to do. That will cover your ass If he asks about the crewman I'm bringing with me, tell him I gave the order."

Carl and TJ went on the dock and talked to the detective in charge. The detective stared at them. TJ wasn't sure if it was Carl's exposed, pock-marked torso, or the drying blood covering them. He seemed unsure what to do when Carl told him to keep the area secure, along with all employees and possible witnesses. Detective Smit wanted answers.

Carl called the commissioner, explained the situation and how he wanted the investigation handled. He handed the phone to Smit. Smit looked at the phone coming from Carl's blood-smeared hand, reluctantly he took it and listened as the commish told him to comply. Smit's round Irish face was beet red when he returned Carl's phone. He turned and strutted off, barking commands to the policemen in his charge.

"Smits' a hardnose. He'll go to his commander, who will go to my commander. The pot will boil over. My name will be shit." TJ said matter-of-factly.

"You worried?"

"Two things worrying me at this moment—seeing you shirtless and my wife. She has tried to call me several times and texted me demanding I call her. She has never done that."

Carl flexed his chest, making each breast bob up and down. Sexy huh?"

"Not by a long shot."

"Guess I need to get cleaned-up and put a shirt on. Might settle some nerves around here. I'm going to commandeer a police van and load up our guests. Go clean yourself up and call her. I wish I could say go home."

"I wish that were possible. She knows and would never ask." TJ went to find the bathroom. He wished he had another change of clothes. Vomit had ruined one set and now blood another. Deane would not be happy. He worried about her urgency. If only he could head home.

He looked in the mirror, not expecting how macabre the person, that was reflected back at him, appeared. No wonder people were gawking. After a brisk scrubbing of the blood off hands, arms and face, he called Deane's cell.

"I'm sorry. I was incommunicado. Why the urgency?"

"Did you not see the calls from your mother and brother? We've all been trying to reach you. Some calls have been coming to my private number and your mother's phone. Threatening calls. One claimed you were dead meat. Others said we were being watched. Leon has posted his men in the neighborhood, watching our houses, accompanying us when we leave. I called your commander, he told me not to worry. He would look into it. He let me know you were okay. Leon tried to get me and your mother to go to his house. We both refused." Deane said this in her no-nonsensical way. TJ heard no sense of panic or fear. Raised in the Hood makes you that way.

"I'm sorry. I wish I could've been there. You need to be careful. These might not be idle threats. Keep my riot gun in reach. And keep your 38 loaded. And with you at all times. Shades drawn, lights dimmed, keep away from doors and windows. I will deal with mama and Leon. I will be there as soon as I can. I may have to move you, so pack your bags and mine also."

"I don't want to leave here, TJ. Isn't there some other way?"

"I wish there was. These bangers have already killed one, maybe two of their own, another may be dead as we speak. They mean business. Be ready, I'll be there in less than half an hour. Tell Leon. Gotta go darling. I'll be there as fast as I can."

32

Great Exuma, Bahamas

Mitch, Kendall, Amy and friend Nick came home from Georgetown later than Jake had hoped. Jake and Thomas had been waiting, parked out of sight. Amy seemed excited to see them, the others not so much.

"Blakely's missing," Mitch slurred, "Alec said she was with you. Rick is pissed, says he's going to kick your ass." He grinned. "Whoa dude, is that blood on your clothes? If that is from the whore bitch? I hope you did her good."

Jake looked down and noticed splotches of blood on his dark blue knit shirt and dark grey cargo shorts. Other drops were on his tennis shoes. Thomas had more blood streaks than Jake drying on his dark shirt and pants.

Jake knew he looked shocked. He was trying to figure out what to say when Thomas jumped in with an incredible story.

"All three of us were down on the dock near the Governor's Inn. Blakely and Jake had just agreed he should move out of the house when some drunk or drugged out dude showed up. He attacked Jake, tried to taser him. Jake beat the hell out of him. Me and Blakely jumped in to separate them. The guy was hurt pretty badly, bloody as hell. She said she would take him to get patched up. Last we saw they were headed back toward the party. We got the hell out of there, picked up Jake's things and came here."

Jake was in awe. He looked from Thomas to Mitch, then Amy staring at him from the doorway to the kitchen. She had turned on the stereo. They couldn't've heard much if any of the story. Mitch seemed to have zoned out.

He stumbled over to the ashtray, searched its contents, found the remains of a handroll and lit up.

Jake walked over to Mitch, who half-heartedly offered him a toke. "Nah man. The reason I came here was because you've got a spare bedroom," Jake said, once more refusing a hit, followed by him having the scorched, sweet and sour smoke blown in his face. "Figured you might let me crash here until I get a chance to talk to Ned. Thomas needs a place for the night also."

Nick and Kendall went to the kitchen grabbed some beers, came back, donned their virtual headsets, plopped down on the sofa, ignoring everyone else.

"Like what's with you Thomas?" Amy asked, beer in hand, smiling at Jake making a face from the smoke. She caught the end of the conversation.

"Authorities are investigating my neighbor's boat, got the place quarantined, meth or some other drug crap. Hopefully I can get back tomorrow. I could get a room, if this is a problem."

Mitch's attention wavered. He kept looking from his friends' game play back to Jake and Thomas. "I don't know man. Kinda like having the place to myself. As far as Ned knows Kendall and Amy are staying here."

Amy spoke up, "Thomas can crash here, and Jake can take our spare bedroom for tonight."

"What the fuck?" Kendall stopped playing, Apparently, he wasn't completely tuning them out. Jake wondered what else he might have heard "I don't think so," Kendall added.

"He did us a favor. Turnabout is only fair," Amy stated.

"Whatever. Just for tonight, nothing more." He chugged his beer, banged his empty-sounding can down on the cheap, empty-can-littered coffee table and resumed the game.

"Want a beer?" Mitch asked, "Got some in the kitchen, cooler by the frig." He joined his friends on the sofa and lit up the remains of another joint from the butt-filled ashtray.

"Think I'll have one," Thomas said, "Jake? Amy?"

Amy shook her head. Jake said, "think I'll head to y'all's place, if someone will tell me how to get in. I need to make some calls, get cleaned up and crash."

"Kendall, you going to be here long?" Amy asked. He ignored her, yelling at having made a big score. "I'll go with you," she said to Jake. Looking once more at Kendall, she said louder, "I'm going to the house." No response from Kendall. He didn't even look up.

Thomas told Jake to wait a minute while he got a beer, that he needed to talk to him before he left.

Amy was asked to wait while they talked.

Jake was by the car when Thomas came out.

"Jake, I hope you aren't going to call the people you're not supposed to."

"Thomas who I talk to and about is none of your concern. I have been in the military. I know what should or shouldn't be said." Thomas started to say something. "Leave it be. Hope you get some sleep. Who knows what tomorrow may have in store? See you then. Tell Amy I'll be in the truck. Nice story by the way. Not sure if anybody heard it or believed it. Wouldn't use that one if the authorities show up. Might want to plead the fifth until we get a chance to get our story straight."

Thomas shrugged and went back inside without saying another word.

Amy had a scowl on her face when she came out. "You don't have to go with me. Kendall may think this is not cool."

"So. Like I really don't care what he thinks. I confronted him earlier about Blakely. He finally admitted screwing her. Said it was just once, like he was drunk or some bs. He's so selfish and immature. I think I'll go back to Charlotte, get on with my life."

Jake didn't say anything. They rode the rest of the way in silence. Jake worrying about his family, friends and his farm. When they got to the house, Jake asked Amy to give him a few minutes while he made some calls.

He hated calling Patrick again. His wife Molly answered. They exchanged the usual pleasantries. He asked if Patrick was nearby.

"Two calls in the same day. I'm glad you called. I've been thinking about us helping you out. We talked it over. Katie told me, twice when she went up there, some older model pickup stopped in front of your house, two guys just sat there. Said it kind of spooked her. Don't know why she didn't mention this before. Your barn getting broken into and this. Sorry, but gotta tell you Jake, I'm a little uncomfortable with Molly and Katie going up there anymore.

Business is going strong and me and Ben are both busy as hell. You got any idea when you'll be coming home?"

"Got a meeting Monday with Ned, the man I work for, could be he'll send me packing sooner rather than later. I'll let you know. I'll see about making some other arrangements, I don't want any of you putting yourselves in danger. If anyone shows up, steer clear and call the police, don't confront them."

Patrick hesitated. "Ten four. Let me know something Monday. Maybe I can think of someone to help you out, if'n you decide to stay."

"Thanks Patrick. Y'all take care."

The next call was going to be the most dreaded. He hoped his daughter, the 16-year-old they called Janie, had her same cell number. A man answered, had to be the grandfather, Francis Henry Michaels, called Hank, car dealer, pool hall owner, local Dixie mafia loan shark.

"Yeah. Who is this?" Hank snarled.

"Good to hear you Hank. I'm calling about my kids. They still up?"

"What's it to you? Don't think they want to, nor do I think it's a good idea for you to talk to them. If it was up to me that would be forever, soldier boy."

"Sorry you feel that way Hank. You still trying to blame me for what happened to Joanna. I wasn't there, maybe you should have been paying more attention and gotten her help. No. It's easier to place the blame on me."

"Fuck you, asshole. If you hadn't kept soldiering and running off overseas, maybe none of this would have happened. Your kids don't need you. Don't call them again or else."

"Don't hang up. My kids may be in danger."

"From whom? You? Only danger I can think of."

"Listen to me Hank. There are some cartels, Russian and Mexican, who have made threats to me and my family."

"You mixed up in some drug shit? I always wondered if you had something to do with Joanna's addictions. I hope these cartel fuckers don't get you before I can."

Jake could see this was going nowhere. He had no way to allay Hank's accusations without saying what he couldn't say. Drugs? That was damn sure the pot calling the kettle black. "Listen to me, Hank. Blame me for Joanna.

Maybe I should have stayed home more. But think what you will, I have nothing to do with drugs, never have, never will. But I do love my children and don't want anything to happen to them. I can't tell you why these bastards are after me. I really don't know. But the threat is real, and I need you to protect my kids. If you want to come after me, so be it. Just believe what I am telling you and guard my kids."

Hank hung up without another word. Jake sat there trying to calm down. He hoped Hank heeded his warning. What he said about feeling partially to blame for Joanna was true. She knew he was a soldier, as did Hank. Hank had bragged about Jake's military status before the marriage. Joanna's return home and eventual overdose death had sent Hank seeking someone to blame. Jake was it. He knew Hank loved his grandchildren. He would guard them. Jake had to believe this. He felt he should be there. Should have been there more than he had. The soldier's lament.

Amy rapped on the truck window startling Jake.

"You ok?" she asked. Her face was knotted with concern.

Jake opened the door and stood leaning on the door frame. She reached out and rubbed his arm. "Yeah. I'm alright. Just tried talking to my kids. Got my ex-father-in-law instead. Wouldn't let me talk to them."

"I'm sorry. I didn't know you had kids."

"Janie, Will and Becca Sue. Sixteen, seventeen and eleven. Live with their grandparents in Slidell, Louisiana. Haven't seen them since their mother's funeral over a year ago."

Amy's look turned to pity. "You lost your wife, their mother? Like that must be awful. Makes me want to cry."

Jake looked at her and closed the door. She moved into his arms, hugged him tight, rubbing his back, the human touch gave him some relief. She pulled back and before he knew it, she reached up, cupped his face and kissed him. At first tentatively, then more intensely, her tongue pushing at his teeth. He resisted only briefly, tried to pull back, she slid one hand behind his neck, kneading the stiffness, pushing herself into him, their breaths coming in nasal gusts, he felt his arousal despite his reservations. She began rubbing against him. He broke the kiss and pushed back.

"Amy..." He wasn't sure what to say.

"Don't say you don't want me." She smiled and pointed to his crotch. "Like I felt you in the truck the other night. First time I've thought about anyone but Kendall. I need this. Like can't you see. Please don't say no. I would be like so humiliated."

"Maybe I should leave. This is not a good idea. Yeah it would be easy for me to say yes. Damn right I want to, but–"

She reached up and stroked his face, her eyes imploring, smiling. "You think I'm like too young. Like maybe I'm trying to hook up with you, get back at Kendall. It's nothing like that. I haven't let Kendall touch me since before that party, after, when I started thinking about you, I fantasized… like don't look shocked, I'm old enough and this is not some schoolgirl crush. I want to have a real man make love to me. Like feel someone else inside me. Please don't say no. Like I've decided to go back home. I promise no one will ever know. Come on."

She grabbed Jake's hand, kissed it and said, "We both need this."

Jake looked at her face aglow, reminded him of his first time, Ariel, his first love before he joined the Army and she disappeared. He looked at Amy's rear as she pulled him toward the cottage door. Memories of the smell and taste of a youthful woman.

Amy's shouldn't disappoint.

33

Miami, Fl

TJ came back through the marina storage building. It was swarming with police and a few FBI agents wearing field fatigues and ball caps. Many marina employees and a few wary boat owners were huddled together in the corner outside the office, where Detective Smitt was having a heated discussion with someone in a suit and tie. TJ rushed out after flashing his credentials. Carl waited by a new-looking, dark-windowed van. TJ told him the situation at home.

"You do realize whoever did this is out there somewhere, possibly awaiting further orders to finish what they started. The calls may or may not be linked to this group. We need to get ahead of them without becoming casualties ourselves. Go get your wife and mother. Make it quick and stay vigilant. Hurry to the center. If this threat is domestic, which it very well could be, we will have to relocate. I'm thinking the coast guard base may be an option. Call when you get home, and, when you leave. Use one of the burner phones. Go."

TJ did a quick search of his truck, making sure it had not been tampered with. Seeing nothing unusual, he jumped in, peeled out, then braked hard after exiting the lot. The police had set up barricades with members of his SWAT unit in full tactical gear manning the exit. They were puzzled by his presence.

Sergeant Doherty wanted to know if he had joined the other side, meaning the feebs, as rumor had it.

"You gotta be kidding sarge. Why would I do that? Just took some time off to spend with my wife. Out here today to do a little fishing. That got fucked up when somebody shot my boat captain. Need to hurry home before Deane gets worried. Story is all over the news. You know how it is."

"Righttt," Doherty drawled. "You know Alvarez, I think you're full of shit. I find out you lied to me, and, he drew out the "and," you and I will have big problems. Capiche?"

"Would hate for that to happen, for both our sakes."

Doherty looked like he was thinking of pushing it, then waved him on through.

TJ floored his truck, the deep rumble of his souped-up V-8 resonated off the surrounding luxury condos lining the lush landscaped boulevard. A few well-heeled pedestrians, out for a peaceful, nightly stroll, some walking their coiffed dogs, glanced his way. He could only imagine their disapproval of his speeding in his not-so-glamorous truck. Shortly he hit the streets of the hood— no plants, abandoned remnants of stripped vehicles, washing machines, refrigerators and other junk, a few street walkers, hookers or druggies looking for a fix-- hood style, combat-zone USA. He could feel their eyes. Leon would have put out his watchers.

He slid to a stop at the end of his block. Just to be on the safe side, he decided to circle the block. He speed-dialed Leon's untraceable phone.

"Here bro," Leon answered and disconnected.

TJ circled wider. Not a soul did he see. It was like a ghost town. He parked in the driveway of an abandoned rental. He knew it was used for transactions. Unlike most in its shape, it was not a crack house. The yard was littered with the usual junk which helped hide TJ's truck. Not that he would have to worry. Leon would have two or more of his men inside and in strategic locations from here to the house where he would be waiting. He texted Carl, *here.*

"Shit bro," Leon said, looking at his blood-stained clothes, then clenching him and going through the hand moves ending in a chest bump. This was after his most trusted lieutenant opened the back door to let him slip in.

"Leon," their mother cautioned from her seat at the table. Like Deane, she was staring wide-eyed at TJ's clothing, but blood or no blood, bad language was not excusable.

"Sorry mama."

Deane stood back, watching the men embrace, then hugged TJ holding herself off, her big brown eyes searching his. "Your momma says she's not leaving her house. You sure we have to leave here? I've never known you to hide. Leon says he can protect us."

TJ pushed back, casting a stabbing stare in Leon's direction.

"Be ready to go in five minutes. You too, mama."

Mama shook her head, her soft eyes now hard. "I may be old, I still my own self. No threat make me leave my home. My son not goina leave either."

"Leon," TJ motioned with his head toward the den, "we need to talk."

"Bro we hear about shootout at club. Shooting at marina, not ask, see from the blood you there. These threats, no word on who making them. Some think Mexican, others Jamaican, Russian. This not normal bro. Cartels recruit from Lil' Havana, they threaten anyone on their turf. This different. The hood not got anything worth taking except dumbass kids. Only t'ing happening is our family being threatened. All dis after I tell you 'bout Double D. Dirty cop get shot, D disappear, then threats. You come here say family leave home, run. This my turf, my family too. I run my men find someone else. You understand?"

"Leon, these men experts, hired guns, expert marksmen. I know. I would have had to be on top of my game to have made those hits. I believe there are two teams. Probably military-trained snipers. They will study their targets, maybe have already done so. They goina have planned all possibilities— in, execute and exfiltrate. They goina be gone before you know they were even here. You listening?"

"Bro, you think military only way you know how to hit someone? We live with hit, be hit, every day. You forget that? No. I know you know. You run, you done."

"You willing to risk your family, mama?" TJ saw his brother's hard look and knew he was going nowhere. Not as long as he was still able to stand.

"That mama's decision."

TJ hugged his brother, hurried back to his bedroom to do a hasty clean-up and change into the clean clothes Deane had laid out for him next to the packed bags on the bed. The bed he wished he could crawl into with Deane. If only.

34

Great Exuma, Bahamas

Jake lay there, moisture rolling down Amy's forehead pooling on his chest, her hazel blue eyes turned up to him.

"Mmm. My girlfriends tell stories, I've read about other people's experiences in magazines, like I never knew what it was like. Wow. How do you know all this?"

Jake looked down at her. They were wet from perspiration and from the shower. She surprised him by stepping in while he was enjoying the warm water washing the bloody remains of the day, first from his clothes, which he wore in the shower, then from his skin, his mind slipping from thoughts of Blakely to Amy, not sure what to think of either. He had almost talked himself out of allowing his libido to overrule the guilt he was sure would follow if he gave in. Her clothing only hinted at the body which wrapped itself onto him. Her shyness slipped away as they soaped and rubbed each other. He almost lost it when his hands and her hands found the others' most sensitive parts. Their breath came in gulps. He shut the shower off, picked her up and stumbled to the bedroom, her legs wrapped around him. Guilt be damned.

"Don't you think you better go to the other bedroom? I don't need a confrontation with your boyfriend, not tonight, not over this."

She continued to rub herself on him. He could feel the sticky wetness running out of her onto his groin.

"I told you. It's like over with Kendall and me."

She slid off top of Jake, her face nestled into Jake's shoulder. He wouldn't be able to tolerate the pressure for long. The nerves in his neck were starting to send a warning. Her free hand found his tumescence and playfully rolled it in her fingers.

"He won't be home for hours. The boys will play their stupid games like forever. Tell me about yourself Jake. Like about your kids, where you come from. You were in the Army? Did you serve in the Middle East?" Her hand moved up to his chest, her fingers smearing their wetness on his chest hair. The smell of their juices mixed with the sweet aftertaste of the tropical fruit drink he had tasted on her lips and tongue when they kissed.

"Not much to tell. I grew up in Lancaster on a farm. My father and his father both had been Army veterans, so I felt it was something expected. Joined before I finished high school. Served overseas, met Joanna my ex-wife while stationed stateside, had three children, she left, we divorced, ended up with medical discharge from Army, live on family farm near York, needed money, so here I am. That's about it."

She was quiet for a moment. "How long were you married?"

"Fifteen years."

"My parents lasted ten years. You think you might try again?" She raised her head, her eyes searching his in the soft glow of the light from the bathroom. Jake twisted sideways thankful for the relief of her head from his shoulder. "You miss your farm, like I can hear it in your voice when you say it. What's it like?"

"I'm country, born and raised, don't have to pretend. My grandparents' old farm is one of the few places near Charlotte where there is no traffic or noise, except during hunting season. For me it has been my refuge, a familiar place to get away from everything that has happened. I didn't realize how much I missed it until I went back there. It takes money to be able to keep it, that's why I'm here."

"Is that because of your ex? My daddy always complained about the money he had to pay."

"Why all these questions?"

She rolled back over searching his face. He was staring at the ceiling. She wondered if she had ruined the mood. She turned to look at him, gave him a deep kiss.

When he pulled back, she asked, "has it been a long time since you had sex? Like you flooded me." She giggled. Her hand moved down to grasp him again. "Kendall thinks sex juices are like something nasty. He would have had me get a washcloth by now." She noticed Jake's frown. "I'm sorry. I sometimes say things I shouldn't. I just wondered if you think our juices are nasty, if all men like think that?" Her hand motions and talk aroused Jake again despite himself.

Jake maneuvered himself around so that he could see and taste her. Ariel, his first love had vanquished all fears of lover's sexual oral sharing as being gay. "If I can kiss you after you've tasted me, why won't you kiss me after I do you? She had asked. "It doesn't make you gay?" Their lovemaking became an adventure from that day on and Jake never thought any more about whether it had anything to do with gayness. He knew he wasn't attracted to other men and clean oral sharing ceased to be a problem with the few women he had made love to since. No woman had ever complained. Neither did Amy.

After they brought each other to a satisfying mutual climax, Jake turned to Amy who was lying beside him, her sculpted body silhouetted in the out light, "Don't get me wrong, but you best get cleaned up and go to the other bedroom. Our scent is all over us. Besides I need to get some sleep."

She sat up, her dirty blonde hair falling on her swollen breasts. She twisted around facing Jake, "I don't care. Like I don't want these feelings to end. This was like the best ever. Don't you think?"

This worried Jake. He hoped she would not cause problems. Now he was feeling he may have made another mistake. "Amy. This means more to me than anything that has happened to me, far longer than I remember and care to admit. You said there would be no strings attached. Please, just enjoy the feelings. They will be so much more when you find that special someone."

She stood up. "Maybe you could be that special someone. Don't you like me? Give it time. Like maybe I'll stay, we can see each other to find out."

Uh oh. "Maybe you should think about it. I'll think about it. But for now, go get cleaned up. If Kendall knows about this, Ned will send me packing, then what?"

"Then we can go to the Carolinas. I would love to see your farm."

"We need to take it slow. Okay?"

She frowned, smiling at the same time. "Not unless you promise to think about it. Like tell Ned to send Kendall home, then we can see each other all the time. You can teach me more. Like wouldn't that be great?" She turned back and forth leaned down and kissed him then walked into the hall and stood there continuing to smile at him. Jake got up, patted her on her firm butt and closed the door.

Oh hell. What had he done? The sex had been just what he needed. But. This was looking like it could be a problem. Could be? Not much doubt. This whole taste of paradise was beginning to look like one gigantic mistake. Swanson had told him to lay low. That looked ever more impossible.

He lay back down. Amy got him to thinking about the farm. Then it came to him. Thomas had said these attacks seemed personal. The farm. What Patrick said about the truck and those official-looking vehicles on the road. There were rumors, Thomas seemed to confirm Jake's suspicions, asshole Thurmond Tindal, former military, military intelligence, was doing something on his land for the government. Jake thought about all the fencing and security monitoring cameras being installed. Ben said the house was a monstrosity, an airstrip, with jets coming and going.

Tindal had been relentless when buying the surrounding land, pressuring Jake to sell. As far as Jake knew, he and Patrick were the lone holdouts. Some of the other sellers mentioned subtle threats from Tindal's man Bud Jenkins. They had caved, Jake hadn't and never would. Didn't seem likely what was happening here was connected to Tindal, or could it be?

He needed to dig around to find out more about Tindal and Jenkins and what kind of shit was going on on Tindal's land. Patrick knew Tindal. Was this part of Patrick's jitters. Jake thought of Patrick as someone not easily intimidated. Patrick knew all the gossip, yet he always seemed to be in awe of Tindal, never gossiping as he usually did about everyone else. Hmm.

He was dreaming about the farm when the door burst open. He reached for his nonexistent shotgun, loaded with alternate shells of birdshot and buckshot, which he kept by his bed at the farm. Kendall, followed closely by Amy, were standing inside the room, both their faces contorted by shock. Jake tried to make sense out of what Kendall was saying.

"Slow down, repeat what you just said." Jake swung his legs over the side of the bed, keeping the sheet on him to hide his nakedness. "Cut that light out." He shielded his eyes with his right hand.

"We almost got busted. They arrested Thomas Devereaux for the disappearance and presumed murder of Blakely" was what he repeated. "You were there, weren't you? That was her blood on you and your clothes? They'll be coming for you just like they did him."

"Wait outside I need to get dressed." He stood up, holding the sheet and pushed the door to behind their retreating bodies. Jake looked around for the clothes he had worn. It came to him. H washed them in the shower. Shit. He grabbed his overnight bag and dug out cargo pants and an LSU tee-shirt. Uh oh, his tennis shoes had blood on them. He put on his steel-toed work boots. Not suitable. He changed to sandals. He went to the bathroom. The clothes weren't there.

Kendall and Amy were waiting in the small living room. Kendall seemed wary like Jake might attack them. Amy had put on shorts and a blouse, her hair pulled back in a ponytail. She was leaning on the jamb of the cased-opening between the living area and the kitchen, a concerned look on her lovely face.

"Tell me exactly who came and what was said. You can sit down. I promise you Thomas and I had nothing to do with Blakely's disappearance, much less murder, if indeed anything untoward has happened to her." Jake walked over to Amy. "Do you have any coffee?"

"No. We have sodas. Would you like one?"

"If you don't mind." Jake turned and walked back to a chair and sat down. Kendall sat on the edge of the sofa, perched on the edge, ready to run Jake figured if he moved toward him. Blakely brought him a Coke and sat back on the other end of the sofa.

"I left my bloody clothes in the bathroom. They're not there now. Amy did you move them?"

Kendall looked from Jake to Amy.

"I found them and washed them. They're like in the dryer. You want them." She got up to go get them.

Kendall continued to stare at her. "Why'd you do that? They're evidence. Oh shit. You dim wit."

"Don't call me that you jerk. Probably Blakely's off like screwing someone else. You should know, huh?"

"Hey. Enough okay? Tell me what happened over at Mitch's place, how about it."

"We were drinking, playing a video game. Thomas took a shower, went to the spare bedroom to crash. Shortly two cars came rushing into the parking lot. There was banging on the door. Mitch tried to hide the ashtray and shit, while Nick went to the door. Two Bahamian police came in and asked if Thomas Devereaux was there. He came out of the bedroom and one of them handcuffed him, said he was under arrest for the disappearance and assault of Blakely Carmichael. The other one went to the bedroom and came out with Thomas' bloody clothes in a clear zip-lock bag. They questioned us. Asking if we knew this and that. Mainly about Thomas being there and what his connection to us was. Nick told them the story Thomas told us. They wanted to know where you were. Mitch told them you left to go back to your place. Nick and I said we didn't know. I didn't want them coming here, neither did Mitch. They took our passports. Said they would need to talk to us again. Nick stayed there with Mitch. I came here to check on Amy."

"Like hoping Jake had killed me or something huh?"

"Not that. I saw how you looked at him. Seemed to be in a hurry to leave with him. That's all."

"Like you thought I was going to screw him like you did Blakely."

Jake didn't like where this was likely to go. He needed to keep the talk on Thomas. "Hey. Hold on. Kendall, did they say what made them come looking for us there?"

"No. They never mentioned it." He turned back to Amy. "You need to get over that. I told you it was just once. I was drunk. You go repeating that, next thing you know the police will be looking at me."

"Jesus," Jake said, "Kendall look at me. You said there were two cars. Who was in the other car? Did they not get out?"

Kendall slowly turned his attention back to Jake. "I forgot about the other car. It was just the two of them came in. Thomas didn't put up any resistance, came out like he was expecting them, stayed quiet, left without any questions or saying he was innocent or anything. Did ya'll do it?"

"Hell no. I had nothing to do with it and Thomas didn't either. Someone is trying to frame him, me too maybe." Jake didn't want to contradict Thomas' earlier story. He had been out of it. Who would ever believe this? He needed to contact Swanson. "I need to make a call. Thomas and I will need a lawyer. Guess I better leave so you two don't get in trouble."

Amy looked concerned. "Why don't you wait until tomorrow. Like no one will be able to help you tonight. We're the only ones like know you are here."

"I can call my dad. He's friends with the prime minister. He'll know what to do." Kendall didn't sound too enthused.

"Wait. Let me make a call, if I can't get someone to help, then we'll call Ned."

Swanson answered immediately. Jake told him about Thomas' arrest and the possibility he could be next.

"Damn. I was afraid this might happen. I told Thomas. Didn't he tell you if you were arrested as far as Homeland is concerned you are on your own?" He paused momentarily. "Right now I'm up to my ears in shit on this end waiting for someone to pull the bucket out from under my feet. Now you just dumped more shit into the pool. Hate it. Yesir Billy Bob O. Hate it for all of us. If I don't drown in it, I'll figure out something." Swanson sounded like he was hyped on something, maybe just adrenalin.

"Kendall says Ned knows the prime minister. Probably will cost me my job. Then again if I'm in jail I won't have a job anyway."

"Might be your best bet. Or, check with Fluor, they should have a legal team for such exigencies. Sorry podna. I'll check to see what else can be done when this shit storm quiets down. Got to go. Talk to Fluor or Ned. Check back. Let us know when anything more happens."

Thanks for nothing, Jake thought.

Jake stood outside on the back deck. A light breeze was blowing wispy clouds past a near full moon. The crazies' howls echoed in his head. He felt and heard the pulse pounding a steady beat. Fight and flight—neither a viable option. Memories of his mill-town youthful gang days—perhaps this was the payback—as if the military debt had not been enough. He was back in a foreign land; this time the enemy a legal juggernaut he felt helpless against.

Blakely? What made them think anything had happened to her? What or who led them to him and Thomas in the first place? Had to be Rick and his cronies, or was it? How did they know where to find them? Was Thomas car confiscated because they suspected their involvement with the Russian crash and deaths? Fuck. They could be royally fucked, literally, by the British Common Law system. Prison here, according to his briefing by the Fluor security cop, was the eighth worse in the world: a single bucket in a three by eight concrete cell with two others all having to piss, shit and bathe in; high incidence of disease—HIV, AIDS, hepatitis, no telling what-all; two years awaiting a hearing. Enough to break even the strongest resistance.

Would Thomas break? Place the blame on him? Jake knew even the strongest broke under the barrage of constant interrogation. Who knows if the Bahamian authorities believed Thomas, and him, were terrorists. Maybe that would expedite their case. Perhaps Interpol would be called in. Better to be brought before an international court than the Bahamian system. Homeland would be worried, forced to come to their aide, or would they? Didn't sound promising.

He needed to know what evidence they had. The Bahamian Coconut Telegraph might be a good way to find out. Call Fluor or Ned first? No. Better to know what he was up against. Kendall should know Terrance or Yeller's number.

Jake finally persuaded him to call Terrance instead of Rodney, his first Bahamian preference.

"I trust Terrance to do more than Rodney. I hardly know Rodney," Jake argued.

Kendall continued to argue until Amy told him to do like he was asked.

Kendall punched in the number and handed the phone to Jake.

"Ya mon," Terrance answered. He was shocked to hear Jake instead of Kendall. After some laughing and off the phone Bahamian jabbering from Terrance, Jake finally got around to telling him bricfly about the problem and wanted to know if he had heard anything.

"Ya wybe sour!" he replied when Jake mentioned Blakely.

"What?"

"Rick say ya roach on her bread. Get the drift? Breakin' ho bread." He laughed at Jake's confusion. Jake felt he was probably stoned. Music, shouting and laughter could be heard threatening to drown out Terrance's voice.

"Look man. I need your help. Rick, maybe Blakely have brought some shit down on me. I need to know what the police know before I talk to them. Tonight, if possible. Will you help me out?"

The sound grew muffled. Jake held on, Amy and Kendall were staring at him. "Must be talking to someone. I'm having a hard time understanding his stoned Bahamian jive," Jake told them. Terrance returned shouting in his sing song way. From what Jake could gather some bloody clothes had been found near the docks at Georgetown and Rick had been questioned, pointed the finger at Thomas and him.

"You hear anything else let me know through Mitch or Kendall. Thanks Terrance."

Jake told Amy and Kendall what he heard.

"Like what are you going to do?" Amy looked distraught.

"He needs to leave is what he needs to do."

Jake wondered who all knew about this and what they knew. The Fluor people would certainly have heard about Blakely. Swanson was right, Fluor should have lawyers. I should talk to Charlie Davenport. Tell him about Thomas. Have him call Thomas' boss. Then I guess I should talk to Ned. "I need Charlie Davenport's number, Kendall."

"Charlie is worthless. He'll be drunk like everyone else is tonight. Call my dad. Then you need to leave."

"You think Ned is going to help Thomas? Somebody needs to be trying to help him. I don't leave anyone in the lurch if I can help it, especially people I know are innocent."

"Is he? Are you?" Kendall asked.

"You better believe it. The police jumped to conclusions based upon Rick believing something happened to sweet little innocent Blakely. As you well know Blakely is not some sweet little innocent kid. I don't know what happened to her. Last time I saw her she was going off with some other man."

Kendall's face turned beet red. He was clenching his fists. "How did you and Thomas end up with blood on yourselves? And what about the bloody clothes the police have?"

Jake shook his head. "There was a scuffle, not exactly like Thomas said. Someone attacked me, knocked me down, tasered me. Everything is a blur. Seems like I may have seen Blakely and that man hurrying away. Then Thomas was helping me to my feet. I don't know for certain whose blood was on me or how it got there. Some of it probably is mine." Jake struggled to piece his jagged thoughts together. Kendal was scowling. Amy looked like she wanted to believe him.

"Most of it I believe was from the other man. Happened in a scuffle. That was earlier, before I was hit from behind and tasered. Fortunately, I have the blood on my sneakers that can be analyzed to determine whose it might be. I'm sure the blood on Thomas will prove his innocence. But, from what I know, the Bahamian judicial system is slow. I don't want Thomas, nor myself sitting in jail waiting for them to find Blakely. So, give me Charlie's number."

Amy smiled at Jake for the first time since she and Kendall had gotten him out of bed.

Kendall saw the smile. Amy seemed to believe him. He damn sure didn't. "What about the bloody clothes found at the dock? Has to be Blakely's, since the police arrested Thomas for her presumed murder. Guess you're going to say you don't know anything about them. You were with Thomas. Makes it difficult to believe you know nothing about them or what happened to her. Seems to me you and Thomas made this all up. Can't get your stories straight."

"Kinda like your rape story, huh?" Amy said.

"Shut up Amy. I was acquitted."

"Like your dad Ned's lawyer got you off. And like I wanted to believe you. That's what's got you worried. Or is it more like because it's Blakely?"

"No. I shouldn't have ever told you. There isn't anything going on between me and Blakely. If the police come, we could be locked up as accessories. This guy needs to leave."

This was going nowhere.

35

Miami, Fl

The Homeland op was losing steam and would soon lose funding. That would take heat off Mark's own operation—one which had taken years for his team to set up. They were a long ways from knowing who all the players were. His boss was certain there was no major united effort—as of now the pieces didn't fit. Everyone was obsessed with the new technology—drones were the soup du jour. They were becoming as common in the air as houseflies, soon, perhaps as huge a threat in the water as Asian carp. His task was to prevent organized crime, international cartels from getting their hands on military capable versions. Homeland's op, at the new president's behest, had the potential to undermine his efforts. The threatened government shutdown could slam the brakes on Homeland's op.

His lovely Hispanic assistant stared down at him, outside light shimmering and outlining her gorgeous body. No underwear today, perfectly coiffed head to toe. He had his feet up on his desk, hand's clasped behind his head, staring out at Biscayne Bay. The Juarez Cartel had sent her here. She was an excellent IT operator and did whatever he asked. Anything and everything. All he had to do was tell her to bend her lovely ass over the desk or drop to her knees and she would comply. Better than his hand, cleaner than high-dollar hookers, but he had grown weary of her. He would never let her stay overnight. He couldn't trust her. Just like the bugs in his office and condo, she was another cartel tool placed near him because her bosses were paranoid, despite his hard-earned credentials. He was the money man, turning dirty assets into clean assets. Like their competitors, the Gonzalez Brothers, family members of the Juarez Cartel, were obsessed with drones. Their potential for surveillance, as weapons and material transports along the border for use in their war with rival cartels and the U.S. government agencies. They were his newest client, though they thought they had exclusive rights to his services.

"Arturo wishes to speak with you." She placed the mini tablet, which she had been clutching to her small, but perfect breasts, into his hand then left, the sight of ass, her thighs swishing when he waved her off. Mark knew she was Arturo's cousin. He'd have sent his sister if he had one.

"Arturo, how are you? Mark asked in near perfect Spanish."

Never one for pleasantries, Arturo jumped right into his concerns. "How soon we have drone?"

"Arturo. I can get you many drones like the ones you already have. But, to get the one I told you about takes time. I talked to someone close to the manufacturer. It is to be developed near Charlotte, North Carolina. This one's special—being developed for Uncle Sam. Testing should take place by the end of the next fiscal year. This threatened U.S. government shutdown could potentially slow the process down. Believe me when I say, this drone is everything I promised you. No one has anything like it."

"Need see proof. El Chapo's son expand. Must hurry. No time for bullshit. What is company name?"

Mark wasn't sure giving the name was a good idea. Arturo could fuck things up. It was enough to have to make sure Tindal Industries was on the level. Intel hinted there were covert talks happening with foreign investors. Lisa would know. Having the Gonzalez Brothers snooping around would be potentially problematic. Or would it? His other current op had become jeopardized by Homeland's op run by Agent Robert Hardy from the Charlotte office. One of his operatives was this Jake Harper, according to Lisa, a man of interest to Thurmond Tindal and his security man, Bud Jenkins. Maybe it was time to open an office in Charlotte.

"Company name is Tindal Industries. I've been thinking maybe we should set up an office in Charlotte. The heat is becoming a problem for us here in Miami. Perhaps it's time to branch out. That way I can be closer to where the drone is being developed."

Arturo was quiet. Mark began to worry. "I talk with uncle and brother. We have members in this Charlotte. I no like Chicago—too cold. Need change. We talk." Arturo terminated the call.

Mark would put Maria on locating and setting up an office in Charlotte. He needed to strike when the iron got hot. Those Russians being shot in Miami, Tobolokov and Caemichael disappearing in the Bahamas. Someone was getting nervous, getting rid of potential problems. The government shutdown seemed inevitable. The FBI and CIA would be taking over Homeland's Op. He needed to find out who was behind these seemingly disparate ends. Arturo hadn't asked about Double D. Strange. Who was Double D working for? Arturo or some other player, perhaps the Cubans? Agent Hardy was headed to Cuba. Christmas in Havana. Just what he needed. Maybe he would know something by New Years.

PART II

36

Miami, Fl

"*B*oom" was written on a business card stuck in the weatherstripping on TJ's driver-side door. Leon's tall, lanky lieutenant had been sent to retrieve TJ's truck from what should have been a well-guarded safehouse. He was about to hand it to Leon.

"Don't touch that!" TJ barked. The man jerked as if he been handling a snake and dropped the card. Everyone else froze. "Deane, I need a clean unused zip-lock and tweezers."

Holzhauser Investment Group was embossed on the other side of the card along with an address in Switzerland and other business information. Andrei Bolstoy?

He and Deane were set to leave. "I need to get a bomb squad unit sent here," he told Leon.

"No bro. They will bring other police and the newsies. That would not be good. Could become major problem. My men find out how this could be. They say no one threatening come here. They run off bag lady. She was pissing, sorry mama, relieving herself by your truck. Had to be her."

"They know who she is?"

Leon shook his head. "They try to find her."

"Leon, I need to leave. Mama and your family need to leave here also. Can't you see they mean business. The police and FBI need to investigate."

"No bro. We investigate. You know better. You can leave after my men check your truck to see it safe. No need bomb squad. Not take long. You know they could take your truck apart in less than fifteen minutes. We have dogs same as your police. Has become necessary. Young bangers getting more vicious—no longer chains, knives, guns. Everything online. How to make bombs. Not care if innocents get hurt. You go off fight in foreign streets—no realize war in streets here. People desperate. Local government want us to kill each other, have reason come here take our homes. No. You no bring police here."

TJ knew much of what Leon said was true. He saw it. They had talked about this numerous times. Homies didn't trust authority. Couldn't much blame them. Miami, one of richest cities in the world, yet so much poverty which government officials wished to hide, sweep under the rug, try to force the occupants to go away. The wealthy people's government.

"Leon, yes, I work for those police, but I live here also. Problem is our people don't trust any authority and we kill each other instead of organizing and working together to fight those who seek to push us out."

"That is what me and my homies do. We organize, protect ourselves. I hear you say we need political power. Most aren't allowed to vote. Those who can, you think they go stand in line? We no stand in lines, same as saying come on man here we are. You know this. You work for the man. Sometimes I think you begin to think like them. This our home. Mama and our families came here, they claimed it. We not give it up and leave."

"Leon this threat's not from the man. This personal. Let me take mama and your family with us until we find who's behind this."

Their mama stepped forward. "No son. Where would I go where I be safe? Leon is right, it always be this way. My parents left Cuba 'cause it worse there. This our home now. Your papa gave his life for this country, so we could be part of it. My home, children, grand babies all I have left. I not run. I know you must go. Take Deane find who do this. I not leave." She drank from her glass of water.

Leon's phone chirped. ''Truck safe now. Homies impressed by your firepower. Say back of truck stink like some street punk get sick."

TJ had forgotten about his weapon storage bin under his back seat. "My weapons better be all there."

"There it is. What I say 'bout you and the man. We not thieves. We protect what's ours." Leon was indignant. He looked at TJ with his eyes flashing. "They bring truck. Need to have word before you go."

TJ led Leon back to Deane's and his bedroom and closed the door.

"This Double D. He talk?"

"Not yet. Why?"

"Word is Mexican Juarez homs sent him here to take care of business with rich Russian. Mex cartels making move. Think cause El Chapo in custody, his business up for grabs. Forget he have son. Say hear Russians get shot. Not like Double D, he not just messenger boy. Business may not be complete. You hear what I saying? This threat to you may be connected bro. Word is the man involved. Watch your back."

"That all?"

"For now. Don't worry 'bout mama or your crib. Card got ever'body jumpy. We find bitch messenger, you see."

"Leon. Don't think I don't respect you. You good man. Papa would be proud."

"Thanks bro. Back at you. Now go. You be safe 'til you leave Hood. After that you on your own. Watch yo' back."

They embraced. TJ kissed his mama and Deane hugged everyone. They slipped out the back door went around to the side. He helped Deane in, loaded her bag and his after checking his lock box. The two men standing by frowned.

"Had to check. Watch over Leon's and my family, your families also." He did some slap handshakes, jumped in the driver's seat and hurried out the drive.

He told Deane, "lay down." She looked hard at him then reclined her seat. He reached over and handed her her .38 he had retrieved from the bedside table. "Just in case."

"Where are we going?"

"Homeland's field office."

"I'm working the late night and morning shifts at the VA. I need to go. There's talk of a government shutdown. I may be working without pay and that will cause some to stay home with the blue flu. We'll be short-handed. Are you listening to me?"

"Deane Not sure that good idea. Leon says word is those shootings today may have been government hit. That threat back there may be connected. Definitely, a warning. Very few people know I am part of the task force."

"You kidding me? Your picture was all over the television. That's how I knew you were okay. Certainly not from you calling to let me know anything. And, you know we can't afford for me to lose my job. I not going in would be cause for termination. At the very least a write-up in my jacket. No more promotions. No more pay raises. The hospital is well-guarded, especially after that recent attack at that other VA."

. "Well-guarded. Those security people some of the most undertrained, inept people in uniform. Wouldn't trust them to guard a latrine."

"We now have metal detectors and automatic, assault-proof corridor doors that lock and seal if anything happens in the whole building."

"Great. You're locked in possibly with some deranged veteran suffering from PTSD who could be better trained than all those wanta-be so-called security people then what?"

"Then I use that martial arts training you insisted I take. I still train in case you don't know. I test for my black belt next month. I think I can handle most threats."

TJ glanced over. Their eyes met. "Congratulations. No. Didn't know. That's good. Problem is, if some hired-assassin is the one, he or she will be armed, possibly strapped with explosives."

"My big hero?" She reached over and squeezed his arm. "You can't be there all the time, you know. While you were overseas…all those wounded vets at the VA… I prayed day and night you would come home not like them. Made me feel guilty. And living in the hood…Leon is right you know—it is changing and not for the better. If it wasn't for Leon, people like me and your mother wouldn't be able to stay in Little Havana."

TJ nodded. "I know. Okay. I'll talk it over with Carl. You'll like him. He's funny, kind of like an old western cowboy, imitates characters like an old rock band groupie. Knows his stuff. Spent time as a prisoner of war. I don't know much about that. Saw the scars. Know he has a bad back but keeps on keeping on, though he says this is his last rodeo." TJ had texted him, five *minutes*. "When we get there, I want you to jump out and run inside the door with whoever is waiting. I'll park and meet you inside."

Two armed men in suit and tie TJ had never met were waiting. One grabbed Deane's door, and they rushed her inside. The other came around to TJ's side; he waved him off and sped off to park on the parking deck. When he exited the elevator, the place was crawling with men and women hurrying here and there. Some glanced his way, others ignored him. He was headed for Carl's office when Mariel rounded the corner. Carl had sent her to intercept him.

"Carl said for you not to talk to anyone. Follow me." They hurried back the way she had come.

Deane was in the breakroom, Julia seated across from her. They were talking. Deane looked up and smiled when he entered. "Do you two know each other?"

"Julia's husband Dave Arando was a patient of mine at the VA. She says he's doing great."

"Thanks to your wife. He has a steady job. Been clean for over a year."

"What's going on?"

Julia's face dropped. "Carl will explain when he gets here. We were all told not to say anything, not even to each other."

TJ went to the vending machine and got two waters. He handed one to Deane, sat down, drank from the other, watching the constant parade in the corridors.

Shortly Carl came in and introduced himself to Deane, "Well little missy, if you ain't the sweetest filly I've seen all day," he said in his most-John Wayne-like-imitation. Wish I could stay and chat. If'n you don't mind I need to borrow your man for a bit."

Deane smiled and nodded. "Just don't go riding off after the bad guys with him," Deane replied.

"No ma'am. Wouldn't dare."

She turned to TJ, "Don't forget, I need to leave here in a couple hours."

TJ followed Carl down the corridor to a supply room. Carl looked around when no one was to be seen, he touched TJ and they slipped inside. He locked the door.

"May not have long. I'm sure someone noticed on the monitor, he said bumping into shelves loaded with cleaning supplies, rolls of tissue and boxes of other sundry items. TJ tried to squeeze in between some boxes on the floor.

"The shit has hit the fan. We've been ordered to stand down. There is a government shutdown. Won't be officially announced for a few more days. The president is using the up-coming Christmas break to coerce the in-coming Dems to make concessions on the border wall. Not going to happen. We've been furloughed. The NSA, FBI and CIA are here jockeying for control. I can't get in touch with Hardy. I suspect he knows or will shortly.

"Our secretary, the spineless bureaucrat, called saying she tried to get special consideration for this op in the interests of national security, but the president was unhappy with the adverse publicity created by the shooting. When I tried to reason with her saying they should see it was indeed a matter of national security, she said she agreed, but that there was nothing she could do. She has been ordered to turn the op over to NSA, who brought in the CIA, then the FBI got wind and here they are. All trying to justify a paycheck, rub it in on Homeland. We have been ordered to cooperate. For some of us, that means without pay."

TJ handed Carl the Ziploc baggie with the card inside. Carl slipped on some reading glasses. "What's this?" He flipped the baggie over and back.

"Stuck in the weather-stripping on the driver-side door."

"And you drove here with your wife in that truck? I'm beginning to think you might be mucho loco."

"Boys in the Hood took my truck apart, had their own bomb-sniffing dogs."

"Damn." He flipped the card over again. "You got to be shitting me. No fucking way. Who? Why would anyone, associated with them, leave a calling card?" He scratched his head. "Who all knows about this?"

"My brother, a few of his men. They don't tend to listen to the news, got their own sources. The card was apparently left by a woman disguised as a bag lady. She even squatted and took a piss by my truck, right under the eyes of my brother's watchers."

Carl shook his head. "Any way to find this woman?"

"If there is, Leon will find her. One other thing. Before I left Leon, he told me Double D was sent here by the Juarez Cartel for something to do about some Russians. And that the hit was made by government men. Didn't say which government."

"Curiouser and curiouser. Ms. Secretary blasted me, said the president was upset with how we were handling certain friends of his."

"Hmm. I've been thinking about those shooters. How did they know we were there? Why Bolstoy and his ship's captain. This threat. Bombers don't usually threaten."

"That's not all. Our two agents in the Bahamas have problems connected with Tobey's and that Carmichael woman's disappearances and her supposed murder. Seems some bloody clothes were found; our agents had blood on their clothing from a scuffle with Tobey. The State Department has been called."

"The thing with the hazmat team and the dead Russians there, now here, has raised eyebrows. The CIA has taken interest in not only this but in the disappearances, which I find curious. The talking heads in Washington have ordered me to distance myself from the whole thing. Puts me in a helluva position and you agents in a worse one. Not you, since you are considered part of the local task force. If I could somehow get those two out of there, I would. But the pot is about to boil over because of this shooting of our two Russian friends. Those boys could end up scapegoats unless I can pull some trick out of my ass. One of our agents is a former FBI man. The word is the feebs will be doing the investigation, maybe something can be worked out. The best thing would be if this Carmichael woman and this Tobey Tobiski, or whoever they are, were to be found alive.

"Now this fucking shutdown. I expect them to use it to put me out to pasture with a cloud hanging over my head. Not without a fight. No siree, billy bob o. Hate you're caught up in this. The Miami-Dade police commissioner is determined to keep his hand in. He says the shootings makes it a local matter. Unless the feebs invoke that national security bullshit, he may be right. Meaning, maybe you can remain in the loop. And, if they call jurisdiction because of national security, I have a good argument for not being furloughed. You with me?"

"What you want me to do?"

"Keep your cards to yourself. They may threaten us, but they don't have a case. If push comes to shove, we'll work through you as part of the police investigation. I know a few sympathetic judges, should be able to get some surveillance permits even if we lose our Homeland National Security Patriot Act rights. Not likely. Never know. Tread lightly until we see how this plays out. Assume your brother's intel is correct about Double D and government agents. I think I can get us another shot at talking to Diego. Any ideas on getting him to talk?"

TJ thought back to his earlier encounter. "Gitmo. With the CIA here, that seemed to shake up Renaldo. Could work with Diego. He seemed to be more open to talk to that woman nurse. Might be the way to go. Play the sympathy card. Think any of the female staff could handle it?"

"Rather not involve them. They're not trained interrogators. Plus, they're officially furloughed. I'm trying to keep them away from these assholes taking over here."

TJ could see Carl was feeling despair. He understood. This would be one that would gnaw at him. Like his last sniper duty, days in the bush, and no target, relief and anxiety, a sense of business left undone which could be fatal for someone else. He checked the time. Deane would be getting worried.

Deane? No bro? She might would. You shouldn't put her in this arena, he thought. Oh hell, they were desperate.

"My wife Deane's a registered nurse, degrees in nursing and counselling, works as a VA counselor, years of experience dealing with vets in all kinds of situations. Could ask her to try to get Diego to talk."

Carl was flexing his back, fatigue and discomfort etched into his pale, round face. He shook his head. "This is not some wounded vet." Carl reached to open the door.

"Desperate times call for desperate measures, was once told."

Carl hesitated. "Let me see about getting us in there without those other dickheads watching and listening."

"Get your tech to kill the feed. We can wear personal recorders."

Carl flicked his blood glazed eyes at him. "You know podna, I'm beginning to think you've done this shit before." He stuck his ear to the door. "Hand me one of those boxes. Grab one for yourself. TJ did so with difficulty due to the cramped space. Carl swung the door inward almost falling over in the squeeze. He nodded for TJ to exit first.

Deane was pacing when they entered the break room. They sat the boxes in a corner next to one of the vending machines.

"Where have you been? I was beginning to believe I was going to have to get Julia to give me a ride. Some jerk came in and escorted her out of here.

He wanted to know who I was. Julia told him I was a nurse. He had the audacity to tell me they needed more coffee at the nurses' station. TJ," she glanced at the clock on the wall, "an hour, hour and half at most, then I've got to be going."

Carl spoke up. "Mrs. Alvarez, your husband and I are in a bad situation. These jerks are here to pull the plug on our op. The dadgum government shutdown as you are aware. Anywho, TJ and I are hoping to have one more shot at saving our rears. We have a hostile here who has refused to talk to us menfolk. He seemed to want to talk to a nurse. TJ feels he may be willing to talk to you because of your qualifications dealing with vets. Would you be willing to help us out? That is, if I can get you in to see him?"

Deane looked back and forth from TJ to Carl. "I wouldn't know what to ask him. I have case files to read before I interview or counsel veterans."

"TJ will brief you if you'd be willing to give it a try."

"You could do it, Deane. I know you could," TJ added.

She looked at TJ's big brown tired looking eyes, "You sure about this? I hope this isn't some excuse you cooked up to keep me here."

"Promise it's not. Shouldn't take long." TJ's eyes bore into hers. "You go in as a nurse to check on him. By now he'll be looking for someone to talk to...if you're willing?"

Deane reluctantly nodded.

"Good. I'll go get a pen recorder and get it set up with the head jerkoff. Pardon my crudeness."

Carl rushed out of the room, leaving TJ in an awkward position with Deane. Never before had their professional lives been as intertwined as they were because of this op. "I'm sorry," TJ said. "There is no one else we can turn to." He reached out to her. She stiffened.

"I hope I don't disappoint you and Carl. He does seem like a nice guy."

"He is. Let's sit over here and I'll fill you in on Daniel Diego."

They sat down in two chairs at a corner table. "This Diego character works for the cartels. We know he came from Juarez, where he is the prime suspect for killing two men across the border. He's the one killed Buster Brown." Deane flinched at the mention of Buster's name.

TJ saw it, hesitated, reached across to rub her hand. "We don't believe that was part of whatever he was sent here to do. He's a hired killer, a cartel hitman. Leon says he came here to deliver a message, which doesn't fit. He isn't a messenger boy. Not that kind of messenger boy. Maybe that's what Leon's source meant. Without disclosing more details than you need to know, and, I'm prevented from telling you, we need to know who he came here to see or hit, his contact, how and why."

"He's been shot in his shoulder. Treat his wound, act like a caring nurse, make him think you care. I believe he'll talk. When I talked to him earlier, I made him believe I was from a rival gang and my boss thought his boss was barging in on his turf, trying to cheat us."

"Use that or tell him Renaldo and Toby talked to the feds, said they don't know him except from meeting him at Clutch's. That's an upscale biker bar. Tell him you're not sure, now that you've seen him you believe what you heard, that he doesn't look like someone who would do anything like what the feds say he has done."

"You're a trained interrogator."

Deane gave him a hard look.

"I meant counselor. Tell him anything to soften him up, to make him think you want to believe he's being framed. Hint at the feds say they're going to send him to a max, possibly Guantanamo because they think he is a terrorist hooked up with the Russian or Mexican cartels."

"You sure you want me to try this?"

"You can do this. I know you can. If not, the real nasty boys are going to take over. Diego will wish he had cooperated with us. And Carl will ride off into the sunset feeling he failed."

"And what about you?"

"I don't know. Somehow, I feel Diego may know who sent that calling card threat. I believe they are the people who he came here about. I won't feel we, our family, will be safe until they are caught."

She squeezed his hand. "I hope I don't disappoint you and Carl. No matter what, I'm still going to work after I do this."

37

Great Exuma, Fl

"If you don't mind, please take this tennis shoe and drop it off at the police station then get the hell away from there." Jake handed a Ziploc freezer bag with one of his bloody tennis shoes to Amy who brushed her fingertips against his hand as she took the bag. Her look and touch sent shockwaves up his arm. He was certain Kendall noticed.

"Don't do it Amy? We're probably already in trouble."

"Kendall, you can't like tell me what to do. You're not my boss." She took the bag, got her things to leave.

"He's not your boss. Not my boss either. I already called my dad, left a message. He'll know what to do. That damn shoe doesn't prove anything."

"You're right," Jake said. "Tucked down inside it is my explanation for how the blood got there and on Thomas Devereaux. I told them a forensic DNA test will show whose blood it is and prove it's not Blakely Carmichael's. I also said I have sent the other shoe to an independent lab in the United States which will verify my statement."

"Yeah. That will never happen. How do you think you're going to avoid arrest until then? You can't stay here. This island is too small, everybody talks."

"It's almost Christmas. If the Bahamas are like most places, nothing will happen before the new year. I don't plan to wait around until next year in some Bahamian jail. You should be glad this happened to me. Seems to me you didn't want me here in the first place."

Kendall shrugged. "I don't give a shit about Rick or you. I'm getting things done my own way. The Bahamians all think I should be running things, not Rick. They despise him. They don't understand why my dad doesn't let me run things. I've been working for him for almost ten years except when I've been in school. I know everything there is to know about how to do things."

"Maybe that's the problem—you think you know everything. My grandfather told me, "son, you can learn something every day, if you're willing and keep your mind open and your mouth shut." He was letting me help him chop wood. I was swinging with all my strength, going for the bleachers and often the axe blade bounced off the log and buried itself in the ground. He took the axe and with hardly any effort split several logs. "It's not how hard you hit, it's knowing the right place to strike, even without a sharp blade, that is the secret. Two lessons everyone needs to learn."

"You're full of shit. Sounds like you think you know everything about me. You have no idea what I know or don't know. I guarantee you I know more about ESI's business than you and Rick combined."

"Guess you don't think I can teach you anything or that maybe you could teach me something. Bet you're hoping I'll be arrested or sent packing. That's why you're so anxious to talk to your dad?"

"I could care less. I will do what I've been doing with or without you. I think you should go deliver your shoe yourself."

"Like you can't kick him out, Kendall. This place is in my name, so your dad won't know we're like not staying with Mitch. I'm going now and like he better be here when I get back."

"Why do you care? Maybe you think he can teach you something, is that it?"

"Like one more thing you'll never know."

"What's that supposed to mean?" he yelled as she went out the door. He jumped up from the sofa and went to the door.

When he turned back, Jake said, "I need to make some calls." He went out on the back deck, leaving Kendall to stew in his own thoughts.

He called Charlie Davenport. Charlie was trying to sober up, so he said, and having a hard time dealing with the issue. He had already been contacted.

"Now that I'm head dog on this project, everything that happens falls on me. Rick has been up my ass. Alec has informed me of what transpired between you two. Then I get the call from the local police informing me of Mr. Devereaux's arrest and inquiring if I knew your whereabouts, naming you as a person of interests in a possible kidnapping and attack on Blakely Carmichael. I told them I did not know your whereabouts. Where the hell are you and what is this all about?"

Jake told him the same story he told Kendall and Amy.

"You need to turn yourself in. I have a call into our legal counselor. I also called Thomas' boss and have tried to reach Ned Estes. It's a weekend, the weekend before the final week of Christmas. Most people are having company parties back home. Not only that but we're getting ready to take the Christmas break, shut the operation down. You picked the wrong time to come down here, get involved in something like this. I was hoping you could help get things back on track. Now this."

"Mr. Davenport, I don't believe anything has happened to Blakely. I have sent one of my bloody shoes to the police. I have the other. That is one of the reasons I called you. I need to get this other shoe to a forensics lab in the states. It will prove the blood is not Blakely's and verify Thomas' and my account of what happened."

"Who was this other man, and where is Blakely? She hasn't been heard from or seen since she was with you and Thomas." Jake heard him take a swallow of something. "From what I hear, the Bahamian authorities are talking to the state department and the FBI. Your best bet is come forward and tell them what you know."

"I've told you what I know. I don't have any idea where she is. I wish I did. What about Thomas? I bet he told the police just what I said."

"It seems Thomas has other problems. Far bigger ones which, even if I knew, I would not be at liberty to say. I'm afraid you don't have many options other than turning yourself in. You won't be able to leave the island and the longer you wait the worse this could get. The Bahamian minister is under a lot of pressure. The project is behind schedule and these incidents are not helping our PR." He drank again, then added, "If you get me that other shoe, I will see that it gets sent to the proper authorities. I repeat, you need to turn yourself in. Let the FBI and your lawyers handle this."

"What lawyers? I don't know any lawyers."

"Then they will provide them. Goodbye Mr. Harper. I hope to hear you have decided to do the right thing. Our company will do what we can to help clear this up." He ended the call.

Thomas had bigger problems; they both did. The FBI. Oh shit. Jake felt certain this had something to do with the car and the Russians. They needed big time help. Homeland was supposed to have handled it. Where was Hardy? Swanson had said everything was to go through him. Now, according to Swanson, Homeland would deny their connection. They were on their own. He hardly knew Ned, but it was looking like he had run out of other options. He should have never left the farm.

He heard a vehicle approaching.

38

Miami, Fl

Carl handed her a pen he explained was a voice and video recorder. Deane was escorted down the hall by the head nurse, who explained Daniel Diego's condition and what had been done.

When she entered the room, she was shocked by the man's size. He had trapped-wounded-beast eyes that followed her as she entered the room. She checked his chart and the monitors, after greeting him with as warm a smile as she could muster. Treat him like one of your veterans, she told herself. God, he was terrifying.

"Hello Mr. Diego," she said laying the chart with the pen pointed toward him on the bedside table. She reached out, took his pulse. "You have an elevated heartrate. Have you been diagnosed with problems regarding your blood pressure?"

He continued to stare without answering.

Deane reached up to remove the bandage. He flinched. "That's a nasty wound. Gunshots usually are. You're lucky. It passed clean through without hitting an artery, only soft-tissue damage. A couple weeks with the right care and the pain will be almost gone. I need to change your bandage. I will give you a little pain medication along with the antibiotics, if you promise not to tell anyone."

She administered the medications she had been given to her by the head nurse.

"Is there anything I can do for you to make you more comfortable?"

His eyes began to lose their focus. Deane checked the monitors. Everything appeared to be the same as before, that was somewhat unusual. She checked his pulse again. His heart rate had slowed. She wondered what was in that needle to have that quick of a reaction.

"Feel better now?"

A flicker of a smile. "Gracias," he mumbled shocking her.

"Morphine. Don't tell anyone."

He nodded.

"I heard them say you are a terrorist and they're going to turn you over to the CIA. You don't look like no terrorist." She gave him her most benevolent, innocent smile.

"Shot me for no reason."

"They said you shot a policeman."

"He dirty, shot me."

Deane remembered what her husband had said about him being from Juarez. She leaned in and whispered, hoping the mic would pick up the sound, "I know you not from here. Word is you came here from Mexico. Some of my homies say you botched a hit on their turf, they want me to tell you, you brought heat when your men shoot policeman and the two Russian cartel men."

He turned his head, eyes glaring. "Not shoot fucking commies. What you give me?"

"You'll go to sleep and never wake up. You'll die in excruciating pain unless you tell me who sent you and why." Deane stood straight, withdrew another needle, stuck the end into the intravenous tube strapped to his arm.

"Wait," he hissed. "Some hom pay me meet people at this Clutch's. Policeman and woman come in. Thought they my contacts. Left, all hell broke loose. Truth I swear."

"Why were you sent? We know you gun for hire. Who was your target?"

"How I know you not kill me anyway?"

"You don't. Tell me or you tell no one. You die in pain."

"I tell you. You get me out of here?"

"Not possible."

"I hear of medicine make heart stop. Other medicine, make heart start again. You know this. I tell you. You do this for me?"

"You tell me truth, Information checks, I do this."

"Contact, government man. Business with Russians, high-tech weapon. All I told. Money in overseas account. Get me out, I split funds with you."

"You have bomb?" He looked puzzled.

"Bomb? What this 'bout bomb?"

"We see. Keep your mouth shut. I check."

"Twenty big ones. Tell them."

Deane gathered her stuff and left. She felt dirty.

Carl and TJ downloaded the pen memory, watched and listened several times on a tablet in the break room. Deane told TJ she never wanted to do anything like that again.

TJ asked her how she came up with her way of doing that. "Wow. If I had been him, I would've been shitting myself." Brought a brief smile to Deane's downcast expression.

Carl was beaming. "You mean this is not the script you provided her?"

"Scripted? Not even close." TJ hugged Deane. "You were great. I'm sorry I ever doubted you would be able to get him to open up."

"You're a natural. Amazing."

"Hope it helps?" Deane said. "I need to go to the restroom. Carl gave her directions and she left.

"My bet is on Tobey," TJ said.

"Then why didn't he get with Diego? And who were the shooters?"

"Maybe he spotted us, or he got spooked when Maggie approached him."

"No. He wouldn't have hung around if he was suspicious. Okay let's say he is the contact. We still don't know who Tobey's employer is? If he is an operative for some government agency, my bet is he is a CIA asset. And this woman, Blakely Carmichael, claimed she was a double agent. They set the plan in motion to shoot Bolstoy and his captain. He goes to Bolstoy, why? It all comes back to Toby and Blakely. I'm missing something." He scratched his two-day old stubble.

"The weapon. The whole reason for our operation. There must be an inside man. He's trying to put together bids for this tech weapon. Tobey went to Bolstoy because he's one of the bidders."

"Was. Got word he was DOA. Sorry, go on. I like how this is going."

"If I had to bet, the Palmroys and the other guests were there with Bolstoy because of his bid for the weapon. Maybe Tobey was on the run because of us having taken Rinaldo and Diego. He warns Bolstoy. Gets him to help him escape."

Carl cut in. "Somehow, he finds a way to the Island of Great Exuma, Bahamas. Finds government agents there with two dead Russians, maybe? Anyway, he must have gotten in touch with someone to find Blakely. She is surprised, again maybe, when he shows up while she is with our two agents. This damn woman has proven to be a chameleon, very quick on her feet, shows superb training and resourcefulness. She zaps Tobey and Agent Deverreaux with a taser, she just happens to have. This, after our agents recognize Tobey, and Agent Devereaux gets into a scuffle with him. Seems to me she was afraid of what he might say, so she continued to zap him so our other agent, your friend Agent Harper said. Harper sends her off to stop the curious party crowd who witnessed the arc of the taser. Our agents take Tobey. Devereaux goes for their vehicle while Harper continues with Tobey. Blakely returns, blindsides then zaps Agent Harper, takes Tobey and they disappear. Subsequently, to cover their tracks, they leave behind bloody clothes. Must be besides themselves because our agents are in trouble."

Carl paused. Listened to someone talking to him through his earpiece. "Got word, he said to TJ, source' says someone named James Dean turned up in the Bahamas looking for Devereaux and Harper."

"Who's James Dean? How does he figure into this?"

"Hopefully Agent Harper will soon shed some light on that subject." Carl didn't sound optimistic.

"Don't worry about Jake. He can handle himself. He's a whole lot smarter than people give him credit for. Jake's well-trained and street-savvy. Which brings us back to this government insider? Too bad we didn't get to question Bolstoy and his guests further. What about the marina employees?"

"FBI has taken them elsewhere. The police and the feds are arguing over who should have access to them. For now, the feds are in control. Unfortunately for us, we're being locked out, thanks to our politically motivated, spineless leaders in Washington. Thanks to you and your remarkable wife, we have something no one, except us, knows. And we have a means to operate through your police task force ties."

Deane who had left to go to the rest room returned. "TJ, I need to be going."

"I'm not sure it's safe, Deane."

"I'm going. I'll be damned if I'll let these people keep me from living my life. That's what we've both said all our lives, why should this be any different?"

"She's right you know. Look I'll ask Julia and Bridgette to take her in one of our armored vehicles. Have them stay at the VA until tomorrow. Both are trained. This will get them away from the circus atmosphere here. They can spend their furlough time there as well as they can here. Maybe I can keep them on the payroll, thanks to you Deane. Perhaps they can be of use via the secure VA net. I'll go find them. You two can have a few minutes alone."

39

Great Exuma, Bahamas

There were no steps off the deck. Jake decided the vehicle he heard had to be Amy. That was quick, too quick. He stepped back inside just as the front door opened. Amy burst through, a look of horror and disgust smothering her usually calm, remarkable features. The thirty-something-year-old man who stepped in behind her was about Jake's size, clean-shaven, military style haircut, a sneering smile plastered on his sun-starved, blunt Slavic-looking face with a nose that had been broken at some point making his face seem even more flat.

"I'm sorry Jake. He was like waiting for me at Mitch's place."

"Mr. Harper your girlfriend had no choice. We need to talk."

Jake stared at him. He had no visible weapon. Jake figured he probably could take him if he had to. Easiest thing would be to turn, jump from the deck and run. Run where? The place was surrounded by mangrove which ended at a bay, a shark-infested bay, so he had been told. The other direction was to the road. Others were probably waiting, perhaps already waiting outside. He wouldn't leave Amy and Kendall to this man.

"That is her boyfriend." He pointed to Kendall. He sat slack-jawed on the sofa, cell phone in his hand.

"Who are you?" Kendall asked, swinging his head from him to Jake. "I knew it." He glared disapprovingly at Amy and Jake, his face contorted in anger and disgust. "I knew I should have not let you come here."

"Shut up Kendall," Jake said. "Answer. Who are you?"

"James Dean, FBI."

Jake was skeptical. "ID?"

He reached into the front pocket of his kaki cargo pants and brought out a badge holder. He started toward Jake.

"Hold it. Hand it to Amy." Jake wanted to get her away from this man.

"This is really unnecessary. I'm not here to arrest you. Thomas Devereaux told me where I might find you. Swanson in Miami sent me to talk to you. I think in private would be better."

Amy spoke up. "He like showed me this badge. He took your shoe. There was nothing Mitch or I could do." Amy was on the verge of tears as she took the holder and came to Jake.

"It's ok. You did the right thing." Jake took the holder from Amy. "Did you come alone?"

"Just me. We need to talk, in private."

"Wait outside. Give me a minute. I need to talk to Amy and Kendall. Don't worry I'm not going to run."

The man looked at him, nodded and went out leaving the door open. Jake crossed to the front door and peered out. He looked at Amy. "Did you see any other vehicles at Mitch's or out on the road?"

"No Jake. Like I wasn't expecting him. He was in a rental car at Mitch's and like came in the door behind me before I knew he was there. Like scared Mitch and me to death. He asked where you were. We didn't say anything until he like showed us his badge and told us he was here to help you. I didn't say anything. Mitch told him. I hope you're not mad at me. I didn't know what to do. Like neither did Mitch."

"Don't worry. I'm not mad." He looked over at Kendall. "Have you talked to Fred?"

"No," was all he said.

"If he calls, tell him to call my cell. If I don't answer, tell him to call the jail. If he doesn't get me, then notify the state department. Got it?"

"Why should we do anything for you?"

"Just do as I ask, ok?"

"Like I'll make sure he does Jake. Isn't there like something else that we can be doing?"

Kendall scoffed. "Not in a million years could you stop me from saying anything. Not you nor your boyfriend."

"You're like always such a jerk. I don't know why I came here…"

"Enough you two. I would appreciate you doing as I ask Kendall. Do it for the sake of ESI's reputation, if for no other reason. Your dad will understand, as should you. I have to go. Hopefully this guy is here to help Thomas and me get this straightened out."

Jake walked out onto the front entrance porch. The only sounds came from Kendall and Amy inside and the ticking of the truck. James Dean stood leaning on the passenger side door of the ESI company truck.

"This better be good. I'm too tired to deal with bullshit."

"I think you'll want to hear what I've got to say."

"Where's your vehicle?" Jake asked.

"Left it next to the apartments where her stone-head friend lives."

"How do I know you're not here to arrest me?"

"Agent Hardy initially asked me to come here to shadow you and watch your back. He told me you and Devereaux were working undercover. If I were here to arrest you, I wouldn't have come unarmed or alone. I read your jacket. I'm former Marines, military police."

"You're not really FBI are you?"

"What the badge says."

Jake didn't believe Swanson would send a feeb. He needed to figure out what was going on. He went over and sat in the driver's seat. "Where to?"

"Nowhere unless you have the keys."

"I'll get them."

Jake could hear Kendall yelling at Amy accusing her of telling James Dean she was Jake's girlfriend. Jake opened the door. They were standing face to face, both red-faced, Kendall with his fists balled. "You need to cool it Kendall. You touch her and next time I see you, I'll put a major hurting on you. Amy, I need the keys to the truck."

"That's ESI's truck. You can't take it."

Amy came over to Jake. "Like I'm not staying here with him. I'm going with you. You can take me to Mitch's."

"Go ahead. Leave with your boyfriend. Fuck you, you whore. I hope they do lock him up. Fuck both of you."

Amy climbed in and slid over to the middle. James Dean grinned and shook his head.

At Mitch's Jake got out followed by Amy. "Earlier, that man made crude remarks to me. It scared me." They stood outside the apartment door, a worried expression creasing her lovely face.

Jake gave her a hug. "I'll make sure it doesn't happen again," he said looking over her shoulder meeting the leering stare on the other man's face. Amy kissed him on the cheek and tried the door. Mitch opened it and she disappeared inside. Jake doubted he would ever be seeing her again. He handed Mitch the keys to the truck. Mitch looked askance. "Don't worry about it son." Mitch nodded and closed the door. Jake got in on the passenger's side. "Okay asswipe, let's go." They headed back toward Georgetown in Dean's rental car.

"What's she like like?" Dean asked, his grin irritating Jake.

"Not something we need to talk about. Fill me in on yourself and what you know. Just so you know, my bullshit warning register has begun to go off. If it gets worse, things will get nasty."

Dean's grin flashed off. "I heard you don't play well with others. Along with being told I might have to defend myself while watching your back. Kind of was disappointed. That is until earlier this evening."

"What do you mean earlier this evening? You been watching me?"

"How well do you know Thomas Devereaux?"

"Only what he told me. Same as you. How long you been watching me? Who are you working for?" Jake wondered if this guy could be working with Blakely and the Russians. Was he another one Blakely had been worried about? Could be the one sent to get rid of her, him, or both as she once claimed.

"I'm afraid I can't answer that."

"Not acceptable."

"Look man. This is not about getting to know each other. All right? I don't want to know more about you, nor, for you to know more about me. Having been in the desert, you should respect that. My name is James Dean. I was briefed by Agent Hardy, with a follow-up by an Agent Swanson. I was sent here by them to watch your back without you or anyone else knowing. For now, that is all you need to know about me. Your jacket is all I need to know about you."

He paused. Jake had been dividing his attention between watching him and watching the road. Jacket? There shouldn't have been any jacket. Meter was now buzzing. This man, last name possibly Dean, had that intense look he had seen on most warriors. Then, Dean grinned.

"Except I'd like to know how it is an older dude such as yourself can tag some primo eye candy like that Amy chick?"

"I warned you. You better start telling me something I believe."

"Like Blakely Carmichael. Were you doing her also? Or Tobias Tobolokov? Maybe a threesome and a lovers' quarrel. Seems to be your thing, eh?"

Who the fuck was this guy? Better still who was he working for and why was he here?"

He chuckled. "Cat got your tongue? Like I said, I was sent here to watch over you. Beginning to wonder why they would want me to watch you. You seem to be more of a lover than a fighter. Let them get away. Tsk tsk. Amateurish."

"What do you know about the Carmichael woman and this Tobolokov guy?"

"Same as you and Thomas Devereaux." Dean looked over at Jake. He saw he hadn't missed the inference. He didn't like the way Jake was looking at him. Good thing he brought some protection. He slid his hand down to the pocket of the door, resting his left hand on the grip of a snub-nose 38 special. He had been told to discourage Harper and Devereaux. Send them packing might not work. Best to defuse the situation until he knew what they knew. Would have to wait until he got them together. The noise by the dock had kept him from getting a good recording.

"Look man, I followed the three of you—Devereaux, you and this Blakely woman when you headed down toward the docks. The Toby guy's appearance was a shock. I had been briefed about him. This was the first he appeared on radar. I almost made a countermove when he came running toward you. That Carmichael woman's taser shot out of nowhere caught me by surprise, stopped me. Your letting her go afterwards gave me pause. I continued to shadow you, I became cautious about who was zooming whom, especially after you had a parting, intimate moment."

He looked over at Jake. Jake had a deadpan expression.

"You were down at the docks? Then you know more than I do? Skip ahead to after she left, and Thomas left."

"You sure Devereaux left? I watched him disappear also. But I stayed with you and that Toby guy. Created quite a bit of commotion and conversation among those who saw you pushing a trussed guy with blood on you and him. Not long after, came the other attention-getting taser strike and the hit putting you down. I was moving in when I saw Thomas coming up behind Blakely after she fired the taser. Thomas took the taser from her. He cut Toby loose, they all hurried away. I checked you out, you were moaning. Other curious people from the Georgetown Inn bar began heading our way to see what the flash meant. Kept me from being able to follow them. I moved out of sight. Shortly Thomas reappeared and grabbed you. You two stumbled past me. I saw him load you in a car, but before I could get to my rental, you were gone. I took a chance and went to the house you were sharing. I followed you to that apartment then watched you leave with that Amy chick. I was outside. Heard her squeals. Damn. Wish it had been me."

"You're not my type," Jake said.

"Funny."

"Not me. Wondering if you are." He saw the angry flash, then the sudden smarmy look—a trained player.

"No. Anyway I reported in to my control. He told me to stay with you. He would get back to me. All hell apparently was breaking loose in Miami. Guess you haven't heard about the shootings of two high-profile Russians in the bay out from Coconut Grove Marina. One has, or should I say, had a mega-yacht, a rich real estate tycoon along with his captain. Both dead. They're looking for the shooters. I was told in an earlier briefing Toby escaped capture by fleeing from that yacht before the feds could get there." Jake was eyeing him suspiciously. "The shootings I read about them on my phone's news feed while I was listening to you getting your ashes hauled." Despite himself, Jake's look turned to an angry squint.

"It was shocking, pun intended, when Toby appeared out of nowhere, right before our eyes. Got me to thinking, trying to put the puzzle together. What was Thomas up to? You know he and his boss were terminated from the FBI because they refused to cooperate with the special council about Russian interference in the election. Then there were those two Russians found dead in a car, apparently run off the road by another vehicle. Police have GPS records putting Devereaux's car in the vicinity in the time period when that happened. Caused quite a diplomatic stir. That's why I was sent here—damage control. Devereaux is to be extradited. You, they want to talk to. Guess we'll maybe get some answers when we get to the jail."

"Whoa. Who said anything about my going to the jail? Pull over." Jake grabbed the steering wheel. Dean slammed on brakes and the car skidded sideways, each struggled to control the wheel. They ended up inches away from a shrub-covered embankment which overhung a sheer drop-off down to an inlet thirty- feet below.

"You crazy?" a shaken Dean shouted at Jake. He had turned loose of his weapon while wrestling for control. He made a desperate attempt to grab Jake who was half out of his roadside-facing door. "Stop, listen. Agent Swanson called back." Jake stopped, standing ready to attack. He held onto the door ready to slam it on Dean if he tried to get out.

"Better be good. I slam this door the car might just slide on over and away."

Dean glanced out his window, made a quick look down to the door pocket, considered grabbing his revolver. "Swanson told me Thomas' clothes had been tested in Nassau. Had Toby's, yours and Blakely's blood on them. Mostly, Toby's. They're in the process of getting him extradited to the states. He's smart enough not to fight it. He backed up your story. They are no longer interested in locking you up. They want you to come in and give your statement is all. Thomas Devereaux has said he will talk to you, only you. Swanson wants me to keep an eye on you and assist you in finding Toby and Blakely. Maybe Devereaux will tell you where we can find them. I'm to remain out of sight, in the shadows. Get back in the damned car, before some other vehicle comes along, sending me and this damn car over the edge and puts you in real trouble."

40

Jake noticed the man calling himself James Dean slide his left hand down into the door pocket earlier. His eyes went there again. Has to be a weapon. One of the reasons Jake grabbed the steering wheel. It was time he, and whoever this man was, have a little one-on-one. Jake slid his free right hand into his pocket, taking hold of his special pen knife: one with self-sharpening handle sides, disguised as a cigarette lighter, flint and all. A simple touch on the bottom and the blade release was triggered. Jake kept his thumb on the razor-sharp blade release until it was out of his pocket.

He could tell Dean was preparing to go for his weapon—a slight twitch in his eyes. His left hand was inching over. Jake slammed the door hard enough to rock the car. At the same time, he moved, slid in through the open rear passenger door window. He had the knife against Dean's neck before he could raise the snub-nose 38.

"Easy or I'll slice your carotid before you can get a shot off." Jake had reached across the back of Dean's seat in case he needed to attempt to block his aim or hopefully take the weapon away.

Dean kept his arm still while he turned the gun barrel past his left side pointing toward the rear. Maybe he could get a shot off. But Jake's reflexes would cut him. Perhaps not deep enough to be fatal. "And how would you explain my death? Your girlfriend and the other member of your threesome know you are with me. How will our people at Homeland get you out of this one, eh?"

"Not if there's no body. Like Toby and Blakely, eh?"

"I'm the only witness that can testify to your innocence in their disappearance. You need me. I don't need you. Devereaux does. Think about it. Why are you doing this? I'm on your team."

Jake was watching Dean's eyes in the rearview mirror—they twitched. His left arm was tensing. The explosion was shocking. The bullet should have hit him. Something deflected it.

Jake cut Dean but not deep enough to cut the artery. The recoil, Jake's thumb digging into the nerve in his upper arm caused Dean to lose his weapon. Jake reached across Dean's neck with his right arm and locked his hand onto the head rest. He squeezed his own bicep, locked into Dean's neck, cutting off his oxygen and keeping him from going for the gun. Dean reached back with both hands trying to break the grip. Jake drove his left fist into the side of Dean's temple over and over, forcing him to remove his left hand to block the punches. Jake grabbed the middle finger, bent it, the pop was loud enough to be heard over Jake's heavy exertion-tensed breathing. Dean's gasps ended in a muffled screech. He went slack.

Jake let him go. His head rocked over. His body held upright by the seat restraints. There was an odor of sweat now mixed with another bodily excretion. Jake checked his neck for a pulse. He was alive. Thank goodness. Otherwise Jake would have had to attempt to rock the car over the cliff to make it look like an accident. To cover himself, he would have to jump back in and take the plunge without any restraints, hopefully surviving. The only other option would be to get rid of the body after he finished him off. No, neither would help his situation. He had been right. They had left behind witnesses. Plus, whoever knew he was here for god-knows-what. That is what Jake needed to find out.

Jake wiped the blood off his hand, forearm and penknife onto the front of Dean's tropical-design shirt. He slid over, opened the rear door, then the front door, slid in and retrieved the 38. He slapped Dean over and over until his eyes regained some focus. He waved the 38 in front of Dean's eyes. He finally focused on it. His right hand took hold of his broken left hand's middle finger. He winced.

"You're fucked, you know that."

"I'm the one with your revolver." Jake waved it back and forth. "You got some explaining to do. Why don't we start by you putting the car into gear and drive us somewhere private-like."

Dean glared at him still dazed, hate and pain etched across his broad face. He reached over with difficulty restarted the stalled car and put it in gear. "All this was so unnecessary. I've already told you all you need to know," he said through gritted teeth.

"I don't think so. Nice and easy now. You try anything, you'll find out what this old ranger is capable of, jarhead. Or are you actually a former U.S. Marine?" Dean didn't respond. "You're right, this was all unnecessary. Wouldn't have happened had you not pulled the trigger. Why don't we start with you telling me your real name and who you really work for?"

"Why don't you tell me what you want me to say. Make it a whole lot easier

"Be a wise ass. Ok, first off, I know you're not with HSI, not a feeb either. If you were in the Middle East, it was as one of those puke mercenary so-called security services. Probably got off on raping innocent defenseless civilian women then killing them and their families to shut them up." He saw Dean flinch. "Getting warm, ain't I?"

"I was a Marine. Trained at Parris Island, located in your home state. I was in Naval Intelligence. My name is James Dean, my parents were big fans of the actor. Born and raised in Rollo, a little town in the Ozarks of Missouri. No, I am not with HSI. Never said I was. Satisfied?"

"Since you say you're from Missouri, what's the state capital?"

"You really want to keep playing these stupid fucking games? Everyone knows it's St. Louis. Now can we get on with figuring out what to do about finding Tobolokov and Carmichael?"

"The capital is Jefferson City, not St. Louis. By the way, my jacket should have told you I did my basic at Ft. Leonard Wood. And I agree you need to quit playing these stupid games. Jake reached down and put the revolver in Dean's crotch." The car swerved. Dean tried to grab Jake's arm, only to have his right-hand thumb grabbed by Jake's left hand. Jake twisted. Dean shouted, "Ok. Ok." "Keep your hands on the wheel and eyes forward. I warned you what would happen if my bullshit meter went off. Now. One more time. Who are you? Who sent you and for what purpose? Or, you'll never rape another innocent woman again. Better hurry. My finger's getting itchy."

"My name is James Dean Kabiski. I'm an independent contractor hired to find Tobias Tobolokov. By whom does not matter. My employer suspects Tobolokov was hired by the dead Russian Andrei Bolstoy to steal high tech weapon plans which Bolstoy planned to sell on the black market. I was to follow him to see who he contacted. I almost didn't get here in time to see the events involving you, Devereaux and Carmichael. I only received a quick rundown on all the possible players and the recent events that occurred while I was on my three-hour flight from Miami to here. I wasn't sure if you, and Devereaux in particular, were on the up and up. I wasn't given the opportunity to question Devereaux as much as would have liked. I suspect he knows more than he told me or the authorities. All I know is he wanted to talk to you. I wasn't sure about you. Neither was my employer. I was hoping Tobolokov or Carmichael would contact you. Or Devereaux would tell you what he knows, seeing as how he was the one that helped them get away. The rest you know about."

"How do I know you're telling the truth?"

"I could've killed you, numerous times. Talk to Devereaux. He'll be shocked you know he helped them escape."

"What made you change your mind about me?"

He nodded to the revolver. "I like my family jewels. Worth more than what my employer is paying me. I still have my reservations." He smiled, glancing at Jake. "You did seem mighty cozy with Carmichael. Guess I'll know in a bit. That is if you don't shoot me."

Jake removed the revolver from Dean's crotch. They were stopped. There were cars backed up coming and going from Fish Fry. It was still packed with the late-night revelers. Seemed like an eternity since he had been by here earlier. His mind was on Devereaux's possible betrayal. That was if Dean could be believed. Mercenary, gun-for-hire, were of low moral value, lying came easy for them. Then again wasn't that what he had become? At least he wasn't a traitor.

"You want to give me my revolver back?" They inched forward as another car pulled out to get in front of them. Dean let the carload of Bahamians in to avoid them possibly causing a collision.

"No. Think I'll hold onto it for now. I need to talk to Devereaux, find out if your story checks. Make sure all the police want from me is a statement. Your fate is not completely up to me, need to talk to some others about what to do about you."

Dean whipped the car over at the far entrance to Fish Fry. "Look man go ahead call whomever you need to talk to. As for me, you either going to shoot me or work with me to find Tobolokov and Carmichael, or not. Either way I intend to do what I was paid to do or die right here and now in front of all these people."

Jake reached into his left pocket and retrieved his cell and the battery which he had removed when he last talked to Swanson. The screen lit up. He saw he had ten missed calls from caller unknown. He had a message, *call me when you get home. Mother.* Jake's mother had died years ago. Had to be Swanson. He needed a secure phone. "You got a burner phone?"

"Use your own phone."

Jake saw a half-empty two-liter water bottle in the floor. He reached down picked it up, unscrewed the cap, poured some of it out on Dean's still damp crotch.

He quickly jerked up. "Hey. What the fuck?"

Jake stuck the barrel of the revolver in the open mouth of the bottle and pointed it at Dean's knee. "Phone. Now."

Dean fumbled into his cargo pant pocket and pulled two phones out. He managed to punch the screen buttons on each. He handed one to Jake.

Jake said, "Other one also."

"You only need one. Go ahead shoot me. Maybe they won't hear the shot. Bet some of them will see the flash."

"Probably think it was a cigarette lighter. Someone lighting a big j. Want to bet being a cripple on your assumption?"

He tossed the other phone onto the seat between them. "You're damn sure ballsy. Ever decide you need a job, I can point you in the right direction."

"Shut up. I'm going to talk to someone about your future." Jake took his battery and sim card out using the tip of his knife. He removed the sim from one of Dean's phones and replaced it with his. He dialed the number and punched in the codes. When he heard it starting to go through the system he waited, when he heard Swanson's voice, he removed his sim.

"Say hello to James Dean." Jake put the phone on speaker.

"Mr. Dean," Carl said. "Is that your real name?"

"Indeed it is, Agent Swanson. Would you be so kind as to ask your trained monkey to stop pointing a gun at me. He's already told me he has an itchy finger."

Jake heard a chuckle in the background. "TJ is that you I hear?"

"That it is bro. Sorry I missed your call. Hear you've been kinda busy."

"Okay. Okay," Carl said. We don't have time for chit chat. Mr. Dean what are you doing in the Bahamas? Let me ask it another way, who in the sand hill do you work for?"

"I'm afraid I can't answer that. Let's just say they want the same thing your people want. Namely to keep these high-tech weapons from ending up in the wrong hands."

"Jake you have a gun? How in the hell did you obtain a gun?"

"Took it from Mr. Dean Kabiski after he attempted to shoot me with it."

"This was after your Mr. Harper had a razor knife at my throat, threatening to severe my carotid artery."

Once more Jake heard TJ chuckling, followed by, "What'd I tell you? That's my man."

"Well Agent Harper, has Mr. Kabiski told you anything of value?"

"Just that he witnessed Devereaux leaving with Toby and Blakely after I was tasered. Says Devereaux is to be extradited back to the states, said he wants to talk to me. Also, that the police are not going to arrest me. They only want to get a statement from me. Does any of this ring true with you?"

"Nothing has been said to me, but, as you may or not be aware, other federal agencies are now involved, cooperation is not their strong suit. Isn't that right Mr. Dean whatever your name is?"

"Not my end of things. I swear to you everything Harper said is true. No matter what Harper does to me will make me divulge who my employer is, wouldn't be good for my long-term health. Check your sources, not going to change my stance. After you waste more time, perhaps then we can discuss how Mr. Harper and I can find out where this Tobolokov man and Carmichael woman have disappeared to. That is what my employer wishes to know. It's in all our best interests."

"Perhaps you might want to change your healthcare provider, Mr. Dean. Kinda late, but I'm going to see what I can find out. For your sake, you better hope I can verify your story. Jake don't take your eyes off him. Call back in say ten minutes. No answer. Keep calling every ten until I answer. Mr. Dean you best hope his finger doesn't get too itchy. And you might want to reconsider your position if I am unable to verify your statements." Carl disconnected.

"Sure could use some food and a beer. What say we go over and grab something while we wait?"

"I'm fine. Think we'll wait right here. If your story checks out, I might reconsider letting you have something."

41

Miami, Fl

Carl had one of his people go into the NSA database located at Fort Meade, one of the most extensive collections of info in the world. Nothing, not NSA, FBI or CIA, nor any other sources had info on Dean, which came as no surprise. He tried to contact Hardy. So far no response. Same with his attempt to get a return call from Homeland Security's Secretary. TJ talked to his police commissioner, who was demanding his department be the lead on the murder investigations of Buster Brown, Bolstoy and Jokovski. The task force was on the verge of being torn apart by the infighting. Everyone was doing their own independent analysis and demanding to be the lead because Homeland was pulled back by Washington.

Carl finally got a friend at justice to verify Devereaux had been indicted and an extradition agreement worked out with the Bahamian authorities. Nothing concerning Jake Harper. His friend wanted to know why he was inquiring about a Jake Harper. Carl said he received an inquiry about Mr. Harper and was following up on it. Carl was afraid his friend might flag the name. No matter, Harper would show no connection to HSI. Carl knew that may not be the case. Apparently, someone inside or outside HSI briefed James Dean.

He let Jake know what little they knew and told him to proceed with caution.

The threatened shutdown put a damper on everyone's mood. No one knew who was furloughed without pay, or, for many, forced to work without getting paid. Carl felt certain he was going to be given early retirement. He had been looking forward to being able to walk out the door and get on with whatever came next. Maybe a small ranch in Montana with a couple horses and a trout stream nearby. He had had a good career, nothing spectacular, but he had done his part and never been rebuked, until now.

"Reluctantly, his team tried to continue their duties. He asked them to continue to find all they could on James Dean Kabisky? Also, to find out how anyone resembling Tobolokov and Dean were able to get to the Bahamas? And, what connections Carmichael and Devereaux had with them?

"Thomas Devereaux, like Tobolokov and Carmichael, fooled us all," he said to TJ, once they returned to his office. "Who was this Dean fellow working for? NSA, FBI and CIA, all, as is their habit, refuse to acknowledge him. And Hardy did he know? Why had he failed to tell me about this James Dean. James Dean, I know everything the public knew about the dead actor James Dean. This James Dean, he's a ghost. Who would have brought someone like him in on this op and there be no trail," Carl repeated, leaning back, putting his feet up on papers, which lay scattered across his desk.

TJ wondered if other agents had been searching through them. Carl's office had looked like a typical head agent's desk last time TJ had been here. Not this time.

"My bet this CIA."

"Yours and my bets would be the same. All the team can find is he was a former Marine, assigned to military police, whatever that means. Two tours in Iraq, an honorable discharge, then nothing for the last three years. He talked to Devereaux at the jail. Can't find how he was able to do that. On whose authority? He tried to say Hardy pulled some strings. Not likely. No way to confirm, Hardy has gone dark. Dean, as you heard, says Devereaux refused to talk to him, other than to say he wouldn't fight extradition back here to answer any questions about this op. This guy Dean confronted him, so I was told. His story has not been verified. Devereaux's clothing was expedited to an expert sent to Nassau. By whom? Should be able to find out soon.

"Lastly, he said Devereaux told him he had told the Bahamian authorities Jake was innocent and knew nothing about what happened to Toby or Blakely.

Again, I repeat, Dean says Devereaux refuses to discuss what he knows with anyone but Jake. What in the hell is that all about, why Jake? My source assured me they have no arrest warrant for Jake, he had never heard of Jake. II hope that's the case and remains so. Dean reaffirmed Devereaux was telling the truth about there being no warrant for Jake's arrest in connection with this Carmichael woman. My team made inquiries. Some unidentified source in the Bahamian Embassy said no warrant had been issued for anyone. Other than Thomas Devereaux. The authorities reserve the right, pending their investigation, to take anyone they suspect into custody, if Devereaux's account is not proven to be true. They do want Jake to come in and give a statement and answer their questions. What do you think, should I let Jake chance it?"

"Don't know. Dead end unless we find Toby and Blakely, and, from where we sit, I believe this goina be the only way Jake's going to prove his innocence. Sure would help if we knew more about Dean and his employer."

"Exactly. Jake may be damned either way. Wish I could talk to Agent Hardy."

"Speaking of Hardy, how'd you two manage to get Jake involved in the first place. He made it clear to me he wasn't interested."

"Hardy convinced him. Not sure what was said." Carl was drumming his fingers on his stomach, a pensive look on his red face. "I hope I haven't signed his death warrant."

TJ wasn't sure what to say. He thought as much of Jake as he did his own brother. Despite Carl not telling him, he knew Jake was somehow involved.

"You've made up your mind. Care to share your decision with me?"

"Went with my gut. Like you said, without Carmichael we'll never know the truth. Devereaux could be lying. Hope I get a chance to question him when he gets brought back. If he is brought back here. Who knows, like you, my gut says Dean is CIA. If so, Devereaux will disappear never to be seen or heard from again. Like Renaldo and Diego. I think Dean could be lying to use us. Need to find out. Sometimes, you have to put what's best for the country ahead of personal feelings. You know that. All we can do is wait to hear back from Harper. I'm hoping we hear something positive, otherwise..." He shook his head.

"Jake's a warrior and survivor. Believe you me when I say, I pity anyone he sees as a threat."

"It's late, rather I should say early." He looked at his cell—2 AM. I sent the others home. Hopefully they'll return in the morning. Our friends left. Said they'd be back tomorrow. Left some poor flunkies here in case something happens. We both look like shit. Why don't you grab a cot in our agent guest quarters? If I hear anything from your friend, which I figure you might need to hear, I'll rouse you."

"What about you? You really do look like death warmed over."

"I'm going to kick back in my chair," he put his feet back up on his desk, "and do what I've done many other times podna. Get some shuteye right here. May be the last time I'll be given the opportunity to do so. Cut the light out when you leave. The agent guest quarters are next to where we had Rinaldo and Diego."

42

Great Exuma, Bahamas

"**Y**ou know I could be more useful on a full stomach."

"Should've thought of that before you dropped in on me."

"Ok Romeo, how we going to play this? My employer has a jet at the airstrip waiting. We could take Devereaux and get the hell away before anyone could do anything to stop us. What you say?"

"Thought your employer wanted Tobolokov and Carmichael. Guess Devereaux was the target all along."

"Devereaux is the key. Once we get him out of here we can find out where the other two are off to. That is if they've not been turned into shark shit. I think they're possibly nearby and Devereaux knows where the bodies are hidden. So, how about my plan?"

"I'll decide after I talk to him. You just have to play nice with anyone at the jail while I do."

"I don't think you and I should go in there together. Might spook Devereaux."

Dean took it slow through Georgetown. The parties were winding down. Most of the vehicles had left the tent area parking. There were more than a few vacant spots on each side of the road. The downtown loop had a good number of Bahamians standing around or seated on the low wall in front of the street vendor wood shacks which were closed, locked for the night. The smell of reefer hung strong in the air. You could get a contact high from being in the area. No police were visible, not even when they reached the low-slung concrete structure that served as the court and jail. Thomas Devereaux' rental was the only vehicle there.

"Looks empty," Jake said, "seems I won't be talking to Devereaux tonight."

Dean parked the car up the street from the jail. "Has to be tonight. Come morning they'll be taking him to Nassau for extradition, too late to catch Tobolokov and Carmichael."

"You planning on breaking him out of there? Not with me you're not. This was your plan from the git-go, wasn't it? Jake pointed the 38 at Dean. "Let's go. Drive to the airport."

"Guess you're not listening. This is Devereaux' idea. He told me he would tell you where they were, only if we got him out of there before he was taken away in the morning. He knows the staties are planning on taking him to some place where he'll never be heard from again. He said tell you it's personal, whatever that means. That you'll want to hear what he has to say."

"Sounds to me like some bullshit cooked up, either by yourself or in conjunction with your employer. No matter what, I'm not about to do any jailbreaking to find out."

"That's too bad." Dean opened the door and got out, taking the key fob to the car. "Here are your options: one, you shoot me. Sure bet the police will show up afterwards. Two, you come with me, we get Devereaux and fly out of here. My employer pays well and will help you resettle anywhere with all new bona fides, even a new face should you like. Either way, I'm going to go in there to get Devereaux and guess who will be implicated?" He ran off.

Jake learned while a teenager how to hotwire a car. After watching Dean disappear around the side of the building, he did the deed and drove several blocks away and texted Swanson, "911," using one of Dean's burner phones.

A groggy sounding Swanson called immediately. "Better be good. Almost had a nice trout on my line."

Jake told him what was happening with Dean.

"Should've shot him," Swanson said sounding more alert. "Knew this guy was up to no good. Your friend TJ and I had him pegged for CIA. Not so sure. And Devereaux, makes no sense. Got to stop them," Carl said thinking out loud. "He's right. You'll be left holding the bag. You sure there's no policemen on duty?"

"No idea. No vehicles except Devereaux' rental parked in a fenced-in area. A light is on at the entrance and the interior was partially lit inside the entrance area. Didn't see anyone. No police vehicles anywhere. You sure you want me to shoot them?"

"I would like for you to. But better not. They take weapons seriously down there. In particular, should you shoot someone. At least you have slowed them down by moving the car. I'm going to try to get in touch with the Bahamian authorities. Then I may have to let the FBI in on this. Damn what a fucking fuck up. If they get away, our part, most likely, is finished. I'll get back to you. Oh, you better get rid of that gun. Take it apart and chunk it in the bay."

Keeps getting better and better, Jake thought watching, trying to determine his next move. Get rid of the revolver? What if Dean and Devereaux get their hands on some other weapons? Jake decided he'd hold onto it a little longer. What did Devereaux mean it was personal? Damn. Could be that was another Dean lie to solicit his help. It was possible a policeman had been bribed. What if Dean hurts or kills a policeman or some other innocents? The guy struck him as the type to not really give a fuck about anyone but himself. If the authorities come, even if Jake isn't with them, he could be accused of being an accessory. Damn. He couldn't wait. He had to stop them.

Jake tucked the revolver in the right-hand-upper-most pocket of his cargo pants where his pen knife was. He looked around to make sure no one was watching, slipped out of the car, hurried to the jail. No sign of Dean and Devereaux or anyone else. The sounds of stoned revelers were distant and not very loud coming from the business district. There was a steady hum of motors coming from the dock area in the opposite direction. He stopped at the jail entrance, peeked in the glass door. There were chairs in rows with a desk and podium on the far wall. No one seemed to be inside. He tried the door. Locked. He walked back out toward the front parking area, keeping his eyes and ears scanning for any signs of life. Nothing in the immediate area.

He turned on the sidewalk and started toward the business area. It appeared safe. He casually walked toward the other end where Dean disappeared earlier. Once he was in the dark, he picked up his pace and started looking for where Dean was or where he could have gotten in. There were small slit windows up high on the end. Too small for anyone to get through.

At the corner, Jake stopped, crouched down and took a quick recce of the back area. Satisfied it was safe, Jake moved out from the building to a rear parking area where there were a few palm trees planted as a buffer. He laid down on the ground behind one of them, scanned the back of the building. There was a metal door which looked like what Jake figured was as it should be. No other penetrations or access potential into the block building.

Had Dean been let in or somehow managed to jimmy the two visible locks? Jake had been trained to pick locks. Stood to reason, Dean had the knowledge also. Or, had he pulled a fast one and slipped away, perhaps with the help of someone else? Jake discounted the thought. Okay, so assuming he's inside, which way would he most likely come out? The front was lit, but, if they planned to get off the island, why should he care who sees them leaving the jail? Jake did not see any cameras. Could be some small recessed ones. Didn't appear likely for this old building where the police appeared not to have anyone on duty. Unless the police were part of Dean's plan? Jake decided the back was the best bet. But, if he moved over to the side, near the front, he could watch the front and, most likely, if they came out the back, they'd come around this end since the other one was fenced in. He ran in a crouch to the shrubs about twenty feet from the other end.

When they came out, then what? Jake figured he should render Dean unconscious, then deal with Devereaux.

The sound of an automobile turning the corner caught Jake's attention. He lay as flat as possible, hoping the occupant or occupants would not be paying much attention to his somewhat-exposed position. They slowed as they came toward the front area across the parking lot. Jake twisted his face in the thin grass and sand, not daring to raise his head for fear of being seen. The car turned into the far end of the lot, it's lights sweeping across him before they were turned off, back on, then off again. He heard footsteps slapping the concrete walk. Tilting his head, he saw two figures moving toward the car from the jail. The back door of the car flew open, and Dean shoved Devereaux in. The door slammed shut, Jake heard Devereaux shout his name, didn't catch the rest. The car shot forward and out of the lot with Jake on foot in pursuit.

Dean had a backup, he thought, sprinting to get the car that brought him here. This had not been part of his calculations. Most likely they would be heading to the airport. Could he catch them was the big question? There were two people in the front. He could have sworn it was a man and a woman. Tobey and Blakely, he wondered, as he fumbled with the wires of the Ford Edge, finally getting ignition. They had a good three-minute head-start, he thought, the tires squealing when he peeled out, hurrying to catch up. At the corner, the avoidance system slammed on brakes sending the car sliding past two Bahamians, who stepped in front of him, both jumping away, one slapping the window next to Jake's head, before the brakes released and he sped away. He glanced in the rearview mirror to catch their raised fists being shaken at him in the fading distance. Hopefully they had not recognized him.

Thank goodness the traffic was light heading out of Georgetown. That was until he drew near Fish Fry. The last of the crowd was leaving, most heading away in the same direction as he was. Jake floored the car passing three of them once there was an opening in the other lane. Had the traffic also slowed Dean, Devereaux and the others down? He hoped so. For the next several miles he drove like a maniac, weaving in and out of the light traffic, passing and going into the curves on the wrong side, the Edge's warning dings sounding off, brakes attempting to engage whenever he came too close to fronts and rears of the other vehicles. He did a power-slide onto the turnoff for the winding road to the airport. Straightening every curve, he was perplexed that he had not come upon the car he was pursuing. Had they gone somewhere else? No, he didn't believe so. That was one thing Dean said that he believed.

The terminal and other buildings came into view, no sight of the other car. He slowed scanning the nearly vacant parking and rental lot just past the buildings. Nothing. He looped back around. There it was. Somehow, they managed to drive onto the runway and were stopped near a jet outside the newly built maintenance and storage hanger. Jake didn't see where the break in the fence was. He slid to a stop next to the metal fence, jumped out of the car onto the hood, then top, swung up and over the slack barbed wire that topped the fence. The barbs dug into his palms. He ignored the pain to his hands and to his neck from the jolt of landing on the concrete on the other side of the fence. He pulled the snub-nose revolver from his pants pocket.

Running as fast as he could, he wondered how many rounds were in the revolver. Should he shoot someone, if so who? They were boarding the plane, its twin turbines making a whining, whooshing roar preparing to taxi for takeoff. Jake saw Devereaux being pushed up the steps by Dean. The other car was empty. Everyone must be already onboard. He couldn't shoot Dean from this distance on the run and be certain of the trajectory. The door swung up and closed, the jet swung across his course and onto the runway. Jake dropped to one knee, fired, hitting both left side tires, so he thought. The plane continued. He fired twice. One tire exploded. The plane slowed down, stopped moving. The other tire began to deflate. Over the noise of the engines, Jake heard sirens coming from the entrance road on the other side of the terminal.

Time to get out of sight and rid of the 38. He sprinted toward the maintenance and storage hangar, veering off into the shadows when he heard one of the big doors sliding open. On the side was a fuel truck and stacks of drums, beyond which was the back fence. He went to one of the drums, struggled to loosen the metal band holding the lid in place, finally managing to slide it open, only slightly, but enough. He could smell the petrochemical liquid, made his head swim. Jake fumbled disassembling the revolver, his hands slick with blood. He pulled his shirttail up and used it to wipe each part, letting them drop into the drum once he figured they were clean of his blood, hoping the solvent would take care of any he missed. Once the grip was wiped, he put it back into his pocket. He put the lid back onto the solvent, tightening the bands the best he could. He went over to the fuel truck climbed up onto the tank, unscrewed the fill lid and dropped the rest inside. He heard the splash. Closing the cap, he climbed back down and stayed hidden by its cab.

Time to call Swanson. He once more dialed 911. Swanson called almost immediately. He sounded weary but was anxious to know what had happened. Jake filled him in.

"Not sure what I should do now," Jake said. "The emergency maintenance truck has gone to the plane and here comes a police cruiser."

"Stay put. See what happens. The FBI should be there in a plane from Nassau within thirty minutes or so. Doubt they can replace those tires that quick. You did good podna. When the feebs arrive, you need to have made yourself scarce. Might think about who you can call to pick you up. That place will be crawling the rest of tonight."

"Dean's car—my fingerprints are all over it."

"Think you could get to it without getting caught?"

"Not sure. My best bet is to get away from here in it."

"Then do it. Call back when you're safely away from there."

Jake was reluctant to leave. How was it Devereaux had been left unguarded. Had he? Wouldn't be the first time a poor policeman had been paid to look the other way. Too often in the Middle East, he had witnessed police and soldiers, supposedly on their side, play along, seemingly to turn sides, due to bribes, threats to family or undetected radical ideology. Happens everywhere. Hank, his ex-father-in-law and crew owned many local police in the good ol' USA. Not the first time. Definitely, not the last.

Jake knew he should leave. He was rid of the revolver. Were the police armed? He couldn't recall seeing any holstered weapons on the few he had seen.

The police car pulled up next to the service truck. The men sent to repair the tire were shaking their heads. What Jake hoped would be the case—no replacement wheels. He had seen enough. Quietly as he could he checked the drums until he found an empty. He rolled it to the ones stacked against the back fence, attempted to climb on top, almost turning it over one time, coming close to falling back off the next time, finally succeeding in gaining his footing, then performing the next level on the adjacent stack of drums. He was more careful climbing over the barbed wire this time, just a couple more puncture wounds. Staying low, he moved around the perimeter of the fence until he was at the car. He reached in the open door, keeping his head down and started the car. Before he got in, he looked over to the scene at the airline. The stairs had been lowered, Dean was fumbling because of his broken finger, to flash his fake FBI badge to the police. As Jake eased the car forward, he saw the woman at the top of the stairs looking in his direction. He was almost certain it wasn't Blakely—from this distance, she seemed taller, leaner, different physique, much darker hair.

Once he drove past the terminal and started down the winding entrance drive, Jake turned the lights on and sped up. He needed to put distance between him and any authorities that may arrive. Swanson had said the FBI were coming by air. He needed to let him know he had managed to escape, and, that the woman most likely wasn't Blakely.

"You feel certain this woman was not Blakely? Damn. Means we still don't know where she is. Now we have two Dean accomplishes we have to account for."

"What about the FBI? Dean and guests aren't going anywhere by air. Oh fuck. I knew there was something wrong back there."

"What are you talking about?" an exasperated sounding Carl asked.

"Their jet is blocking part of the landing strip. The FBI plane may not be able to land unless they move the one Dean and friends are on. What if Dean's pilot knows this and Dean decides to force the issue by demanding new wheels be delivered? Doubtful if Dean has remained unarmed. The Bahamians could be fooled by his badge or coerced if they refuse to listen. Depending on who Dean's employer is, they may have a chopper on its way."

"Agent Harper, you have a vivid imagination. As much as I hate to, I guess it's time to tell you, you've been furloughed without pay and most likely will be terminated. Not my call; only Hardy could possibly do anything about the situation, I haven't been able to reach him. You need to get the hell away from there and see how this plays out for you tomorrow. I mean today. Jesus, it's 3:30. Go somewhere and get some sleep. I'll do what I can to get some answers. Call me if there's any problem."

Swanson called the FBI number he was given for Nassau and relayed Jake's concern. The agent said he would contact their plane which was fifteen minutes out from Exuma and give them the news. Carl asked what their plan would be if they couldn't land. The agent said, "They would have to return to Nassau and board the agency's helicopter. If the SAC can get permission. With the furloughs and all, their flights were limited. Meaning, at best a good two-hour delay. The SAC would have no better alternative."

Frustrated, Carl called the DEA station at the nearby Exuma Island. The night agent answered. He identified himself.

"There is a disabled jet at the Great Exuma Airport with members of a cartel onboard attempting to flee the island. A chopper is needed with armed agents to assist the local authorities. They need to take an unknown number of men and one woman into custody until the FBI can get there. How soon can you be there?"

The agent said he would alert the station chief. "He will be the one to determine the response."

Fucking government shutdown was making things impossible. Didn't any of those childish morons know they were jeopardizing national security in their petty political game? His op was far more important for border security than some half-ass wall which wouldn't stop the cartels. They were after high-tech shit like what he was trying to stop. Ignorant glory hounds. Looking more like his career was ending the way those assholes wanted it.

Jake was floored by the news of his possible termination. Would they attempt to take the money back they had paid him? Fuck Hardy. What did that mean? And, his problems with the local police, had they been resolved? He hadn't given a statement. Was that even the case? Furlough or no furlough, pay or no pay, Devereaux was his only chance unless he could find Blakely. He wasn't too confident of finding her. Would Dean stay with the disabled jet? If it was me I wouldn't. What were the alternatives? If not flying, had to be by boat? Devereaux' boat. Possibly? He could wait there. At least it was a place for him to get some much-needed rest. And if they show, then what? Maybe Devereaux had a weapon onboard. Devereaux had thought going there was too risky. Three thirty, four by the time he got there. Most likely no one would be awake to see him.

43

Driving up Queen's highway, more tired thoughts hit his tired mind. The hazmat team, what had been done with regards to the Russians' boat? Would they have taken the boat, or would it still be there under guard. Hopefully, no one was watching Devereaux' boat. And the car—they can track the GPS built into the car. What does it matter? The ones he was most concerned about were tied up with the plane. For what was left of tonight he hoped. He needed to try to get some sleep. Later he would have to formulate a plan. That is if Devereaux, Dean and friends didn't show up at the boat.

He passed by Mitch's place. Made him think of Amy and the sex they enjoyed earlier. He could stop. Most likely she would be delighted. Tempting, but he shouldn't involve her just to satisfy his rekindled ardor. He told himself not again with her. Best for her. Best for everyone. More and more it was looking like he would be heading back to the farm, terminated by HSI and ESI. Not being able to afford any woman's company, once again. Would he be able to hold onto the farm without these jobs? Government promises. He should not have listened to Hardy.

44

"I saw him, it was definitely your boy." The dark redhead, named Renai, was staring at Dean who had re-entered the plane after talking to the Bahamian police. "He was looking right at me. He drove off while you were out there chatting up those natives."

"He's no longer a problem. He's been terminated."

"Fortunately, not by you," the pinched face pilot Boyd said. "Mark would have been upset if you had shot him."

"If I had wanted to shoot him, he would be dead. He had a knife at my throat, I had to do something."

"You underestimated him," Renai added. "You knew he was a trainer with the elite Philippine Scout Rangers, and you almost screwed yourself. I don't know why Mark sent you."

"You mean instead of you. Perhaps you would have joined him in a threesome with the Carmichael bitch or the Jones gal."

"Enough you two," Boyd said. "We need to figure out what we're going to do with our friend Thomas Devereaux. According to what was picked up from Agent Swanson, there could be a DEA team headed our way. Your fake FBI credentials won't work with them. And there's the possibility, the SAC in Nassau will send a chopper. We can't let them get their hands on Devereaux. Our cover will be blown, and we'll be in a world of shit. You talked with Mark, what did he say?"

"He wants us to get Devereaux to tell us what he knows about the Carmichael woman's and Tobolokov's disappearance. Tobolokov probably knows who Bolstoy's contacts were. That damn friend of Harper, TJ Alvarez came close to getting Diego to talk, amazingly his wife did. We need to know who his contact was, Mark is certain it had to be Tobolokov. How did he get to the Bahamas? What is the connection to the Carmichael woman and Devereaux? The dead Russian agents, who sent them, and, why were they sent to threaten the Harper man. If the Carmichael woman's story is to be believed, why was she a threat? This dead Victor and this other Russian Boris, who is supposed to be behind the threats, who did they work for? Mark wants answers. The government shutdown buys us time. It won't last forever. America's and Israel's enemies are ahead of us. Somebody is attempting to sell them weapons that will threaten the free world's security. Carmichael, Tobolokov and Devereaux are our only leads. We've got to get Devereaux to talk. That is our mission."

"You should have let the Harper man talk to him," Renai said. "Your jailbreak was amateurish. Our whole mission is at risk because of him. Perhaps you should have been upfront with him. Devereaux was willing to talk to him."

"Renai, Mark did not want the Harper man told any more than I told him. He was HSI's man, we were not let to them know anything about our team. Got it? Now, Boyd, you need to get in touch with the DEA and get them to call off their team, stall them. We need to find another way off this island."

Renai said, "I can try sodium pentothal on him, perhaps Rohypnol, get him to drop his inhibitions, I'm sure your voyeuristic tendencies prefer that."

"If I wanted to watch you perform, all I'd have to do is watch your training videos."

"You bastard."

"That's right. Do whatever, just make sure you don't make him too drugged to move. Boyd track the Harper man's movements to make sure he no longer poses a threat."

Dean wondered why Mark had such a soft spot for the Harper man. Had to be something more from his past that was not in the dossier. He logged into the backdoor of the NSA's Daisy Chain and typed in Jackson Harper, Army Ranger, South Carolina, DOB 04/09/84.

He skimmed through the stuff he'd read before. Two things he noted not contained in the earlier file that rang a bell under contacts: ex-father-in-law, Francis Henry Michaels, "Hank," suspected member of Dixie Mafia; and further down under person of interests connection—neighbor, Thurmond Pinckney Tindall, Colonel US Army, ret., NSA, ret., Tindal Industries, military contractor, seeking government approval of weapon manufacturing facility on adjoining land.

Interesting—Colonel Tindal, Tindal's Terrors, feared and despised military intelligence team in the First Gulf War. Right-hand man was Major Bud Jenkins. Was this what Devereaux meant by personal? And, Mark taking a proprietary interest in Harper's well-being? He logged out of the NSA so-called "secure" database, which their IT team hacker had shown was anything but.

Boyd took the key fob and using another program entered the car ID and pulled up last known location—Rolleville. Devereaux' boat? Harper was headed to Devereaux' boat. He pulled up the marina location via real-time satellite. Too hazy, not clear enough to get a fix. A few more hours until daylight. The boat, a way off the island.

Daniel Boyd Jacobs started tracking the DEA team. He told Dean he was not able to get the station commander to call his team back. ETA was in less than thirty minutes. They would need to break into the rental lot to steal a car. Time was critical.

Dean leaned over his shoulder to watch.

"Perhaps I should requisition us a vehicle?"

"Go."

Jacobs was on his feet and hurrying off the plane while Dean went to the back to check on Reba Heloise Renai's efforts with Devereaux.

Her attitude bordered on insubordination, but her work spoke for itself. She was totally dedicated in the use of medical training and the art of seduction, which, though he chided her, he stood in awe of her willingness to use her beautiful body as a weapon. Especially, in light of her having been abducted as a child and sold into prostitution. She had been in one of Saddam Hussein's private brothels. Being Jewish had made her treatment heinous. It was a miracle she survived physically and mentally. She had not been recruited, she volunteered. Dean was glad she was on their team. He only wished she would share her bodily delights with him. She had made it clear, never going to happen. One could only fantasize.

Devereaux had a dazed lascivious twisted grin on his sweating face. Renai sat on his lap facing him, her curvaceous bare backside turned toward Dean. He looked at the crack of her shapely buttocks and wished it was him she straddled. He hated to interrupt.

"Reba."

She stopped her lap dance, rose, rearranged her clothes, swung one leg down, stood up and buttoned her pants and blouse. Dean couldn't help but notice Devereaux' clothed erection. Confusion spread across Devereaux' face. Reba turned around and walked past Dean.

He followed her out, closing the door. She poured herself a flute of white wine from the small bar. He watched her smooth, slim neck as she swallowed. If only. She seemed to read his expression and smirked.

"Satisfy your fantasies?"

"Hardly. Pun intended. Afraid we'll have to pursue our pleasures another time. Jacobs had no success. The DEA chopper will be here in less than half hour. We need to be moving. Jacob has gone to find transportation. Pack everything incriminating and useful for your questioning. Get Devereaux ready to disembark as quickly as possible. Is he mobile?"

"With help." She drained her flute and began wiping down the glassware and bar."

"Forget that. Get ready to move. I'll pack the electronics. Jacobs will help with Devereaux. We'll do what we can before getting out of here. May have to burn this damn pricey asset."

"Mark won't like that," she said, "might want to check with him first."

"He may already be in Cuba. Go. Hurry."

45

The night view coming down the hill into Rolleville was almost as spectacular as the daytime panorama. The softly lit cathedral, the sparkling lights of the boats in the bay as a backdrop were a picture Jake would never forget. Hopefully he would get the chance to enjoy it after tonight. The dock area was faintly lit, the parking lot was full so Jake rode a couple blocks away, continually checking his phone reception until it showed no service. He parked in a small unoccupied backlot near wooden shacks. In a matter of less than five minutes, he moved through the dark alleys toward the bay area.

The only life he ran across were a couple hungry-looking mongrels, called potcakes. The story was many were brought here by boaters and abandoned. Always amazed Jake that there were so many cruel and uncaring people all over the world who regarded fellow animals as lesser creations. Jake was more of a Buddhist or native American in this regard. He believed all life served a higher purpose.

He worked his way through the parking lot near the docks, stayed low in case some early riser was up. A few boats lights were on, but none near Devereaux' boat. The Russians' boat berth was empty. Jake stood, ambled down toward the docks, trying to appear like a weary, late-night partier returning to his boat. Wasn't difficult. He stepped onboard, tried the sliding glass door. Locked. He thought about lying down and crashing on the deck. He went cautiously around the outside rail-run to the forward deck area. The door there was unlocked. He entered the suite, thought about looking for a weapon before he crashed. He stumbled up the steps, went to the storage compartment. Inside were the usual stuff—life vests, scuba tanks, masks, snorkeling gear, speargun, and several razor-sharp tipped spears. He took those, a sheathed knife, a flare gun and a fire extinguisher. That ought to do it.

Jake put the bulkier items on the outer side of the queen size bed. He loaded a spear in the gun and laid it on the bed next to him, pointed away in case he accidently engaged the trigger. He slid the knife under the other pillow, lay down and closed his eyes. Soon the gentle rocking of the waves sent him off into la la land.

Dean was satisfied with their cleaning efforts. He decided burning the plane would create more problems than were necessary. Let the delivery and maintenance crews deal with the blowback. He gave the maintenance guys money, adding an undeniable threat in case they felt the need to do anything except claim ignorance of anyone but him. As far as they knew, he grew weary from waiting. He left them a made-up cell number where they could reach him once the plane was ready.

They loaded all their equipment and Devereaux in a requisitioned van.

"Devereaux's boat. We'll take it, be long gone before anyone has any idea where we disappeared to," Dean told Reba when asked the plan.

"And the Harper man?" Reba asked.

"Haven't decided."

"If he's armed?"

"Our Mr. Harper has a soft spot for females. You'll have to make sure he doesn't use that itchy finger. The revolver only has one round left."

"One is all it takes."

"My money is on you." Dean smiled.

She didn't.

The wet lick ran across his cheek, his sleep-addled brain registered the sensation, unable to comprehend. The weight on the bed told him someone was there. The pressure on the side of his neck increased when he reached for the weapons.

"Huh uh uh. Be a shame to cut your own throat." The voice was clipped, somewhat nasal. Definitely feminine. "Easy I mean you no harm. Don't make me change my mind."

There wasn't enough light for Jake to make out who the speaker was. Defensive countermeasures raced through his mind. This was a first for him—

a woman threatening his life. He knew he had the advantage in terms of strength, perhaps in trained techniques. Big problem, his awakening mind realized. She held a weapon at a vital part of his anatomy. Any move could prove disastrous.

"Salty with a hint of sexual secreted undertones," she said. Her nimble hasty movement up off him, was surprising. Jake jerked upright, felt the tip of a spear in his chest. "Easy. Someone wishes to talk with you. Get up, don't make any sudden movements. hate to have to hurt you." She eased back, kept the spear pressed in the center of his chest. They moved around the bed. Jake felt certain he could slap the speargun out of her hand; he felt more certain others were waiting with more lethal weapons. They twisted, she moved the spear to the center of his back, marched him up the steps to the galley.

The dim light from the screens of the computer monitors showed a smiling Dean standing at the other end of the galley. Seated at one of the monitors was a man with a pinched face like a bird of prey, who looked him up and down then turned his attention back to the equipment which he was studying with great interest. On the table bench seat was the prone figure of Devereaux.

"Greetings Mr. Harper. Good to see you again. Have a seat." Dean motioned with his chin toward the bench seat—the other end was vacant.

Jake didn't move despite the unpleasant prod of the spear. Dean, nor birdman, had weapons showing, wonder woman could easily be sent back down the stairs.

"Is Devereaux dead?"

"Wouldn't be of much use to us if he were. Now would he? Mr. Harper, we're not the enemy. If I had wanted you dead, the earlier shot would not have missed or my lovely cohort could have killed you as you slept. Please have a seat. Reba, remove the weapon from his back." Dean moved over to sit in the other chair next to bird man.

Jake put his fingers onto Devereaux' neck, felt a pulse, moved around to face Dean after checking the woman he called Reba to see where she moved to. She had moved away from the steps, the speargun in her right hand pointed down, her left hand behind her back resting on her rounded hip.

"Your show. I guess you're here to take the boat."

"Seems someone disabled the plane with a couple well-placed rounds from a revolver, mine, I do believe. I would appreciate having it returned."

"Left it at the airport inside some barrels and a fuel truck tank."

"What a pity. Was a family heirloom." He crossed his legs, relaxed, feeling totally in control. "Mr. Harper, I would love to chat, I'm in somewhat of a hurry. Your choice. Stay here to deal with the authorities. Or, come with us. We can drop you off at the nearest port away from the Bahamian jurisdiction. Possibly better, you continue with us. Since you are no longer employed by Homeland and probably will be terminated by your other employer, you may consider my offer a good alternative to losing your farm to Colonel Thurmond Tindal."

Jake knew he flinched, couldn't be helped. How did Dean know so much about him? Who was his source? Agent Swanson had only tonight delivered the news of his termination. Hearing Tindal's name was like a cold slap. The fact that Dean knew about him and about his dire financial situation stunned Jake. Could part of the answer be Devereaux? Had this been the personal information he wanted to tell him?

"What else did Devereaux say?" Jake asked.

"Not much. Claims Tobolokov and Carmichael are both dead. I don't buy it. Trouble is we've been on the run since you refused my earlier offer to allow you to hear what he had to say."

The sound of other boat motors' rumbles reminded Jake that daylight would soon be upon them. He was tempted to take Dean up on his offer. He seemed sincere, but Jake had learned that well-trained spooks were well-trained liars. Once they were out of here, he would be at their mercy. The thoughts of voluntarily or involuntarily ending up as shark bait didn't appeal to him. "As much as I wish to get out of here, I'm afraid I must decline your offer. I'll take my chances with the authorities."

Before Jake could react, all three moved as one. He kicked out at birdman who deftly deflected his attempt to take out his knee. Jake's swing connected with Dean's jaw, slowing him down, then he felt the needle pinch to his neck. He backhanded Reba, his muscles began to fail, knees gave way, the last he remembered his head bounced off the carpeted floor.

When he slowly became aware of having re-entered the real world, he noticed Rolleville's bay sounds—voices, vehicles, boats, all manners of human activity. He looked around. He was in the back of a sour-smelling van. He checked his pockets, his cell phone sans sim card, and pen knife remained. Dean had retrieved his cell. The one Jake had taken. He sat up. He had a tremendous urge to piss, fortunately, there was a half-full water bottle against one side panel. He relieved himself, recapped the bottle and set it in the front console drink holder to remind himself to bring it with himself when he got away from here. He climbed into the driver's seat after crossing the appropriate wires left dangling beneath the steering column.

He rolled the windows down the rest of the way from the partial opening left by the Dean crew. He put the van in gear. He needed a shower, a change of clothes, something in his stomach and a new phone. Hardy would be happy. Fuck you Hardy. He needed to get rid of the van, either go to the job site, or turn himself in, get it over with.

He left his bags and other clothes in the spare bedroom at Amy's house. He was shocked at the time—10:45. He had been out of it for almost six hours. The airport incident should have been cause for a search for Dean and company.

Twenty minutes later, he came by Mitch's. No company vehicles in front. A couple of minutes later, he pulled behind Amy's house. The van wheels began to dig into the sand, Jake stopped, took the piss bottle, went in the back door.

The bedroom was as he left it. Jake brushed his teeth, took a dump, followed by a long cool shower, shaved and was getting dressed when he heard the door open.

Amy jumped when he stepped out, then hurried over to hold him tight. "I was scared something happened to you. I like called the jail. No one answered. I went to the project. Mitch said he hadn't seen you. Nick was there. I didn't like dare ask him. That nasty man, I was like scared he did something to you, was going to come back here to do what he said he wanted to do to me." She tried to kiss him.

Jake turned his head. She kissed his cheek and stepped back. He held her arms, slid his hands down to take hers. "Amy, I need you to keep as far away from me as you can. I shouldn't be here."

"What did I like do? I thought last night you know, like meant something." Her eyes began to moisten.

He pulled her to him and rubbed her back. "Last night was the best thing that has happened to me since I can remember. Trouble is never far from me. You deserve better…"

"No. No. Last night was like the best ever for me too. Please don't like push me away. I love you." She pushed back again and grabbed Jake's head and they had a deep soulful kiss.

"Amy, Amy, Amy," was all he could say. He pulled loose and went back to the bedroom. She came in, closed the door and began undressing. Her body was more beautiful looking in daylight than he remembered from last night. He tried to turn away.

She came over, reached around, rubbed his growing erection, then unbuttoned his pants, unzipped him, sat back on the bed, pulled him to her, placing her lips around his penis, her eyes looking up into his. Jake wanted to resist. The tensions from the nights and days before, he needed this. He pushed her back and entered her. They started slow, the pace quickened, her nails dug into his shoulders urging him on until he collapsed completely spent and rolled off her. She leaned over and kissed him, grinding her lips into his.

"You like cannot say that wasn't like the best. I want to stay here like forever. We can like do it over and over."

A part of him was upset with himself. He had told himself not to ever let this happen again with her. His little head had over-ruled his big head. What man could resist someone as eager and ravenous looking as she was? He knew it couldn't last. He leaned up and tried to look just in her eyes. His neck hurt. He adjusted his hand to help support it. "Amy, I would like nothing better, but–"

"Then like just do it." She tried to pull him down for another kiss,

He pulled back and sat up. He needed to shower and change clothes. "I need to either go to the project or go to the jail, see if they intend to arrest me. First, I need to get something to eat."

She sat up and slid next to him, her hand reached to caress him. He took her hand in his.

Jake felt good being here with her, sharing their bodies, having a laugh. Hard to believe she was such a willing lover. Lover? Little head again, his downfall. He leaned over and kissed her. "I really have to get going. Let's take a quick shower so everyone doesn't smell our lovemaking. You can take us to get something to eat, while I decide on my best course of action."

"Okay. Like Action Jackson." She jumped up, Jake watched her firm, well-toned, shapely butt run toward the bathroom across the hall. He joined her. Once more they kissed, stroked and sensuously probed with soapy fingers while they let the warm water run over themselves. Surprisingly, Amy was able to bring Jake off again. He knelt and returned the favor.

Amy took them to a restaurant on the other side of Moss Town, and Jake enjoyed his first Caribbean crawfish, which was the size of a lobster. Amy smiled at him the whole time. It had been years since he received such female attention. He couldn't help but feel it very well could be his last.

He should have just let it go. Hard to admit defeat, he guessed.

He had Amy drive them up the circuitous airport drive. Near the top where the road bent around to the terminal, they saw a police car stopped in their lane, emergency red, blue and clear light bar flashing, a burly Bahamian policeman leaning on the car. Two more vehicles were between his car and them.

"I'm going to get in the trunk. If he stops us, ask him what's going on. Go as far as you can and take all you see in. Make it as fast as you can, that damn trunk is going to be hot as hell." Jake pulled the back-seat release, climbed between the seats into the small trunk space. He wiggled around to get situated so his neck wouldn't drive him into unbearable pain. He left the seat down partially until they were close enough that he might be seen. The policeman didn't stop or say anything to Amy. Once they moved on to where Jake felt it was safe enough, he lowered the seat partially back forward, relishing the cool air blasting from the car's AC.

Amy glanced at Jake in the rearview mirror. "Like the area past the terminal circle is blocked off. There are like a bunch of men in suits huddled in a group on the other side of the blocked off area. What do you want me to do?"

"Circle around and get us out of here."

"What now?"

Jake wasn't sure. It was looking like he should think about packing up, head stateside, shake Thurmond Tindal's tree, keep the farm out of his hands. He had gone all-in with a hopeful hand, game wasn't over, yet.

"Guess we'll have to go back to your place, watch some football or something."

"I have a better idea," she said. She reached over, rubbed his crotch.

What had he unleashed?

PART III

46

"How's it hangin' bro?" TJ asked. He and Jake had not spoken since before he learned of Jake's termination the week before.

"Sad to say without. I guess I shouldn't complain, at least I'm not in jail, still have a job."

"Whoa bro. Something I missed here. You sound like someone who has been getting some. Last I knew you were still being celibate." TJ looked over at Deane his comment piqued her attention.

"Unfortunately, I am once more. Had a nice time with this fine young lady, she's gone back to the Carolinas now. ESI's owner decided no more women friends for his employees down here. Sent the old manager to another project and put me in charge." Jake was seated at Rick's old desk. Things were quiet. Too quiet. Most people had gone home or wherever for the Christmas to New Years' shutdown of the project. "How about you and Deane?"

"Deane's working her VA job without pay because of this damn shutdown. I'm back at my job with Miami-Dade working with the joint task force on this Russian thing. Big battle with the feds, not getting anywhere. Most of the task members worried about when they're going to get paid. Christmas a slow time. Deane and I haven't been a single income family since right after we got married. Makes things tight. Hopefully, it be over soon. What about you, you coming this way for the holidays?

"Nah man. I'm the low man on the totem pole down here. Ain't diddly squat happening. I'm just part of the skeleton crew left here to keep an eye on things. They're scared the islanders will make off with a bunch of shit or sabotage the project for job security. From what I've seen and heard, most of the Exuma natives are taking or bartering for what they want, even when everyone is here. No matter, I figure why waste money flying back home. Ain't nobody there for me anyway, other than that young lady. Kinda feel some guilt because she's so young and needs to live a little. Besides she wants to have babies. I can hardly support my other children or myself. So, I'm stuck here without."

"Did you say babies bro? Moving kinda fast, aren't you?"

"Babies?" Jake heard Deane chime in.

"Damn bro, you little old to be starting another family." TJ laughed.

"Sure better make some money."

"Don't go saying that. Be done put the mojo on me."

"What you goina do for Christmas?" TJ asked. "You know you would be more than welcome to come here. Be part of the Hood Christmas. Tried to get Carl to come for dinner. Says he might. He says they trying to force him to retire. He's determined not to go anywhere until Hardy tells him to. We haven't heard a word from him in over a week. Carl's worried, even though he says he's not. You wouldn't have happened to have heard from him, have you?"

"No. Don't expect to. Kinda pissed at him for lassoing me into his op then leaving me hanging in the wind. The Bahamian authorities are still watching me like buzzards waiting for the kill. They were hoping I'd leave and not come back. Getting containers released and expat subs okayed continues to be a problem. Now this shutdown is making getting shipments released from the states potentially a bigger problem, especially for ESI, meaning me. Their prime minister is not happy, Fluor people are less happy, Ned refuses to admit not paying taxes and fees created this mess. At least he paid those after Fluor paid him for work completed."

"Everyone hopes things will get back to normal after the first of the year. Meanwhile, like I said, I'm stuck, not much here to make it feel like Christmas, weather is in the eighties. I'm running around in shorts. Funny thing some of the Bahamians are wearing parkas and toboggans." They both laughed. "Remember the one named Alvin? The one I thought was tied up in the stuff going on here, still think it. Anyway, when I took over as manager, I gave two thirds of the Bahamians pink slips. Bunch of them led by Alvin came to my work trailer, threatened me with boards and tools. "We goina feed you to de sharks," Alvin said. Had to do some fast talking."

"Guess it turned out okay, seeing as how we talkin' bro."

"Still kickin' and back to doin' without. Anyway, just wanted to check with you and Deane. See how you doing."

"If we don't hear from you, have a good holiday. Go get drunk. Who knows maybe you'll get lucky again? Just be careful, there is such a thing as condoms, you know."

Jake returned his attention to the computer, browsing the Internet dating sites. The woman Elena sounded interesting. No picture, her answers and bio came across as intelligent and she didn't shy away from his bio, he stated he wanted someone he could enjoy in and out of bed. She wanted to get to know more about him. She lived outside New Orleans, a place he loved to visit. Self-sufficient, not wanting more children and loving the country were important attributes Jake liked. He had steered clear of Rick and Kendall up until they departed with Ned. Amy had wanted to be with him. They were able to slip a couple more epic lust-laden moments together before her forced denouement.

Staying on this island with few people here and nothing to do made him feel like a prisoner. Jake spent the majority of the weekend giving his statements to the FBI and Bahamian authorities. Evidently, Ned or someone had spoken to the prime minister. The Bahamian police weren't pleased with their minister's decision to allow Jake to remain for the duration of the project, warned Jake they would keep a close eye on him. He was not to leave Exuma without notifying them before he did. As for the threats? Seemed they left with the departure of Devereaux, Dean and crew, Blakely and Tobey. The past week uneventful.

Jake talked to the Bahamians, Fluor's other field managers, and observed the interactions of ESI's men. Alvin would disappear whenever Jake came to the building, he was supposedly working in. Rodney, on the other hand, must have been warned or was good at reading people, he seemed to be working every time Jake slipped in to check on his crew's work progress. He would talk to Jake in a professional way and went out of his way to ingratiate himself by seeming warm and friendly. Jake overheard Rodney's and others' morning conversations about the porn sites which Mitch said they were so caught up in. Invariably, it led to talk about the hot Cuban hos. Played into Jake's inexplicable fascination with Cuba.

Most of their stories were about the cheap, good-looking pussy to be had there. The last morning before the project was to shut down, Rodney brought him a card with a Bahamian who now lived in Havana and could help him out with lodging and other things to do in Cuba.

"That was if Jake might want to slip off and go there," Rodney said with a gleam in his eyes.

Sitting at the desk, on that Friday, having given the men their checks before they headed to the bank and then back to their homes on the various other Bahamian Islands, he had sent a message to Elena. Jake looked at the card, pondered taking a chance, thinking the opportunity might never happen again, weighing the prohibition on leaving the island, plus the presidential ban on unauthorized travel to Cuba. Rodney said call his friend, go to Nassau, catch a Cubana Air flight, be there in a little over an hour, wouldn't cost more than a hundred dollars a day, room, food and lots of pussy. What was never asked or answered was how to go without being noticed or detained trying.

The Internet went down, as it so often did. Jake decided he would go to Georgetown to the Scotia Bank ATM, check on available funds in his BOFA account. The maximum withdrawal was three hundred, with the fifty plus in pocket, he would need at least another three fifty. Better to have extra, just in case. He really shouldn't be spending the money, but Ned's allowance would cover it and his first check should have been deposited.

The ATM was out of cash. Shit. What was he going to do? Ned had left him with the company credit card and the RBC check book. He could pull cash out, repay it when he got to Nassau, if he decided to go. He walked to the Royal Bank of Canada's ATM and tried the card. Asked for a pin which he didn't have. There was a short line outside the bank, a Bahamian policeman was at the door letting the customers in and out one at a time. Jake thought about it. Get in line, cash a check if he can, if not, then no Cuba.

He was able to cash the check. Hopefully, he could replenish the one thousand Canadian dollars before Ned found out. The internet indicated Cuba had exchange locations, was best to use Canadian money or Euros.

Jake rushed to the airport and bought a ticket to Nassau. He had an hour to run back to the apartment he now shared with Mitch, pack a bag and get back in time to board his flight.

In Nassau's airport, he checked the ATMs. He was out of luck. He wandered around until he found where Cubana Air's boarding location was. There was a short line, mostly women, looking about nervously. Jake wasn't sure what to do. He didn't see anyone snooping around watching the area, no police, no suits meandering around. He decided it would be best if he called Rodney's man in Havana. He went out of the terminal to a private area. No answer. He left his name, number and message, including Rodney's name.

Back at the boarding area, the earlier line had already boarded. There were three Cubana Air attendants, two dark-skinned lovely ladies and a short, swarthy man, behind the desk. Jake decided to risk it. He had come this far, felt it was now or never.

He walked up to the desk to one of the ladies and inquired about purchasing a roundtrip ticket to Havana. She smiled, told him in English, the next flight was in two hours, cost two hundred seventy-five dollars. Jake placed the money on the desk along with his passport. She told him he not need passport. She asked the nature of his visit and for how long. Jake told her personal for a week. She typed in the info and handed him a ticket and a Cuban visa good for one week, warning him in a friendly but stern manner not to miss his return flight or overstay the date on the visa. She handed back his U.S. passport without stamping it. That was a relief. He thanked her.

Jake went outside and tried Rodney's friend again. Nothing. He tried Rodney's phone and left a message. The sun was bright, the air noticeably cooler. Jake stretched out one of the concrete benches in the sun and closed his eyes. He dozed off and awoke to the sound of voices. He checked his phone. No calls. Thirty minutes to boarding time. He hurried back in. There was a long line, mostly twenty to thirty some, light-skinned, American-looking women, a long blonde-haired hippy type dude, what looked like a couple Euro/American casual businessmen and a few Cuban stiff-necked men. No one was talking, the women's eyes occasionally darting glances, none meeting his eyes. Jake figured they were some group on a cultural exchange visit allowed by the state department. Unlike him. Why were they so nervous? Made him self-conscious. His main worry were the Bahamian authorities. He had not seen one. He kept his sunglasses on. His LSU baseball cap pulled down low.

47

Havana, Cuba

They boarded. No assigned seats. The same airport attendants were the flight attendants. Jake ended up near the front, seated between an older man at the window and two of the American women to his right. The attendants continued standing during takeoff. Shortly afterwards, they were pushing carts up the aisle selling souvenirs, cigarettes, cigars and bottles of beer and liquor, mainly Cuban rum. No signs saying no smoking, stay in your seats or fasten seat belts. Some people were up and moving about freely.

The women in the surrounding seats began talking to each other. The older man, named William Burke, turned out to be a sports fisherman, part-time contributor to Field and Stream Magazine, coming back after a twenty-five-year hiatus. Jake became nervous when William told him back, when the airport was located in a cow pasture, nowhere near any civilization, the plane would stop on the broken concrete runway, and Cuban military soldiers would escort them off the plane and take them to the concrete block building to retrieve their bags. Jake asked about transportation. William claimed there would be bus service, a few taxis, no private rentals.

After the attendants made their trip from back to front and back again with the cart, they went to the cockpit, returned with questionnaires which they distributed, and told everyone to fill it out. The information was all about the nature of the visit, length, etc., including where you were staying. Oh shit. Jake had no idea. What would they do if he didn't put down anything, arrest him? No one knew he was going to Cuba. He could be arrested, disappear, no one would have the slightest idea where to begin looking for him. The depressing thought was there wasn't really anyone who might give a shit. TJ and Deane, but it could be months before TJ would think to look. And Cuba would be the last place TJ or anyone else would think to look for him.

He listened to the women and overheard one seated behind them tell someone Hotel Nacional. Jake tried to see what the woman beside him put down. She must have noticed he wasn't writing and was looking at her paper. She immediately covered her info up with her hand, like Jake was trying to cheat on a test or something. To put her mind at ease he asked if she had an extra pen. She curtly told him no. William handed him his when he finished. Jake put down Hotel National.

Shortly before landing the attendants retrieved the questionnaires. They didn't look at them. Jake wondered who would, would they follow up, see if he was at the hotel?

Jake was surprised and relieved when they landed at modern Jose Marti Airport and pulled up to a disembarking chute. Prior to landing Jake overheard the hippy dude, seated in the next rear section across the aisle next to the casual-dressed businessmen, reference a place called Jaimanitas, where both were going. They decided to share a cab.

Inside the baggage claim area was a center rotating carousal. Along the walls were cubicles for merchandise, all closed with screens pulled down except for one which was a currency exchange area. No one was behind the counter, standing next to it was a soldier in green fatigues armed with an AK-47. There were two other soldiers similarly armed at two other locations in the room. The bags had not been unloaded, so Jake wandered over to the exchange window and waited. After a couple minutes of being five feet away from the armed soldier and no one appearing across the counter, Jake walked back to join other passengers at the now spinning carousel. The hippie dude came out and walked by one of the guards and through a set of swinging doors. Jake grabbed his bag, went through the doors.

The terminal was a stuccoed-concrete and glass building extending upwards two stories. Directly in front of the ramp from the baggage area were pictures of new automobiles advertised for rent. William, the outdoorsman with his scary scenario, had fortunately been proven outdated. At the top of the ramp to the left was a semicircular, well-appointed bar. Seated on stools were five women in miniskirts looking like they belonged in a glamour magazine. Standing beside them was the hippie, a beer in hand. Jake stopped at the back of the bar area gawking at the women's nice derrieres, wondering about them, worried what he should do about transportation and a place to stay.

Outside, a small taxi pulled in, some people got in. A small bus was the only other vehicle in the traffic circle. Soon another of the casually dressed businessmen came up the ramp, he went over and hugged two of the foxy ladies, exchanged kisses on each cheek and in a Slavic sounding language said something to them. They all stood and filed out past Jake, boarded the bus, and left.

Jake decided he needed to get some answers to his dilemma. There was no one he thought safe to ask other than the hippie. He got a cerveza, and walked over to the hippy, who introduced himself. Said people called him Ace. Jake told him his plight.

Ace laughed. "Pretty ballsy coming here without knowing anything about the place. I'm waiting on this guy named Mark; he and I are going to share a cab. You're welcome to join us. We're going to a place, kind of a suburb of Havana, no doubt you can find a place there."

Hippie Ace worked on yachts at a marina in Miami and had a Cuban wife and infant which he visited every weekend. Jake told him he was working on a resort construction project on Great Exuma. Mark showed up. Introductions were made, Ace explained Jake's problem. Mark grabbed a cerveza, and they took their bags, went out front and hailed a cab. Ace had the driver stop at the end of the airport drive at a convenience store. He went inside to buy a twelve pack. While he was gone Mark offered to let Jake accompany him to see a man named Koko for accommodations.

"Maybe we can get a place for both of us. You can watch my back and I'll watch yours."

"Sounds great," Jake replied, wondering about the guy and what was meant by watching each other's back.

Mark Castle seemed to be a little under 5-10, maybe 165, had an angular jaw, brown hair and deep set greenish brown eyes which continued giving

Jake a calculating stare. He smiled and said, "I'm an advertising exec with offices in Miami and New York City. My major account is Jet Blue."

Jake wasn't sure about the guy, his bs radar was going off. He turned his attention to their Cuban cab driver who was watching the store, occasionally cutting his eyes toward Mark and him, only to break away when their eyes met. Jeff returned with the beer. He and Mark offered to pay him. He refused. Handing out the cans of cerveza. The cab driver declined.

They drove out the Avenida de la Indepencia, made numerous turns through towns with austere white-washed buildings and neighborhoods where the homes reminded Jake of some New Orleans' neighborhoods post-Hurricane Katrina—flaking soft pastel colored clapboard or chipped stucco-concrete with rusted metal or broken and missing tile roofs.

Ace and Mark drank their beers and talked. Jake drank, listened and would politely answer when asked a question. He gave a sanitized version of his life, leaving out the military and marital, family parts. Mostly he watched and listened. One thing which puzzled him were the lack of people. Where were the automobiles normally seen on the streets, vintage ones Cuba was noted for?

The stories. Ace having a wife and child living in Cuba and his ability to travel back and forth on weekends was interesting. Jake wondered why she didn't move to Miami but didn't feel like asking. Mark's story was much more intriguing. He claimed to have come to Cuba to see the place his mother's father had lived at before the Revolution. His maternal grandfather, he said, had been Fidel's priest. Strange, a priest, married with children, how was that possible? His grandfather had been deported to Europe following the revolution. Jake noticed the driver paying close attention to Mark's story.

Ace talked about living on a boat and his job maintaining wealthy people's yachts. Mark said his company had recently opened an office in Miami and he moved from NYC to manage it. Jake figured much of *their* stories, like his, were sanitized.

Mark watched Jake while he and Jeff talked. Jake, Dean said had a weakness for women. Good, so did he. Could prove useful. The big question was why was he here? Had someone learned his team was here? He would have to keep a close eye on Jake and be careful when he checked in with his team berthed nearby at Hemingway Marina. Jake was supposed to be no longer working for Homeland. Had Agent Hardy brought him here, if so for what? Jake seemed friendly enough, yet he saw Jake giving Ace and himself an appraising eye. What are you thinking Jake? You could not know about me. Few people did. Would have to watch him and Hardy, see if they communicated. The cartel business and the team's mission had just become more complicated.

Ace directed the taxi driver to pull over to the right curb at a y intersection in one of the somewhat nondescript neighborhood centers. He pointed across the street to a white-washed, l-shaped concrete structure with a small courtyard in the corner of the l. "That is where Koko lives and has his office."

Mark insisted on paying the cab fare. They bid Ace farewell after he told them where he lived. They agreed to meet him at the neighborhood watering hole at 5 o'clock.

There was a door to the right in the corner. Sounds of a television could be heard through the open doorway. They hesitated to enter. Mark called out "hola." A nice-looking, matronly woman appeared out of somewhere to the left of the narrow hallway. Mark told her they were here to see Koko about a place to stay. She looked him and Jake up and down, walked down the hall to the end where the tv sounds came from. The volume went down, she came back followed by a man dressed in an off-white guayabera and loose-fitting pants of the same color over stylish loafers, sans socks. He was swarthy and walked with a light step for someone his size. He was approximately 5-6 or 7, 170—rugby halfback material, Jake thought, a round Hispanic farm worker with thick dark hair and dark, no bullshit, eyes in contrast to his welcoming smile.

Mark introduced them. Koko said he had been expecting Mark. Mark explained Jake's situation. Koko gave Jake an appraised look, then told them to follow him. His English was surprisingly good.

The office had a cell phone and laptop computer sitting on a metal desk in the corner with a wooden chair in front and a cushioned chair behind it. Koko sat, gestured for Mark to sit in the other chair. Left Jake standing in the doorway. In another section off the office, Jake noticed were caned, tropical-design-cushioned chairs and ottomans and a fabric recliner in front of a television. There was a small, older woman seated there watching an English-speaking program with Spanish subtitles.

Koko had them fill out an application form while he looked through a spiral bound notebook. When they were finished, he read their application, told them he had two rooms in a home not too far away at a cost of thirty CUCs per person per night. Mark looked at Jake, who nodded. He watched as Mark laid 40 Canadian dollars on the desk and Jake, relieved to find Koko took Canadian money, did the same. They received a receipt, Koko stood, excused himself, left the office area and went back down the hall. Shortly he returned with a slightly taller, more fit-looking version of himself who introduced himself as Tomas.

Koko said, "Tomas will take you there. First let me introduce you to my family. He led them to the sitting room where the first woman they met, his wife Esmeralda. The other, eldest lady rose from the recliner. Her name was Lynesa something or other, Esmeralda's mother. Then from the other part of the house came a young, very sensuous teenager in tight shorts and a T-shirt with a picture of Carlos Santana on it. Her name was Carmen. Jake tried to not stare. Mark didn't take his eyes off her and she in turn displayed a radiant coquettish smile as she was introduced. Koko hurried her back out of the room telling her to bring refreshments. She returned shortly with a pitcher of Mojitos. The men had a drink and the women went back to doing whatever it was they had been doing.

Tomas loaded their bags in an antiquated Lada. The exhaust poured into the unairconditioned interior making Jake feel uncomfortable. Luckily it became more bearable when they started moving and the fresher air poured in through the opened windows. They wound their way through a neighborhood with homes that looked well-maintained to the point where, if blindfolded and plopped down with the blindfold removed you would think you were on Meeting Street in his hometown of Lancaster, South Carolina, with their 1950s era residences. It was in front of one of these homes, that Tomas stopped. Tomas went with them to the door and introduced them to the residents, Sr and Sra Esquivel. The inside of the house like the way the couple were dressed were vintage 1960s Americana. It unsettled Jake. He felt like he had been caught in a time warp. Sra Esquivel took them upstairs to their rooms, small with dormers, separated by a small bathroom.

They told Tomas on the way to their quarters about meeting Ace at the community cerveceria. He said he would take them there, if they so desired.

He offered to be their guide, put his car and driving services at their disposal for five dollars per day plus cost of fuel. Mark and Jake readily agreed.

The cerveceria was in the middle of a park-like square, two concrete buildings with several picnic tables with benches in between. As they approached, they could hear the sound of voices, laughter and reggae music. Rounding the corner of one of the buildings, Jake caught a glimpse of a light-skinned, pinch-faced guy arm around what appeared to be a drunk young woman exiting the other end. Jake could have sworn it was Dean's man. Ace was sitting at the nearest table with one Cuban male and five attractive Cuban women. He yelled at them to come meet his friends. Mark and Tomas went ahead of him, then Mark dropped back and asked him if everything was alright? Jake told him he thought he recognized someone, but, wasn't sure.

"Come on. Relax. This is what we came here for. Right?" Mark waited until Jake nodded and moved forward.

What the fuck was Jacobs doing here? He was told to stay at the marina and monitor the equipment. Dean better have Reba making sure Devereaux was kept quiet and out of sight. So far, all efforts to get him to talk were in vain. What was Jacob's thinking? His intel efforts indicated something big was in the works. To happen in Cuba. He would need to tighten them up.

Pussy had to be. Like himself and Jake, fucking warriors, literally and figuratively. Eat, drink, fuck and be merry, for who knows what tomorrow brings. Like all mercenaries, they all saw a chance to get laid as part of the benefits. And what better place to get laid than in Cuba, where the women saw it as a way to defy a repressive government, a chance to enjoy the food, drink and personally forbidden places, enjoyed at the expense of what they believed were rich foreigners, who may take them or their sisters away from their futureless life on their poor totalitarian island.

Nevertheless, orders must come first. He would not tolerate his team not following orders. Jake knew their faces. Jacobs' being here may come back to haunt them.

He would take care of that problem later. For now, he needed to get his mind on making sure Jake relaxes and doesn't have time to think about Jacob's appearance. Jake was his immediate problem. Alcohol and women often led even the best warrior to drop his guard.

Jake couldn't believe this was possible. All these young women were acting amazingly friendly, Rodney hadn't lied, least wise about all the hot women. Ace poured drinks from a bottle of Havana Club Rum for everyone. It was the smoothest rum he had ever tasted.

Tomas' too young but Cuban gorgeous sister was there. He introduced her, then they left after he gave Mark his cell number.

The bottle was empty. Jake volunteered to buy the next one, incredibly only seven and change for a two-liter bottle. Everyone was getting smashed except Ace, who seemed to be playing host, or was it facilitator? Jake felt the alcohol. Apparently, Mark did also, he was making crass joking comments. The girls seemed to be eating it up.

Jake thought through the growing buzz; he hadn't been with a woman since Amy. Strange—before Amy it had been years. Joanna had been the last, certainly not the first. The first had stolen his heart. He played the field while taking college classes and living it up stateside. Several women thought he had impregnated them. One got an abortion without telling him, another self-aborted, after which he vowed if he was going to play, he must be willing to pay. He wasn't anti-abortion but felt the woman should include the man in the decision. That resolution led to his marriage to Joanna. They married, doomed from the start. He loved her more for being the mother of his children than for who she was. That guilt plagued him, especially since her death. That accusation by Hank, her father, hit home.

Here he was, surrounded by lovely ladies seeming to offer themselves to him. Maybe this was a pay to play situation. That would be a first for him. The alcohol dulled his caution. He wasn't sure he could perform well enough to get his money's worth.

"Jake," the one with expressive eyes sitting next to him said, "you should take me with you."

"I believe I'm more to his liking," the raven-headed one on the other side replied. "Tell her Jake."

A rough-looking boney guy with what looked like prison tats came over from the far table and sat down at their table and drank from expressive eyes' glass, he glared at Jake, then he winked at raven hair. Jake felt her clench his arm. Her friend, from whose glass he guzzled and finished off, closed her eyes then shook her head to something he whispered to her. When they opened, it was like the light had gone out. Ace stood and said he needed to get home. The conversations around them seemed to diminish. Jake started to stand but raven hair held onto his arm. Eyes stood when the tat guy did, she took the remains of the bottle Mark bought, left the table and followed tats. They went back to tats' former table. Jake started to stand. Mark looked at him, shook his head and said, "I'm ready to go back to my room. You want to leave or stay?"

Jake felt like he should do something about what happened, then decided it would not be wise. He had left a place where a woman had gotten him in trouble, best not repeat the problem here. Especially here.

Jake, raven hair, Mark and his pick-up, ambled along going past some closed businesses. Mark and the other gal stopped.

"Elsa says we can't have guests at the place where we are staying. She and I are going to get a room nearby. What about you two?"

Raven hair, who said her name was Alice, had been holding on tight to Jake's arm, she looked up at him waiting for, from her look, a definite yes answer.

"I think I'm going to head back to the place we're staying. It's getting late and I don't want to take a chance on being locked out." Alice's grip relaxed, a silent message passed between her and Lila.

"You not like me?" she asked Jake.

"What about tomorrow? I've had too much to drink, maybe we can get together tomorrow."

"I go with you to your room. Maybe they let me stay, okay?"

Jake didn't feel like arguing. "Ok."

Mark and Lila took a left at the next block. Alice and Jake continued walking. She asked for the address. He let her direct their slow, staggering course.

"Will your friend who left our table with that jerk be okay?"

"Jerk? I do not know that word. He bad man. Been in prison."

"He her boyfriend?"

"No. You wish to be with her?"

Jake stopped and brushed her lips with his. She quickly pushed away. They walked on.

When they reached the house, Sra Esquivel came to the door when Jake knocked. She looked at Alice, said something to her in Spanish concerning jinateras not being allowed. Alice bristled. There was a quick exchange which alarmed Jake. Sra Esquivel turned to Jake, told him her house was not a casa particular. That he could not entertain women here. He apologized. "I'm sorry. I did not know."

"She must leave. Do you wish to stay?"

"Yes. I will be back shortly."

She closed the door. Jake turned, went to where Alice waited near the street. He told her he needed to go in.

Alice shook her head. "That man at Cerveceria. He cause trouble if I not have money."

Jake thought tats must be her pimp. "I'm sorry. There is nothing I can do."

"Please you give little money. I have baby. Need money for her."

Just my luck, Jake thought. He reached into his pocket and pulled out a note. It was a twenty. He handed it to her, turned and went back to the house. Sra Esquivel evidently had been watching, opened the door before he got to it. She shook her head. Jake walked by and went up the stairs.

He was upset with himself for falling into such an obvious trap. He tried to sleep. It was humid hot, with no breeze coming in the open windows. Noises from outside didn't make it any easier—there was music, dogs barking and, oddly enough roosters crowing hours before dawn. He never heard Mark come in.

48

Mark came in an hour or so after Jake. Sra Esquivel told him they could no longer stay after tonight. Mark wondered if Jake's bringing the other jinetera had anything to do with her decision. He slipped up the stairs, quietly went through to the bathroom, peeked in on Jake. His back was to him. He was alone. Probably a good thing. After he had paid Elsa and enjoyed her services, they talked a little in between bouts. Elsa said she was a cuenta propista, a free-lancer, unlike her friend Alice who was a jinetera. Elsa told Mark Alice had a baby, the father was the scrawny asshole with the tats. He had been in prison for being a pimp. Elsa said she wasn't like Alice, she did whatever she had to to pay her bills. Mark almost laughed. Instead he rolled her over, went at her from behind. He would have to ask Koko to find another place. He thought about Jake.

Tomorrow, he would need to have a heart to heart with his team. Instead of coming here for pussy, Jacobs should have been trying to locate Tobolokov and Carmichael, monitoring the networks to see where Agent Hardy was. They needed to find the Cuban generals. Unlike the clowns in Washington, Mark saw no way the generals would sell any Chinese or Russian technology without going through the cartels. Supposedly only his contact knew he was playing both hands against each other. With Bolstoy out of the picture, what other oligarch would be willing to take the risk of dealing in such a venture? Mark could think of several. Someone was eliminating competition.

Meanwhile, the Juarez Cartel kingpin had put Mark in a precarious position of dealing through Arturo, his nephew, who wanted to come to Cuba to meet directly with the generals. Even threatened Mark if he wasn't soon successful. Who were the generals dealing through? He needed contact. They had to know he was here. Had Tobolokov or Carmichael been a go-between and already made contact? Didn't seem likely. So far there had been no sign of them in Cuba. Then there was Jake. Was he here to help Hardy, or, and it didn't seem likely, here to meet with Carmichael? The scene was getting crowded.

Agent Robert Hardy was summoned to the embassy by Ambassador Amherst Mann. The ambassador wanted to know why Hardy had not checked in with him upon arrival. Hardy told him about the op and his suspicions that there were Americans, perhaps within one of the other agencies involved in selling their technology to their enemies. Ambassador Mann asked Hardy if the sickness from some mysterious source at the embassy could be connected. Hardy said he didn't know. Seemed the ambassador was more worried about the supposed *sonic sickness* that had caused a recall of diplomats and staff of his and a dismissal of Cuban diplomats from Washington, than he was about the selling of secrets. Before he was dismissed Hardy requested the ambassador keep the reason for his being in Cuba from his staff, most of whom every nation knew were CIA agents posing as diplomats or assistants. When asked what cover story he should use, Hardy said to say he *was* here to investigate the cause of the sicknesses. But, he would rather the ambassador say nothing unless he had to.

The ambassador showed him photos of American tourists who had entered Cuba in the last month. Hardy had sent these to Agent Swanson who seemed overjoyed to finally hear from him. He and Carl caught up on what had occurred since they last met, while Carl scanned the photos.

"Holy shit. What is Jake Harper doing in Havana?" Carl remarked when Hardy sent his photo separate.

"I was going to ask you the same question."

"Like I told you, our fucking secretary in Washington had me dismiss him. He's supposedly been told by the Bahamian authorities not to leave the Bahamas. He told TJ he had been picked to stay on Exuma for the holidays. What in the sand hill is he up to?"

"I intend to find out," Hardy said. "Ask TJ if he's heard anything more from Jake, but, keep Jake's and my presence here under your hat, don't mention it to TJ or anyone, including our esteemed secretary."

"Don't worry. Everyone's so upset about the shutdown, they're either calling in sick or claiming they're too broke to afford transportation. Many just show up here in body but not giving a shit about work. Some have started looking for other employment. Can't blame them. The only reason I show up is to piss on the wish that I go ahead and retire."

"Glad you're still there. Hopefully I'll get some results, be out of here by the new year."

Jake, Jake, Jake. What are you doing here? Hardy needed to find him before he did something to foul up his investigation. Or, some other agent, from one of the other agencies got wind of his presence, namely whomever Carmichael, Tobolokov and Dean worked for. He told Carl to have their best hacker check the Havana hotel registers for Jake's name.

An hour later, Carl called back. He talked to TJ who said the only conversation he had with Jake was the one where he indicated he would be in the Bahamas for the holidays. TJ wanted to know why Carl was asking, Carl told TJ it was for his monthly reports. Hardy and Carl both hoped TJ bought the answer. Carl then checked with Bridgette, she found nothing at the major hotels. She would keep looking. Finding any of the other parties so far resulted in sore feet and back, no results. So much, in these situations, depended upon luck. The whole fucking country could use a lot of luck.

49

Caracas, Venezuela

Blakely and Tobey were at the back of the crowd watching the women supporters of President Maduro at the front before the stage. They were there to protest the OAS coalition and now U.S. ally and opposition leader, Juan Guaido and the OAS Representative and spokesperson Gustavo Tarre Briceno at a boisterous, loud rally. Briceno said the weapons supplied by Russia and North Korea were inferior and new contracts needed to be renegotiated with new partners. Guaido, the exiled elected president tried to climb the police-barricaded state building to claim his position. The police held him and his party's elected members at bay. Maduro refused to concede. Putin backed him. The clueless women of the anti-U.S., anti-war movement Code Pink were chanting, "Hands off Venezuela," enflaming the desperate crowd.

Tobey leaned over to Blakely and said, "this could get nasty. We better get out of here."

They escaped Exuma by way of a special charter arranged by Pietr Okneyev after Devereaux stopped Jake Harper from taking Tobey. Blakely felt bad for Jake. She told him enough to be dangerous to their mission. The Russians were divided. Fortunately, Tobey decided, or was directed, to join with her. For now, they were forced to side with Okneyev. America's HSI came close to blowing their covers with everything that happened in Miami. Then, Boris sending his goons to the Bahamas, threatening her, made her realize her position had become too precarious. Devereaux took care of Boris' goons. Some sharpshooters eliminated Colonel Bolstoy and his Captain Jokovski. She felt certain this happened with Tobey's help. Okneyev's freighter brought them to Caracas. He planned to meet with other parties, perhaps Russian and some Cuban generals, involved in a drug for weapon scheme involving one of the Mexican cartels and some unknown American.

Tobey and herself were both deep undercover Interpol operatives who had been working for years to infiltrate the two Russian mobs. Blakely had never met Tobey until he showed up on Great Exuma. Good thing Devereaux gave her fair warning things had gone awry in Miami. He had been informed by Homeland and passed along the news that Tobey could be headed their way with Homeland in pursuit.

She previously arranged with Okneyev an emergency plan. She put This into motion when Jake sent her back to waylay the crowd. Devereaux contacted her when Jake sent him to get his car. Thankfully Devereaux agreed to sacrifice himself for the cause. At first, he argued they needed to take Jake to deflect suspicion, give themselves an out. As much as she liked the idea, she didn't want to make things any more problematic, possibly fatal, for Jake. She had not heard from Devereaux since arriving in Caracas.

The reported Venezuelan unrest was making Okneyev and the generals nervous. Initially a show and bid session for the Venezuelans and Cubans had been arranged to take place off the coast here. Now there was talk of moving it to Cuba. Neither she nor Tobey had detected any radiation aboard Okneyev's freighter. They needed to get somewhere to relay this and the information about their movements to their individual controls. Blakely was getting nervous, she and Tobey needed to get away from the crowd. Too many newsbies and intelligence operatives were here. Okneyev was acting strange. Some of these people could be his.

50

Hemingway Marina, Cuba

"**S**omething has to give, Dean shouted. "You can't expect us to stay bottled up on this fucking boat for over a week while you fucking have your way with the women."

Dean knew Mark didn't like being talked to this way, but he shouldn't be blaming him because Boyd slipped off the leash and strayed outside the damned marina where Cuban women weren't allowed without being with a foreigner. Neither of them felt Mark should have privileges denied to them. His claims that they might be recognized seemed far-fetched. Who would have ever imagined the Harper man would turn up in Havana? Dean figured he would have been sent stateside, back to playing Old McDonald, porking that sweet treat Amy. And how was it he and Mark ended up at the ceverceria at the same time as Boyd did? Plain bad fucking luck. The way he saw it, Mark was the one taking the risk. The Harper man needed to go. Mark should get the fuck away from him. They needed to be out there, looking and listening, gathering intel, not stuck at the marina and on Devereaux' boat staring at computer screens 24/7. Seeing those Cuban women and not being allowed to take part in enjoying what they so wantonly displayed was tearing his nerves up. If he didn't get laid before long, he was going to start begging Becca, or worse.

Reba overheard Dean's shouting at Mark and empathized with him. A rarity. Being cooped up on this boat with three men, the scent of animal testosterone dripping off the walls, she needed fresh air, some action. Everyone was at each-other's throats. Boyd and Dean had nearly come to blows numerous times; she too felt the need to lash out. The boat had become their prison. They took turns venturing out into the prison yard, the marina. This was not enough. Boyd and Dean were like dogs sniffing for females in heat. She grew weary of their sexual jokes and inuendoes, worse were the looks she was receiving. Dean's comment that she needed further training in her duties, him rubbing his crotch, she wanted to break his other fingers.

Her efforts to pry information from Devereaux proved futile.

At the marina, stuck on this boat, she was nothing more than a nurse maid for three non-housebroken assholes. The best part of them had run down their mother's ass. She needed to get off the boat, away from the marina and these men. She wouldn't mind seeing Havana, a beach would be nice, a hot bath and massage would be stupendous. Activity was what she needed. Adventure. That was one of the things she enjoyed about her job. Getting even, her first incentive, defending Israel, America and civilized democracies were her underlying motivations.

Being an agent had its rewards and benefits, but lately she had begun to feel lacking. More and more, she had begun to think what it must be like to have a mate, to share a home, children. She wasn't sure if she could have children of her own. The things she had suffered in her childhood under Saddam Hussein's men. Doctors said it would be difficult for her to conceive or bear a child normally. She had eggs, that was her best hope they said. Perhaps invitro fertilization, letting another woman bear the embryo. But first she needed sperm, even for invitro. There was no lack of ways to obtain that. Could she find a male whose sperm she wished to use to help give her a child? Did she want a husband? She often questioned her orientation. She never felt comfortable with the thoughts of a man, or woman, as something viable. Their lives would be an unshared reality. Her life as an agent would sit between them, like an affair, never to be discussed, always there creating festering wounds of lies. There was always a fellow agent. Only a team member could possibly be talked to. She looked at whom she had teamed with. Never. She'd rather shoot herself. To think, her life was tied to these whore-dogs, "till death do we part." May the gods be merciful.

"I think I may have something," Boyd said excitedly.

"You probably do. It's called venereal disease," Reba replied.

She and Dean went over to where Boyd sat staring at one of the two monitors, waving his hand in a shushing motion, pointing to the plugs stuck in his ears. They stood frozen waiting. A big grin like a crack in his egghead spread from ear to ear. After several clicks with the keyboard mouse, the words appeared on the screen.

"Unrest. Too risky. Moving demo to Cuba. Will update."

Nothing else. They waited, transfixed, excitement had spread to each of them.

"Who? What and where did this come from?" Dean asked.

Boyd typed in some prompts. "Somewhere off coast of South America. No id on phone. Receiver unknown. But these signals could have originated anywhere and been bounced around from place to place."

"Unrest? Could be any of those countries. Venezuela has been all over the news. Heard couple of Cubans in that shithole they called a pizzeria talking about it. They're coming here. We've been sitting here with our thumbs up our asses waiting on Mark to find someone or for us to learn something and they've been elsewhere. I like Venezuela for this. Good work Boyd. I'll get in touch with Mark. Give him the good news. Now, we just need to figure out where in Cuba, then we'll be there to find the who." He clapped Boyd on the back, turned and hugged Reba. She reluctantly hugged him back.

Mark and Jake had not seen their hosts when they came down the stairs to wait Tomas arrival.

Koko didn't seem surprised they came back requesting different arrangements. He gave Tomas another address. Jake noted the change of Tomas' normally sedate expression when he heard the address.

The house was at the far eastern end of the community with water visible in the background, continuing beyond the end of a half-circle intersection. There was a fence with a gate at the end of a longer than average concrete drive leading to the side of a large l-shape, lavender trim, pink stucco home. A middle-age Cuban man dressed like most, older Cuban men in plain white guayabera and loose draw-string pants and black leather shoes, medium build with a no-nonsense expression, opened the gate. Tomas stopped his car and introduced them. The man's name was Louis. He nodded his head at each introduction and stood back without further ado. Jake looked out the back window to see Louis close, lock the gate with a hasp lock and take a seat by the post. Didn't seem like a bad neighborhood.

Nice homes, far apart. No one out and about. Hmm?

At the door they were met by a pleasant Cuban lady dressed in a plain dress with sandals. Tomas introduced her as Maria, Louis' wife.

"I am the maid, cook and anything else you need seniors." Maria added. "Let me show you to your rooms."

She led them from the side entrance vestibule, a nice kitchen on the right. The adjoining room had to be the living room. Well-kept Nineties era loveseat between a window and another exterior door to the left. A sofa on the far wall, a wooden chair with its back to the door opening to the vestibule faced a small television on an end table next to the loveseat. On the right were floor to ceiling plain faded-pink curtains, closing off the cased opening, behind which he heard soft classical jazz playing. Jake noticed all the walls were plain white, like the ten-foot high ceilings and the polished marble floors that extended into the hall where there were two large bedrooms on the left separated by a large bath containing a footed tub, marble-topped sink and a modern toilet. At the end of the hall was another exterior door facing the road. It was closed and had a heavy-duty brass lockset. The right side of the hall was plain plaster with no doors.

Mark chose the bedroom toward the back. Jake was left with the front, corner bedroom. The four-poster bed felt more forgiving than the hard bed the night before.

After depositing his bag, he and Mark went with Maria and Tomas to the living room. The jazz was no longer playing and there was a tall, stately, shoulder-length blonde-haired lady dressed in what appeared to be an American fashionable, below-knee, wrap-around skirt and button blouse wearing nice strapped sandals—could've passed for Beaver Cleaver's mom.

She held out her hand palm down. Jake didn't know if she expected them to kiss it or what. He slid his fingers into her palm and gently touched the back of her hand with his thumb, felt rather awkward and nodded his head. Mark simply nodded his head. Maria made the introductions.

"This is Sra Doctor Camilla Edelina Fernando Castile."

"Camilla," she said in a very professional sounding tone. "Sr Harper and Sr Castle, please call me Camilla."

"Just Jake. Camilla, you have a lovely place."

"Certainly is," Mark said. "What's behind the curtains?"

"My private area. There is a dining room and library and a staircase that goes up to my bedroom suite. Please honor my privacy. You may move about in this area of my house as you wish. Maria is an excellent cook and she will see to cooking breakfast and dinner. You need only tell her what you would like, Louis will do his best to obtain groceries. I'm afraid there may be a limit to what he can acquire. All finances will be handled by Maria. I do not know if Sr Castro told you, I rarely allow visitors to stay, so please do not cause me to regret my decision. Our country's economy suffered setbacks. The situation is not good. I hope you understand."

"I do," Jake said. "Thank you for letting us stay here. Maria had your title as doctor. What is your specialty?"

"I am a clinical psychologist. I teach at the University of Havana. And yourself?"

"I am working as a construction manager on a resort project in the Bahamas. Always wanted to come to Cuba, decided this was my opportunity."

"And you?" she turned to Mark.

"I do advertising," Mark replied sounding less than enthusiastic.

"I see," Camilla replied. "You hear of Myer Lansky? He once lived in this casa. He built it."

She gave Mark a piercing look.

"I must attend to some business. Please excuse me." She went back through the curtains leaving Jake wondering what had caused Mark's attitude and her strange remark and hasty retreat.

They went back outside to the side entry's patio which had a wrought iron table and four chairs. Maria asked what they might like for dinner. Jake told her, "I'm game for anything Cuban. Whatever your specialty is."

Mark said that would work for him.

She asked them how they would be paying in CUCs or other monies? Mark asked if it mattered and what were the charges.

"Thirty CUCs for room, five dollars for me and five for Louis plus cost of groceries."

They agreed, each gave her fifty Canadian dollars. She walked down the drive to send Louis to find what she needed to make the meal.

Mark turned to Tomas. "Will we be able to bring female guests here?"

Tomas laughed. "Yes. You need me to find you women?"

Jake couldn't believe Tomas offered. "You can do this? No hookers."

Mark said, "yeah, some nice young ladies for tonight would be great."

Tomas asked them to wait. He went down the drive and talked to Maria. She came back with him.

"Tomas say you want female company for tonight. You want young or not so young. Sra Camilla, she not allow girls of color here."

Incredible, Jake thought, delighted there would be female company, but wondering about the implied prejudice.

Mark grinned. "Young, but not too young, nice looking women companions would be great. Jake probably would like more than one."

Maria looked Jake up and down. "Two maybe. More than that someone your age might not can handle."

Jake could feel the heat of embarrassment on his face. "Mark was kidding."

"I know some very nice young women. I see maybe I can arrange. Tonight, I cook for you. Cuban women expect you take them places. Perhaps you wait until tomorrow for meeting these women."

"I'd prefer to take these women out tonight, maybe have you cook for us and these women tomorrow. That okay with you, Jake?"

"If it's not too much trouble for you Maria."

Maria went inside brought a pitcher of lemonade out and three glasses. "I arrange women to meet you." She went back inside.

Sra Camilla must approve. Maria knew Sra Camilla was upset with Koko putting her in a bad situation. This was big risk. She already scared because her casa was in place government wanted. Agents could come, arrest them, take casa. To have foreigners here was forbidden. Why Koko do this?

"How did you know Maria could make arrangements?" Jake asked Tomas. "You know these people, don't you?"

Tomas cast a glance toward the house and down the drive deciding what to say. Koko and Sra Camilla had not been speaking much. He wasn't sure if she or Koko would want him to say anything. And Maria agreeing to bring companions here. Perhaps he should warn them they could be arrested.

"Sra Camilla is family. Sometimes she allow strangers here. Koko know she need money. Louis and Maria work for her, for other people when they can. Maria, like most Cubans, we do whatever we can. Could be problem. You are not registered. You should be in hotel according to new laws. Koko, Sra Camilla, all, including you are in violation of the law. You must never say you stay here, have other guests. Never mention girls stay here. They would be arrested, treated as unregistered jinatera. These girls will be special, could be Maria's family, must be good to them. You want other, I help. Sra Camilla, she decide."

Oh fuck, here I go again, Jake thought. He noticed Mark had moved off and was walking toward the water. He looked across the table. "Tomas, how big of a risk are we talking about? I mean is it likely government agents will come here?"

"Always possible. They go Koko first. He man collect monies, taxes in this area. People talk. That why you never say where you stay. If asked, you say talk Koko. He has business license. They come here Louis not let them in too quick. He send them see my uncle. Whether you have other guests here at night, that is Sra Camilla decision. Better we leave soon. I take you anywhere. If you not here, there no problem they come."

Mark felt his phone vibrate. He moved away to read the message. The generals and Russians were coming. Good and not so good. Cuba had too many miles of coastline on the mainland and many more on the outlying other islands. They could be coming by air or boat or both. He texted back to Dean, *Keep at it. Check all ports of entry for arrivals. Be ready to move.* He heard footsteps slipping on the coral shells behind him. Mark closed the phone and slipped it back into his pocket. Jake came up beside him.

"Sounding kinda iffy for having female guests stay here tonight. You heard Tomas, what do you think?"

"I say it's up to Camilla and Maria. Maria gets some sweet little ladies to come, we take them out, get them out of here after we do our thing. After all that's one of the reasons for being here, at least it is for me. What you say?"

Jake looked back toward the house. Tomas was sitting at the table watching them. "Tomas says we need to make ourselves scarce during the daylight hours. He's waiting to take us anywhere we want. I say let's get out of here while Maria does her checking. I'd like to see Havana, maybe see places Hemingway went, maybe his house. How about it?"

Mark looked around as Jake talked. Damn shocking. There were Cuban naval vessels right across the bay. What the fuck were they doing there? This wasn't on any map he knew of. Looked like it was a naval port. He needed to get pictures. "Yeah. Sure, sounds good. Tell you what how about taking my picture." He pulled his cell back out, hit the camera icon, zoomed out and snapped off some shots of the boats, then zoomed back in and took some shots of Jake before handing him his phone.

Jake snapped a couple of pictures after Mark moved around. Only then did he notice the boats. There were a couple navy patrol boats and closer to them was a submarine with some sailors on deck staring in their direction. "You see that. Those are Cuban naval vessels. A sailor was looking this way. I think he noticed us."

Mark used Jake's phone to take his picture, handed it back and pulled his phone back out of his pocket, took some more shots as the submarine headed out of the bay toward the ocean. The sailor disappeared below deck.

"Even if that sailor noticed us, he won't give a shit. Nothing to worry about. Come on, let's hit the road, grab some lunch and see some sights." Mark would send the photos to Dean. This could be worth checking out—a naval base not on any map. He couldn't figure why Jake hadn't seemed excited. What was he doing here?

Jake was really beginning to wonder about Mark. He seemed too interested in taking those pictures. Hmm? He would need to pay closer attention to him.

51

While the Miami Homeland's agents, who reluctantly showed for work, searched futilely to locate Jake, Blakely and Toby, Thurmond Tindal's newly set up lab in York County, South Carolina, worked on its drone project under the direction of Dr. Lisa Guthridge and team leader Dr. Leonard Perkins. Lisa wanted to wait until the new year to make the relocation, but Tindal's man Bud Jenkins sent a team, under Leonard's direction, to begin the immediate breakdown and moving of the lab and her team to their new location. She anticipated some members of her team to rebel. Despite their bitching and moaning at disrupting holiday plans, most were pleased by the new setup and the opportunity to continue the project which they feared would not happen when Tindal Industries bought Marberry.

Mark told her he was with the Harper man, had to limit keeping in touch with her. He asked her to keep her eyes and ears open for any communication between Tindal or Jenkins

with foreign nationals. Lisa informed Mark the majority of Tindal's recent ground and maintenance hires were Hispanic.

"Many bear gang tattoos. Getting access to Jenkin's office is problematic. He has a retinal-scan lock system and cameras. He indulges his voyeuristic tendencies via access to almost every part of the property. Including the lab and my team's personal quarters."

Lisa told him she would continue to penetrate the network's everchanging firewall. So far, her efforts only pointed to communication with potential foreign investors by Jenkins.

"Jenkins is having marital difficulties. He came right out and told me as much. Seems I'll be fighting off his advances. His tongue practically hangs out of his mouth every time I get near him. I know he's watching me, most likely monitoring my computer and other communication."

"Perhaps you can use that to your advantage," Mark said.

The comment stung. She was using the ploy. Mark didn't know she was. For him to casually suggest it. Seemed Mark was not as enamored with her as she hoped.

"Is that what you're doing, taking advantage of the opportunities there. Wherever there is?"

"I know to separate business from pleasure. The mission always comes first, you must learn to keep this in mind, emotions cloud judgment."

Lisa heard voices in the background. Some were female. That Mark would encourage her to use her sex to gather information from Jenkins turned her stomach. She was not a whore. Teasing Jenkins was as far as she would go.

Jenkins' source at NSA contacted him immediately to inform him he had intercepted communication from several sources in Tindal's area with someone named Mark in Havana. One intercept concerned one of the names Jenkin's had asked him to locate, Jake Harper. The intercept placed him close to Havana Cuba. Jenkins instructed him to find out who Mark was, where in Cuba he and Jake were and what the hell connections he had with Jake. His source said the information was going to cost Tindal and him dearly.

"Pietr," Jenkins said upon his answering the call minutes after ending his call with his NSA source. "Seems Jake Harper is still alive and well in Havana. You agreed to take care of him for me."

"I lose two men in Bahamas. Two others manage escape authorities. You fail to inform me this man Harper connected to your government."

"Jake Harper is not connected to this government, or any other government. Your information is wrong. I need him taken care of. Should I find someone else?"

"My sources here with me say he government. He in Cuba? They finish this for me. I send them once I find. You pay what I decide you owe me, yes?"

"You take care of Jake Harper and find out who a man named Mark is, I will give you first shot at a new weapon being developed. Believe me this will be well worth your doing this."

Pietr Okneyev wondered if perhaps the Harper man was alive because Blakely had developed feelings for him. If this weapon his fellow Russians and Cuban generals were purchasing happened, he decided he would no longer need this Tobolokov. Perhaps it was time to test Blakely's loyalty. Maybe she had outlived her value to him."

Why this Jake Harper in Cuba? Had Blakely told him something? Not possible, even she didn't know his plans. Could other man named Mark be agent? He was too close to finalizing the deal. Perhaps he should do as Jenkins asked.

Tomas took them in his exhaust spewing Lada around Havana. They visited the Hemingway home. Jake saw several of the famous six-toed cats, decided to not bother touring the home. They enjoyed a daiquiri at El Floridita standing next to Hemingway's bronze statue situated at the corner of the dark mahogany bar. Earnest's corner stool was chained off to keep anyone from sitting on it. The walls were covered in pictures of Hemingway with Archibald Leach, aka Cary Grant, Tennessee Williams, and other famous personalities of that era.

From there they walked the streets of the central city. Some had recently been renovated, many in need of rehab, crumbling interiors hinting at fading grandeur. In Park Central, artists displayed their arts and craft, reminding Jake of Jackson Square in New Orleans. As he strolled across the plaza, the bright sunlight rippling on the pavers and the gathered crowd, he caught the sight of a young man shadowing them, a pencil and pad in his hand. Jake stopped as the man cautiously approached him once they reached the steps of a former cathedral. He showed Jake what he had been doing with his pencil, an amazing caricature of himself done in the few minutes taken to cross the square with both him and the artist moving. Jake bought it for five CUCs. Mark refused the artist's offer to sketch him.

They ended their tour by driving along the Malecon past the mob built, Habana Hotel Riviera, the Hotel Nacional, where Jake was supposedly staying, and the American Embassy set back from Revolutionary Square where Castro gave his yearly speech denouncing the United States and other imperialist democracies. Jake thought it seemed ironic that Castro had given his speeches within the sightlines of a sniper inside the U.S. Embassy, while declaring himself as the target for U.S. assassination attempts. Machismo.

As they drove past the embassy, Tomas, who had been telling them historical anecdotes about the various sites, said, "There is much talk of Americans becoming sick from sounds inside the embassy. Many sent home. Your president send Cubans back here in retaliation. Many Cubans think Americans do this to themselves, make Cuba look bad to rest of world. I hear others say Russians do this using miniature drones armed with sonic weapons. The Russians not want America and Cuba have good relations. Want Cuba stay communist. Friends hate Russians, want things American, wish to go United States." Jake and Mark gave no reply.

Next Tomas took them through Miramar's stately tree-lined upscale residential district, where numerous mansions were set back behind gated fences. Once the homes of prerevolution wealthy Cubans, now homes for foreign ambassadors. Jake could have sworn he saw Agent Hardy leaving the U.S. Ambassador's residence. He noted Mark was giving the residence his full attention as well.

Mark turned toward Jake in the back seat, wanting to ask, *"was that someone you knew back there?* Instead he asked, "Entertain some nice young ladies tonight and see some sights outside Havana tomorrow, sound good to you Jake?"

"Fine by me. Any place you have in mind?"

"Why don't we leave it up to Tomas. Tomorrow can be up to you Tomas. Then maybe we can see some beaches."

Tomas had been quiet. Jake checked his face in the rearview mirror. He didn't look back. "Okay with you Tomas?" Jake asked.

"I think on this," he replied. Tomas knew taking foreigners anywhere was supposed to be approved by his uncle and the government. In Havana was no problem. Other places could be risky. He would need to talk to his uncle.

The sun was setting, as they returned to Camilla's casa. Louis opened the gate and nodded to them when Tomas drove through. Maria came out to greet them.

"Tomas, young ladies ready in hour, little more."

Jake watched Tomas get back in the car. "Since you will be driving, why don't you bring your girlfriend? It will be our treat."

Jake followed Maria inside. When he went to his bedroom, he heard water running in the bathroom. Mark had beaten him to the shower. He decided to do some snooping. He went back down the hall. Mark's door was locked.

They were seated in the sitting room having a glass of lemonade when Tomas arrived. Maria came in following four lovely teenage looking girls, all smiling. Jake was taken aback—so young, why four?

Maria noticed the puzzled look on Jake's face. "You not like young women, I arrange others," she asked, as if the girls were not there, listening.

"No. These young girls suit me," Mark replied. He moved over to a dark-haired girl and introduced himself.

Jake didn't know what to say. All eyes seemed to be on him. Tomas had come in without any sign of a girlfriend.

"Tomas, you think all of us can fit in your car?"

The girls' faces were beaming now.

"Someone sit on someone else."

"No problem. Our treat, right Mark?"

Tomas took them to an outdoor Italian restaurant. The food was good, amazingly inexpensive including the wine, which the girls drank in moderation. Jake noticed most of the patrons were not Cuban. The men seemed to pay close attention to their group. Maybe because Mark grew loud after consuming a whole bottle of wine himself.

One of the young women seated next to Jake at the long table had apparently lain claims to him. The other two seemed to have acquiesced. One had ridden on Jake's lap with her hands holding the seat in front of her. Her soft derriere bouncing on his lap would have been stimulating if not for the constant chatter between the other girls pressed tightly against them and the exhaust fumes. His neck stiffened and ached, which didn't help.

Tomas dropped them off at Camilla's. He left with the other two who didn't seem to mind not having been asked to stay the night after having enjoyed being treated to a night out. Louis, still seated at the gate, let them in without saying or acknowledging them or the girls.

Mark wasted no time. He led his selected young lady back to his bedroom. Jake felt awkward not knowing what to say. The nervous young girl named Teula didn't make the situation any better. She claimed to be twenty-one but was probably sixteen, eighteen at the most. Why would Maria offer these girls up if they were family and why would their parents allow this? The obvious answer was money. He had read Cubans were much more promiscuous.

When asked if this was her first time with someone, Teula's eyes did not meet his. Soon she asked to use the restroom. Jake took her to his bedroom, checked the bathroom. Through the walls he could hear Mark having his way with the other girl. Teula had followed him into the bathroom, he went back out, closed the door and sat on the bed. Teula came out holding her clothes to her chest, wearing nothing it seemed, except her plain white underpants which contrasted with her dark skin. She had heavier thighs than Jake preferred, not surprisingly, youthful baby fat on her hips and waist. Jake had mixed emotions about the situation.

Teula came over to the other side of the bed, laid her clothes on a chair in the corner, pulled back the bedding and lay down, hastily covering herself with the sheet. Jake watched her, then decided to turn off the lamp before undressing and joining her. He lay back feeling this was going nowhere, he couldn't. After a while she asked if he wished her to do anything. Jake told her not to worry, she could stay the night, everything would be okay.

She turned into him and brushed his lips with hers. Her breath told him she used toothpaste. Jake wondered if she brought it with her. Damn. What was he going to do about this situation?

"I not know what to do. Tell me." She snuggled closer to him. He could feel her nakedness.

This made him uncomfortable. A new first. A naked woman asking for sex and you're at a loss for what to do. Not woman, girl, close to your daughter's age. The same age as Ariel, his first. The one who owned his heart. He tried to move away, she followed.

"Teula, you don't have to do anything, okay? I'm too old for you. Don't you have a boyfriend, someone special?"

She made an almost silent laugh. "I not want boys from here. Is not easy unless you jinatera. I want you feel good about Teula."

Jake lay there not sure what to say or do. He wished she had been older. Even a jinatera would have been better. "Teula, why don't we lie here and talk?"

"You wish I be like friend Ilya?" she asked. "This not Ilya first time. She tell me what she do. How it feel. I wish to know. If you no like me, I must leave. She say ask for money first. Maria say you know this."

Jake reached down to his pants laying on the floor beside the bed and pulled out some bills. Not worrying about what denominations, he handed her two. She turned on the lamp and he saw he gave her a five and ten. He also saw how nicely firm her breasts were with their dark areolas and large nipples. He saw the woman she was beginning to be.

Teula turned off the lamp and turned back to him, putting her head on his chest. Jake felt her tears and pulled her up so he could ask her why she was crying.

"I sad. I want you like Teula. You not want me? I not know how make you want me. Maria ask me. I tell her I not know."

Teula reached over and rubbed Jake's penis. Despite himself, as was his little heads habit, it rose into her hand. She continued to hold him, her hand moved back and forth. Jake reached down and pulled her hand away.

"Teula, I'm sorry. I can't do this."

"You must. I need learn. You no hurt me. Ilya say feel good. Her first man he gentle."

She slid on top of Jake and began rubbing herself on him, down and up. Her breath touching his face. Jake pulled her face down and attempted to kiss her. She didn't know how to kiss. She kept her mouth open. He stopped the attempt. He held her, trying to stop her motions.

"Teula, you could become pregnant if we have sex."

"No. All girls have birth medicine after fifteenth birthday celebration. Not worry. This feel good." She sounded breathless.

Jake knew if she kept rubbing herself on him, he would soon have an orgasm. He rolled her off.

You're going to hate yourself if you allow anything to happen, he thought. She reached down, took his hand and placed it on her hairless sex. He pulled his hand away. He gently caressed her face. Felt her tears. He kissed her eyes, rolled onto his side and brought her to him.

"You don't have to please me."

"Ilya says men like her take them in her mouth. I wish try this. Make you want Teula." She started to move down. He stopped her, pulled her back up. "No. I don't want you to do that." He held her tighter. He could feel her naked body trembling.

"You not like Teula?" She cried.

"Let's just go to sleep, okay?" Jake felt better about himself. What they did was no more than what most teenagers did when first experimenting with sex. He could hopefully live with himself for what happened. Not if he went any further. He wasn't a teenager. He believed she was.

Enough lessons for the night. He held her close, ran his hands up and down her back until he felt her relax. He rolled away from her. She pressed herself against him and whispered something about in morning.

Jake didn't get much sleep. Teula held onto him keeping him from being able to relieve the pressure on his neck. She blocked his normal switching positions. His half-conscious thoughts drifted from being frustrated about his luck with Cuban women to thoughts about his farm then to those concerning Robert Hardy. Had he been the man leaving the ambassador's house? Jake was certain it was him. He wanted to talk to him. HSI had frozen the account with the money promised him. How much did Hardy know about this, and, Toby, Blakely, Devereaux and Dean and crew? Finding Hardy was something he had little hope of doing. Too many eyes would be on them both. Jake lacked transportation and zero knowledge of how and where to go.

It was still dark outside, when Mark tapped on his door from the bathroom. Jake squinted when Mark opened the door, the bathroom light finding his eyes.

"Ilya says they were told to leave before daylight. Hope you weren't planning on sweet morning repeats."

Mark closed the door. Jake pulled Teula's hand off his arm and sat up. He reached over, gently rocked her to waken her. She looked at him, a confused frown on her oval face, then she smiled.

"Good morning. Your friend says you have to leave before daylight." Jake reached across and turned on the lamp.

A panicked expression vanished the smile. She sat up, threw back the covers revealing a slight belly roll that drew his eyes to her neatly trimmed pubic region before she swung around and jumped out of bed. She hastily dressed, as did Jake. After a few minutes in the bathroom for each of them, they joined Mark and Ilya on the outdoor patio. Louis walked up to them. He said he would escort the girls home. He turned and walked back into the shadows toward the gate. Ilya and Teula gave Mark and Jake hugs and departed. This, after each asked if they wanted them to come back again. Mark said he would like that. Jake said he would let Maria decide. Teula looked crestfallen.

When they disappeared down the street, Mark asked Jake how he liked his first taste of communist pussy.

"Never entered my mind about the politics."

"Man, that Ilya was really enthusiastic. How about yours?"

"Too young. Not much to tell."

"I certainly did my part to give mine a taste of capitalism. Haven't had pussy that young in a long time. "

"Yeah. Tell me about it. No, on second thoughts, forget I said anything."

"Don't tell me a warrior like yourself had that sweet young thing lying next to you and you didn't get any. Perhaps you haven't shaken the desert dust and those forbidden Muslim women, with their hidden treasures, off you yet. These girls here don't have the same moral inhibitions and taboos most women have. Cuba's beauty has always been her bountiful treasures freely shared, despite or perhaps because of their political repression. You need to enjoy yourself more. Loosen up. Isn't that what you came here for?"

How you going to answer that one Jake, Mark thought. Maybe Jake wasn't the pussy hound Dean indicated. Dean? He needed to find out if they had any luck hearing where the Russians and Cuban generals were relocating.

Jake knew Mark's reasoning was like everyone else's, even his when he decided to come to Cuba. But a line had to be drawn on girls as young as Teula. He wouldn't cross that one, even if the girls and their government-controlled youth rebellious-society said it was okay.

"Maybe I'll get lucky next time."

"That's the spirit. Next time you get first dibs."

"I'm going back to bed. Wake me when Tomas gets here."

Jake lay there thinking about Teula. Then what Mark said. It hit him—Mark mentioned desert dust, forbidden Muslim women. He never told Mark about his military service. How could he know. Jake didn't believe it was a lucky guess.

52

Caracas, Venezuela

Getting back out of Venezuela proved more difficult than getting in. Toby was tasked with following Okneyev. She looked for anyone looking suspicious. Tobey lost him. Where did he go? Who was he meeting? Perhaps the Cuban generals were here after all. Okneyev's text said he would be leaving soon. To meet him back at the boat.

She relayed the lack of nuke discovery aboard the freighter. She sent another coded message about the possible change in plans to her Interpol contact. She requested a boat to get them out if Okneyev ditched them. Pietr Okneyev could pull a fast one, leave them behind. Have other plans. Eliminate them. The contact told her to make sure Okneyev didn't give them the slip. He felt it too risky for the offshore watchers to bring them onboard. Such a move would certainly blow their cover. End the op.

Blakely didn't trust anyone. Not her contact. Not Toby. Damn sure, not Okneyev. The Russian criminal got to where he was by killing those who stood in his way. And, anyone he suspected as a threat. As soon as they discovered what was required, Blakely would make certain he was renditioned. Let the Americans have him. Guantanamo would be a good place for him.

Americans. She had come to think of herself as American, even though her Jewish gypsy roots were not very popular in the Midwest where she spent half her teenage and adult life.

Jake Harper reminded her of Dieter, her recruiter, former lover, now her controller. Jake seemed kind-hearted, decent, a grown-up boy scout with his all-American looks. Blonde hair and blue eyes that flashed when he was angry. She hated having played him. If only.

Her burner phone vibrated. Toby texted, '*Okneyev headed to dock. Make it quick. Something has happened*'

Boyd intercepted the message. Dean relayed the news to Mark, adding, *Boyd thinks Tobolokov is with Interpol.*

Bridgette at HSI's field office in Miami also intercepted the text and notified Swanson at once. Carl was delighted with the news. Answered many questions, posed more. Who was Okneyev? What were they doing in Venezuela? He had Bridgette to send a message to the American embassy in Cuba requesting Agent Hardy contact the Miami field office. She used a series of hacker tricks to bounce the message around the world so the message originator would be, for all but the best, unknown. Carl then told her to contact their agent in Venezuela monitoring the crisis there.

"Ask if he has any info on Russians or Cuban military presence there?"

The reply came quickly. Intel said the Russians and Cubans were there in support of Maduro. He wanted to know why she asked, Bridgette did not answer.

Carl told all agents reporting to work to find out who this Okneyev was.

Turned out he was a wealthy Russian Oligarch, dealt in black-market arms, drugs, and human trafficking. The breakthrough they were after. He needed to inform Agent Hardy of this, ask him if he found Devereaux's boat *Dev'sDelight.*

Wait a cotton-picking minute, Homeland's equipment was onboard that boat. Carl hurried to see his tech people.

"Mickel is it possible to locate missing equipment, listening devices, computers, the kind of Homeland equipment we had installed on Devereaux' boat?"

"Our expensive and sensitive equipment is registered and can be tracked via the serial number and MAC." Carl gave him a quizzical look. "Stands for

Media Access Control address. The network administrator will have all that information. Using that I can locate any device."

Carl felt they were going to finally get some useful intel.

"Get the information of the equipment installed on Devereaux' boat, find out where it is pronto."

"Hopefully the admin showed up at the admin office."

"Any problem let me know. Okay my compadres get me the intel asap and don't let the snoops know what we're up to."

Bud Jenkins' source at NSA also intercepted the message and informed him. His attempt to reach Pietr Okneyev was unsuccessful. It was important to know how much Interpol knew. Did they know about his connection to Okneyev? He had to assume they did. Okneyev needed to clean house, severe loose ends. Why wasn't the son of a bitch answering his supposedly secure phone?

Blakely entered Okneyev's luxury suite aboard his freighter. Toby was not invited and was stopped at the door by Okneyev's two bodyguards. The same neckless dorks did a thorough search of her, confiscating her phone. Good thing she had ditched the phone she had been using.

Okneyev stood at his shiny brass-topped bar drinking, Blakely assumed, his favorite Vodka. There was a black case which he set down along with his crystal jigger glass. He offered her a drink, which she accepted, despite her disdain for Vodka. He did not offer for her to sit, nor did he. His broad Slavic shaved head glistened in the bright light directly above him. His normally friendly smile was replaced by an intense scrutiny of her, his brown eyes dark and foreboding. Made her wonder what had happened. And what was in the case he was toying with.

"How long have I known you, Miss Blakely Carmichael?"

"More than five years, Mr. Pietr Okneyev, as I'm sure you know." Inwardly, Blakely felt like a taciturn child facing a stern parent. She knew if she showed any sign of weakness whatsoever, Okneyev would pounce, swiftly and violently.

"You came to me as a gift to be my personal whore. Those arrests in America of those poor girls doing what rich American men and some women do." He shook his head, then bowed it. "Some of my people will pay for this misfortune. If I had done what the man some once called boss wished me to do, that would have been you. Yet I treated you like a daughter, is this not true?"

"I did not know I came to you to be your whore. I was sent by your former boss to learn if you planned to kill him. I was not told how. Just to do whatever it required. You were good to me this is true. I happily helped you to get rid of him. For this you have always treated me like family. I am grateful."

"Yet you failed to do as Boris directed. This man Jake Harper is still alive, is in Cuba. Why I ask he still alive?"

Blakely began to speak and Okneyev held up his left hand, the one with the end of the little finger cut off at the middle joint, the result of a loyalty oath, a feudal fealty ritual.

"You bring member of rival crew claim work with hired marksmen, kill Andrei Bolstoy. Bolstoy dead, yet no one vouch for this Tobias Tobolokov. Other than you?" He stopped and looked at Blakely with an inquisitive squint.

"I told you what happened and how Tobolokov ended up being with me. As for Jake Harper, Boris asked me to help a man named Victor to get rid of the man. Victor beat me and threatened to kill me. I knew this was not your way toward me. Next thing I knew, Boris and Victor had died at the hands of an American agent named Thomas Devereaux. When I made the move to get rid of the Harper man, Tobolokov showed up, along with this Devereaux man making it impossible for me to know what was going on. That is why I got in touch with you. I brought this Tobias Tobolokov with me at your request. I have never vouched for him. I know nothing about him."

Boris poured them both another shot of Vodka. "Then you kill him, prove yourself innocent. Yes?"

"If that is what you ask in order to prove my innocence."

Pietr downed more vodka, squinting at Blakely as though he was contemplating what to choose from a menu. "A meeting will be arranged with Harper man. Tobolokov will accompany you. Once find Harper man, friend Mark, you get rid of Harper man, Tobolokov. Youring this man Mark to me. You do this. Then we will finish our business. All will be made right. Yes?"

"Yes," Blakely said smiling in relief.

Okneyev's face relaxed, just as she hoped it would. He poured himself another shot of his beloved vodka. "Skoll." He downed his, and Blakely reluctantly followed suit.

Blakely gave it her best effort to look calm, though her heart was pounding in her ear. Who was Mark and where was he and Jake?

53

Jamanitas, Cuba

Dean's text threw Mark a wicked curve. He needed to get to the marina. Tomas wasn't due for another couple hours. With Jake in bed, now would be his best opportunity to slip away and coordinate their efforts to find where the demonstration was to happen. He went to his room to lock the door, then told Maria he was going for a walk and would be back in an hour or two.

Jake couldn't get comfortable. He felt guilt for having touched the young girl, anger at Mark's cavalier attitude regarding these girls and his subsequent remarks. He heard Mark lock the door to the bathroom, then his door to the hall. Was he going somewhere? Jake peeked out the window, watched Mark heading down the drive, stop to talk to Louis, who had returned from wherever he had escorted the girls. Louis let Mark out the gate.

Jake decided he needed to find where Mark was headed. He put on his tennis shoes, hurried out locking his door. Maria stopped him asking if the young girl had been to his liking. Jake said she was nice, but he preferred more mature women. Maria smiled said she was sorry he had been disappointed. She promised older ones for tonight.

Jake asked her if Mark had said anything to her. Mark told her he was happy with his young lady, had asked her to return for tonight.

"Did he say where he was going just now?" Jake asked.

Maria looked inquisitively at Jake. "No. He say he go for walk, be back in hour, two. I make Huevos Rancheros. You wish eat now or wait for Sr Mark return?"

"Thank you, but I can wait." Jake turned and left before Maria could say anything more. He went to the gate and asked Louis if Mark had said where he might be going.

Louis said Mark asked directions to Marina Hemingway.

"He has my cell phone. I need to catch him. How do I get to the marina?" Jake had his phone in his inside cargo short pocket in his wallet/phone anti-hacking protector. He hoped the keys in the outer pocket disguised the impression it made.

Louis gave him directions and let him out the gate.

After he got out of Louis' sight, Jake started jogging. The pounding jarred his neck, so he slowed to a brisk walk. Numerous turns right then left brought him to a street with a bridge over the Jaimanitas River. On the other side he came to a tree-lined boulevard with a guard post. Mark was just passing through. Jake watched until Mark got on ahead, then went to the guard manning the gate. He showed him his ID and filled out the registration form. By the time he finished Mark had disappeared. Jake had seen him heading toward the dock area while he was filling out the form.

The rows of boat berths seemed to be all filled with yachts, some with sail masts, many others without. Where had Mark gone? There were too many boats and Mark was liable to spot him. Jake was certain his being here would precipitate an angry confrontation. He couldn't think of any believable reason for being here.

The next thing Jake knew a hand clasped his shoulder. Startled Jake dropped and spun ready to launch an attack in defense. Hardy stepped back twisting sideways as Jake pulled the intended groin punch in time.

Hardy straightened his stance and asked, "Hold up Jake." Then, "What in the hell are you doing in Cuba, here at Hemingway Marina?"

"I could ask you the same thing Bob. Are you following me?" Jake stood up, stared at Agent Hardy and did a quick inventory of their surroundings to make sure he had come alone. Good thing he was checking. There was the auburn-haired Reba coming out of a nearby opening of a three-story white-washed concrete building, headed in their direction.

"Don't move or look back, Bob. There's a woman who is one of James Dean's crew headed toward us. If she sees me, we will have a problem. When I twist my head turn with me in that direction in ten, nine, eight, seven, six, five, four, three, two, one, now."

Reba walked within spitting distance. Remarkably she seemed not to pay any attention to Jake's and Hardy's pirouette. Jake kept his eye on her nice swaying ass headed toward the far dock.

"We need to follow her. You go in front and I'll stay behind your wide ass."

"Didn't think you liked men's asses. Remind me not to drop the soap if ever you and I end up in a shower together." Hardy turned, they followed. "Now that would be the kind of ass I would think you preferred to watch," Hardy said.

"I would say fuck you, but you might get overly excited," Jake replied as they watched her go down the last row of docks. "Let's go down this line of boats." Jake hung a left and Hardy did also, keeping himself between Jake and Reba's line of sight. "We should be able to see Devereaux' boat from over here. Has to be where she's headed." Jake stayed on Hardy's left side, they walked out the parallel dock keeping their eyes on Reba as best they could. Near the end Jake saw her climb aboard Devereaux' boat.

"Any ideas on what we should do now?" Jake asked.

Mark and James Dean walked out onto the aft deck. "Fuck. What is Mark doing on that boat?"

"Who is who?" Hardy asked.

"James Dean is the kinda flat face on the left. The questions are: who is their employer, what are they doing here, is Devereaux on the boat, and what the hell are you going to do about this?"

"I have no authority here, therefore my hands are tied. We could notify the Cuban authorities, but that would open ourselves up to increased scrutiny. We don't know who all in Cuba, in and out of government, including our own people, are in on the selling of the technology."

"Well Bob, I guess this leaves you with keeping an eye on them to see what they do next."

"And you."

"Oh no. I've been fired in case you don't know. I'm just a curious bystander. Furthermore, Homeland welched on our deal. They froze my account which had the deposit in it. You're on your own. I intend to enjoy my vacation and go back to finish the project in the Bahamas." Jake turned and began heading back off the dock.

Hardy caught up, they walked in silence until they were off the dock.

"What if I said I would personally guarantee you a portion of the funds, say a quarter of what we agreed upon. That is if you help me out here for the remainder of the week keeping an eye on Mark and report anything suspicious to me."

Jake stopped. "Half. The first years' worth. I've more than earned it with the shit I did in the Bahamas." Hardy hesitated, so Jake once more began walking.

"Okay. Deal," he said with finality. "If I can't get HSI to reimburse me, I'll have some hard explaining to do with Loretta."

They continued walking. "What do you plan to do if they leave here?"

"There is a Coast Guard cutter out in international waters. We have the equipment Homeland installed onboard Devereaux' boat being monitored. I'm going to book a room in the hotel over there and keep an eye on their onshore movements. I need you to stay attached to your friend Mark. Our intel indicates the meeting will be taking place somewhere along the coast here any day now. Oh, and by the way, you'll be interested to know we picked up news concerning your ole housemate Blakely Carmichael. Seems she is working for Interpol. She's in this up to her eyeballs."

"You gotta be shitting me," Jake said, his mouth hanging open afterwards.

"Shit you not. And, she is apparently on her way here with whomever is involved in the other side of the op. Our guess is some rich Russian oligarch. Best you keep your eyes and ears open in case you run across her."

"If I could catch her, get a picture even, that would clear me of the lingering suspicions with the Bahamian authorities. Not to mention her friends back in the Bahamas who think I caused her disappearance." Jake and Bob stopped walking. Jake kept a wary eye toward the docks in case Mark appeared. "Suppose Dean was on the level about Devereaux helping Blakely and Toby, he may be with Interpol also? How is it Homeland didn't know?"

"HSI may have someone higher up who did know. It is also entirely possible Devereaux is an FBI agent working with Interpol, assigned along with Blakely, perhaps Toby, to be part of Operation Flamingo. That I'm an agent in charge with Homeland doesn't mean I would be given all the information on all personnel assigned to the op. Like you and Agent Alvarez, often field agents working undercover are just that, undercover."

"What about James Dean?"

"What about him?"

"He claimed he was working for you?"

"No. I do not know him. He too could be with one of our sister organizations. As I told you from the beginning, cooperation among the agencies, though better than before 9/11, is a long way from being what it should be. Everybody is hoping to get credit for being the one to bring down the bad guys. Too often, as you well know from serving in the military, your allies can often create the biggest nightmare for a mission." Hardy put his hand out. "Thanks Jake, you may be the reason this op succeeds. Watch Mark and look out for Blakely and these other players. The sharks are circling, that means they smell blood. Make sure it's not yours. We're on our own down here and eliminating competition isn't always pretty."

They shook hands. "Just make sure my money is there, okay? And, my account unfrozen."

"Ok and good luck. If you have anything for me, text me." Hardy asked for Jake's burner phone and entered his number." Text one to call you. Two for a face to face." Jake took his cell back. "Looks like your friend is leaving the docks. You best get going."

Jake did a quick looksee for Mark then picked up his pace as Hardy split off and headed toward the hotel.

What was going on? First the Mexicans were pressing him to get them invited to the dance. Then Arturo calls accusing him of using the cartel's money for his own pleasure. He did not believe Mark when he said he was in Cuba on cartel business. Afterwards, Mark contacted Lisa. She told him she saw someone fitting Arturo's description talking to Bud Jenkins two days earlier. There were now Hispanic men assigned to the security team along with the yard and field maintenance crew. They leered and made obscene gestures at her, made her nervous.

He had assured Arturo, then Lisa, he would be coming there by the first of the year.

Arturo didn't sound like anything he did could make him happy. Probably never would. He said his brother had bought a house in Charlotte and was setting up a computer repair shop to use as a front. Mark told him that was a good idea. Arturo failed to mention Bud Jenkins. Interesting. Could Bud Jenkins be the missing piece of the puzzle? He told Lisa to watch and listen more vigilantly. She didn't sound ecstatic.

After the calls he talked to his people with him aboard the boat about Devereaux' possible Interpol connection.

"We thought he was working for Homeland," Dean said. "I find it hard to believe he's with Interpol. He killed those Russians. You ever known Interpol to openly kill anyone? That Harper man was with him. He was a witness. Why would you leave a fucking witness if you did something like that?"

"Unless Jake Harper is also working with Interpol," Boyd added.

"Not after what I witnessed. Devereaux helped Carmichael and Tobolokov when Harper had him. Devereaux's the one hit Harper. Presumably because, in my opinion, Harper had been doing what Agent Hardy told him to do."

Mark turned to Reba who entered the salon with food for Devereaux. "Reba, you have any opinion about Devereaux being Interpol?"

Reba set the food down, poured herself a way too early flute of white wine, went out on the deck without replying. Dean and Mark followed.

With her shapely backside pointed at them, she raked a hand through her hair, her face tilted up to catch the rays of the rising sun. She sipped her wine, then replied, "Anything is possible. Devereaux is well-trained. Better than most I have encountered. Perhaps I could tell him what we think. See how he reacts."

"Do that. Also tell him we think Jake Harper is also Interpol. And see if he knows a Thurmond Tindal and Bud Jenkins. Tell him if he will work with us and come clean, we'll let him go free, perhaps share information."

Reba drained her wine, They re-entered the salon. Reba carried Devereaux his food and a bottled water.

Mark told Dean and Boyd he thought it unlikely Harper was working with Interpol. "He may be here on vacation. Nothing better to do for the holidays. And like most workers on the Bahamian project and now being one of the many furloughed government flunkies, he came to Cuba simply to get away, enjoy the holidays. It's my opinion he seemed too overwhelmed at the airport. If he came here on assignment, he would have been better prepared. Agent Hardy being here makes our mission more difficult, especially because I'm with Harper. The good thing is if I'm wrong about Harper, he'll most likely contact Hardy and I'll be there. Right now, my biggest concern is Devereaux' pals with the Cuban generals and their Russian money boys. We should have heard something by now. You picking up anything, Boyd?"

"Nothing. Last word was they were headed this way."

54

Playa Giron, Cuba

Before Blakely left Okneyev, he informed her they would be putting her ashore near Matanzas Province not far from the Playa Giron, famous as the site of the failed invasion by the CIA backed forces in 1961. Okneyev laughingly said this seemed appropriate for their planned rearming of the Cuban military with the new technology in their fight against the imperialist America.

"The Cuban generals believe my freighter not noticed; many freighters come here load, unload oil, petrochemicals, foreigners are forbidden bringing their pleasure craft here, we bearing the Venezuelan colors. You go ashore have your comrade Tobolokov, find your friend Harper, bring man called Mark. Two days be on our way."

"How am I to find them?"

"Find you. Cuban friends arrange you place near Plaza Independencia, Hostal Alma. They arrange message. The men come."

"How is this possible?"

"Know your friend Jake, this man Mark look for you, Tobolokov's names."

"You're using me as bait. This means you don't trust me, am I right?"

"Do this, you prove trustworthiness." He handed her the case. "Inside substances, must use very carefully, not let touch skin, eyes, nose. This for Harper. Syringe for Mark, make compliant. Once you do these things, must take this Mark to dock, boat waiting, bring you, him back freighter. Two days, two nights you, friend Harper, you enjoy time together. You must go now."

Blakely felt her mission was doomed. She would not be onboard to find out whom the other players were. Okneyev had set a trap and she felt certain Jake and Toby weren't the only people to be eliminated. Where had she gone wrong? Had Okneyev's people intercepted her communications? How was this possible? They were encrypted, bounced around in that place called cyberspace. Had to be a leak somewhere. All these years and it ends here? Not without a fight.

Once more she was left wondering who was this Mark, ally or foe? What part did he have in this fucked up op drama? She hoped for Jake's sake he was on their side. Who and how many were they up against? If the Cubans were working with Okneyev to get rid of them, there was little hope they would survive or ever be heard from again.

55

Jaimanitas, Cuba

Jake waited up the block from Camilla's casa for Mark, walking along looking at the wall of pastel murals, what he figured were portraits of famous local community members.

"I thought you may have mistakenly taken my phone," Jake said when Mark came up to him. He held his phone up. "It was in my lower cargo pocket. I decided I needed to check my bank balance to see if ESI had made the deposit into my account. Louis gave me directions to Hemingway Marina said that was where you were headed. Money was there but didn't see you. You plan on renting a boat?" Mark didn't even flinch.

"The thought crossed my mind. Too expensive."

What was Jake up to? Had he been tailing him?

"Guess we best get back. Tomas should be here shortly. What say we hit the countryside today, maybe a beach?"

"Sounds good to me."

They were eating Maria's delicious huevos rancheros when Tomas arrived. While they finished eating, he went inside to talk to Maria. Maria and Tomas came out. She poured them more fresh juice, then told them she would not be having any women for them tonight that Tomas was taking them to Club Habana, where many women would be. Tomas nodded smiling.

Tomas was driving on a four-lane expressway through countryside seemingly unoccupied by humanity. In the distance were hills, everything lush and green. On the outskirts of Havana, they had ridden by dilapidated apartments, ditches filled with what looked like raw sewage, scruffy, shirtless children watching sullenly from open doorways or sitting on bare ground. There was an emaciated man walking behind an oxen hitched to a plow turning over the ground. Jake asked if there were many small farms or did the government own them all? Tomas said all land was the peoples and the government was the people and yes there were small farms. Mark remarked how skinny the man was and how healthy the cow looked.

"If it were me, I'd be eating steaks or hamburger."

Tomas replied, "Better to kill your wife than the cow. Cow dies they perform autopsy to see if animal died from abuse."

Further outside Havana, they passed several armed soldiers in fatigues on each side of the highway. At the third sighting as they approached, two soldiers were waving them to stop. Tomas told them to pull their ballcaps down low, slope down in their seats and let him do all the talking. After looking at papers Tomas gave them, several questions were asked, seemingly satisfactory answers given by Tomas. They were allowed to proceed. Jake heard Koko's name given by Tomas in one reply, the rest was too fast for him to comprehend.

Off the main highway, up in the hills, they visited a former French coffee plantation with concrete walled enclosures approximately two by three meters that Tomas said held slaves during the colonial period.

Next, they went to a place with old weathered wood structures around a lake which Tomas said had been a vacation get away for wealthy Havana residents prior to the Revolution. One of the structures housed a novelty shop where Buena Vista Social Club was playing and pictures were displayed of famous Cuban jazz players.

The next stop brought them to where Tomas said they could purchase sandwiches and swim in a stream. They purchased sandwiches and beer, ate at one of many picnic tables where Tomas said he would wait while they enjoyed a dip in the stream down below.

The stream ran over rocks and sandy ground inside a verdant landscape with many young people on its steep banks, eating, drinking, smoking, sunbathing and occasionally taking a dip in deep pools.

Jake climbed down to feel the cool water sluicing over him in one of the pools. When he came out, he saw Mark talking to a man and woman on the opposite bank. They were conversing in Russian. Jake studied the young man and the young attractive female. She was wearing a short sundress, sans underwear. Even from the twenty feet separating them, Jake could see her shaven pubic area. He became self-conscious of his staring, looked up to see her smiling. She asked something and when he didn't respond, she asked in fairly good English, if he spoke Russian also? Jake told her he didn't. She then turned back to her male friend and rejoined the conversation with Mark in Russian. Shortly they got up and walked away.

Mark slid down the bank and lay back in the pool while Jake mulled over Mark's ability to speak at least three languages. Later, as they went to rejoin Tomas, Mark told him he could speak seven languages. He had learned them in Europe where he had attended university, or so he claimed. On the trip back to Havana Jake closed his eyes to ponder what the conversation Mark and the Russian couple could have been about. He heard his name a coupla times.

Mark talked to Tomas, but his mind was on what the Russians were doing there and why they had singled him out. How did they know he spoke Russian? Their questions were about him and Jake, who they were. What had brought them to Cuba? Their story was they were students studying at the University of Havana. Mark didn't believe them. He didn't believe in coincidence. He didn't think Jake bought the bullshit story he gave him, any more than he bought Jake's bullshit for being at the marina that morning. What had Jake seen? This could be a problem. The time was approaching to either confront Jake or separate himself from him. The op was entering the stage when he needed to give it his full attention. Right now, he felt Jake would only be in the way, probably getting Agent Hardy involved, which would create a world of problems for him and his involvement with the cartel. The whole op could blow up in his face.

Okneyev was counting on Jake or this man Mark finding out she was in Cuba because they had the capability to monitor her presence. Blakely was skeptical of this being possible. Most likely the Cuban authorities would be the means to spread the word, sealing their fate. She had to get word to Jake. How was the question? The only way she could think of was to contact his friend Agent Hardy of Homeland Security. Assuming Hardy knew Jake was in Cuba and knew how to contact him. Which created another dilemma. If Okneyev was able to intercept her communication, then he would know she had contacted Homeland. She would never be allowed to leave the freighter. She had no choice. She would wait until she was onshore and send word to Dieter, let him handle the communication. Hopefully he could find a way to get the word to Jake without bringing Hardy, the Cubans or anyone else to the party.

She decided to let Toby handle Mark. Give her a chance to meet with Jake. Hopefully, find a way to save them all. That was if Jake showed and would be willing to work with her.

Tomas took them to a nice restaurant in an upscale neighborhood. The place was like an antiquated inn with stone floors, a fireplace where a chicken was being roasted on a slowly rotating skewer, heavy wooden tables and chairs, crystal water carafe and glasses with expensive looking silverware and candelabras. There was limited seating. They sat in a corner next to a table of a family of four, who kept eyeing them as they ate. Especially when Mark, having consumed more than his share of the alcoholic beverages, began asking Tomas politically charged questions about Cuban society. Jake seemed to be the only one to notice the disapproving looks and facial expressions of the family members, who promptly left when they finished eating.

Jake was the first one to leave while Tomas and Mark waited for the patron to return with the change. Jake saw the man from the next table talking to two men further down the street. He waited by the car. Two men, both dressed in dark clothes, donning thin mustaches, dark shades and walking with an attitude, approached him, asked for ID, questioned him about his presence in Cuba. Why he was in this neighborhood? Mark and Tomas came out, were IDed. Tomas was led aside. A brief heated exchange occurred between Tomas and the two men. Tomas was smiling when he came back to the car.

"I hope we didn't cause you any trouble," Jake said. "When I came out the man who was seated next to us was talking to those two."

"Fuck them," Tomas replied. "What they going to do. It illegal for he and his family to be there also. They dare not testify against me. Fuck them. I'm not scared. I spend year in prison for saying what they no like to hear. Fuck them. Koko take care of problem." He laughed. "No worry. Everything be okay. We go Club Habana tonight."

Club Habana was in the same area of Havana as the embassy residences. Diagonally across was a multistory building with a mural of Che Guevarra lit up covering the entire face. The tree and shrub-lined drive was dimly lit leading up to the club. Before Tomas' car came to a complete stop, they were mobbed by a bevy of females surrounding the car. They must think we are someone famous or important, Jake thought.

The doors were pulled open, and the women were all clamoring for attention. "He's mine," became the argumentative pleas emanating from the clutching hands which pulled Jake and Mark this way and that. Finally, Jake was able to extricate himself, when another vehicle approached, half the gals moved off to intercept it. Tomas shouted something to the remaining five, pulled the grinning Mark and Jake aside.

"They no enter club unescorted. You must choose ones you want. They expect you to pay everything."

"We'll take all five. Come on," Mark said and marched off with four of the gals, leaving Jake and Tomas to follow with the fifth.

Amazingly enough, the doorman allowed all of them in after Mark and Jake paid.

Inside was like a gigantic music hall with several levels around a stage area where a band was playing loud rhythms of Jazz, calypso and swing style songs. Mark bought three-liter bottles of Habana Club Rum and passed around cups filled with ice from several trips to the long bar at the back of the room. Soon everyone was talking loudly. The gals took turns sitting on laps, kissing and squirming their asses in a clothed lap dance, an attempt to achieve the desired effect, get money.

The evening continued in much the same manner. Jake remembered one group of musicians who had a musician who danced on one hand while he played his trumpet with the other. Mark ended up doing some acrobatic flips and a break dance breakout, including spinning like a top on his shoulders, then catapulting back to his feet. Across the dance floor, Jake saw the schoolteachers from his plane. They had young men entertaining them. Jake watched through an alcoholic haze. It ended when the gals asked a hundred to accompany them back to their place. Jake offered fifty and Mark was willing to pay sixty. The gals one by one disappeared. Tomas offered to get them other women. Jake declined. Mark eventually agreed he was too drunk to do any good.

When Jake arose the next morning, his mouth was clammy and his breath nearly nauseating. He went to the bathroom and took a cool shower. There was no sound coming from Mark's room. Jake tried his best to hurry getting dressed, hoping Maria would allow him an extra demitasse of the rich dark Cuban coffee.

He said hello to her and went outside into the sunlight waiting for her to bring the coffee, juice and fruit. He felt dull and drained.

"Sr Mark, he leave early. Say tell you be back in time Tomas take you beach."

"Did he say where he was going?"

"Not say. He drink coffee, juice, say he need to walk. Look like you. You have much fun at club last night?"

"Yes ma'am. Too much fun. Maybe Mark is right. Think I'll go for a walk also." Jake drank his coffee then juice, went back got his cell phone and wallet, locked the door and hurried off after texting Hardy a two. That was when he noticed the missed two texts by Hardy over an hour earlier.

Louis was opening the gate as he rushed down the drive.

"Your phone again, senior?"

"Something like that Louis. Thanks for asking," Jake replied. He hurried down the sun-washed pavement wondering what he would find when he reached the marina.

What he found was Devereaux' boat was no longer tied up and Mark was nowhere in sight. He headed to the hotel where he found Hardy eating fruit and a bagel seated at a corner table.

"Beginning to wonder if you received my text," Hardy said as Jake sat down across from him.

"Late night. I feel like death warmed over."

"We received a message which might pick you up. Your friend Blakely has arrived. She is staying at the Hostal Alma in Matanzas Province. I've confirmed she's there. As is our friend Toby. She is expecting you."

"Me? What makes you think that?"

"Message was explicit, your mystery friend Mark, seems the Russian Oligarch Pietr Okneyev ordered her to meet with you and him."

"A trap?"

"You think? Question is why you? And how did he know about Mark? By the way I guess you noticed Devereaux' boat has disembarked." Hardy drank the rest of what Jake figured was coffee. He sat staring at Jake.

"You do look like shit. You've got to snap out of it. Blakely is booked for just two nights. That means something is happening today or tomorrow. Perhaps she knows what. My guess is Okneyev suspects something and is getting rid of loose ends. There has been increased airwave traffic before and after each transmission." What Hardy failed to say, some of the traffic was coming from a point near his farm. The feds were in that area. He had a team there helping with the security setup for Tindal Industries' weapon research facility. Good thing Jake knew nothing of this. Swanson's team should be checking these and all other signals, tracking down their source. He needed to break his silence once more soon. They were close. He could feel it.

Jake shook his head. "You asked me to watch Mark. For that you promised to make a deposit. If I go over to the ATM in the lobby, will I find the funds in my account? I bet not. Now you want me to stick my neck into another noose. For this what will I receive, more unbankable promises or some more patriotic bullshit?"

"You said you wanted a picture of Blakely to clear your name. Here's your chance. As for Mark, do you know where he is?"

"No. And unless I get my money I'm going to go back to my room, try to get over this fucking hangover. Mark be damned."

"Mark saw his friends off. Then he skedaddled out of here minutes before you arrived. You should have passed him on your way here. As for your money, I swear on my mother's life, I will have your money one way or another. I put in a request for funds, they will have to be approved. Homeland doesn't know why I'm here. We had a leak, have a leak, until we know whom, I decided to keep my purpose for being here ambiguous. The ambassador thinks I'm here about the sonic sickness issue. You and Carl, perhaps TJ, are the only people who know the real reason. This op is my make or break career moment. I'm close I can feel it, I need your help. It is dangerous. We have no backup. No promises. No patriotic speech. This is an all-in moment. I'm asking you, in or out?"

Jake saw the plead in Bob's eyes. He had never turned his back on a friend and had never let any of his military comrades go it alone. His head hurt, his stomach rebelled, his neck was stiff. He twisted it trying to relieve the pressure. "You're one convincing asshole. Maybe you should enter politics. That is if we survive this one. What's your plan?"

Bob broke into a grimacing grin. "I have the Coast Guard vessel monitoring, shadowing Devereaux' boat. The captain is an old buddy of mine. I figure Okneyev is meeting his marks somewhere near Playa Giron, the Bay of Pigs. Their little inside ironic play on humor. My bet is Devereaux' boat is on its way there and Mark will follow via air or land transport. The question is, will he include you as requested?"

"Like you said, I should have seen him on the way here and didn't. He told Tomas that he wanted to see a beach today. He may have contacted Tomas and arranged with him to drive him there." Jake pulled out his phone and called Tomas' number.

Tomas answered on the third ring.

"Sr Jake. I at Camilla's casa. Maria say you go for walk. Mark call say he no need me today. You wish my services or no?"

"Hold on Tomas." Jake told Hardy what Tomas said. "I believe maybe I should have him take me," Jake told Hardy. Hardy nodded. "Tomas, I should be back there in twenty minutes. I have a friend wants me to come to Matanzas Province. Can you take me there?"

Tomas hesitated, then said, "I talk to Koko about this, call back."

"Could be a problem," Hardy said. You say this Koko is probably tied into the Cuban government? This could be bad news. Wish you hadn't asked him. Maybe you should tell him your friend called back and said he would meet you here."

"And how do I get there without raising suspicion? Tomas tells Koko everything. My cancelling will make Koko wonder, especially after Mark took off on his own."

Tomas called back. "Sr Jake, Koko say it okay. Wants you come see him, make arrangements so no one cause problems."

"Be there in twenty minutes."

"Koko wants to see me to make arrangements, so Tomas and I have no problems. I think I can trust Koko. Don't see where I have a choice. May be a good thing if Koko has someone watching me. He'll think Blakely is an old girlfriend. Could give me some protection."

"If he's not in with the group connected to Okneyev. In which case you'll be walking into the trap with his assistance."

"Guess it's too late to back out now. What about you?"

"I need to find Devereaux' boat, Okneyev's freighter. Probably see if I can find a secure location nearby where you're going, so I can monitor you and Devereaux' crew. Be careful Jake. Mark will most likely already be there, he won't be the only one."

56

Matanzas, Cuba

Mark did not return to Camilla's. He brought everything he needed when he left earlier after receiving a text from Dean. After meeting with Dean and sending them to find Okneyev's freighter, he caught a cab and asked to be taken to Matanzas. The driver informed him it was illegal for him to do so. Unfortunately, Cubana Air once had a flight to nearby Juan Gualberto International located 20 kilometers east of Matanzas in the Veradero section, Cuba's attempt at having a Cuban Cancun. Problem was the flight no longer existed. Mark rented a car paid the exorbitant insurance and damage fees plus the rental charge, asked for directions to Matanzas and hit the Autopista Nacional.

Two and a half hours later, he arrived outside Hostal Alma and waited for Carmichael or Tobolokov to make an appearance.

Toby saw Mark as soon as he arrived. He waited knowing sooner or later he would get out of the car. If he did or not, at some point once he determined he was alone, Toby would signal Blakely to act as decoy, catch this man Mark from behind, inject him and try not to attract too much unwanted attention while they got him back to the hostal. A big risk, but the best they could hope for under the circumstances.

Three nagging questions: who was meeting with Okneyev, who was in on setting him up and where was the Harper man?

Koko led Tomas and Jake into his fenced in back yard. They sat in sturdy metal lawn chairs, not unlike the ones Camilla had in her courtyard.

"Tomas tells me you wish to visit a friend in Matanzas Province. The beach in Veradero is a popular place for foreigners, but not many Cubans other than the poor wait staff are allowed. Sr Castle, is this where he has gone?"

"That is what I was told. I wish to go to the town of Matanzas to meet a friend who invited me to visit her."

"Is she Cuban?"

"No. She is American."

"Sr Castle goes to beach and you go to Matanzas. Why not travel together?"

"Mark, Sr Castle preferred to go alone. Better for both of us. Mark might make my friend uncomfortable."

"Your friend Mark he seem to like Cuban women. Do you not like Cuban women? I hear you nice, but not take advantage of the young ladies, unlike Sr Castle."

Jake could feel himself reddening. He hoped Koko did not notice. "I have children and prefer not to indulge myself in young ladies not much older than they are. I do not mean to insult anyone."

"Highly unusual. Most foreigners they come here to indulge their fantasies. These young ladies are not the usual jiniteras most men become acquainted with. They are poor young ladies hoping to meet a special foreigner. I understand about daughters. Mine will have her fifteenth celebrated before the new year. One can only hope she will be like her mother and grandmother, perhaps someday meet an honorable man such as yourself. I believe you are an honorable man Sr Harper. Honorable men do not take advantage of others. Or lie. Tell me, Sr Harper, why are you here in Cuba?"

"Cuba has always fascinated me, even as a child. I don't know why. When I had a chance to come here, I took it. I must admit it was in the hopes of indulging my fantasies. In that respect I am not unlike most who come here. I wish to see more of Cuba. I am a country boy, always have been, always will be. I have a farm in the United States and plan to live out the rest of my life there. That is why I wish to see more of the countryside outside Havana, the farms and natural beauty, breathe fresh air. If this is a problem for Tomas or yourself, then tell me so, and I will find some other way."

"Sr Harper. It can be dangerous traveling in Cuba by yourself, especially if you are American. There are many in my country who do not trust Americans. The young people want American goods, emulate American movie stars, think all Americans rich. Compared to them, you are. I know there is poverty everywhere and some who would do you harm. Even in America, it is so. I do not wish you to become a statistic. This would be another problem for our two countries. There are police and soldiers who watch, they not everywhere. Sadly, some of them do not always act honorably. I have given Tomas a letter from me. This should help, but you must do what Tomas tell you. He will watch for you. For this you will pay his expenses. Is this agreeable?"

"On one condition?"

Koko raised an eyebrow. "And what condition must you ask?"

"That you and Tomas call me Jake or Harper without the signor."

He chuckled. Jake held out his hand and they shook.

"Ok Jake. You must be here to attend the party I give for my daughter. You will be an honored guest."

"I appreciate the invitation. Will Camilla allow me to stay at her place when I return."

"Yes. But you must pay, even if you not there."

"Thank you Koko

57

Mark had seen pictures Dean had taken of Blakely Carmichael along with hazy pictures of Toby Tobolokov. She was an attractive woman. Dean said rumors had it she was a big flirt, seemed to be familiar with Jake among others. Mark wondered how and what she knew about him?

For an hour, a man passed by on different sides of the street. Mark kept expecting him to stop by the car, ask for his identification and ask the reason for sitting here. He would tell him he was meeting a lady here and she was late. The man passed by another time. He needed to piss. Where were they? Did they know he was here? Perhaps they were waiting for Jake to appear. He hoped Jake did not know or would not show.

Toby sent Blakely their arranged code. Mark was moving right up Melanes in the direction of Plaza de la Libertad, located a block away. Blakely left the balcony, went down and out the back through the small patio area shared by guests of the Hostal Azul, cut over to Santa Teresita which would intersect Melanes at the corner of the plaza. She hurried past the corner trying to locate Mark among the many tourists. He had stopped at the granite edifice of Jose Marti and the Indian maiden breaking free of her chains. Off in the distance was the town hall, its clock said the time was almost noon. Blakely moved around using the other tourists and the trees as cover. Next time Mark moved she would make herself visible, lead him around to the farmers market where Toby was waiting out of sight. From there it would be a short walk back to their hostal.

Mark caught a glimpse of someone resembling the Carmichael woman off to his left. He dodged his way through the crowd trying to keep her in sight, far enough away so he could get lost behind other bodies or the trees. He figured she might be headed back to her hostal, but she kept going beyond the street he had come in on. Had she seen him? Was she deliberately leading him away from the plaza, perhaps leading him into a trap? It would be better to go back to the hostal and wait for her there.

Blakely stopped, acted like she was trying to figure out where she was. She glanced back. He was no longer there. Where had he disappeared to? Had he not been following her? He must have not been and was headed back to his car. She would get Toby to get back there ahead of her, then she would lead this man Mark into another alley so Toby could do the deed. Where was Jake? She left a message with the owner to let Jake into her room if he came asking for her. Would he come asking?

She found Toby. He was dressed like one of the locals, floppy farmer hat and all. She told him the new plan. His plan was for her go to the passenger side of Mark's car to distract him while he slipped up on the driver's side to inject him. Might work. She let her fingers touch the other syringe in her pocket, her backup, just in case. She hoped she wouldn't have to inject Jake. Better than what Okneyev wanted her to do.

Toby said, "Mark may not be in the car. Whichever one of us has the chance they must take it and the other must catch him. That way anyone watching will think he's just another drunk tourist. We have to be very careful."

"Too risky. Policeman could see us. We're here to find out who he is and why he's important to Okneyev."

"You're right. But taking him to my room could lead to other problems. We need to get him somewhere secluded, away from here."

"Okay. One of us will sedate him then you can take him away in the car, I'll wait until the Harper man arrives. I'll join you, with or without Jake, in the morning."

"This Jake, I think you've got a thing for him. That's not good."

"Not a problem. I can handle myself with him. He's scared of getting too close to me, especially the way you're implying. I'll do what I've got to and you do what you must. Why don't you take some fruit from here with you?

Might help with your disguise. You can eat it while you're out there keeping an eye on Mark. Wait and keep your eyes open for any problem. When it's clear, signal me, I'll distract him then you move in. Hurry we need to make this happen while everyone's eating or hanging out inside to avoid this damn humid heat."

The unexpected always seems to happen to the best laid plans.

As Blakely approached the hostal, she was taken aback. Out front on the sidewalk beside Mark's car was Mark, a young Cuban and Jake. They were having a heated discussion. This called for quick thinking. Be bold. She continued her course.

58

"Hello Jake. Hello Mark. I'm Blakely," she said extending her hand to the young good-looking Cuban, who said his name was Tomas. Tomas gave her an appraising look. Jake and Mark stood staring.

"What, no hello? No hug or kiss? I know this must be awkward me inviting you both to meet me here. I figured I might as well get everything out in the open. Tomas, if you would be so kind, I have two rooms here, please take these gentlemen's bags up. The owner will show you where. Doesn't matter which room you put the bags in, we'll sort it out later. I need some time with these two before we join you."

"I know of no bags to carry, senorita. Perhaps they should stay in one room and I in yours."

"Tomas you're a credit to your race and gender. If you would, have the owner give you food or drink and please wait inside for us." Blakely leaned over and gave Tomas a kiss on the cheek. His eyes never left her less-exposed-than-usual bosom. He was all smiles, as he strutted off.

When he disappeared inside, Blakely quickly spoke asking Mark, "Who the hell are you?"

"Your other lover, apparently."

Jake looked from one to the other of them. "What are you doing here Blakely and how did you know how to get in touch with me? Mark, the truth, what are you doing here?"

"Like I said, this fine piece of feminine flesh invited me."

Blakely kept smiling. "I did invite Mr. Castle here same as I did you, Jake, albeit for some of the same, and, different reasons."

"Stop talking in riddles, Blakely. If you wanted a threesome, I'm sure Mark and your friend Toby will gladly accommodate you. Speaking of Toby, where is he?" Jake could see he had ruffled her feathers. Mark seemed to be mulling the possibilities, clearly enjoying himself.

"I don't know your relationship. How much you know about each other. Perhaps I should discuss my invitation with each of you separately."

Jake continued to look perturbed. Mark seemed to be enjoying Jake's discomfort.

"I'll leave the decision to Mark. I have nothing to hide."

Mark shifted his weight. "You mentioned someone named Toby. Is there another man waiting for you, perhaps someone dressed like a peasant farmer, who peeked out from the corner a few minutes ago?"

Blakely's smile faded. "If that's the way you wish to play it. Yeah, I have someone else with me. We were sent here to kill you Jake. Don't look shocked. I told you before, someone wants you and me dead. This man is doing it at the behest of someone else. Who, I do not know? Thomas Devereaux thought he knew. I believe he was going to talk to you about it. Apparently, that never happened. As for you Mr. Castle, or whatever your name is, this Russian wants you to be his guest aboard a freighter out there somewhere. I was to bring you to him, not sure why?"

"Perhaps he needs some advertising for his company. I handle many international accounts." Mark put on his most charming smile. "Damn Jake you never told me you had someone trying to get rid of you. If I had known, I might have reconsidered sharing living quarters with you."

"Bullshit Mark. I saw you at Hemingway Marina talking to some supposedly government agents aboard Devereaux' boat. Who are you? Better still who do you and your friends really work for? You speak Russian which I heard. Are you like Blakely playing both sides?"

Blakely spoke up, "I'm not playing both sides, Jake. I'm trying to figure out who is selling state secrets to the Russians. Does that include you, Mr. Castle?"

Mark stepped back. "I want nothing to do with this international crap you two seem to be involved with. Like I said, my business is advertising, nothing else. Tell your friend Toby if he comes any closer, I will jam whatever he has in his hand up his ass." Mark turned completely, facing Toby.

Blakely immediately stepped in and plunged a needle into the back of Mark's neck. Jake tried to block her move. He was too late. Toby hurried forward and caught the slumping Mark. Jake watched them struggle to pick Mark up. Wary, he moved back away from them.

"Help us, damnit Jake. We need to get him into the car before that plain-clothed policeman returns."

Jake felt he had no choice. The three of them put him in the passenger's seat. "Toby get him out of here. Do like we discussed. I need to talk to Jake." Toby hesitated. "Don't worry about me. Jake would never harm me. Tell him Jake."

"That depends. What are you going to do with Mark?" Jake asked.

"Get him away until we know what he's up to. I understand his people have Devereaux' boat. What happened to Thomas?"

"He was on there, last I knew. I want to talk to Mark also. Where are you taking him?"

"Go Toby."

Toby took off. Last they saw he turned the corner and was lost from sight.

"Answer me Blakely."

"Come on Jake. This incident may have caught unwanted attention. You never know who feels it is their patriotic duty to call the police. Your compadre Tomas is waiting for you. You need to explain Mark's absence."

They joined Tomas in the dining room. He sat at the bar drinking some brownish liquid in a glass of ice. Jake told Tomas Mark decided to go on ahead to the beach. "I told him perhaps we would join him there tomorrow." Jake wasn't sure Tomas heard him. His attention was clearly focused on Blakely. He only looked at Jake when Blakely told him she and Jake were going up to her room.

"There is another room if you wish to relax or you can take a walk around. You ever been here?" She asked.

"No senorita. Jake, I wait here for you."

Blakely took Jake's arm. They left the sullen-faced Tomas and went up to her room.

Blakely sat on the edge of the bed. Jake chose to sit in the cushioned wooden chair.

"This is not some black widow scenario. I didn't bring you up here to mate then kill you, Jake."

"Where is this Russian who sent you here?"

"His freighter is out there offshore, hiding in plain sight among the many others. He hatched this plot to get Toby and me away while he conducted his other business."

"Sent you here to kill me and bring him Mark, so you said. I still don't know why someone wants me dead. Seeing as how you were sent here to do the deed perhaps you can enlighten me?

Blakely leaned toward Jake exposing more of her cleavage. She enjoyed how well this worked, almost laughed at Jake's attempt not to look.

"If it's any comfort, I was supposed to get rid of Toby also. I'm certain Mark and I would have suffered, then met the same fate. Okneyev doesn't trust anyone and his modus operandi is to get rid of competition or anyone who could pose a threat."

Jake noticed Blakely eyes kept straying to a black box sitting on the end table between him and her. He stood, reached out to pick it up. Before he could, she snatched it away.

"Is the modus in there? What is it, drugs or poison?"

"Both. It's too dangerous for anyone to touch, smell or get the stuff on any part of their body. Please believe me. Don't dare open it." She laid it back on the table. "Jake, I meant it when I said we could be good for each other. I'm sorry I played the slut. I'm not like that. I try not to hate myself whenever I have to play that role. Makes me numb, can't let myself feel anything. Afterwards I feel used."

Jake didn't know if he should trust her. A part of him wanted to. A part of him wanted to throw her back and fuck her hard. He could feel himself stiffening.

Blakely read Jake's silence as a possibility.

"I wasn't lying when I said I have no sexually transmittable disease. I can see you're still interested." She moved in close, her eyes holding his, she lifted up and brushed her lips across his, her hand reached down, her fingers lightly touched his arousal.

Brought back memories of her earlier attempts back before everything started happening, including Amy. He wanted to turn away. Her touch froze him.

"Why should we deny ourselves this opportunity," she said her lips against his, each word a tingle. "A part of me is afraid I will never have a chance again to truly make love to someone. Please Jake. I've never begged anyone." They kissed. Her fingers became more animated. She pulled back, watched the softening of his eyes. "Make love to me, then we can make plans. Maybe we'll have a chance at getting to know each other if we like how we feel afterwards."

Blakely moved back and started undressing. A part of Jake wished she wouldn't. The other part ruled the day. He set the case on the chair and began to undress. Their eyes never leaving each other until they lay in each other's arms, she on top, kissing him with fierce abandon.

She moved down, kissing and licking.

Their lovemaking started frantically, ended tenderly. She lay with her face on his chest running her fingers in swirls, teasing his nipples, then brushing his chest hair.

"Jake have you ever been in love?"

"Once. I thought I was with my ex-wife. The closest I've come since is with my children. Love doesn't seem to be in my cards. And you?"

"I thought I was once also. It didn't work out. Guess it wasn't meant for me either. Doesn't mean it may never happen. Maybe we haven't allowed ourselves to be open for it to happen."

"Yeah. Maybe." Jake liked lying here, but the other reason for being here wouldn't allow him to relax. "Blakely, this was great."

"But. I know there will be the but. By the way, I like yours," she said rising up on one elbow so she could look once more at him. She was scared this would be the last time. This bothered her, and she didn't like the feeling,

"Jake, I do not know who wants you dead. We need to find Thomas. Hopefully, he is alive and on his boat. I also need to know who Okneyev is doing business with on other matters."

"Would this have anything to do with Thomas, Toby and you being Interpol?"

She sat up and looked down at Jake who was lying back his hands laced behind his head staring into her eyes.

"What makes you think we're Interpol?"

"Come on Blakely. You want me to trust you. I think I just proved I am willing. So how about we level with each other, figure out how we might work together. Isn't that what you said? I believe it's in our mutual interest." Jake rubbed her back. "You also have a beautiful ass, by the way."

She lightly punched him on his thigh. Too close to his tender parts for comfort.

"Let's say I am. Who are you working for?"

"Homeland Security in the Bahamas. I was supposed to be simply eyes and ears for them, same as for ESI. You and Thomas changed all that. Especially when my life was threatened. You and Toby disappeared. Left me to defend myself. I was fired from Homeland when the government shut down happened. Surprisingly, despite the problem your disappearance created, Ned had me take over Rick's job with ESI. Ned sent him to another project, Kendall and Amy home. Nothing was happening during the holidays at the Bahama project, so I came to Cuba for a surreptitious vacation. Homeland found out, bribed me to help solve the same question you're somehow involved with. My job was to stick with Mark to see what his involvement is. Your turn."

"Pretty much what I told you, before I left the Bahamas. I'm sorry. I was told Devereaux planned to take the blame. I didn't know." She rubbed Jake's thigh where she punched him, then started absent-mindedly rubbing his penis.

"I was sold to Okneyev by my traitorous uncle. He trained me to be a spy, then, as Okneyev informed me, my uncle sold me to be his whore. He never used me like that. Okneyev treated me like his daughter, sent me to the United States, paid for me to go to college. Made me manager of his bar and other businesses. On one of my visits back to Ukraine to see my family, I met this young handsome Italian who made me believe he was in love with me. Not long into the romance, I discovered he was using me. One female among others. He threatened to have me locked up for being a member of a Russian cartel unless I agreed to work for him. I had no idea what I had become involved with. If Boris had found out, I would have vanished without a second thought."

"Later my Italian heartbreaker told me he was Interpol, said they wished to pay me for my services. I became a double agent in a manner of speaking. My uncle was made to die. Thomas and you killed Okneyev's men in the Bahamas. The op in the U.S. blew up in Toby's face, shortly afterwards. Thomas said Homeland and you were getting too close, you were going to blow our cover, I panicked. Okneyev was not happy. He had plans for me in the Bahamas. I don't know how, but I think Okneyev found out I am with Interpol. Here I am. He wants me dead, I'm sure of this. Homeland's op is taking place and my control wants me to find who is involved. If I go back, I'm dead. If I don't, Interpol may think I'm no longer trustworthy. Either way, I can't win. At least I got one last wish. Making love to you."

She started crying. Her tears dripping onto her hand that had been kneading Jake's penis.

"Hold me Jake. I'm scared." She let go of his penis and wrapped her arms around his neck. He kissed her and hugged her tight.

After a short pause, Jake pulled back. "There might be a way to find out who is involved." He stood, began pacing. "Devereaux' boat left the marina. I bet they are headed here. The Coast Guard is sitting out in international waters, which could be useful." Jake looked down at the black case. Maybe she had an antidote. He stepped in front of Blakely, reached out to wipe away a tear.

"Mark knows how to get in touch with his people on the boat. If he's CIA, which is what I believe, he's after the same information everyone else is. That drug you gave him, do you have an antidote?"

"No. It should wear off in a couple hours." She looked up at Jake expectantly, sounding sullen. "Toby is going to question him when he comes to, if no cooperation, he has enough dosage to last until morning, when we, I mean me, are supposed to bring Mark to the boat and back to the freighter. I never wanted to be a murderer Jake. I could never do to Toby, or you, what Okneyev wants."

"I believe you. You need to get Toby back here with Mark."

"They are not far from here. There are miles of farm crops not far from here. That's where he took him. I'll text him. Mark should still be under."

"We need to be with them when he wakens."

"What about your friend Tomas? What will you tell him?"

Jake stood. He sat back down. "I'll send him back to Havana. Tell him Mark will give me a ride back in a couple days. Go ahead get in touch with Toby?"

She reached over and picked up her phone. A chill passed through her as she thought about the case that was no longer there and what she was supposed to have done.

Blakely texted Toby the code telling him to return for her. He would assume she had taken care of Jake as was arranged. He texted back *45*.

For the first time since leaving the freighter, she felt there might be a chance they would come out of this alive. Her relief reawakened her feelings for Jake. Feelings she hadn't dared allow herself for far too long. She looked up, then down at him. "He'll be here in 45 minutes," she said in a near whisper. "We have time for one more go."

"Blakely, I don't think we should, or I can."

She leaned down, whispered to the little head, then kissed it. "I believe we can." She looked up into his eyes, then resumed convincing him.

59

Tomas was reluctant to leave Jake and the beautiful senorita. After Jake watched him leave, he went back to the room. Blakely had showered and changed into jeans and a plain brown T-shirt along with tennis shoes. Her hair was pulled back into a ponytail that stuck out through the hole in her brown, slogan-less ball cap. She glowed.

"Jake, I hope you will always remember this day and cherish it as much as I will."

"How could I not?"

She stepped up on tippy-toes and kissed him.

"Did you check out?"

"Yep. Wish we didn't have to leave." She went over to retrieve her bag. Jake took it from her, she refused. "Got to return to the bitch in charge mode. Toby will not respect me otherwise. Keep your eye on him. I really don't know him well enough."

"I thought you were a team?"

"First time I laid eyes on him was the same time you did. I knew about him, had been told to work with him, same as Thomas. Thomas is undercover FBI liaisoned to Interpol for this op."

"And you're the queen bee?"

"In a manner of speaking. I usually work alone. Not in my nature to share or be a team player, so forgive my reticence. Have you given anymore thought on how we pull this together?"

"The man you accused me of having a gay meeting with is Special Agent Robert Hardy. This is his op. I'm just the hired hand. Seeing as how I can no longer coordinate with him, I figure once we get Mark to cooperate, we should get Devereaux' boat to pick us up and we recon the freighter. About as far as I've gotten."

"There are Cuban generals involved, as well as others, including cartel interests. Okneyev is the go-between. It has been assumed the key man will attend. That may not be the case. Usually people like him remain in the background. Nevertheless, it is best to know who is involved, always you have to start somewhere, often working backwards. The Cubans are sticking their necks out big time. We determine who they are and go from there. This is what I think we should do. Knowing what cartel or cartels involved won't be so easy. Hard to get leverage on them with something like this. Once they have whatever they're buying, no one will be able to touch them unless they use it against some entity other than another cartel. The police and governments protect them."

"Not always. Look at Noriega and El Chapo. What the United States is worried about is having another Cuban military threat nearby with high-tech capability. Or the technology ending up with a terrorist group."

"Same reason Interpol is involved. We better go down. Don't want Toby getting out of the car." She hugged Jake and gave him a quick kiss.

They drove back out into the countryside heading south toward the coast. When Mark showed signs of consciousness, Blakely directed Toby to pull onto a road that dead-ended at a swamp.

At first Mark kept up the pretense of being an advertising exec. Jake escorted him to an area filled with crocodiles and snakes.

"Finally got laid, Jake. Smelled it on you when I came to. Saw the change in yours and this lovely vixen's faces. I don't know why you wish to believe her. Must be because she laid a good one on you."

Jake saw Toby's eyes go to his in the mirror. He didn't look happy.

"That's for me to know, Mark. Let me tell you something. She was told to bring you to Okneyev for questioning. I talked her out of doing that."

"You must have really laid it to her ol' pal."

"Mark, I know you are CIA. I suspect you know I'm not some contract foreman here strictly on vacation, so cut the bullshit. Okneyev is meeting with potential buyers while you stand here wasting our time discussing my sex life. Work with us. Let's nail the motherfucker. You can have all the credit you want. Get your people to pick us up down on the coast. We can observe whoever is coming and going and you can do whatever you wish with that information. Blakely has agreed to let you run with it. What do you say?"

"Jake, even if I were who you claim I am, what reason would I have to trust those two? They are part of the Russian group admittedly sent here to kill you, and when I refuse to talk, they'll kill me too. As for my friends and the boat, the coast where we are headed is off limits to all but commercial vessels. By the time you got to a place where they could pick us up, you would have missed the opportunity, that is even if my friends were to cooperate and the Cuban Coast Guard didn't catch you first. Your best bet is to go somewhere and fuck yourselves silly. That's what I'd do if I were you."

"You're not Jake or me asshole," Blakely said.

They turned around. Jake glanced back, saw movement and walked over to Blakely. Mark took a step forward.

Blakely raised her hand. She clutched the black case. "We could inject you again and leave you to become those crocs next meal. I'd prefer not to do that. You thought we would be too late, that wouldn't be because that was your friend's plan all along, would it?" Mark smirked and remained quiet. "I thought so. Here's my final offer. I have access to Okneyev's computers. I'll trade that info for the names and photos your crew are or will be taking."

Jake looked at her in amazement. "Were you going to give me this information?"

"I held this info as a final bargaining chip. On Devereaux' boat is highly encrypted equipment. I intend to offer the info to your services in exchange for being promised admission into the witness protection program. Thomas knew this and planned to help me bargain with the feds. That was until Mark and friends kidnapped him. Is he still alive?" She asked Mark.

"I don't know this Thomas you're talking about."

"Last chance, either you let me talk to him or you stay here and draw your last agonizing breaths." She stepped toward him. "I have two options in this case. One is a slow prolonged and painful death. The other is the same sedative. Either way, you'll suffer unless you prove to me Thomas is alive. We have your phone. Give us the code and you'll leave here, alive, provided

Thomas is still alive. Otherwise." She took another step toward Mark while opening the case.

Jake saw the fierce determination on Blakely's face. He could knock the case out of her hand. Problem was it could fly open and potentially infect them all. Jake didn't want to die. Not here. Not this way. "Blakely don't."

"And what? Without the witness protection program, I'm dead. Move away Jake. Either this jerk does the right thing, or I'll make sure he never leaves here."

Mark shook his head. "Too bad. Both of you." He started toward them.

Blakely opened the case and flung it at Mark. He nearly fell back into the water. He flailed his arms, knocking the case in the water. The dust hung in the air, some settled on his hands, arms and face, which he began clawing at. Jake saw the look of horror on his face as he brushed by them, touching Jake on his arm when he did. All kinds of thoughts of impending doom raced through Jake's mind. Was this to be his fate?

Blakely snickered followed shortly by giggles then she bent over laughing. "You should see the look on your face," she said between gasps for breath followed by more laughter.

"What is wrong with you. Are you crazy? Tell me you have an antidote," Jake said rounding on her.

"Wish I had a picture of the look on his face and yours." She grabbed Jake wiped some of the dust on her palm wiped it around her mouth then quickly, before he could react, kissed him. "Smell that Jake. Does that smell like death to you? It's talcum powder, my love."

Jake pulled back. It did smell like talcum powder.

"I told you, I am no murderer. Well, that may not be entirely true. Depends on if Okneyev was telling the truth. In which case he and his guests will get a taste of his own medicine. Skol indeed. Never did like vodka." She continued to snicker.

"You should take up acting," Jake said. Then he started laughing.

"I did consider it. Studied drama and business in college. Even starred in a play."

Tobey joined them.

"Did he get away?" Blakely asked him.

"Ran by me like he was on fire, hollering and beating at his arms and face. Got rid of his shirt is up the road. Shall I try to catch him?"

Jake and Blakely both bent over laughing.

"What's so funny?"

Blakely told him between bouts of mirth. He joined in the laughter.

Catching his breath with relief Jake said, "We better get going. I need to go where I have cell service and warn the Coast Guard to alert the Cubans before any innocents board that freighter."

"Jake, Jake, Jake, always thinking of others. That's one of the things I love about you."

"We also need to see if we can find out about Thomas. The Coast Guard should have intercepted his boat by now."

"You knew this and didn't tell me?" Blakely's facial expression turned serious.

"I was hoping Mark would bow to your threats. I still don't know what part he played in this psychodrama. What about you, Toby, witness protection?"

She didn't answer, just started walking back to the car. Jake and Toby followed.

"Where to?" Toby asked.

"I guess for me it's back to Havana. I can't legally leave until January 2nd, Jake said. "What about you two?"

"No idea. Guess we could see if the boat that brought us here from the freighter is there like it's supposed to be. We could commandeer it, then see what happens. Hopefully Thomas is alive, and his offer works out."

"Toby, what about you?"

"I think I'll see what my controller at Interpol wants. Maybe he can figure a way for me to retire. I'd like a small business in a little village on the coast somewhere."

"Jake you know they'll be after you as well as us. Someone wants you out of the way. Thomas may be able to shed some light on that for you."

"Are you two in a hurry to get going?" Jake asked.

"The boat will be there until tomorrow. That was the schedule."

"OK. I read the area between here and Cienfuegos is beautiful. Why don't I tag along. That way we can see what's what and go from there tomorrow."

"Only if what's what includes you sharing a room with me tonight," Blakely said.

"Wouldn't dare miss an opportunity to have another taste of paradise. And…"

Jake didn't get to finish his statement. Toby plunged the needle in his neck. Blakely felt Jake sag against her.

"Why the fuck did you do that?"

"We can't wait another day. You heard what he said. The Coast Guard is out there. Our job is to locate Thomas. You had your fun. It's time to do what needs to be done. We'll take him with us and drop him off back at the hostal. Our control wants Mark. And, we need him to help us locate Devereaux. We need his boat. It's our only chance to get out of here."

Blakely looked down at Jake. She hoped someday she would be given a chance to make it up to him.

"And how do you suppose we'll find Mr. Castle?"

"He'll have tired himself out by now. There's nothing but swamp on each side of the road. Shouldn't be hard to find him."

'We don't have a weapon. He's not going to willingly get in the car."

"He'll be too tired to put up much resistance."

Mark tried to fend them off. Didn't take long for them to subdue him. They used his belt to secure his hands behind his back. They threw him in the trunk, tilted the rear seat forward on the driver's side giving Blakely a clear view of him and Jake strapped in on the other side behind her, his chin slumped forward onto his chest.

Blakely went inside and rented another room at the hostal. She and Toby waited until the hostal owner went up the street then they carried Jake in and left him on the bed.

When they reached Okneyev's runabout that brought them ashore, two of his men were waiting onboard. They had no weapons. Blakely went down to the dock to ask the two men for assistance to bring Mark down to the boat. Toby stayed out of sight with the trunk lid open. The only weapon he had was a tire iron. When the two men reached in the trunk, he brought the iron down onto the back of one of the men's heads. As the other one jerked up, Blakely brought the trunk lid down hard on his head stunning him. Toby finished the job with the tire iron.

They pulled Mark out, gagged him with the bandana from one of the men's heads, used the men's belts to bind his arms to the door window opening, loaded the two men in the trunk and frog-marched Mark down to the boat. Several people on other boats and nearby watched but made no move toward them none of them dared say anything. Blakely figured they thought she and Mark could be police or government agents. They knew not to question or intervene.

Toby was the one with seaman experience. He captained the boat. They buzzed Okneyev's freighter, saw no one on deck. Nearby were two other vessels, both bearing insignia designating them as Venezuelan. Had they followed them or were they already waiting? Blakely was worried. Was Okneyev alive? Were the Cuban generals onboard? The amphib and the nuclear explosive to arm the missile, was Okneyev ready to make the exchange? She had not told Toby she poisoned Okneyev's vodka.

"We need to get onboard the freighter," Toby said. They were out of sight of the freighter, hid behind another freighter. They were able to see the other vessels. They too looked deserted.

"I don't see any way to do that without backup. We need Devereaux and Mark's crew. Either that or we notify the Coast Guard."

"Are you crazy? We'll be taken in. Our careers finished. The Castle man has agreed to cooperate. I say talk to him."

Mark wondered why Jake wasn't with them and what connection he had with these two and their plans? Blakely refused to answer any questions concerning Jake. Had they let him go? Was Homeland closing in? Toby and Blakely, who were they? Who did they work for? Dean overheard Blakely tell Jake she was a double agent. Where did her loyalties lie? Was she helping the Russian, helping him set a trap? He needed answers. He chose to cooperate. He knew this was his only chance. By now the authorities would be alerted by someone back at the dock. He couldn't afford to be taken in by Cuban authorities. He figured his best bet would be to get them to go to Devereaux' boat. His men were armed. They outnumbered these two. He and his men needed to get back here and board that freighter. Problem was, there was no way to know who was onboard. They certainly will be armed. What could be done about the nuke? Boyd might know. He hoped so.

"You can't board that freighter. Toby's right we need to get my men. Maybe then we'll have a chance."

"How do I know we can trust you?"

"How do I know I can trust you? We both have few options. Time is critical. That subamphib drone may be onboard Okneyev's freighter being armed while we sit here trying to decide between a suicide mission and a possibility of succeeding. Contacting the authorities is out, you two made certain of that option. The US Coast Guard dare not come into these waters. That eliminates every option except us teaming up. If you'll give me a phone, I'll contact my crew and have them meet up with us." Blakely didn't reply. "Damnit. Are you with the good guys or not?"

Blakely and Toby went topside.

"He's right. We need his men."

Blakely sat down on the bench-seat. "I've got a plan. We let Mark contact his guys. After we meet up with them, me and you will take this boat back. Mark will come with us made to appear our prisoner. His crew will board the other boats, make sure any occupants are neutralized then board the freighter. Okneyev will be happy we brought Mark. I don't think he'll eliminate us in front of whoever his guests are. He'll want to finish business with them first. If I'm right, he'll have some crewmen take us somewhere away from where he's making a deal. The three of us should be able to overcome the crewmen. Hopefully, Mark's crew will be successful and together we'll crash Okneyev's party. Sound like a plan?"

"A lot of ifs. I don't trust this guy Mark. The big if is thinking Okneyev won't kill us in front of his guests. He's ruthless. He may kill us to impress the guests and his crew. I say we get Devereaux, take this boat, get the fuck out of here, notify control and leave the cleanup to the big boys."

I made contact already. He's afraid international warrants will be issued for our asses. Our only hope is to stop this deal from going down. Think it over, decide for yourself. I'm going to present my plan to Mr. Castle."

Mark agreed the plan might work. Anything, so long as he had his crew. He would send a code to Washington informing his control of the danger. Problem was diplomatic channels were out of the question. They needed a special team, a top-secret op. Anyone on that freighter would be neutralized.

60

Jake couldn't figure out where he was at first. When he realized who, what and how, he was pissed. Blakely had fucked him and it didn't feel good. Where was she and Toby? He needed to notify Hardy. He said go through Carl. He checked his pocket his cellphone was there. Fuck Hardy and Homeland, he called TJ.

Hey bro. How's paradise?"

"Was good. Got a big problem. I think I know where the deal is going down, who the players are."

"What you talking about bro? Carl said you were terminated."

"Hardy hired me to help him. Problem is the only way to contact him is through Carl. Is Carl in touch? The situation is critical."

"Last I heard Hardy went black. Carl said he was headed to Cuba. Oh hell Jake, are you in Cuba? I need to call you on a secure line. I'll get Carl. We'll call you back."

"Damn son. What is this about you being in Cuba? TJ said you were working with Hardy. Where is he?"

"Last I knew he was headed to Guantanamo. You might want to check. Problem is I believe the deal is going down in Cuban waters. Okneyev's freighter would be my guess. Blakely Carmichael and Toby pulled a quick one on me and Mark Castle. My bet is they're headed to Okneyev's freighter. Hardy said the Coast Guard was trailing the freighter. If I'm right, they're already in Cuban waters off the Bay of Pigs. The Coast Guard can't come in here. This is way over my head. I figured I better let someone know."

Carl knew. This checked with their intel. Why hadn't Hardy told him about the Harper man? If Hardy had a deal with him, it was outside channels. He was in a better position to give them intel. His people could continue to scramble the communication.

"Okay podna. Here's what I need you to do. Go down to the coast. See if you can rent a boat. We need eyes on that freighter. Think you can do that?"

"I'll try."

"Get another burner phone. Use this code when you call." Carl recited the code. "Got it?"

"Got it."

"Get going. Call when you get a boat. We'll track you."

It was midafternoon before Jake reached the coast. The dock area was swarming with Cuban authorities. A Cuban Coast Guard vessel was leaving the dock when Jake arrived. Jake called Carl.

"This place is swarming with Cuban authorities."

"An international warrant has been issued for two westerners who supposedly killed two Russian seamen and stole their boat. Sounds like Carmichael and Tobolokov have created a huge problem for themselves."

"Yeah well it makes renting a boat a problem for this westerner. I need to get out of here. Got any ideas?"

"Head west. Look for the first access to a beach. Let me know when you get there. I've got someone with a boat I'll have them head that way by water. He's a big black Cuban and understands some English. Call him Pedro."

Pedro had an old fishing boat, a Boston Whaler type with a small cabin, looked and sounded like it was just operable. Pedro listened, nodded his bald head, didn't join in any small talk. Jake told him what they were looking for. He already knew. They headed back east, then south, then back east. Jake worried darkness would beat them to the freighter. There were a lot of freighters waiting to load or unload off Cienfuegos. Carl's people located Okneyev's boat by using a drone high in the sky, undetectable. Jake directed Pedro. The reception was remarkable, better than Jake had back on the farm.

Jake told Pedro to stop when they came into view of the Ro-Ro cargo ship. The drone spotted the other boats next to the freighter. Carl grew excited when his spotters told him one of the boats nearby, out of sight was Devereaux. Carl told Jake the satellite was returning to base. Another would take over in a couple more hours.

"You're it until then."

Pedro had a serviceable pair of binoculars. He dropped a fishing line for him and Jake, pulled out a fresh-looking couple of cigars, offered one to Jake who declined, lit up and settled back like this was where he wanted to be. Jake watched the freighter and tried to look happy that he was getting to fish.

What was Devereaux' boat doing out here? Was Blakely and Toby onboard?

DevsDelight came into view headed toward Okneyev's freighter. It disappeared. A runabout entered Jake's sights. It pulled up to a section of cut lines on the side of the freighter. A docking platform began to slowly lower. The outside area was higher and longer than the center section. Jake watched the platform lower down until the center section went below the water line. The runabout entered the center section. The platform began to rise. Jake saw three people, two men and a woman, step out onto the gangway portion of the platform. The man in the center appeared to have his hands bound behind his back. Jake couldn't believe his eyes, he was certain these people were Blakely, Toby and Mark. He reeled in his rod after telling Pedro to get him to the freighter pronto. Pedro reeled his rod in, used a finger to put out his cigar, started the boat and gave it full throttle. Jake was surprised at the acceleration and speed of the boat. It was like the motor had been switched out.

Jake didn't know what he had in mind. Couldn't believe he was headed toward definite danger without a plan or any weapon. Pedro sensed Jake's dilemma. He opened a compartment, pulled out two fully automatic M4s and six clips. Jake took one of the M4s and three clips. Next Pedro pulled out four M84 flash grenades and handed Jake two. All action, not a single word. Who was this guy?

They reached the area of the platform as it started retracting. Pedro swung the boat sideways against the hull, yelled "come" to Jake, climbed on top of the cabin, grabbed the runabouts propeller well and swung himself up onto the back platform, reached a hand back and Jake grabbed hold. The man was unbelievably strong. He hoisted Jake up with little effort.

A crewman saw them and charged. Pedro's back was to him. Jake pushed Pedro aside and punched the guy in the throat. He dropped, gagging, his hands holding his throat. Pedro produced a KBar and stabbed him through his hands into his throat. Jake was already up and running, his M4 in his left hand. He heard Pedro behind him, his steps barely discernable because of the lift's noisy hydraulics. Before they went far, the angle of the ramp grew too steep and they had to jump. The hard landing jolted Jake's whole body. His neck pain would be unbearable later. Pedro landed next to him. They moved off toward a door where an overhead light shined down on a metal landing. There was noisy clanging behind them from the runabout lift raising the boat inward and upward.

When they stepped through the door at the top of the metal stairs, it was as though they had entered another world. The corridor was shiny stamped metal, clean, looked like brushed chrome. There were doors on each side. Jake opened one on the right, Pedro one on the left. Crew quarters. They continued down the corridor. The others were locked, no sound penetrated the doors, their occupants hopefully elsewhere. Jake counted eight on each side.

"Sixteen possibles," Jake said. Pedro shrugged.

There was an elevator at the end on the right. A staircase with an emergency sign above the door on the left. Jake wondered why you would go up in an emergency. Because of flooding below he guessed. They took the stairs. The stairwell was painted bright white. Near the top they heard voices and footsteps coming from above. They hurried back down and waited behind the door.

Two men dressed in crisp blue naval outfits came through the door. Jake grabbed the nearest one, put him in a chokehold. Pedro broke the other one's neck with a quick twist. Jake dropped breaking his man's neck. They drug them back to the first unlocked room.

At the top of the stairs were two doors, one on each side of a large landing. The one on the left was locked. The one on the right was not. Pedro took the lead. He cracked the door, no sound. They stepped through into another corridor. The sound of dishes rattling came from somewhere out of sight near the end. A man in white carrying something passed through from right to left. Never looked their direction. Pedro and Jake walked beside each other down the polished concrete floor. At the end to the right, through a set of stainless-steel doors with an upper glass inset, they saw four people dressed in starched whites busy preparing food. Pedro started to enter and Jake shook his head. They didn't appear menacing. Two were young women. He couldn't do it. He hoped he didn't regret the decision.

They turned and went to the other door. Once more, Pedro cracked the door. Voices, clatter of dishes, silverware and people talking. One voice, with a Russian-tinged British accent, was berating someone. Sounded like his back was to them. Pedro nodded, stepped inside. Jake caught the door and followed, letting the door close quietly. The man they saw earlier saw Pedro. His eyes grew large. Pedro put his rifle barrel into the back of the speaker. He started to turn. Jake told him not to move. Jake had his rifle pointed to the man in white. He stepped past Pedro and the man with the accent, used the butt of his rifle to catch the white-clothed man under the chin. He dropped to the floor.

The accented man looked wide-eyed at Jake, then smiled. "Mr. Harper, you look exactly like your picture. Comrade Okneyev would have been pleased to see you. Do you wish to speak with him? Perhaps you won't mind waiting. You see he is rather busy at the moment. Tell your friend I am unarmed. Easy fellow, I rather like my family jewels."

"What is your name?"

"His name is not important."

Pedro slapped him across his ear. The man shook his head, raised a hand and massaged the wounded ear. "Please. No need in being brutal. You may call me Chekov."

"Well Mr. Chekov, I guess we'll just have to interrupt Comrade Okneyev. You're going to take us to him."

Chekov chuckled. "I'm afraid that is not possible. You see Comrade Okneyev is no longer onboard this ship. I hate to be the one to inform you, but you see, you made your grand entry onto a floating bomb. I was explaining the situation to that poor fellow you so rudely bashed when you interrupted me. The other marauders were in the lounge area last I knew. Shall we join them? We can toast our brief acquaintanceship."

Pedro prodded Chekov in the back and Jake followed. When they entered the lounge, Mark was seated at the bar. His hands and legs attached to a stool. Jake came over to him and looked him over. "How's it going Mark?"

"All tied up at the moment. If you're looking for your girlfriend, she and her friend are trying to locate the bomb. I guess this gentleman told you about the bomb? If you untie me, we can celebrate our reunion."

Jake asked Pedro to cut him loose. Mark rubbed his arms and ankles, then went behind the bar. He took a bottle of vodka down and retrieved a couple of shot glasses.

"I wouldn't drink that if I were you. Might want to wash your hands also. Blakely spiked Okneyev's vodka with the real poison."

Mark jerked back, turned to the bar sink and scrubbed his hands.

"She said something about him taking a couple bottles with him. I didn't quite understand the remark. Goes to show, never trust a woman. Does your buddy have a name?"

"Calls himself Pedro. I believe this chatter is wasting precious time. What's the fastest way off this boat?"

"Okneyev locked us in before he departed. The locks require a retinal scan. They are rigged to set the bomb off if they are tampered with. The only way off is topside. Even if you were able to break out the practically unbreakable glass, there is no guarantee the glass wouldn't trigger the explosion. And, the only way down would be to jump, over three stories, you'd land on the metal deck, chances of survival less than ten percent. Probability of not breaking most of the bones in your body, practically zero. Checkmate. Game over. He fucked us."

"I saw *DevsDelight* disappear to the other side of this floating timebomb. What were they up to?"

"There were two other boats bearing Venezuelan flags and insignia that my crew were going to commandeer. After which they were going to come onboard through another ramp door and join us in taking care of Okneyev's men. Boyd was going to use online experts to disable the bomb if necessary. That was the plan. Seems your girlfriend had other plans. That's why she tied me up. She wanted to make sure of Boyd's cooperation if she or Toby managed to find the bomb. Chekov was supposed to keep eyes on me. She threatened him, told him not to release me. Fuck you Chekov." Chekov shrugged. "I have no reason to trust her. For damn sure she doesn't trust anyone, not even you, apparently."

"How long do we have?"

"No one knows."

The freighter began moving.

"What the fuck?"

"Okneyev said he would take the freighter out into open water. He can operate it remotely. He figured the US vessels would move to intercept and get caught in the blast. He laughed, said it was appropriate to have the blast happen off the coast of the Bay of Pigs. Have to hand it to him, he outfoxed everyone. Might as well drink up."

"Pedro, do you think you can disable the controls on this damn thing."

Pedro nodded, turned and hurried off.

"Don't kill anyone you run across." Jake wasn't sure he heard him or would do as told.

"Doesn't say much does he? You figure if he can disable the boat, it'll buy us time. Good thinking. Hope Okneyev gives a damn and doesn't signal the detonator if we stop moving. Who knows, perhaps the Cuban generals can hold sway over his murderous impulses."

"We need to find that bomb. To do the most damage, where would Okneyev have to place it? My guess would be at the waterline near one of the access doors in order to achieve his objective of doing damage to a boarding vessel and crew. Mr. Chekov, who are you? Why were you left behind?"

Chekov was seated listening to their conversation. He looked at Jake. "I am the service manager for this vessel. Okneyev felt my services were no longer of value to him."

"You must know something about this freighter."

"I know very little. My duties didn't require my going anywhere except on these two levels. Okneyev's crewmen handled everything else."

"Whose quarters are those on the lower deck?

"The crew and my staff's."

"I need all the doors unlocked. Need to check them as a possible place for a bomb. Can you do that?"

"I have a master key. Come with me."

"Mark, you and I need to go below deck and try to locate that bomb."

"You're talking the equivalent of four football fields and it's not all open. Could take a day or more."

"Guess we best get to it. We'll start with the rooms, then check near each opening. Blakely and Toby should have covered part of this damn vessel. We should run into them at some point."

The bomb wasn't in any of the rooms. The hydraulic-operated rollout door where they entered and the area around it showed nothing out of sorts. There were three more rollout openings. Chekov took them up, down and around to the second opening. Nothing.

Up, down and around, the next two rollouts were in a cavernous bay area with vehicles on two levels. This is where they found Toby. Rather this was where Toby found them. He stepped out from behind one of the vehicles, a Glock 26 in his hand.

"Harper, lower your rifle and you and your buddy step back away from it."

Jake pointed his rifle at Toby. Toby didn't fire his weapon. "Where's Blakely?"

"Here," came her voice from a side entrance. Pedro shoved her forward. "Your friend is a man of few words. We couldn't get into the control room. He would have blasted his way in if I hadn't warned him not to. Tell him I'm not the enemy Jake. Please."

"Pedro, did you disarm her?"

"He did. Haven't been felt up like that. Ever. We haven't located the IED dirty bomb. Okneyev, or whoever planted it, could have placed it in the control room or in one of these vehicles. We won't have to wait long to find out. My guess is less than an hour, probably closer to half an hour."

"IED dirty bomb. IED. I have an idea. Let's get everyone to the crew quarters."

"What are you talking about Jake?" Blakely asked, hands on hips. She looked like she was going to cry.

"I'll show you." Jake told Chekov to lead the way. As they were going back Jake asked Chekov if they had any H2O2 biocleaner and peroxide? He said they did. Jake told him to bring some rags, the two items and some tape along with his staff members.

When they reached the lower deck crew quarters, Jake told the others to bring mattresses from the other rooms into the end room. "Pedro, give me your M84s and see if you can find a container of diesel fuel."

Chekov and his staff stood in the corridor. Jake took the items one by one into the room. He told Chekov get his people and bring buckets of water. "As many as you can find."

Mark brought in a mattress, leaned it up in the corner. Blakely drug hers in followed by Toby.

"We need all of them. Blakely line them up on each side wall.

"Do you care to share your plan?" She asked. She was breathing hard. "You plan on an orgy?"

Jake grinned. He had his back to her, taping the M84s together. "I'm going to attempt to blow a hole through this outside wall with an improvised explosion, an IED."

Jake heard Mark and Toby. They were having a heated discussion. They stopped when they saw Jake taping the M84's to the outside wall.

"That's thick metal," Mark said. "Got my doubts this will work. Could set off the other bomb."

"Unless you have a better idea, keep bringing the mattresses. Mark see if you can call your crew."

"No. The signal could trigger the nuke. McGyver would know that."

"Yeah. Well. Keep those mattresses coming."

Pedro came back with a five gallon can of diesel. He looked at what Jake was doing and nodded. "Help them with the mattresses. When Chekov's guys get here with water start wetting the mattresses down."

Jake helped lay down the mattresses, they wet them and lined the walls. He kept one of them dry, lined it up with the M84s, cut a hole, pulled the foam out, stuffed the rags in soaked with $H2O2$ and peroxide. He carefully pushed the mattress in place, had Pedro and Toby bring four metal closet lockers to lock it in place and hopefully direct the blast. They stacked other mattresses against the lockers. Jake squeezed through on the open side, poured the diesel fuel so it ran over and under the first mattress, then he poured a trail on the floor, a liquid line following his struggle to squeeze out.

"Okay everybody, down to the bottom deck. Get life preservers on." Chekov handed Jake a butane lighter. When everyone was out, Jake waited until Mark sounded out "Ok". He lit the fuel, watched the flame snake its way toward the load, and ran. Pedro held the door open for him. They ran down the steps and jumped the last four when the whump and vibration shook the steps. Blakely handed Jake a life preserver. Pedro grabbed the rifles, handed one to Jake, then grabbed a huge fire extinguisher. They hurried back up the stairs. Everyone followed.

Acrid smoke filled the corridor. Pedro reached out to push the door out of the way. He felt the heat and jerked his hand back, then kicked the remains inward. He extinguished the fire. Everyone was coughing, their eyes and noses streamed. Jake handed Pedro a couple of rags from his back pocket, then wrapped two more around his hands. It was a chore working their way through the debris. Jake knew his attempt must have failed, otherwise the air would have been sucked outward. The wall had a bulge in it, the metal looked melted, no hole.

"Everybody get back. Go down get some fresh air." Jake was pissed. He stepped back to what had been the door opening, pointed his rifle at the bulge and opened fire. Small holes, with light shining through, appeared. He reloaded another magazine and opened fire, this time directing the bullets, cutting a jagged opening. Pedro joined him. The smoke started seeping out. Jake tied a rag around his face. His eyes streamed. He wanted to scream.

They had created a circle of holes. "If only I had a saw," Jake coughed out in frustration.

Pedro scratched his head. He turned and rushed out. Momentarily, he returned with a reciprocating saw and two demo blades. They took turns cutting until they made a hole large enough that even the heavy Chekov could fit through. The smoke continued to pour out through the opening. Jake sent the grimacing, grinning Pedro to get the others. He looked out the hole. It was going to be a twenty-foot drop. Toby stood at the destroyed door opening. He told him to grab a blanket from one of the other rooms to cover the jagged metal. Everyone began pushing and shuffling their way into the room. They cheered. The cheering stopped when Blakely through smoke, dust and tear-streaked lips exclaimed, "That's too far down. I'm afraid of heights. "

Everyone began murmuring among themselves. Pedro shoved people aside, took the blanket from Toby, wrapped it over the bottom of the hole, stuck his legs out and pushed off. Jake looked out, saw him splash down, turned back, grabbed the protesting, struggling Blakely and with Toby and Mark's help tossed her feet first out the opening. She screamed all the way down. Toby, Mark, Chekov and the others jumped at intervals once the ones in the water moved back. Jake was the last one out.

No sooner did he hit the water, when the bomb went off on the starboard side of the vessel. The vessel tilted up. Everyone started swimming away as fast as they could. Jake felt the concussion of the blast. He lost consciousness.

When he came to, the first sight was Bob Hardy sitting in a chair, his chin on his chest. He was lightly snoring.

"Hey jerkoff, where am I?"

Hardy looked up, eased up out of the chair, opened a door and called out, "in here." He walked over to the bed. "You're onboard the Coast Guard vessel. We rescued you and a few others."

"A few. How many? What about Blakely, Toby, Mark and Pedro?"

"Sad to say, I don't know. There were other boats. We dashed in, picked you and three others up and left. The Cuban Coast Guard warned us off. You're lucky we found you. Shit, you're one lucky son of a bitch."

A medic came in.

"I'll need a full report as soon as you are able. See you later Jake. I'm going to get out of here and let the medical people do their thing."

EPILOGUE

Jake stayed on the Coast Guard vessel until the next day. His neck and head ached. Despite his aches and pains, he dictated a report for Hardy. Jake was taken ashore in a small rubber dinghy and dropped off near Cienfuegos. He caught a ride back to the hostal and called Koko. Tomas returned to pick him up. All he told him was Blakely decided to return home and he decided not to join Mark at the beach. Tomas, his usual self, let it go. He told Jake Koko would be happy Jake would be attending his daughter's, Tomas' cousin's fifteenth party.

Koko cooked a whole pig, head and all, on a hand-turned rod over a huge half barrel, filled with sweet smelling charcoal. Everyone tore off the tender strips of flesh and ate their fill, accompanied by beans and veggies laid out on a long picnic table. Jake washed his down with drinks of fruity rum drinks. There was latin dance beat music. Many young, luscious looking friends of Koko's daughter danced. Jake stood off to the side, watched and talked to Koko. Koko was amused by Jake's questions regarding Mark and any prior connection they had. He laughed off Jake's attempts to learn any more about his last name being Castro. He told him there were many Castros, like there were many Harpers. Jake knew not to mention what Maria said. Jake figured he was what she said, Castro's mafia-like lieutenant. Even if he was or wasn't family, he collected a fifty percent share of all commerce which went into other Castro's personal overseas' accounts, making them and their families rich capitalist communists.

The next day, a Sunday, Jake woke up, packed and went through Camilla's house—no Maria, no Louis, no one. He went to the boulevard, several blocks away, hoping to catch a cab to the airport. None ever came. He was running out of time. He called Koko. Within ten minutes Koko came in a new Fiat sedan. Koko drove fast, zipping around corners, passing the few other vehicles--time seemed to stand still for Jake. On the way, Koko told Jake about the explosion and the half-sunk freighter. Jake listened. He dared not ask questions. He wondered about the others. He hoped they all made it and weren't in a Cuban jail.

At the airport, Koko took a different approach to the terminal. They came to a secured gate manned by Cuban soldiers, the barrier was raised, the soldiers saluted him. With time to spare, they pulled up to a private entrance, other soldiers opened the door. Koko took Jake around the line of other ticket holders to the counter. Something was said to the attendant, his ticket and exit visa were stamped. He and Koko walked away from the other gawking ticket holders. Koko shook his hand. They hugged him. Koko gave him a business card, told him to come back. Koko left.

The flight back was more raucous than the flight to Havana, everyone celebrating, buying bottles of Havana Club rum, Cuban cigars, souvenirs, and swapping stories. A happy, hungover, aching Jake observed, did not participate. In Nassau, he hurried to the Custom's que. He needed to catch a flight back to Exuma. Someone had other plans for him, waiting on the other end of the line was the top Bahamian policeman, ESI's and other expat companies' main nemesis on Exuma.

"Mistuh Harper, hope you have good holiday. Care to tell me what you do in Cuba?"

Jake was tempted to say none of your business. He said, "Having fun. Hope you enjoyed your holiday."

He took Jake to an administrative office where he questioned, more like interrogated him. Jake said little, told him to call the prime minister. Jake was there for five hours, after which he was escorted to the concourse for the last flight to Exuma. A firm warning from the authorities. Made the months interesting. He was ESI's manager. They tried to make his job difficult. He found ways around their attempts. He emailed and tried to call Mark and Koko using the information on their business cards. No success. Person not found. Figured. Bonafides were bogus.

Over the following months, Jake put the threats behind him. Enjoyed the memories of Amy and their last tryst. She was back in Charlotte. Their communication grew less and less, then ended shortly thereafter. Jake often thought about Blakely. Figured he would never hear from her again. He came to know and like Elena McElroy through the online dating ap and long telephone conversations. When his time in the so-called paradise ended, he flew to New Orleans to meet her in person.

Months of celibacy, no Amy, no Blakely made their union a much needed wonderful N'Orleans' Bacchanalia. They wed not long after and settled into life on the farm.

The following summer, baseball season in full swing, Elena's daughter Jennifer and husband Beau drove up from Mandeville, Louisiana for a visit. Beau was a big Yankees fan. Jake was a BoSox fan. The Boston Red Sox Triple A team was in Greenville, S.C. They decided to catch a game.

At intermission, an announcement caught Jake's attention. A little league team from the Bahamas was in attendance and would be honored. Jake watched through binoculars the team march out onto the field, each kid introduced, along with the coaches. Jake was shocked, one of the coaches was Alvin Moss. Jake stared at him through the binoculars.

"Alvin. Unfreaking real. There's Alvin."

Elena, Jennifer and Beau wanted to know what the hell he was so excited about. He told them the story of Alvin and the other Bahamians busting down the door to the container office after they received their pink, termination slips.

"That was my first managerial decision when I took over the job. Alvin threatened to feed me to the sharks."

"Obviously that didn't happen," Beau remarked. "What did?"

"Shocked me. I stood up. I knew I had to deflect. I pointed to the ones who had not been let go. Told them they should leave less I change my mind. I told the others, "hey you guys know there's not enough work to be done to keep you all. You had to see this coming. The other companies have done the same thing. Check with Four Seasons, I hear they're looking for full-time employment." This cooled everyone except Alvin and a couple of his buddies. Rodney convinced them to leave. That was the end of it, except for Alvin. I received word to watch out for him."

"Come on Beau. We need to get some more refreshments," Jake said.

Elena and Jennifer warned them not to cause trouble.

Alvin exited the field with the team. He peeled off to go to the refreshment stands.

"Hello Alvin."

Alvin stopped, looked up, he opened his mouth, but words failed to come. Jake saw the recognition click in his eyes.

"Remember me?" Jake asked. He kept his emotions in check. "You were going to feed me to the sharks. Said I was in your country. Well, welcome to my country. Surprised you don't have any of your Russian buddies with you. Oh, that's right, they disappeared, went over a cliff I believe. And Tobey Tobolokov, that name ring a bell?"

Jake started walking toward Alvin. For every step Jake took, Alvin, hands up, palms out, stepped backwards.

"Harper, you be wrong. I upset dat you fire me, meant no t'ing."

Jake picked up his pace.

Alvin started backing up. "I tell dem I want no more of dis. They come for you Harper. You see. Our family neva be safe."

His eyes bulged when Jake continued his advance. He turned and ran, pushing and shoving people. Jake and Beau watched him disappear. Jake thought about pursuing him, ask what he meant. He didn't want to have Beau present and have to explain to him and Elena and her daughter about the threat. Good thing Beau apparently didn't hear or didn't understand the meaning behind Alvin's words.

Jake thought it was over. Wishful thinking. Elena, like many others, knew nothing about his work with Homeland.

'You see the look on his face?" Beau said between laughs.

Jake's laugh was brief, not wholehearted. He took what Alvin said seriously. Hardy had sent him a final email, told him not to disclose anything about the op, warned him to be cautious, he would be watched. Jake took the warning to mean Homeland and other government agencies would be watching. Had Hardy meant otherwise? Why hadn't TJ said anything? Had he also been warned?

Hardy included an update in his email. The Coast Guard intercepted *DEV'SDELIGHT*. Its crew was taken to Guantanamo. No word about Mark, Blakely, Toby, Pedro, Okneyev or the Cuban generals. Or if the op was over. Was it considered a failure or a success? Jake was given no thank you. No mention of the promised compensation.

Jake often wondered if what Blakely said about the Russian Okneyev's possible demise was true. If so, what did Alvin mean? Who else was out there wishing him harm? Blakely's warning of continued danger, he thought was no longer true. Devereaux' remarks about Tindal came to mind. Jake knew Tindal wished him out of the way. Was he involved? The more Jake learned of the activities on Tindal's property, watched and listened to the constant hum of heavy equipment coming and going. And, the talk of a big government project with hints on the news of employment opportunities from a government project announcement coming soon gave him pause. The constant push by Tindal's associates wanting him to sell, accompanied by threats of adverse or government imminent possession. Could Tindal be involved? Jake felt now, more than before, this was a distinct possibility. He had hoped it was over. Seemed his hopes were wrong. What now?

"You ready. How 'bout we grab some beers and get back, catch the end of the game," Beau said.

Jake nodded. His mind whirring with thoughts of the threat and what he should do about it. What could he do about a threat when he wasn't sure of the source? What should he tell Elena? The excitement she had when she came to live on the farm seemed to be waning. Her daughter's visit seemed to perk her up. They had a serious conversation, after Tindal's latest offer, about the possibility of selling the farm, buying a house near Jennifer and his children to use as a home base, and use the rest of the money to travel. He agreed that sounded nice. He overheard her telling Jennifer of their plans, as if he had agreed. If he told her about the threat, she would see this as another reason to sell and go near her ex-Marine Gunny, CIA father.

Jake needed to talk to TJ. Maybe he knew more. TJ hinted he and his wife were strongly considering moving to the Carolinas. Maybe this would make

Elena feel less alienated. She seemed to hit it off with Deane at their wedding. TJ could watch Jake's back like he did overseas. Jake needed backup.

It wasn't over.

To be continued

Next

GIT JAKE
FRAGMENTARY EVIDENCE

Warrior veteran, roguish, Ron Marshall is a graduate of UNC Charlotte, where he lettered in wrestling and LSU, where he played rugby. His major courses of study included economics, architecture, landscape architecture and construction management. He has worked up and down the eastern seaboard, along the Gulf Coast and in the Bahamas. While working as a construction manager for a resort in the Bahamas, he visited Cuba. His experiences while in the Bahamas and Cuba inspired this novel.

He and his dog Streak spend their time on his farm in the Carolinas and visiting friends and family in Louisiana, or wherever he finds interesting people and places to inspire his writing.

Coming Soon Book 2 of the Jake and TJ Novel Series
FRAGMENTARY EVIDENCE
For Info Visit: ronaldkmarshall.com